PRAISE FOR THE NOVELS OF MADELINE HUNTER

LORD OF SIN

"Snappily paced and bone-deep satisfying, Hunter's books are so addictive they should come with a surgeon general's warning. [Hunter] doesn't neglect the absorbing historical details that set her apart from most of her counterparts, engaging the reader's mind even as she deftly captures the heart." —*Publishers Weekly*

THE ROMANTIC

"Every woman dreams of being the object of some man's secret passion, and readers will be swept away by Hunter's hero and her latest captivating romance."
—*Booklist*

THE SINNER

"There are books you finish with a sigh because they are so rich, so tender, so near to the heart that they will stay with you for a long, long time. Madeline Hunter's historical romance, *The Sinner,* is such a book."
—*The Oakland Press*

THE CHARMER

"With its rich historical texture, steamy love scenes and indelible protagonists, this book embodies the best of the genre."—*Publishers Weekly* (starred review)

THE SAINT

"[An] amusing, witty, and intriguing account of how love helps, not hinders, the achievement of dreams."
—*Booklist*

THE SEDUCER

"*The Seducer* is a well-crafted novel. . . . characteristically intense and frankly sexual."
—*Contra Costa Times* (CA)

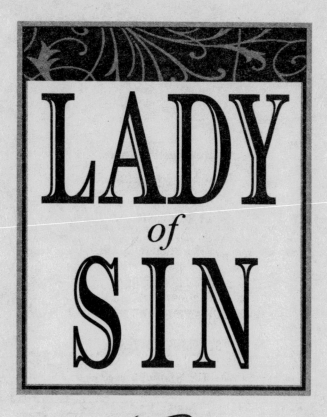

LADY
of
SIN

Madeline Hunter

A DELL BOOK

LADY OF SIN
A Dell Book / March 2006

Published by Bantam Dell
A Division of Random House, Inc.
New York, New York

This is a work of fiction. Names, characters, places, and incidents
either are the product of the author's imagination or are used fictitiously.
Any resemblance to actual persons, living or dead, events, or locales
is entirely coincidental.

Dell is a registered trademark of Random House, Inc., and
the colophon is a trademark of Random House, Inc.

ISBN-13: 978-0-553-58731-9
ISBN-10: 0-553-58731-5

Printed in the United States of America
Published simultaneously in Canada

www.bantamdell.com

OPM 10 9 8 7 6 5 4 3 2 1

For Thomas,
who has grown into a man whom it is a joy to know
as both a son and a friend

LADY
of
SIN

CHAPTER ONE

Nathaniel Knightridge dwelled in a special hell, one where men of action and command are rendered powerless by events beyond their control.

Chained in that underworld of the spirit, he awaited the dreadful result of his impotence. The chill in his body could not be warmed by either the fire he sat beside or the brandy he freely imbibed.

The spirits dulled his mind enough to keep his futile fury contained, but not so much that he did not hear every damned tick of the damned clock. It constantly poked at his soul from its place on a far table in the sitting room of his apartment at Albany.

He stared at the fire's flames, all too aware that his vigil paled compared to another being endured a few miles away.

"Sir." The address came quietly. Tentatively.

Nathaniel slowly turned his gaze to the doorway. Jacobs, his manservant, stood there. Jacobs's aging, cherubic face wore a caution born of Nathaniel's angry outbursts all day long.

"A lady is here, sir. She went to your chambers and your clerk directed her here. She insists it is most important."

"If she is here, she cannot be too much a lady."

"Oh, but she is." Jacobs proffered a silver salver. "Her card, sir."

"Tell her I am not receiving."

"But it is—"

"Send her away, damn you."

Jacobs left. Nathaniel poured more brandy. He did not need to look at the clock to know the time. A half hour remained, no more.

He gulped enough of the spirits to send his mind flying for a few blissful moments.

It did not last. Soon he was back in the chair, half-foxed but mercilessly aware. Of the clock. And of voices. Jacobs's and a woman's. Their alternating high and low rumble approached and grew louder until the words became audible.

"I tell you again, my lady, that Mr. Knightridge is not receiving."

"And I tell you that this cannot wait. I do not have the leisure to waste another day looking all over town for him."

Despite the muffling effects of the thick door, that voice sounded familiar. Nathaniel's dulled sense tried to poke around his fogged brain to identify it.

The door opened. Jacobs entered, looking apologetic and helpless. A woman sailed in behind him.

Nathaniel took in the dark hair beneath the crepe bonnet's cream brim, the middling height of perfect posture, the crimson mantle trimmed in fur. Her hand grasped the ivory handle of a parasol.

As she brazenly intruded on his private misery, she passed one half-draped window. The overcast day's silver light revealed her lovely, determined face.

"Oh, God have mercy," Nathaniel muttered.

"Charlotte, Lady Mardenford," Jacobs announced.

Charlotte waited for Mr. Knightridge to stand and greet her. Instead he propped his elbow on his chair's arm and rested his forehead in his hand. The pose communicated weary resignation. It also obscured his eyes.

Dark eyes. Deep set and compelling. They contrasted dramatically with his golden hair.

Those eyes could mesmerize like an actor's and he used them to deliberate effect. Mr. Knightridge did not perform in the theater, but he was known to command different kinds of stages. Those in courtrooms and drawing rooms.

Women were especially vulnerable to his magnetic presence. That was one reason why Charlotte had sought him out today despite her determined efforts to avoid him the last month.

The other reason for her visit, the one that had led her to this apartment today and not his chambers tomorrow, involved his seclusion in this shadowed sitting room and his disheveled appearance.

He finally acknowledged her with a sour, exasperated glance. A long strand of his collar-length hair hung over one eye in a lazy, sinuous curve. His waistcoat was unbuttoned and his collar and cuffs loose. He was the kind of man who still looked handsome when he was unkempt. Disarray became him. She could do without the roguish danger he projected in this state, however.

She removed her mantle and handed it to the servant, who retreated. She positioned herself so that she could not be ignored.

Mr. Knightridge remained in his deeply upholstered, high-backed green chair, his tall body slouched and stretched. He looked her over slowly. Annoyance hardened his countenance.

Then it faded, as if other thoughts had claimed his mind.

He turned his face away and gazed into the flames. His hair, swept back from his high brow except for the errant lock, permitted his profile to chisel the space around it. With its high cheekbones and straight nose and full lips, it was a classically handsome face but not very soft even in the best of situations, which this definitely was not.

The chamber fell silent, except for the ticking of a clock on a far table.

Charlotte had not expected the visit to start this badly. Then again, she had not anticipated joyful welcome either. After all, she and Nathaniel Knightridge did not like each other very much.

"You are being rude," she said.

He sighed. "No, madam, you are being rude. My man told you I am not receiving, and I will not humor this inexplicable invasion. I am in no mood for social calls today. Jacobs will see you out."

"This is not a social call. I am here to discuss business."

"In case you did not notice, I am almost drunk and intend to be thoroughly so, very soon. I am in no condition to conduct business, so it must wait."

"It cannot wait."

"Then find another man to irritate with it."

They had never rubbed well together, but he was being unusually blunt today. His behavior would be inexcusable if she did not know the reason for it.

She set down her parasol so he would know she did not intend to leave. The action drew his attention back to her.

"This may not be a good day to put aside your weapons, Lady Mardenford."

"I have never needed weapons with you."

"You act as if you do. You carry a parasol like a sword. You have one with you even in winter when the sun does not shine. I keep expecting you to stab me with it."

"I would never stab you. I might hit you with it if you gave me cause, but never stab."

"If you insist on staying, I may give you such cause. Hence my warning."

"You are being deliberately provocative today. While you have never been what I would call gracious, this is extreme."

His gaze sharpened, then warmed as it took her in again. Male calculation reflected in his eyes. Deep, predatory sparks in them made her nape prickle.

It was a boldly familiar gaze, and it aroused both caution and concern in her, along with an irritating, sensual stirring. It was not a look that a gentleman should let a lady see. It entered her head that his inebriated state not only freed him from the normal constraints but also permitted him to perceive and remember more than he did while sober.

"You are a fine one to speak of being provocative. It is no mistake, I think, that you donned that dress for this visit. It shows a lot of shoulder. When I see that much of a woman's skin, I know she wants something." He smiled, not kindly. "What is it you want, Lady M.?"

She felt the skin he observed flushing. Her cross bodice did show a bit of shoulder and neck, but not enough to warrant comment. Nor had she chosen it because of this visit. She had a full day scheduled and could not bear spending hours on the town trussed into the stiff stomachers that had become fashionable again for some malicious reason.

Just like Mr. Knightridge to assume a woman dressed only for his benefit.

She composed a sharp response, only to realize he wasn't waiting for one. His mind had turned elsewhere again. She thought she knew where.

The clock chimed the three-quarter hour. It startled him out of the reverie into which he had drifted.

"You really should leave. Your visiting me alone could create a scandal."

"If anyone saw me arrive, which no one did, they would assume I sought your counsel, just as I am doing. Besides, the whole town knows we do not have a warm friendship. My reputation is quite safe with you."

Since he showed no inclination to invite her to sit, she took it upon herself to do so. She perched on a cane-backed settee that faced him. From her new position she could see a decanter and glass on the rug beside his chair.

"When you hear why I have come, you will not mind the intrusion," she said.

"I promise you that I will, since I already do."

"Hear me out, that is all I ask. As you know, I am hosting a meeting in four days' time. The goal is to begin petitions to send to Parliament requesting changes in the laws governing married women. Including, of course, the laws on divorce."

"I received your invitation. You did not need to call."

"I feared you would not accept because of our— well, our occasional disagreements."

"Occasional? Madam, you and I are incapable of forming a right understanding on any subject."

That was not true. Twice they had come to complete agreement. One time they had not even needed words to know the other's mind.

Of course, he was unaware of that. She was the only one who had incurred a debt because of it.

She forged ahead. "I have come to explain why you need to be there. Three times now you have served as defense counsel in trials that touched on the misery some wives endure—"

"Four. I have been involved in four such trials. There was one you would not know about. But go on, please." His voice sounded bored, as if she engaged half his attention at best.

"You have seen and heard firsthand how some women suffer. You know better than most the inequities under the law. If you attend the meeting, your mere presence will lend weight to our cause."

"The testimony of lawyers who argue divorces in the ecclesiastical courts will aid you more. My experience only touches on the cases where a bad union leads to tragedy, and those examples will only turn many against you."

"I think you are wrong. There is great sympathy for women who have needed the voice you lend. Also, your fame alone will attract others to the meeting."

He began to respond, but stopped. His eyes glazed. What little attention he gave her flew away.

His hand reached down, found the decanter, and poured liquid into the glass. Lifting the glass, he rose and walked away.

Toward the ticking clock.

"What say you, sir? Will you attend?"

He stood at the other side of the chamber, his back to her. He tilted his head to drink.

"You want me there because I am notorious."

"Not notorious. Famous."

"It is the fame of a circus performer."

"You are much admired. The ladies in particular will appreciate your presence, as you well know."

"You want me because I will attract a crowd? Worse than a circus performer, then. I will be your dancing dog at a village market."

"You will dance to a very pleasant tune. I daresay you will have your pick of the gawkers when all is done, so there will be compensation."

She expected that to recapture his attention. At least she expected a barbed response. Instead he did not move or speak. He just stood there near the clock. Silence fell until only its ticks sounded.

She searched for something else to say, something to disperse the terrible atmosphere gathering. Normally Mr. Knightridge and she ended up arguing when they spoke at all, and a row would be better than this.

Anything would be preferable to the awful expectation that thickened the air.

Time stretched and slowed. The clock's sounds got louder as the silence deepened. They became a beat matching the throb in her chest. From the way his stance grew taut, she knew the hour's chime was imminent.

"My apologies, Lady Mardenford, but I am too drunk to behave civilly. You should leave now."

Yes, she probably should.

She could not. She sensed his turmoil and it

twisted her heart. He stood tall, strong, and straight, but he looked very alone there. Almost . . . vulnerable.

She owed him much more than he would ever guess, and sharing this terrible vigil was the least of it.

She knew when the moment was almost upon them. He threw back the last of his brandy, then went deathly still. She realized she was gripping the arm of her settee so hard that her fingers hurt.

The clock chimed twice.

The sounds echoed in the chamber for a long time, then left a quaking silence.

Nathaniel abruptly turned. He hurled his glass. It flew across the chamber into a window, smashing a pane on its path out to the city.

The sudden movement and explosion made her jump.

She could see his face now. Eyes blazing and teeth bared, he wore a mask of fury. Beneath the anger, however, deep in those eyes, something else burned. Raw anguish.

She had not expected such a violent reaction. She had not known it would affect him this deeply.

It had probably been unwise to come. She should have left when he asked, but she had not. Now she was glimpsing something she had no right to see.

His hard gaze moved from the shattered window to her. His glare made her swallow hard.

She stood and took a few steps toward him. "It was not your fault. You did your best."

His eyes blazed as he realized that she knew what

this hour meant. "An innocent man just hanged. Man, *hell*. He was a *boy*. It does not matter that I did my best. It wasn't good enough, damn it."

"You do not know for certain Harry Binchley was innocent. Perhaps—"

"He committed crimes enough in his short life, but not this murder."

"You cannot be sure of that."

"I *know*." He advanced on her. "Do you think I do this for my amusement? For the *fame* you say I have? I know the guilt or innocence of those I defend or I would not speak for them."

He walked right up to her until he was so close she had the urge to step back. "I look in their eyes and it is all there. No matter how jaded or cold those eyes may be, the soul is visible if you look deeply enough."

He looked in her eyes that way. His gaze pierced them until she feared he really could see her soul.

She fought to hold the invasion at bay. She scrambled to throw up barriers to protect the corners that no one should ever see. Even she did not inspect some of them.

His gaze softened, as if he had perceived more than he expected. To her horror she saw flickers of confusion, even tentative recognition in his eyes.

"Your condition makes you too bold, sir. I remind you that I am not one of your defendants."

In light of his distress, she tried to strike a note of understanding, even kindness, in the reprimand.

Instead she only managed to weaken her voice. She heard it shake like that of a frightened girl.

It checked him, however. And amused him. Like a jouster long experienced in tilting with his current opponent, he saw the gap in her armor.

He did not back away, but held her attention with a very different gaze. Hard, angry, and decidedly male, it alarmed her more than the last.

"You knew about this afternoon," he said.

"I was aware of it, yes."

"Did you come to gloat?"

"Whatever our differences, I hope that you do not think I would take pleasure in a man's death, or your discomfort."

He had not backed away. She still wanted to, but did not care for what that would imply.

His gaze shifted, and meandered over her bonnet and face, down to her shoulders. "Why are you here?"

The manner in which his gaze lingered and slid had her skin warming. "My meeting—"

"That could have waited."

She really wished he would move back and not hover like this, projecting a dominating, raw power. She silently cursed the way she was reacting, and the evidence that she had become susceptible to him. She had found ways to make sure she was never at such a disadvantage in her life, but those strategies now failed her.

She prayed that he did not know why.

"I will admit that I guessed—that I thought that

you would be most distressed today. I thought if I made my call now, it would comf—distract you a little. Help the hour to pass."

"How like you to think that talk of political meetings would ease a man's need."

Well, goodness, that was uncalled for, and close to disgracefully ribald. "Forgive me. It was stupid of me to think you might need company, when clearly all you required was that decanter."

"It was not stupid. It was very kind. Quite soft, actually. A very warm, womanly gesture. I am touched." He smiled slowly. "However, if you truly want to help, if you really want to distract me, there are better ways. When I saw that dress, I dared hope you had realized that."

He reached over and slowly skimmed his fingertips along the low, curved edge of her dress's neckline.

She almost jumped out of her skin, except her skin liked that touch too much to allow movement. She savored the alluring stroke and the memories it evoked for a delicious few moments.

Then she backed away. "You are indeed drunk."

He followed, step for step. "As I warned you. I have an excuse. I am sure we can find one for you too."

That flustered her badly. She was against the wall now, and he blocked any gracious retreat.

His fingertips stroked again. A feathery, delicious skimming sensation. He gazed in her eyes with a confident dare. She tightened her jaw and tensed her body to try to contain the lively tremors streaming through her.

"Mr. Knightridge, you are forgetting yourself."

"Indeed I am, and I thank you most kindly. You have succeeded in thoroughly distracting me from the hell of the hour and my dark thoughts. That was your intention, no? To offer solace?" His hand slid up her skin in a trailing, seductive caress of unbearable titillation. It roamed around her neck until it cupped her nape in a gentle hold.

She did not believe he was thoroughly distracted. His manner bore an edge, a danger, that suggested the darkness not only still lived in him but also drove him.

She tried to shrug his hand off, to no avail. She made to move away from the wall, but with one step he blocked her again.

"What a generous woman you are, Lady M. All this time I thought you were an irritating, argumentative, interfering, opinionated female, but I was wrong."

"It was not my intention to distract you like *this,* for heaven's sake. Get hold of yourself, sir."

"I would rather get hold of a woman. That would be very comforting right now. I assure you, nothing else will suffice." He made a display of looking over each of his shoulders. "I'll be damned, it appears you are the only woman here."

His hand pressed against her neck, easing her forward. Panic and shock broke in her.

"Sir, it is ignoble of you to importune me in this

manner. Your inebriation does not excuse it. I *insist* that you move and allow me to leave. I will *not* be—"

The next thing she knew, he was kissing her.

How outrageous. How *disastrous*.

How . . . wonderful.

If you could silence Charlotte's sharp tongue, she was a very appealing woman.

That was Nathaniel's first thought on kissing her.

He was behaving badly and he knew it. He was not really drunk enough to excuse the impulse he followed. He was angry enough not to give a damn, however. Angry at the world, at his failure, and, since she was available, at her.

His little goads and teases had indeed kept the darkness from engulfing him. Now desire overwhelmed all thoughts of the day's sickening events. He welcomed the oblivion.

It had been some time since he had kissed a woman. Not since Lyndale's last party. His body remembered the intense passion of that night and ached to repeat it. His muddled senses dredged up the sensations and wonders of that dream and his floating mind experienced them again.

Suddenly he was not in his sitting room but in a darkened salon embracing a mysterious, sensual goddess who knew no restraints.

The lips he kissed were unbearably soft and warm. He swept his tongue in a welcoming, velvety mouth and a low, lyrical sigh played on her breath. A beautiful sound, full of assent and anticipation. He kissed her again and his head bumped her bonnet.

Bonnet? She had been wearing no bonnet. A silken veil covered her hair and a mask obscured her face.

The bonnet interfered with both his kiss and his fantasy. He plucked at its ribbons and cast it away. He pulled his lover into an embrace and savored her soft warmth. He looked into her eyes.

Desire and vulnerability looked back. He had not realized what a potent combination that could be, or the reactions it could stir. Even with that mask, he could see where her soul dwelled. Her face might be hidden, but her essence was open to him.

He blinked and reality intruded. These eyes were not looking out from a bejeweled mask. They were not gazing through the pale light of candles. They were owned by a woman not at all mysterious or anonymous, and it was the middle of the day, not night. The middle of a terrible day.

But the eyes seemed the same. And the expression, and the desire. He realized that his befuddled mind was confusing time and place. He was seeing other than was here, but he did not care.

He kissed her again and submerged himself in that ambiguous world where the past and present seemed to merge. Only now he knew it was Charlotte he kissed, even if it felt as if it was the other.

She did not object. He did not have to seduce. She embraced him and accepted and shared, her tongue well silenced now, but not still. The lovely sighs of the memory sang in his head, joining hers.

It felt good. Blissfully removed from reality. The pleasure offered escape as nothing else could.

He cupped her breast with his hand. She arched into it with a little cry. He felt for the hooks closing her dress. She moved as if she welcomed the offer of freedom.

His arousal roared out of control. He wanted to bury his face in her soft breasts and his hips in her thighs and his erection in her tight passage. He would know peace for a brief while before he faced the ugly world again.

He picked her up and carried her to the sofa across the room and set her on his lap. Kissing her hard, devouring her willing passion, he made quick work of the hooks and loosened her stays so he could reach her breasts.

"You are very soft. Very lovely." He kissed the breast he cradled in his hand. "It does not matter that you choose not to speak. I do not need words to know everything about you."

He brushed his thumb over her erect nipple. A muffled cry of pleasure filled his head. A sweet, beautiful moan followed. It pulled him back into the memory.

Her skin tasted so sweet as he kissed her neck, her bare shoulder. His lips moved down, savoring, his tongue flicking at soft velvet warmth. Finally her perfect breast was in his mouth and her delirium at the pleasure carried him to a place where nothing but sensation existed. Pleasure and peace swept him, followed by the urge to lose himself in her lush, feminine comfort. He caressed down her silken nakedness. . . .

Garments interfered. A soft mountain of skirt and petticoats. She was not naked.

He pressed through the cloth for the body beneath. He began lifting the fabric so he could reach her legs.

A tight grip on his wrist stopped him. The soft body in his embrace turned to stone. A new cry penetrated the bliss. One of shock.

"Nathaniel, listen," she whispered in a furious scold.

"Did you say something, my dear? If you expressed impatience, I can only respond that I am dealing with your obstructing garments as quickly as I can."

She smacked his shoulder. "Oh, pay attention for once in your conceited life." She pointed away, to the opposite wall. *"Listen."* She began squirming out of his hold.

Fantasy and reality collided, breaking both into pieces.

"I know he is here." The loud, imperious voice outside the chamber made the afternoon reassemble itself at once.

Jacobs's voice matched the other in volume. "My lord, your son is indisposed. He is unwell. I will tell him you called."

"What twaddle. Indisposed, hell. He is probably

just sleeping off another night's drunken revel. Go back and tell him I am here."

Charlotte's head turned and her eyes widened. "It is the *earl,*" she mouthed silently. She looked down at her exposed breasts with astonishment, as if she had never seen them before. She seemed to stop breathing.

Suddenly sober, viciously so, Nathaniel set her on her feet and rose as well. "Have no fear. Jacobs will hold him off."

He quickly set to righting her garments. She scrambled to help.

"This is *dreadful*. If I am found like this—"

"Move your hands. Your stays—the lacing is—"

"Hurry."

In a hectic flurry of clumsy actions and Lady M.'s desperate exhortations for speed, they managed to get the stays half-fixed and her bodice up. He began on the hooks in back.

"Stand aside, Jacobs. My son is not in his chamber, ill. I can hear him in that sitting room and I will see him *now.*"

Charlotte froze, then pivoted toward the door, horrified.

"This way." Nathaniel took her arm and sped her to a side door. She broke free, ran to get her parasol and bonnet, then hurried back, tripping twice on the hem of her loose skirt.

He opened the door. "Those stairs lead down to the kitchen. Jacobs will get you out once you are ..."

He made a gesture to indicate the work still to be done on her garments.

Her face burned. She looked close to raving panic. Clutching her dress closed in back and her bonnet and parasol to her breast, she crossed the threshold just as the other door began opening.

"My apologies your visit ended so poorly, Lady M. I am most grateful you called."

She cast him a deadly glare that said he would pay dearly for this day.

Nathaniel closed the door just in time to turn and see his father striding into the chamber.

"Father, what a treat. To what do I owe the rare and inconvenient favor of your attention today?"

CHAPTER
TWO

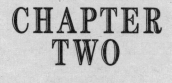

Charlotte cursed herself. It had been stupid to come here today. Reckless. *Insane.*

Now here she was in a small basement kitchen, having her dress fastened by a servant she did not know. A *male* servant.

It was so humiliating that she wanted to thrash someone with her parasol.

The idea to come here had seemed so sensible when it first struck her. She knew the responsibility Nathaniel would feel for that young man's execution. She had empathized with the anguish it would cause. It had seemed perfectly decent, even necessary, to give the comfort of company to Mr. Knightridge so he would not suffer the vigil alone.

The next time she decided to do such a noble deed, she hoped someone locked her in her bedchamber.

Of course, she had not expected him to kiss her. She had certainly never anticipated that if he did, she would capitulate so completely. Memories of her abandon caused a new flood of humiliation.

Jacobs finished with the dress. Charlotte accepted her mantle. Jacobs's face remained as bland as a dumpling while he escorted her to the kitchen's garden door. She suspected he had shown other women out this way. Disreputable ones.

Well, she had behaved most disreputably herself. She deserved to be sneaking out of Albany like a soiled dove.

She mounted the stairs and slipped along the covered walkway that led to Albany's back entrance on Vigo Street. Beneath the roof's deep shadows, she trusted no one would recognize her if they should be glancing out the windows of the other apartments. Just to be safe, she would never again wear this mantle or bonnet.

The cold air bit her burning face. She walked to her carriage and gave instructions that she was going home.

As the carriage moved, she sank back in the seat. The full implications of the scandalous episode overwhelmed her.

Bad enough to melt like an ingenue when he kissed her. Bad enough to end up half-naked on his lap. But to almost be found there by his father, the Earl of Norriston—to have to rush to dress and sneak out—to have his servant know *everything*—

And the worst part, the most dreadful and frightening part, the memory that had her stomach sick and her head splitting, was the look in Nathaniel's eyes when he gazed into hers.

And the bold confidence of his advances.

And what he said as they embraced on the sofa.

I do not need words to know everything about you.

She hoped she was wrong, but feared she was not. He knew far too much about her.

He had realized that she was the woman with him at that party.

"You look like hell." The Earl of Norriston examined Nathaniel with the same critical expression he had used since his five sons had been children. Those steely eyes rarely saw much in his progeny to give him pleasure.

Right now it was clear the earl was most displeased with his youngest son. Nathaniel did not care. He had long ago ceased attempting to reconcile his life with his father's lack of approval.

"Good Lord, is that a love bite on your neck? Fix your collar and show some discretion."

Nathaniel absently pulled at his collar. The passion that produced the mark intruded on his mind, making him smile.

The earl lowered his tall, imposing form into the green upholstered chair. He noticed the decanter beside it. "Drinking already?"

"Yes, and a goodly amount too. Whatever you want with me, another day would be better."

"I expect your drunken state explains the broken windowpane."

"I lost my temper."

"Still sulking about that Binchley fellow, eh? Pull yourself together. He was guilty, and it is a relief your theatrics did not get him off. The law is not a game, you know. It isn't like your chess or tennis matches."

Nathaniel turned away. He struggled to quell a rising anger. Expressing it would do no good. The earl did not like that his youngest son was a lawyer of any kind, and detested the criminal defenses that Nathaniel mounted.

As he found the calm to face the conversation to come, he wondered if Charlotte had made a clean escape. The other bachelors who had apartments at Albany were rarely at home in the afternoons. It was unlikely she was seen leaving. Still—

"What is that smell?"

Nathaniel turned to see the earl sniffing the air.

"Is that perfume? You had a woman here today, didn't you?"

"I have my women elsewhere. That is incense that I burned last night." Nathaniel lied with conviction. It was a talent he had acquired as a youth. It made dealing with his father easier.

"Incense? Papist twaddle."

"It was incense from Calcutta."

"Then pagan twaddle."

"Well, I like to experiment with twaddle in all its glorious manifestations. Now, why are you here?"

Not to offer company or comfort over the failure

with Binchley, that was already clear. The earl would never do that, or see it the way Nathaniel did. His father was not a man to perceive any responsibility on Nathaniel's part, even if he had thought Binchley was innocent. It had taken Lady Mardenford to comprehend the hell that came with this day.

That had really been very kind of her, especially since they were not even friendly. With his increasing sobriety he realized how brave and thoughtful she had been. In payment he had importuned her and left her open to scandal and humiliation.

That she had not objected very hard to his advances really did not matter. His behavior had been inexcusable.

The seductive lure of memories involving the mystery goddess hardly made it better. He doubted Lady M. would take kindly to the excuse that while he caressed her he had been full of thoughts about another woman.

Flashing images of the passion on the sofa flickered in his mind, resurrecting the sensations. Her eyes, her breasts . . . The odd confusion of past and present nudged at him, demanding some attention. The lapse of restraint on both their parts had been a little peculiar, now that he considered it with halfway sober senses.

His attention narrowed on his father. He would sort out what had happened with Lady M. later, and make the necessary apologies, for what little good they would do. Right now he resented the intrusion that had sent her running half-dressed from the room.

"I have come on two matters," the earl said. "Collingsworth approached me."

"What does the good baronet want?"

"He controls a living near Shrewsbury. It is yours if you want it."

"How generous of him. Is, by chance, this living tied to the requirement that I share it with his daughter?"

"That goes without saying."

"It sounds to be a fine arrangement for you and Collingsworth. He marries a daughter into an earl's family, and you obtain his help for that investment you are planning in Wales. However, I fail to see how it benefits either me or his daughter."

The earl sighed with annoyance. "It is a handsome living and it is time you married. She is a good match."

"I will decide when it is time, and she is not a good match. She is in love with another man. Everyone knows that."

"Girlish twaddle. She will get over—"

"I do not intend to count on that. Tell Collingsworth that I will not be able to accept his offer. I would not, even if his daughter were indeed a good match. It would be blasphemous for me to become a clergyman."

"You've the education for it."

"I never took orders or a living because I've neither the temperament nor the conviction for it."

The earl's laugh did not arrest his sneer. "No, you have the temperament for the courtroom. Common

Pleas is not dramatic enough, so you embarrass the family with performances in the Old Bailey. Better than a real stage, I guess. Thank God I convinced you to spare us that scandal."

Nathaniel chose to ignore the goads. There had been rows enough over all this in years past, and he was both too old and too indifferent to engage in another.

"I would appreciate your ceasing these attempts to find such livings for me, Father. It should be clear by now that I will never accept one."

"You could be a bishop, damn it. You could sit in the House of Lords someday if you would do as I say."

"Make one of my brothers a bishop. Edward and Nigel must resent the way you passed them over on this grand plan."

"They do not have your talents. It takes brains and guile to work one's way up in the church."

It was the closest thing to a compliment that the earl had given in years. A little disarmed, Nathaniel moved the conversation to other things.

"What is the second matter that brought you here?"

"One that will be more to your liking. You are going to be asked to serve as prosecuting counsel in a trial."

Nathaniel took that in. How like his father to be so ignorant that he thought this would be a welcome charge.

"You probably never noticed, but I have never served as a prosecutor."

"Then this will be your chance to better yourself. Do it well, and you could be on your way to becoming a judge."

"You misunderstand. I have been asked before. I refused."

The implications were lost on the earl. "Well, you can't refuse this time. You are needed. It is that Finley fellow. It must be handled right and everyone says you are the man to do it."

John Finley was one of the criminal lords who held court in London's rookeries. Nathaniel was aware he had been caught, but aside from deciding at the outset he would not defend if asked, he had not paid much attention to the case.

"He is a thief and murderer, and anyone can prosecute if the evidence is there."

"He is also a blackmailer. It is how they caught him, when he went to get the blunt. A man of importance will be laying down information against him." The earl paused for effect and added a meaningful stare for emphasis. "This Finley can't be allowed to speak his lies in the court. He cannot be permitted to sully a good man's name in revenge."

"The judge will see he does not."

"That can't be counted on. If the judge permits a defense counsel, which the likes of you have made almost certain, Finley may show up with one of those lawyers like you who uses tricks and innuendo to obscure things."

One of those lawyers like you. Nathaniel had to admit his father was right. If he thought Finley was innocent, and he was defending him, he would not hesitate to use the potential embarrassment of a witness to his benefit.

"Who is the good man who will be testifying?"

"Mardenford."

Nathaniel's interest immediately sharpened. The Baron Mardenford was Charlotte's brother-in-law. He had inherited the title six years ago upon her late husband's death.

The earl sighed. "It will be all around town in a day or so, I expect. Damned shame. You know how people talk. This Finley approached Mardenford demanding payment to keep quiet about family secrets. Knowing there are none, Mardenford went straight to the police and helped them set a trap. You can see the danger, however. Finley can spin any tale he wants in court and the whole world will hear it." He shook his head. "Damned brave of Mardenford to come forward. Surprises me, truth be told. I would not have guessed he had it in him."

Nathaniel debated the matter. He did not spend all his time in the Old Bailey. He defended only a few people a month, and he chose them carefully and always out of duty to justice. The accused had so few rights in trials that he did not feel any compulsion to accept the role of prosecutor, however. Any fool could obtain convictions.

He felt some obligations in this case, however. Not to the baron, but to his family. Should Finley be allowed to impugn Mardenford, it would taint everyone connected to the name, including Charlotte.

After this afternoon, he probably owed her some token of apology besides words.

"What is known about this Finley?"

His father shrugged. "I wasn't told much. He recruits children, it seems. The police say he has a whole family, so to speak. Sends them out as pickpockets and whatnot. This town is dangerous enough and does not need men who run schools for criminals."

Nathaniel rose and paced to the broken window. The cold air flowing through the ragged shards of one pane helped crystallize his thinking. With his father's last words, the events of the day all twined together into one braid.

Harry Binchley had been trained in crime by a man like this Finley. He had been taught to steal as a child. By the time he reached fifteen, his life's path had been long set.

That path had led to the gallows today.

For once he agreed with his father. This town did not need men who ran schools for criminals and exploited children for their own gain.

He returned to the earl. "I will give you an answer tomorrow, when I am securely sober. However, if asked to prosecute, I will most likely accept."

"You appear melancholic, James," Charlotte said. "Very quiet. I hope that bringing Ambrose here to visit was not an inconvenience."

"My apologies. I am distracted by a message I received before we came. It is never an inconvenience to spend time with you and my son. Hours like this are always a pleasure."

Her brother-in-law spoke from his chair by the fire in the library. A book lay open on his lap, but she had noticed no pages had been turned.

She sat on the floor nearby, sorting blocks with Ambrose. All of her attention was not on their play, however. The back of her mind sorted other things, those having to do with her visit to Mr. Knightridge that afternoon.

The baron and his son helped her almost ignore those embarrassing memories, but they clamored for attention and decisions.

The blond child's face glowed with delight as he impishly knocked down a stack of blocks they had built.

"You are very good with him. Very good *to* him," Mardenford said, watching now. "I thank God you offered him your love after my Beatrice passed."

"It is I who am grateful. I did not think it was possible to love another person like this."

She watched little Ambrose make another stack. She snuck a tap against one block to push it over so it would not unbalance the tower.

Ambrose had still been an infant when his mother died two years earlier, and so helpless that her heart had been touched. She had never guessed, however, that as he grew, her love would too. In the last year it had invaded new corners of her heart, and blossomed with a sweetness that just deepened and spread.

Her role as surrogate mother had given birth to precious emotions denied her through her marriage. Because of her husband's poor health, the world did not assume she was barren. She did not either, in her mind. Her heart, however, secretly believed the problem had not been Philip's health but her own inability to conceive. She knew that she might never bear a child of her own, and not only because she lacked an interest in marrying again.

She did not mind that so much anymore. Loving Ambrose had revealed that one need not give birth to a child to see him as one's son. However, she suspected her devotion to the child had created a situation that her brother-in-law found too comfortable.

She showed Ambrose how to build a wall around their tower. As the child worked it out, she gave his father her attention.

"He needs love like this all the time," she said.

"His nurse is very affectionate."

"You know what I mean, James."

His expression showed that he did. Pale, long, and soft beneath his brown hair, his face reflected mild chagrin.

"I know I must remarry, Charl, for the boy and for the title. I will eventually. However, right now I cannot reconcile with the idea."

She said no more. She understood all too well.

James and Beatrice had enjoyed a good marriage. Since James was a little dull, and Beatrice a little dim, they had suited each other. It had not been a grand, dramatic passion, but perhaps that was for the better.

After all, she and Philip had not dwelled in drama either, but she had missed him badly when he died.

She gave James a sympathetic smile. She would like to explain things to him, things that would help him perhaps.

She would like to say that she understood the ennui of the spirit that he was experiencing, because she had felt it too. She wanted to warn that it could last forever if he was not careful, because it almost had for her. There was comfort in those dulled emotions. Even a type of peace. One could drift there for a long time and then suddenly blink and realize years had passed.

She gazed down at the blocks. It was like living in a tower, watching the world but not participating in life. The safety became seductive. Eventually its appeal had nothing to do with the mourning that started it all.

She did not explain it. While she and James had a close friendship, this was too personal. She might serve as mother to his son and as hostess at his dinners, but she could never confide to him how her tower had recently crumbled.

She could never admit that in a fit of desperate fear of being imprisoned forever in that place of safety, she had set fire to its foundations.

"Have you received word from Laclere Park?" he asked.

"Fleur writes that she is uncomfortable and ready. Dante writes letters that make no sense. The child will come soon and they will send for me at the first sign." Her brother had taken his wife to the family estate in Sussex to await the birth of their first child. She glanced down at little Ambrose's soft, tiny hands and wondered if she would soon have another child to love.

"Have you been receiving responses to the invitations?" James asked. She could tell he was trying to be companionable despite whatever preoccupied him.

The query made her memories of the afternoon loom. She had just received one response before James and Ambrose arrived. Nathaniel Knightridge had sent a note indicating he would attend.

That promised to be a little awkward now.

"They have been arriving," she said. "The usual acceptances, and the predictable rejections. Now I wait for answers from those who should accept but perhaps will not."

"Do not hope for too much."

"If my efforts begin discussions, that will be a victory in itself. Parliament will be on notice that people care about this. This first step will be followed by a second and a third. I will see this reform before I die. It is past time."

James did not respond. He did not entirely approve of her cause, although he had agreed to present those petitions to Parliament despite his misgivings. Her brother Vergil, the Viscount Laclere, would have done it. However, since their sister had been involved in a recent scandal regarding her marriage, everyone agreed it would be best to have it done by someone without connection to such things.

Ambrose was almost finished with his castle. He reached for a final block, and his little elbow hit the tower. It tumbled and his face folded into the misery that heralded tears.

She gathered him up and held him while he cried. She looked over to find James watching. He appeared sad, and she worried that he was picturing the woman who should be holding the child on this rug in this library instead.

It was his home, after all. When he inherited the title on the death of his brother, he had not demanded she leave the family mansion. Instead he had bought another grand house for his bride, so that Charlotte would not be displaced. It had been a generous gesture that spoke of a sensitivity rarely found in men.

The sobs subsided. Ambrose fell asleep in her arms. She pressed her lips to his downy hair and kept him in her embrace. Loving this child had been the first spark that led to the fire that reignited her vitality.

She dwelled in the sweet emotion, but the sorting was still taking place at the back of her mind. By the time James took the child and left the library, she had made a decision.

Before she saw Nathaniel Knightridge again, she needed to discover if he knew all that she feared.

"I appreciate your company, Lyndale," Charlotte said as she strolled through Belgrave Square the next afternoon. "I have not had the opportunity to congratulate you on your wedding, aside from my note upon seeing the announcement the other day."

The Earl of Lyndale kicked a stone nonchalantly. The wind tossed his dark hair because he carried his hat. "The need for speed was the usual reason, as I am sure you surmised. I regret your aid in planning the more sumptuous ceremony was in vain, but I do not regret that we married sooner rather than later. I would have eloped the day after she accepted my proposal if given the choice."

Charlotte had to laugh. "Oh, how the mighty fall. It is delicious to see you laid low by love. If the reason for haste is the usual one, more congratulations are due."

He beamed delight. Just like Ewan McLean, the Earl of Lyndale, to be indifferent to whispers about that quick marriage. But then, any marriage for this man had been so unlikely that there were bound to be whispers no matter what.

Prior to inheriting the title last autumn, he had achieved a notorious reputation. His bachelor parties would be long remembered. He had a swing hanging in his second drawing room, and displayed an astonishing collection of erotic art there as well. For many he still was a lord of sin, and his sudden marriage to a woman of neither fortune nor good family only seemed the latest of his outrages.

Charlotte broached the subject for which she had sought out this man. They had an old friendship and she hoped he would not interrogate her too closely. She also counted on him to show his usual lack of propriety when she steered the conversation toward indelicate matters.

"I imagine your parties are over now. The special ones, that is."

"Yes, they are a thing of the past. All of my orgies will be private now, with a guest list of two."

"I hear the last one was quite impressive. A Roman theme, the whispers say."

"It was a fitting grand finale, although I never intended it as such at the time. In truth, it did not impress *me* much, but perhaps I had already outgrown such things."

"I will confess I was always curious about them, and what really transpired."

"If so, you should have attended one. You were always invited. Now your chance has passed. I am thoroughly domesticated and only the normal, furtive affairs will occur in my house among guests in the future."

She prodded him to reminisce more. "It was said that ladies of good birth would attend wearing masks."

"That was common, yes."

"I have always wondered if that was effective. Could a mask obscure an identity sufficiently? For example, were you always fooled?"

He cast her a roguish glance. "I am not sure this conversation is proper, Lady M. What a relief that my marriage has not made you treat me like a dullard, however. Now, as to the parties and your belated fascination, since the lighting was very low, and the masks covered all but mouths and chins, they could be effective."

Thank goodness.

"Assuming the woman did not speak," he continued. "There was one lady of very high standing who only whispered. Her laugh, however, was most distinctive and always gave her away. Everyone pretended it did not, of course."

Charlotte had surmised that a voice could identify a woman. When she attended Lyndale's grand finale she had barely spoken at all, and then only in the lowest whisper.

I do not need words to know everything about you.

"How interesting. So a man could be very . . . familiar with a woman and never know who she was. They could meet the next day with him totally unaware of their prior . . . meeting."

"Certainly. With only a few candles lighting the chamber, others would remain ignorant as well."

She barely stifled a deep exhale of relief.

"Unless, of course . . ." Lyndale shrugged and gave her a confidential look.

"Unless what?"

"Well, she would remain unknown to the man unless they shared intimacies again, is all I was indicating. Unless he was the sort to only notice his own pleasure, he would probably recognize the similarities."

Oh dear.

Lyndale tipped his head close to hers. "Is there some reason you are quizzing me on this, madam?"

he asked in a teasing tone. "Some reason you sought me out on this cold winter day to stroll and chat about bygone orgies? Do you have a friend who attended my party and now fears for her reputation?"

She felt her face getting warm. "As it happens, yes. Please do not inquire further. She is most distraught. It was not like her at all. She succumbed to curiosity and now regrets it. She confided in me and I offered to find out how dangerous her situation is. I would have asked my brother Dante, but he has taken Fleur down to Laclere Park."

"Have no fear. Discretion is my second name."

Actually, it was not. Lyndale was infamous for being tactless and for blurting things he should not. And Nathaniel Knightridge was one of his friends.

"Truly, sir, you must promise to tell no one of this conversation." She spoke emphatically so he would know it was important.

He paused in his steps. She stopped and faced him. He looked her over with a speculative gaze in which suspicion began growing.

"Lady M., I am not celebrated for being astute, but I find myself wondering if there is a friend at all. By chance was it you who—"

"What a preposterous suggestion. If you recall, I was not even in town that week."

"You announced you were leaving. That is not the same as actually being gone."

He kept peering at her. She tried to appear indignant, but she felt her face getting hotter.

His eyes twinkled. "Considering your dismay, I do

not think I am wrong, let alone preposterous. My word, this is rich. Now I am dying to know just how naughty you were."

"Your assumptions are unwarranted. I will not tolerate your scandalous speculation."

His brow furrowed. His eyes reflected a searching memory. She realized with horror that he was seeing his party again, and examining its various participants.

His face fell, stunned. "Good heavens, *you* were the woman with Knightridge. I am right, aren't I? Really, madam, you were very naughty indeed. Does he know? Has he guessed?"

She wanted to die. She began to refute him but he held up a hand, silencing her.

"Do not distress yourself. My lips are sealed. I will admit that I am truly shocked for once in my life, but in the least judgmental way. Actually, I am inclined to congratulate you."

"Congrat—! You are still an insufferable rogue, McLean."

"And you are a more interesting woman than I realized, Lady M."

His eyes twinkled again. He bit back a laugh.

She smacked him with her parasol and hurried away.

CHAPTER
THREE

~~~

S he was transported?"

"That was her reprieve after we appealed to the King's Bench."

"Better than hanging, I suppose."

"Yes, better than hanging."

Nathaniel did his best to charm Mrs. Strickland into opening her mind. Her attendance at Charlotte's meeting indicated the mind might already be slightly ajar, although Nathaniel suspected this was one of the ladies who had come to gawk at the dancing dog. As a woman with influence over a certain judge, she carried more power than her diminutive stature and childlike face implied, however, so it behooved him to do his best jig.

Mrs. Strickland's brow knit as she assessed the case they had been discussing. Out of the corner of his eye, Nathaniel noticed Charlotte watching his conversation out the corner of one of hers.

It was the most attention she had given him all afternoon. Her greeting and few words had been cool and formal, her smiles fleeting and blank. She acted as if the visit to his apartment had never happened.

He had not yet decided whether to allow her to pretend they had never kissed. Memories of her in erotic dishabille had invaded his mind for several days now, so he doubted he could be so noble.

"If her husband was a danger, she should have sought relief from the Church on the basis of cruelty, not killed him." Mrs. Strickland spoke with severe righteousness.

"She was impoverished, and such appeals are expensive. Nor would she have found much relief. Her husband's threats would not have sufficed as proof, nor would his thrashings of her. Only violence of a deadly nature gets much credit from most of those judges, although there have been some welcome exceptions lately." He donned his most sincere expression. "I assure you it was self-defense. When arrested she still had the bruises on her neck."

That only vexed Mrs. Strickland. No doubt, since she was married to an unusually pliable gentleman, she could not fathom the reality of men who were brutal.

A woman walked past them and Mrs. Strickland's frown disappeared. As her sparkling eyes followed the passing figure, sympathy and confusion replaced skepticism.

Penelope, Charlotte's older sister, had with her mere presence reminded Mrs. Strickland that bad husbands could be found in every stratum of society.

Mrs. Strickland noticed Nathaniel watching her. An embarrassed smile softened her face. She glanced meaningfully toward Penelope. "One hears things," she confided.

"I regret to say that this time the gossip is true." Normally he would not be so indiscreet, but things were being heard only because Penelope had revealed them for that purpose.

Not in a courtroom, however, and not for Charlotte's cause. Penelope had let whispers tell her story only in an effort to save a man's life. As a result, most of good society knew some very sordid details about the abuse she had experienced at the hands of her husband, the Earl of Glasbury.

Mrs. Strickland excused herself to chat with another man. Nathaniel wondered if she would eventually make her way to the table in the second drawing room where the petitions waited with ink and pens. Of more use would be some words spoken into an ear on a pillow near hers. Not Mr. Strickland's ear.

He looked for Charlotte again. Her head was bowed to listen to the confidences of another woman. The meeting took the form of a social assembly, although Charlotte had made a speech about its purpose and pointed out the petitions. Now, as people chatted and drank punch, a gentler persuasion was under way.

Having given enough testimony for a while, Nathaniel made his way into the second drawing room's relative quiet. He strolled over to peruse the petitions. There were two, one for men and one for women. While every citizen's voice was important, the masculine ones would carry much more weight in Parliament.

"More men have signed than women," a quiet voice observed.

Nathaniel turned to the dark-haired man who had arrived at his side. "Well, there are many men who would like divorce to be easier too. It was shrewd of Lady Mardenford and her allies to restrict this first petition to that matter. Was that on your advice, Hampton?"

Julian Hampton's vague smile was in keeping with his reserved character. "I suggested that men might find sympathy on this issue, but that few would welcome a reform of the property laws that enrich them in marriage."

Nathaniel gazed down the signatures. "Yours is not here, I notice."

"I will sign discreetly on the fourth or fifth page."

As discreetly as he attended this meeting, and observed from the walls instead of joining his lover in her conversations, Nathaniel assumed. Hampton and Penelope would marry sometime in the months ahead, when the heat of the scandal and notoriety surrounding them had cooled.

Hampton lifted the petition and checked the names. "Yours is not here either."

"An oversight." Nathaniel dipped a pen, bent, and scrawled his name.

He felt Hampton move, and sensed yet another

presence. He straightened and turned. "Mardenford. Have you come to sign?" He offered the pen.

"Actually, I was looking to speak to you." He addressed only Nathaniel. He had not greeted Hampton, but instead given him the cut direct.

Hampton noticed. With a wry smile, he excused himself.

"That was rude," Nathaniel said.

Mardenford's long face narrowed more as his thin lips pursed. "He should not be here. He and the countess should be more discreet."

"They could only be more discreet if they retired to abbeys. The whole world knows they are in love and will marry. I think both the delay and discretion are stupid. It is refreshing that they do not bow to those who would have them do penance by withdrawing from society entirely."

Mardenford shrugged as if it was of no account, but of course, to him, it obviously was. "My Beatrice would not have received either of them."

No, his Beatrice would not have. She had been pretty and gracious and shallow. Nathaniel did not doubt that she would have proven incapable of doing a single thing that was not decreed as acceptable.

She had suited her husband well. The current Baron Mardenford was not so much dull as undistinguished. He was interchangeable in his interests and conversation with a hundred other men of his rank. He possessed neither a colorful appearance nor manner, and would never be memorable let alone eccentric. He was part of the wallpaper of the world into which Nathaniel had been born.

His elder brother, Charlotte's husband, had been much the same, but more amiable. When Nathaniel had heard that Charlotte Duclairc was to marry Philip, Baron Mardenford, he had thought it an odd match. Philip was nothing like her brother Laclere, who commanded a room upon entering. Nor did he have anything in common with her other brother Dante, who could charm a snake out of its skin.

It struck him now, as he strolled to a window with Mardenford in tow, that perhaps that had been Philip's appeal. She would have known all about the heartaches waiting for women who married charming wastrels like Dante. As for her elder brother, the Viscount Laclere, living with such a strong-willed man might put a woman off such a character. Especially if she was strong-willed herself.

"If you did not want to greet Hampton, you did not have to join us. He is my friend and I will not have him insulted while I converse with him."

"I wanted to speak to you, and it required some privacy. I thought it unlikely I would find you alone again this afternoon," Mardenford said. "I heard that you will prosecute Finley. I was relieved by the news, I will admit."

"My father requested that I accept. Being a devoted son, I could not refuse."

Mardenford appeared nonchalant, but there was worry in his eyes. "I trust he will not be allowed to speak lies about my family."

"That will depend on his defense counsel to some extent."

"I have heard he has none."

Nathaniel's gaze sharpened on the bland face masking a deep ill ease. "Will the judge refuse him one?"

"No lawyer will speak for him, the way I heard it."

Nathaniel bit back a curse. The lords of the realm had done an excellent job protecting their own. With a coercive word here and an intimidating word there, they had ensured that no lawyer would take Finley's defense.

And the only one who might have, simply in duty to fair play, the only one whose birth made coercion and intimidation ineffective, had been claimed for the prosecutor's role.

"Well, it appears you have nothing to worry about."

Mardenford's eyes cleared at once. He beamed with relief. He might have been in the Old Bailey himself and just heard his own acquittal.

"I should rejoin the others," Nathaniel said. "I think your sister-in-law expects me to cajole more ladies toward sympathy before we are done."

He walked away with a simmering annoyance. He did not mind dancing to Charlotte's tune for a few hours. He resented that he would soon be doing so to Mardenford's.

He was not leaving.

As her guests drifted out, Charlotte could not ignore that Nathaniel was never among them.

His presence had unsettled her all afternoon. She felt him in the room. She had the sensation he kept looking at her, but every time she checked he was deeply involved in conversation with someone else.

He might at least be a little embarrassed upon seeing her again. She was so conscious of the awkwardness that she had become as taut as a tightly stretched string. It was really unfair that he appeared completely at ease.

Of course, that could mean that he had decided to pretend their last meeting never occurred. Maybe he would claim drink had obscured his memory.

Perhaps it actually had.

"It is a little rude to keep frowning at him."

The lyrical voice jolted Charlotte out of her thoughts. Her sister-in-law Bianca's wide skirt pressed against her own as Bianca leaned her blonde head close to issue the soft reprimand.

"It is even ruder to have been distracted from what you were telling me," Charlotte admitted.

Bianca's large blue eyes glanced over to Nathaniel. "Well, he is highly distracting."

"And he knows it."

"I realize the two of you do not get on, but you might look more kindly on him, as your sister does. You cannot deny he has been a great aid to her and to the family."

Charlotte could not deny that. It made her beholden to Nathaniel Knightridge, however, and she did not care for being so. Especially now.

Yesterday she had discovered that she was about to become more beholden to him.

She had learned two days ago that James was to testify at Finley's trial. The news caused a sick worry to lodge in her heart. She knew firsthand the horrors that blackmail could produce, and the way revelations could destroy a person's life. It went without saying that Finley possessed no damaging secrets, but he could lie in court and many would wonder, would talk. There were men who would have paid him off just to avoid the destructive rumors.

When word came yesterday that Knightridge would prosecute, the chill of fear had left her at once, replaced by a secure sense of safety. Knightridge would know how to protect James and the family; she did not doubt that. He would not allow little Ambrose to be tainted by unfounded lies.

"It is just he vexes me so," she muttered, sneaking another glance at him. He utterly commanded his corner of the room. Tall, lean, and broad-shouldered, he was immediately visible even with his golden head bowed toward Penelope's earnest expression. His aristocratic manner and sartorial elegance did not completely contain the magnetism that overwhelmed a courtroom when he unleashed it.

That overwhelmed her, too, as she had learned to her dismay. She had never before been at such a disadvantage with a man, not even her husband. Philip had always inspired feelings of peace and comfort, not this annoying, confusing turmoil.

"I know all about men who can be vexing,"

Bianca said with amusement. "Your brother and I did not like each other much when first we met."

"The situation between you and Laclere was *very* different," Charlotte said. "Mr. Knightridge and I *truly* do not care for each other." She snuck another glance. "He is just so ... so ... *so*."

Bianca laughed. "That you often cross swords proves that he is more *so* for you than for most."

Yes, in more ways than one. That was the confusing part. There was much about the man she could not bear. His conceit. His damnable arrogance. The vaguely mocking note in his polite tone as he explained during their arguments how he was right and she was wrong.

So how could she have twice now succumbed to him in ways that would shock Bianca? It made no sense.

Of course, they had not been arguing during those inexplicable lapses. They had not been talking at all.

"Well, he has served your needs well, at least," Bianca said.

Charlotte's body tensed. "What is *that* supposed to mean?"

"He has worked his charm on your behalf today. Come, let us go see the petitions. I have forced myself to wait although I wanted to count names every few minutes."

Charlotte followed Bianca toward the second drawing room. When they passed Nathaniel, Charlotte could not resist glancing toward him again.

At the last second, just as she began to avert her

gaze, he glanced to her in turn. For the smallest instant a very intimate power pierced her. He communicated no embarrassment with that look, nor apologies.

The effect was immediate, stunning, and worrisome. As she stumbled after Bianca on watery legs, warmth flushed her skin and sank deeper, lowering to where it ought not travel at a respectable political meeting. She barely composed herself by the time she reached the table with the petitions.

"Impressive," Bianca said, running her finger down the list of male names on one petition. "It is a good beginning, with so many prominent signatures."

"Now we must fill it with thousands more, from tradesmen and merchants and farmers." Charlotte was grateful to escape into the practicalities of the cause. "Come fairer weather, I will make a progression through the nearby counties doing so. Sophia has offered to hold assemblies in Devon."

Her voice faltered on the last few words. Even before she heard the evidence that someone was approaching them, she felt Nathaniel enter the room. Her blood hummed.

"Admiring the evidence of your triumph, ladies?"

Bianca greeted Nathaniel warmly. Charlotte felt her own smile stretch, as if someone squeezed her cheeks to force it.

"Your triumph, too," Bianca said. She lifted the other petition and pointed to several names. "I saw you conversing with these ladies, and think your persuasion accounts for their signatures."

"I am sure it was Lady M.'s speech that moved their hearts."

"You are too kind, sir." Charlotte took both papers. She turned and busied herself with laying them down very neatly. She fussed with arranging the pens and inkwell just so. She fought to quell her jumpy reaction to the masculine power enfolding her.

An awkward silence developed behind her.

"I must take my leave," Bianca said. "I am sure that my husband has called for the coach." She embraced Charlotte with one arm and moved her face close for a farewell kiss. "You are being rude again, dear. It is not like you and borders on inexcusable," she whispered.

That settled her faster than a slap. She *was* being rude, and it was not like her. She collected herself and turned to see Bianca leaving the room.

Which meant she and Nathaniel Knightridge were alone.

Nothing changed in his manner or stance. Even his expression remained the same. She sensed an alteration anyway. A quickening in the tempo of time. An alertness in her essence. A myriad of reactions left her vulnerable to a new, essential intimacy flowing between them.

He remembered their last meeting; she did not doubt it. He had not been inebriated enough the other day to forget. The only question was how much he knew about their prior passion. Her conversation with Lyndale had not reassured her as she had hoped, but left the matter ambiguous.

She swallowed her discomfort on that point, and found some grace. "Thank you for attending, Mr. Knightridge. Your aid was most welcome."

"Since you made such a special request, I could not refuse."

That certainly made it plain that he remembered. Nor was he going to pretend he did not. She thought that ungallant of him.

"I have heard that you agreed to prosecute John Finley," she said, thinking it best to speak of something other than the events surrounding that special request.

"That is true."

"I do not think you ever served as prosecuting counsel before."

"I made an exception this time. It was the least I could do as an apology to you. One is due, for my bad behavior when we last met."

He appeared sincere. There was not the slightest gloat or insinuation in his expression.

He was doing this for her, to make amends. That disarmed her. It also increased the aura of intimacy binding them.

"If my ignoble retreat from your home secured your talents on Mardenford's behalf, I suppose I can overcome the embarrassment."

"It was not your departure for which I sought to make amends, but your arrival. I realized later it was a very kind gesture to seek me out. A month had passed since the trial, and I do not think anyone else remembered what the day meant. For them, Binchley was dead already. His story had become a fading broadside. I regret that I did not appreciate your sympathy and instead treated you rudely when you arrived."

A familiar irritation poked at her composure. He was drawing some rather peculiar lines in this apology.

"I do not mean to be ungracious, but I would think that if apologies are due at all, the latter part of my visit requires them more than the earlier events."

"I disagree."

She lowered her voice to a tight whisper. "Mr. Knightridge, perhaps your condition left you too befuddled to grasp what occurred. I visited you for the reasons you say, and you importuned me."

"I think that you are exaggerating."

"Exaggerating? You forced yourself on me, to be plain about it. I came close to being compromised due to behavior of yours that, in its badness, far exceeded your rudeness upon my arrival."

"I do not remember it quite that way."

"Since we have started down this sorry path, allow me to refresh your memory. You—"

"My memories are very fresh, thank you. Remarkably vivid. In particular, I remember a woman in my arms who was well pleased, and very eager."

Her mouth fell open. She glanced past him to be sure no one had entered the room to overhear. "Mr. Knightridge, how dare—"

"I also remember your kissing me back very erotically, with enthusiastic passion." His gaze lowered to her chest in a way that made her nipples tingle.

"Sir—"

"I remember stays undone and the most lovely breasts in my hand and mouth." His gaze rose until it locked with hers. "A man would have to be a fool to regret any of that, Lady M. It would be hypocritical of me to apologize for that part of your visit, and equally so for you to demand such a lie."

She gaped at his boldness. She tried to find something indignant to say. Unfortunately, his shocking frankness had her body warming and her mind clouding.

He stepped closer. He dipped his head toward hers until his dark eyes were mere inches from her own. She was sure he was going to kiss here right here in the second drawing room while the remaining guests drank punch beyond the doorway.

She should step away. Only she couldn't because she was remembering too. His words had called forth the sensations again and they were too seductive to deny.

"I remember every caress and kiss we have shared, madam, and I will not pretend otherwise," he said quietly. "I tried, but have discovered I am incapable of maintaining the deception."

She closed her eyes for the kiss that was coming. She waited for those firm, warm lips to press hers. She waited for his strong arms to embrace her and hold her close.

She waited for the fire of passion to blaze through her soul yet again.

Nothing happened. No kiss. No touch.

Confused, she opened her eyes to see the back of Nathaniel's frock coat passing into the main drawing room.

CHAPTER FOUR

～

Memories filled Charlotte's head as she tossed in bed that night. Beautiful, cherished images invaded and lingered, demanding attention and reconsideration.

She saw Lyndale's private drawing room, full of shadows dotted with pools of candlelight. Musicians played by the windows and she could hear gaming in an adjoining room. The earl's notorious collection of art was barely visible. Like the figures on the sofas and chaise longues, only its vaguest features could be seen.

The atmosphere and lighting demanded whispers and furtive kisses. Instead people spoke freely. Joyfully. Except for the Roman costumes and the women's masks, if one ignored the entwined bodies barely visible here and there, it appeared a pleasant, normal party.

That had surprised her. She had expected something

very rare, more like a bacchanal one might view in a painting. These guests wore the right garments but they seemed too much of this world. Of her world.

She recognized some of the men. She stood there in her own costume, wondering if her mask obscured her identity enough. Now that she was here, she did not know what to do.

"Are you realizing that you do not belong here?" a voice said.

She froze. She knew that voice. Worse, it sounded like he knew her.

She looked over her shoulder. Apollo sat on a chaise longue in the corner. Not reclining, but resting his back against the wall behind it. A belted white linen tunic covered his body to his knees. Golden hair fell around his face and bronze sandals laced up his shins. He sat alone. He did not participate in either the conversations or the pleasures.

Nathaniel Knightridge suited the role of the god of light very well. She could not stop looking at him.

His gaze reflected no recognition. Nor did she see the kind of interest that several other male guests had sent her way already.

"Sit here. No one will approach you." He gestured to the end of the chaise longue.

She walked over, wondering if the nearby candle would give her away. It did not, but it revealed much more about him. He appeared melancholic and re-flective. He barely paid her attention as she perched on the edge of the cushion.

He closed his eyes and listened to the music, but

eventually he looked her way again. "Are you disappointed? Did you expect naked people writhing on the carpet? Nude women served up like so many platters of food?"

"I suppose," she whispered.

His gaze drifted over her. A little of that male interest showed this time. "Did you come to watch or play?"

"Neither."

"Then why?"

Why, indeed? She had no answer now. The idea had made sense an hour ago.

"Perhaps you just did not want to be alone."

His statement made her stiffen. A tremble shook inside her. She stared at the musicians and tried to contain her profound reaction to his simple observation.

He cocked his head so he could see her face. He looked so deeply that it frightened her. She felt horribly exposed.

Comprehension entered his eyes. A warm understanding. He did not know who she was, but she sensed that he knew everything else.

"We have much in common tonight," he said. "It is not a bad place to hide from oneself. The music is pleasant and the joy of the others lightens dark thoughts."

His perception stunned her. She knew Mr. Knightridge well, but he was not the man in front of her now. The Nathaniel Knightridge she knew had never been this gentle and understanding. He had never shown this side to Charlotte Mardenford.

Nor had he ever appeared so . . . defenseless. This Apollo wore an air of very mortal vulnerability as he brooded alone in the shadows.

Hadn't he lost a defense recently? A murder case? In her madness over preparing for this party, she had not been reading the papers, but she believed she had heard a boy selling a broadside about it on Oxford Street early in the week.

That must be the reason for his odd mood. He had failed, perhaps for the first time in his life. Just as well he did not know who was seeing it affect him like this.

"You do not have to hide from yourself," she whispered. "You are not really a god, and you did your best."

His whole body stilled. His face turned severe. She expected him to get up and walk away. Angry eyes sought hers and looked deeply again. Invasively. But he had no shield either, and she saw too much too. His skepticism and anger faded, leaving only warm lights that drew her deeper.

They stayed like that forever, silently connected by that gaze. She grew breathless from the astonishing bond. She learned so much about him, things she could never put into words. He examined depths and corners she never showed the world, or even acknowledged to herself. Their attachment enthralled her. She melted beneath the understanding he offered. Her soul stirred and glowed and yearned for more.

She almost wept. *Yes, yes, you are guessing right, you are seeing the truth. Yes, I did not want to be alone, I will go mad in this separateness. Yes, I know the pain you feel for that failure, I know how you doubt yourself. Yes, I know how you hide behind strength, just as I do. Yes, yes . . .*

They were both strangers on that chaise longue, even if he wore no mask. Strangers to each other and even to themselves. Parts of herself that she did not know existed stirred to life within the freedom of her anonymity.

He held out his hand to her. She did not think at all before accepting whatever he offered. With his touch the world disappeared. No voices. No music. Just the two of them, bound in spirit, connected physically now.

He drew her closer, beside him. "Are you afraid?"

She shook her head, then nodded.

"Sit here with me. You do not have to say anything. I do not need words to know everything about you."

There had been words anyway. Before the first kiss he asked if she was married or in love.

"Long ago," she whispered. "Years ago, I once loved." Tonight it was a different woman loving in a different world, however.

He nodded, as if that confirmed what he already knew. "Long ago," he said. "Too long."

The passion arrived in a torrent, fast and unstoppable, an extension and expression of that gaze. The deep knowing never waned. It transformed the pleasure. It produced an instinctive trust and made every touch holy. Wonderful emotions blazed through her and burned away the dull veil that had draped her world.

Just remembering that passion made her heart ache. She stretched out her arms and swept the empty spaces of the bed that flanked her. She closed her lids over damp eyes and tried to save the perfection. She wanted to keep that night unblemished. She could live off the memories forever then.

It did not work. Questions kept sneaking into her heart. They threatened to alter how she saw that passion. She held the doubts at bay for a while, but eventually they found their voice within the relentless silence of the night.

She had known that seeing him again would jeopardize the beauty. She had managed to avoid him for a month after Lyndale's party. Visiting him this week had been a rash mistake.

No, it had not only been that. She had known what he was experiencing as that execution neared. She had sensed what it was doing to him.

Her empathy had been an echo of the intimacy they had shared. Helping him became more important than her own pride and fears, even if she assumed he would never know the real reason she intruded on his home.

I remember every kiss and caress that we have shared.

When she had entered the sitting room behind Jacobs, Nathaniel's expression was exasperated, uncaring and resigned. She had thought it was because he did not know what they had shared, and he anticipated a contentious conversation.

Except maybe he did know, and had tried to pretend that Lyndale's party never happened. If that was true, it changed everything.

She was not sure that she could face him again. Her behavior at that party had been shocking. Ruinous. She had thought that one person would not condemn her for it, however. Her lover that night would not see any sin. She had assumed that the man she embraced was as far removed from that salon as she, transported to a private world where an intensification of life's energy existed and where souls replenished their vitality.

Now she had to admit that perhaps she had experienced the magic alone. It may have been an illusion, a self-deception, embraced in order to build an emotional excuse to satisfy a physical need.

If he had known who she was and later reacted the way he did in his sitting room, her partner at Lyndale's party had remained firmly ensconced in the reality of carnal pleasure and experienced nothing more. He probably thought that she was merely a promiscuous widow who knew no shame. He might have been so bold the last time because he assumed her visit that day had been a wanton's excuse to pursue him.

Unless she wanted to risk learning the truth about

that visit, and about that precious night, she had better stay away from him completely.

The next Monday, Nathaniel entered Newgate Prison at dawn. Already a crowd had formed outside its doors as the curious jostled to procure tickets to view the trials in the Old Bailey.

Others waited to request permission to visit relatives in the prison. Women carried baskets of food to supplement the prison's poor provisions. Some appeared worried, but most wore the dull faces that said they had conducted this vigil too often.

Inside the building, Nathaniel pushed his way past the lawyers waiting to see the accused criminals they would defend. They greeted him as a fellow member of their odd brotherhood. There was no recognized criminal bar, a matter that Nathaniel and they were close to rectifying. For the present, most of these men were, like him, lawyers who conducted trials in other courts most of the time. They aided defendants at the Old Bailey as time, interest, and a defendant's purse permitted.

Defending was not respectable work and the lawyers waiting to do it were not an impressive group. As the son of a lord, his place among them was unusual. They accepted him, however, and also accepted that he was able to pass by them all and immediately gain access to the warden's office.

Within ten minutes he was deep inside Newgate, following a guard through the warren of stairways

and corridors and crowded yards. As he passed one of
the women's cells the bawds cooed like a chorus of
doves, then broke into cackles and curses when he ignored them. In a crowded men's cell past the next
yard, a boxing match was under way.

He had never grown accustomed to the prison. Its
stench still repulsed him. The sounds were all sad
ones—metal on stone, the moans of illness, the gruff
orders of guards. Even when laughter pealed, it carried a desperate, wailing note.

Finley had been placed in a tiny cell high in the
building, indicating he was considered a dangerous
and important inmate. His place was among the cells
of the condemned, perhaps to save trouble in moving
him after his conviction. The privacy came with
shackles that tethered him to the wall. He lay on dirty
straw, his clothing soiled and his long, dark hair
streaming in filthy strands over his face and short
beard.

At the sound of Nathaniel's entrance, he turned sly
eyes to the door.

Bright eyes. Too bright, like those of a man drunk
from rum, only these lights sparkled in ways hard
drink never creates.

"Leave us," Nathaniel said to the guard.

The guard hesitated, then shrugged and left. The
door remained ajar. Finley noticed, looked down at
his shackles, and laughed. He rose to his feet.

"Took that bitch long enough to send you. The
trial's today."

"No one sent me. I am not your lawyer, if that is

what you think. I do not believe one will be assisting
you."

Finley cursed. "Guess they all want to see Old
John swing."

"It would seem so."

"Then who the hell are you? Not a warden, from
that coat and shirt."

"I am the prosecuting counsel."

Finley cocked his head, as if that made no sense.
Which it didn't.

Nathaniel was not sure why he had come. Curiosity, perhaps. Mostly he had been drawn here out of
a peculiar sense of honor. Finley would certainly be
convicted of several crimes today. Information would
be laid against him for murder, robbery, and blackmail. It had seemed to Nathaniel that if he was going
to aid in sending a man to his death, he should look
that man in the eyes before they stood in a courtroom.

He looked now, but these eyes were impenetrable.
Hardness, he could delve beneath. Fear provided no
solid barrier. But this brightness shielded Finley from
him more thoroughly than a steel wall.

He had expected to see evil. Had counted on it. Instead he saw nothing.

Suddenly Finley sprang, with hands outstretched
like two claws. The move made Nathaniel jump back.
The shackles' chains ran out until they jerked Finley
immobile into a frozen pantomime of attack.

He grinned until all his teeth showed. A high-
pitched laugh filled the chamber and echoed down

the stones. Then the laugh died abruptly, as if the mind had lost connection with it.

Finley threw himself on the straw and stared at the ceiling. "What is your name?"

"Knightridge."

"Fancy name. Fancy coat. You must be that other one's friend. He'll be lying today. Blackmail, hell. I gave him information about the boy and wanted payment, is all." He turned his head and grinned at Nathaniel. "But I'll be 'splaining all that when I have my say."

"No, you will not."

"I get my say. You can't stop that. Even Old John gets his say."

"The court does not permit a criminal to commit slander with impunity. Your right to speak on your own behalf does not go that far. The judge will not permit it, nor will I."

"He says blackmail; I get to tell how it really was. I fed the boy, didn't I? Kept him whole. If a man has been feeding a golden goose, he should at least get a feather for it."

"What boy?" He knew better than to pay heed to the ravings of this rogue, but he asked anyway.

"My boy. Born better than you, he was. Born to be a lord. I told him that, your friend. Told him I had the family's lost golden goose and would sell it to him."

"Was by any chance this boy snatched from his cradle by faeries?" Nathaniel asked sarcastically.

Finley shrugged. "Don't know how he got lost.

Just know I found him. Took a while to understand it all."

"Mr. Finley, you do not have any lost boy. You did not offer Mardenford to return a lost child, since none has been lost. His son is happy in his home even as we speak."

Finley grinned again. "Maybe he is, and maybe he ain't."

"I assure you he is."

"Well, I get my say anyway. Get to explain what I said to his lordship."

"You said nothing about golden geese or lost boys. You approached Lord Mardenford and threatened to expose unnamed secrets unless he paid you dearly for silence. Your misfortune was choosing a man whose life has been so colorless, so lacking in incident, that he knew better than anyone that there was no scandal to be revealed. I doubt there are ten men of wealth in the realm who could be so secure that you were bluffing, but you managed to fix your sights on one of them."

"We'll see if the jury agrees."

"No, not on this. You will *not* be impugning his name with lies and fantasies."

Finley gazed up at him. The brightness in his eyes did not dim, but something else did. His energy, and maybe his hope. It was so clear, so *palpable,* that Nathaniel had to look away.

"I'll not be swinging," Finley said. "You'll see."

Yes, he would be swinging. The execution of guilty men normally did not disturb Nathaniel much, but he could not ignore his impression that this man was not entirely sane.

It was not just the bizarre and incoherent story about the boy making him think so. Mostly it was those unnaturally bright eyes.

He stepped out of the cell. As he walked away he heard the desolate sound of the lock falling into place. He aimed for fresh air, and a place of privacy in which to prepare for his first prosecution.

"Dead?" The judge roared his astonishment. His shout quelled the buzzing surprise that had swelled in the courtroom with the warden's arrival and announcement.

"Killed himself." The warden shifted his weight, trying to find an authoritative stance. "Strangled himself."

"This is shocking," the judge said. "You were charged with this man's keep. If there has been negligence—"

"No negligence, I swear. He had better custody than others. If a man is determined to end his own life, there is not much that can be done to stop it."

Nathaniel advanced until he stood near the judge. "Yes, but strangled? I visited that cell just an hour ago and there was no way for him to hang himself."

"Not hung. Strangled. Used his chain. We found him with it around his neck and wrapped under his boots. He must have pushed with his feet to tighten—"

"I do not think that is possible," Nathaniel said.

"You come see if you don't think it is. We did not move him, since there needs to be an inquiry."

"I expect any inquiry will be brief," the judge said. "It appears Mr. Finley decided to cheat justice, and steal from the law its rights to him. Considering the man, I am not surprised. We will proceed with the next trial."

Dismissed from his duties before he ever took them up, Nathaniel gathered his brief and left the courtroom on the heels of the warden.

The warden turned on him as soon as they were out of the building. "I do not care for your insinuation that I was lying about the cause of death, Mr. Knightridge."

"If you thought I impugned you, forgive me. I just do not see how a man can strangle himself. He would become unconscious before dying, and cannot continue pulling a chain if he is."

"You come see, if that is what you think. His legs were straight out, and the chain was taut. You may not think it is possible, but this bastard found a way." He sighed and shook his head. "Police will have to come, and there'll be a coroner's hearing and all. A lot of fuss for a man who was going to swing anyway, if you ask me."

Word of the death spread among the crowd that milled outside. They took the news with good cheer, and a few even shouted thanks to the warden.

Nathaniel viewed the animated faces with distaste. He had never accommodated himself to the way the populace enjoyed the death of criminals. There was something unseemly about it, as if a man's bad character permitted the darker inclinations of civilized people to enjoy free reign in response.

He had witnessed his first execution when he was a boy, and his shock at the crowd's glee had never completely left him. The condemned had been youths about his age and that only branded the memories on his brain. One had been crying for his mother his whole way up to the noose, and that mother had been shrieking for help to save her innocent boy. Everyone in the crowd either laughed or ignored her, but Nathaniel had never forgotten that poor woman's horror.

His tutor had taken him to that execution as a lesson in sin and justice, but he had left the scene learning other things. He knew for certain that as the son of an earl he would never find himself on a gallows as a child, no matter what he did. His mother would always get a hearing if she begged for mercy. When he got older he sometimes attended the criminal trials, and saw the poor and powerless condemned for small crimes that did not merit death as punishment. He had also seen guilty verdicts for people he was sure were innocent, which was even worse.

So he lent his voice to them once he became a lawyer. He tried to see that truth was heard and justice achieved. He had won every defense he mounted too. Except one.

Not everyone outside Newgate was gleeful over Finley's demise. As Nathaniel walked down the street, he approached a clutch of six boys loitering in the shadow of the prison. The eldest looked to be about fifteen and the youngest no more than seven. The two youngest ones were crying, and a boy a little older, maybe ten years in age, embraced their shoulders in comfort.

The image of sorrow and compassion arrested Nathaniel's attention first. As he neared, however, his gaze settled on the older boy's face. He had foreign blood in him which made his eyes and hair very dark. The face, however, was very English in a long, narrow way.

Nathaniel's attention drew theirs. The group rearranged itself and held a quick conference. A tall, straw-haired lad stepped away from the building, into Nathaniel's path.

He gestured to the rolled brief. "You a lawyer?"

"Yes."

The others moved closer, curious. They smelled of poverty even more than they displayed it in their patched and ill-fitting garments. They reminded him of those boys he had seen hanged when he was very young.

The little ones stopped crying. The youth who had been giving comfort watched from behind their low heads, his bland face masking a deep worry that flickered in his dark eyes.

"You came from there." The tall one gestured to the Old Bailey. "Is it true what we heard? John is dead?"

These must be Finley's boys, part of that family he

collected and trained. Nathaniel shifted the brief so it blocked the path to his pocket. "If you mean John Finley, then I am sorry, but, yes, he is."

The young boys looked ready to cry again, and even the older ones grew subdued.

"Good for 'im, then," the tall boy said with forced bravado. He turned to the others. "John said 'e'd never swing. 'Member? And he ain't goin' te."

There was a lot of nodding and grunting and *good for John*'s. Nathaniel's gaze kept returning to the distinctive-looking boy with the dark eyes.

Suddenly those eyes looked back, very directly. There was maturity beyond this boy's years in those eyes, born of experiences that Nathaniel could not fathom. He also saw sorrow and vulnerability, as if this one alone understood that Finley's death left them all without protection.

It was not that glimpse of the soul that surprised him, however, but rather a note of familiarity that sounded in his instincts. He sensed that he had seen these eyes before. Lighter and less wise, perhaps, but essentially the same.

The boy looked away, and Nathaniel turned his own attention to the tall boy still blocking his path. "What will you do now?"

The leader grinned over at the others. "We'll do fine, won't we, lads? Old John learned us how." He glanced down at Nathaniel's brief, and wiggled his eyebrows up and down. "Most ain't as smart as you 'bout covering their purses."

The other boys thought that was hilarious. The

somber mood broken, they jostled each other and began drifting off.

The one with dark eyes made sure the two little
ones kept up. As they all moved away, he glanced
back at Nathaniel.

Again that note of familiarity chimed.

Born better than you. Born to be a lord.

CHAPTER
FIVE

⌒

The next week proved disconcerting for Nathaniel.
Memories kept distracting him. They intruded
at the least welcome moments, occupying his mind so
thoroughly that he forgot what he was doing.

The first memory concerned John Finley. He suspected that he bore some responsibility for the man's
suicide. If Finley had been deranged, their conversation in his cell might have pushed him into a fit of
madness.

That conversation also absorbed his thoughts.
Seeing that boy outside Newgate made Finley's tale
less bizarre.

Had Finley also seen the boy's resemblance to
Mardenford? Had he truly approached the baron
claiming news of a lost relative? If so, why would
Mardenford claim it was blackmail?

Probably Finley had not been explicit. He may
have only dropped allusions, and demanded some

payment before revealing his discovery. If Mardenford did not know of any lost relative, the entire episode would have made no sense to him.

And what about that boy? If a relative at all, he
was probably the unknown by-blow of a cousin or uncle. For that matter, the resemblance could be a coincidence.

Or not even there.

It had not been a specific similarity that Nathaniel
had seen. If asked to point out just how and why his
instincts had sounded that chime, he would be hard
pressed to do so.

Despite his continued efforts to argue the whole
episode into submission, it would not retreat.

Those dark eyes haunted him.

Another, more pleasant memory also kept intruding, but it was just as distracting and a torturous nuisance.

His mind kept seeing Charlotte's face, flushed and
entranced by passion, lips parted and eyes glistening,
as he caressed her naked breast. That recollection
provoked arousals and calculations that left him
awake at night.

By week's end he had meticulously planned the
seduction of Lady M. several times. In each plot,
their fulfillment more than matched that experience
with the mystery goddess at Lyndale's party.

A week after Charlotte's meeting, Nathaniel
found himself in Gordon's gaming hall, lazily playing
vingt-et-un while most of his mind planned yet an-

other sensual escapade with the cool, self-possessed Lady Mardenford.

In addition to imagining Lady M. in potential ecstasy, he was also remembering his partner at that party in the actual throes of passion. The reality of his Venus and the anticipation of Lady M. tended to keep merging in his head.

The constant thoughts of both women, and the erection barely hidden by the gaming table, made it painfully clear that he needed a woman. He was deciding what to do about that when a tall man entered the hall and caught his eye.

The Earl of Lyndale walked over and sat down beside him.

"You have left your new bride?" Nathaniel asked. "I did not expect to see you on the town for at least another week."

"Given a choice, I would be at home. Unfortunately, my wife's sisters are visiting tonight. I decided to leave so she could warn them what insatiable goats husbands are."

Lyndale laid down a large wager. He was dealt a ten and a nine. Any other man would hold, but Lyndale called for another card. He was dealt a two.

"Uncanny," he muttered. "I can try to lose, and still I win."

"Good fortune is smiling on you in many ways. It is odd to object."

"Oh, I do not mind. However, it lures me to tempt fate. To see how far I can push it."

"Not too far, I hope. You would be a fool to risk what you have recently gained."

"I would never tempt fate where she is concerned, Knightridge. When you have met the woman you were born to love, you will understand that."

The recent memories of his Venus returned right then. He realized that while he needed a woman, he did not want just any woman. He was not even sure that he really wanted Lady M. She was just the first woman he had kissed after making love to a mystery that touched his soul. He had even imagined he was with his Venus while he caressed Charlotte in his sitting room.

He realized he had wanted Charlotte to be that other woman that day. He had wanted to lose his fury and impotence once more in that unknown woman's generous softness.

He had attended Lyndale's party in a dark mood. Although often invited, he had never availed himself of the sensual opportunities before. That night, however, he had been a different man, one adrift from his moorings and appalled by his failures. Harry Binchley had been convicted two days earlier, and a melancholy had descended on him that only got darker and blacker with each hour.

He had gone to that party so he could remain alone but not isolated. He had not even seen the party's joyful games from his dark corner. His eyes were closed while he listened to the music. Then he had opened them, and she was standing there in that white gown and mask, appearing unsure of what to do now that she had arrived.

She had known. As they sat together on the safety of that chaise longue, separate from the others, together in spirit, he had looked in her eyes and seen that she understood all of his anger and doubts. With clear eyes and a reassuring touch, she had soothed his helplessness in the face of losing that boy's chance to live. They did not speak of it, not one word, but she had known, just as he had known about her loneliness and fear. Their comprehension had been complete and mostly silent.

Their passion had been inevitable after that, and indifferent to past or future or surroundings. It had been a night spent thoroughly alive within an incomparable bond.

No, it was not Lady M. whom he really wanted. His body might desire her but his soul yearned for someone else.

He called for some whisky for Lyndale and himself and they continued their play.

"Say, I have been intending to ask you about something," Nathaniel said. "It has to do with your parties."

"There will be no more. A score of men have inquired before you. I think I will take out an advertisement in *The Times* to make it clear."

"I assumed there would be no more. I am curious about something, however. The ladies who attended—I assume you know who they were."

"Invitations were sent."

"So every woman at one of your parties received an invitation?"

"Usually."

"Then you knew who they were."

Lyndale took a good swallow of whisky. "There is no good in wearing a mask if the host demands your name. Since my parties would be ridiculous if women did not attend, I never compromised those who did. If they wanted anonymity, so be it."

"Then a woman could arrive who had not been invited."

"It was known to happen. I had no reason to object, since, as I just explained, the men always showed but one could never count on the women. If some lady decided to attend uninvited, all the better."

"That is all very instructive to orgy planning, Lyndale, but not very useful to the matter that interests me. I asked because I need to learn the name of one woman in particular. She attended the last party. She wore a jeweled white mask, and was dressed in a filmy white costume that was more Greek than Roman."

"Indeed. Well, I cannot help you." Lyndale peered tightly at his cards.

"Is something wrong?" Nathaniel asked. "You look odd."

"I do not look odd. I look passive. Expressionless."

"Exactly, which is odd. You are never expressionless. I think you know who she is."

"Who?"

"The woman I was with at your last party, damn you."

"Damn me? Damn *you*. How could I know? I was barely in attendance myself, and spent my time in the gaming room." He pushed away his cards. "All done here. That is enough for me. I think I will go home and throw out the Cameron sisters and take my wife to bed." He stood.

"Who was she, Lyndale? I ask as a friend. It is important that I find her."

Lyndale looked down with a truly odd expression. Annoyance and sympathy merged on his face.

"If she mattered at all, you should have begged for her name before you parted. I could not give it to you even if I knew it. The lady relied on my discretion. I suggest that you set about swiving every woman in London with similar height and bearing. Eventually you might again kiss the same lips that finally made it important."

The distracting memories continued all night, braiding together in Nathaniel's dreams.

By morning he decided to take steps to remove one of them. With a few inquiries he should be able to ascertain if Finley's story of a lost boy possessed any possible truth.

The easiest way to learn the answer was to ask Mardenford. Since that would not be welcomed, he chose the next most sensible source of information.

That afternoon he called on Lady M.

He was not sure he would be received. However, after a brief delay, the servant ushered him up to the second drawing room, where the petitions had been signed the week before.

The servant opened the door to reveal a relaxed, domestic tableau. Charlotte was on the carpet on hands and knees, barking like a dog at a small blond child posed in the same position. The little boy barked back and added a few growls for good measure.

Their game made Nathaniel smile. A glance at the other person in the room caused the expression to freeze on his face, however.

Lord Mardenford watched the display from a chair that faced the door. His attention was not on the antics of his precious heir. Rather, his heavy-lidded gaze rested on Charlotte.

More precisely, it rested on Charlotte's rump.

There was no mistaking the man's thoughts regarding this woman's position. If his eyes had held only lascivious lights, Nathaniel would not have cared. There was more in them, however. By the time Nathaniel was greeted, he had concluded that Mardenford held affections for his sister-in-law that were not appropriate.

Nathaniel experienced a prick of annoyance. He also felt something more primitive. The quick glare that Mardenford shot the intruder confirmed that a similar instinct had risen in the baron. The air between them crackled with the mutual suspicion of competitors.

"Mr. Knightridge, this is my nephew Ambrose. Come join our pack," Charlotte said. She pretended to try to nip the child.

Ambrose at first giggled, but then suddenly decided it was no more fun. He dropped down on his seat and his mouth turned down. Tears were coming, and one look at Nathaniel towering above did the trick. He threw himself into Charlotte's arms as if his life were in danger.

"I have ruined his play," Nathaniel said.

Charlotte's embrace quieted the sobs to sniffles. She shook her head. "He is tired. He should have gone home to his nap long ago, but I began another game, which led to yet another, and now he is undone."

Lord Mardenford still sat in his chair. Other than a greeting, he had not said anything.

Charlotte turned to him. "You should take him home now, James. Apologize to his nurse for me. It was selfish of me to keep him here so long, and I fear he will be a handful at supper."

Mardenford lifted the drowsy boy. Despite his passive expression, Nathaniel smelled his resentment that he would be dismissed because of the boy, while another man would stay.

Charlotte seemed oblivious to the bad humor her brother-in-law exuded as he walked to the door. She held out her hand. Nathaniel helped her to stand.

"You caught me unawares, Mr. Knightridge. Normally I do not receive callers on Thursdays, since that is when Ambrose comes."

"I did not realize that. You should have sent me away."

Charlotte sat in the chair that James had just vacated.

Knightridge was correct. She should have sent him away. When she had resolved to avoid him, however, she had not expected him to turn up at her house. He had truly caught her unawares, and refusing to receive him seemed very cowardly.

She was also curious about the reason for his visit. Receiving him had been a little perverse, much like poking one's tongue at a sore tooth.

"If I had sent you away, would you have returned another day?"

He settled down on the sofa. "I think so, yes."

Good heavens, had he decided to *pursue* her? He had insinuated that he might the last time they were in this drawing room, but when he had walked away . . .

Her better sense scolded her that she was playing with fire. The attentions of a man who thought she was promiscuous were insulting, not flattering. However, she could not pretend she was not intrigued. She had never been truly pursued before. Not for love and not for an affair. Philip had just been there from the first when she came out, available and amiable and . . . safe.

After she was widowed, no man had tried to woo her either. Just as well. She had not been interested in such things. High in her tower, she had considered the turmoil of the flirtations and romance that she observed below distasteful and exhausting.

And dangerous. In her own family she had witnessed the joy great passion could bring, but she had also seen its devastations. The year before she came out, her sister Penelope, estranged from her husband, had taken a lover. Not the lover she had now, but a different one, who betrayed her. She remembered her brother Dante solemnly entering Pen's chamber one day, and then the low rumble of his private conversation in there. She could still hear her sister's pitiable sobbing during the hours that followed. Pen's grief and humiliation remained unabated in the weeks ahead.

Yes, passion was dangerous. It could rob you of yourself, and leave you alone when it ended, with nothing of substance inside you.

She looked at Nathaniel, with whom she had shared such a passion. Did he know? Nothing in his demeanor indicated he did. Her fears that he did might have been nightmares, or her conscience trying to sully her dream. She still hoped that she had been a stranger to him. There was a type of safety in that. She had been able to taste the power, but not be owned by it.

And yet . . . the passion beckoned still, in all its dangerous glory. He did too, and affected her just by sitting nearby.

"I have been thinking about your petition," he said. "I am curious how you intend to collect signatures in the counties."

She explained her plans to make a circuit in the Southeast come fair weather, and the promise of her friend Sophia, Duchess of Everdon, to do the same in the West.

"That still leaves a lot of Britain," he said.

"I intend to find others to take up the banner in other regions."

"If we put our heads together, I am sure we can identify those who will help us."

"'Us'? Are you saying that you are willing to join our cause yourself, Mr. Knightridge?"

"I already have, no? I even played the dancing dog. You do not have to look so skeptical. We have been allies before."

He was not referring to her cause, but to a trial last autumn where he defended. She had gone to him in the early dawn one day, to advise him to search for certain evidence. "We were only allies because I bullied you into it. You dismissed my suggestion at first, and then took full credit for your triumph when it occured."

"Is that the reason for your bad humor with me these last months? Let me apologize now. In fact, I will have a broadside printed announcing the role you played."

The exchange had turned a little sharp, as it often did when they spoke. He seemed to notice. With an apologetic smile, he retreated. "It was not my triumph, but that of justice. In my relief at the result I did not think to thank you for your help, and that was unforgivable."

She accepted that graciously. In truth, she did not want credit or thanks, and would not have noticed their absence with anyone else. The lack of both from this man had seemed too typical, however.

This apology was not. She never thought she would hear Nathaniel Knightridge admit he was wrong about anything, let alone something involving her.

"Now, about the petitions. I am at your disposal and will aid you as I can."

She did not know what to say. He was a splendid orator and would be very useful. Since their circles were not identical, he could speak to some members of good society with whom she had little conversation.

"What about your late husband's family?" he suggested. "Would they aid in their counties?"

She named the cousins and relatives on whom she thought she might rely, and listed the ones on whom she was certain she could not. The latter list was much longer.

He listened with an expression that made his face very serious and handsome. He appeared to hang on her every word.

"It is a big family. Are any of them in the military? The cousins, I mean? Are they the sort who have traveled quite a bit, going abroad and such?"

"I do not think so. It is not a family inclined toward adventure. I hear that the aunts were surprised when my husband and his brother made a grand tour."

"I am sure theirs was more extensive than mine. I only had three months in France and Italy."

"Oh, they went everywhere. Greece and Spain, and even Algiers. They were traveling with their tutor at least a year. It was right after James left university."

"It sounds fascinating. I envy their visits to the more exotic cultures. Did your brother-in-law ever tell you about those journeys, and the people they met along the way? I would think the stories could entertain one for hours."

"James never speaks of it, but Philip did sometimes. He would get nostalgic. I think his memories were more interesting than his later life. He told me a few stories—"

The words died on her lips. She suddenly heard Philip again, voice in a trance of memory, describing a fire dance in a Spanish town on the ocean's coast. He had seemed a different man as he spoke. It had been as if he were reliving a long-lost youth, even though he was only twenty-seven when he died.

The recollection did not make her sad, but it silenced her anyway. She lowered her gaze and let the gentle memory have its time.

No voice spoke during that pause. Mr. Knightridge made no attempt to fill the quiet. She appreciated that.

The images flowed through her mind, of that fire dance and of Philip both watching it and later describing it. For a few moments the scenes lived vividly, but slowly the little pageant floated away into the clouds of her mind.

She raised her gaze and turned her attention back to Nathaniel.

Her breath left her.

He was watching her with the same expression she had seen in the candlelight at Lyndale's party. His countenance reflected understanding, not pity, and the warmth in his eyes mesmerized her. She did not doubt that he respected the quiet nostalgia the memories evoked. He understood that honoring a man and preserving his memory were not the same as mourning him forever.

The intimacy of that night returned in an onslaught, as if a wave crashed the walls of her heart to pieces. She flooded with warmth and peace and a stark vitality that thrilled her. And trust. An inexplicable, soul-drenching trust flowed through it all that made the danger insignificant.

He ceased being the irritating Mr. Knightridge and became again the astonishing and generous man with whom she had lived an entire lifetime in the space of a few hours.

Did he feel it too? Had she imagined the best of that night?

Was she lying to herself again now?

She cast about for the thread of their conversation, to take it up again. She attempted to look away, but what bound them would not permit speaking or avoidance.

He just rode the silence with her, tethered by a powerful bond.

And then he held out his hand to her.

He did not think before he reached out to her.

It was an impulse and he did not know its source. Nor did he care. It was merely a physical response to a profound understanding that touched him as he watched her stillness in the silence.

Her hand met his. Her gaze held no questions. They both discarded the armor and swords with which they normally engaged, and all that was left was a deep comprehension.

He tugged firmly and she came to the sofa and his arms. He embraced her. A mixture of sweet intimacy and pounding desire scattered his thoughts.

He rested his palm on her face and looked in her eyes. So open, so guileless. Who ever thought Charlotte would need protection, or lessons in guarding her soul? Yet he suspected that his own deepest self was just as exposed to her.

That did not matter. He gazed in this woman's eyes, fully aware of who she was this time. There was no confusion with any mystery goddess.

Except . . . the prod on his instincts died before forming. The impulse to kiss her shut it away.

Her lips were waiting for his. The gentlest tremble pulsed through her mouth with their first connection. It told him everything. That her surprise at their unexpected desire matched his. That she feared what she could not deny. That their arguments had been rearguard battles to fend off something that would leave them both helpless.

He kissed her harder and his desire climbed fast. He did not need to hear her sighs to know she was with him, but their sound entranced him. So did the way her lips and mouth and body accepted him. Not with submission, despite the signs that spoke of a woman overwhelmed. Her yielding communicated trust, not defeat.

He lost himself. He knew her responses better than his own. The complete understanding affected everything, especially his desire. Making love to her became important, essential. After this time, she would never be a mystery again and he would never find himself adrift as he had been these last weeks. They would fill each other again and again and—

He paused, his mouth sealed to hers.

It had happened once more, that confusion between Charlotte and the other. The power of that night was again casting a spell over his perceptions.

Unless...

He broke the kiss and looked at the face turned up to his.

He tried to picture it mostly hidden by a jeweled, white mask.

It was a ridiculous notion. But...

"Open your eyes," he said.

Her lashes fluttered and parted. Her gaze touched his and a flaming arrow of recognition shot right to his soul.

"Impossible," he muttered. This woman did not attend parties like that. Not even the slightest rumor of a flirtation had touched her reputation since she was widowed. Many men wanted her, that was clear in their gazes and faces, but she did not encourage them even for amusement.

"What is impossible?" she whispered.

He looked long and hard. Memories collided, of these eyes in his sitting room, and ones remarkably similar in the dim lighting of Lyndale's salon.

Surely not.

"It is nothing. I just . . . it is nothing," he said. He could not kiss her again, however. Not with the other intruding like this.

Except . . .

He studied her, almost sure even though the idea was shocking. Short of asking outright, there was no way to know.

Madam, did you give yourself to me in a night of passion at a party that everyone knows no reputable woman would attend?

Her expression vaguely changed, as if a veil of thin gauze fell over her face. A distance instantly separated them. The resemblance disappeared so quickly, he wondered if he had imagined it.

She turned slightly, so they were not so close. She did not leave his arms but reality descended, making the intimacy awkward. She did not demand he release her, but he knew she wanted him to. His hold relaxed and fell away.

Her mind seemed to be working hard. She appeared confused. She was thinking the same thing he was, no doubt. That this passion was mad. It made no sense.

"Why were you asking about the relatives?"

She startled him. She had not been weighing the oddness of their impulses, nor had she been especially overwhelmed by passion. While he had been grasping for ecstasy, she had been sorting through their conversation.

"Relatives?"

"My husband's relatives."

She angled back to scrutinize him. Absolutely no resemblance to the mystery goddess remained.

"Why were you asking those questions? The ones about Mardenford's family?"

"I was inquiring whether they might help your cause, remember?"

"Not those questions. I mean the ones about traveling to foreign lands and such."

"I was making polite conversation. That is what polite people do."

Her eyebrows straightened over a skeptical glare. "You came here for something, and I do not think it was for the cause."

"Perhaps I came for a kiss."

He said it lightly, but she contemplated the response at length. "No, I do not think you planned that kiss. Nor have you ever sought my company for polite conversation before. Tell me why you were asking those questions."

He had intended to broach the matter cleanly, but had been distracted by their passion. Therefore he had no compunctions about satisfying her demand.

"I spoke with Finley right before he died, and he confided to me the conversation he had with your brother-in-law. I am wondering if he might have actually known something important."

Her reaction did not bode well for any future kisses. She reared back in shock until her body tilted away from his. "Are you now curious whether his lies are correct? What sort of man are you? To dig and poke to discover if maybe there is a scandal—"

"I do not care a fig about scandals, and if this were the normal sort of gossip, I would not feel obligated to pursue it."

"*Obligated* now. You do think highly of your duties, Mr. Knightridge."

She was using *that* tone. The crisp, challenging, annoying one that said he had a comeuppance due, and she for one was not impressed with him, etc., etc.

The one that made him want to shake her. Or kiss her and caress her until she whimpered in submissive pleasure.

He ruefully admitted that *his* recent impulses had not been entirely without precedent, even if his motivations and actions had been. He had on occasion in the past imagined conquering the impregnable fortress of Lady M. He recognized those calculations in other men because he had done some calculating himself.

"Listen to me, and you will perhaps comprehend my concern. Finley said there was a boy, a relative of your late husband's family, that he knew about. A lost boy, he called him."

"This criminal spins a ridiculous tale and you believe it? I always knew you were conceited and irritating, but I never knew you could be stupid—"

"I *saw* him. The boy. In the yard as I left the courtroom. There were a group of them, waiting for word on Finley, and one of them—he had a resemblance to your brother-in-law."

She fell silent. Her eyes turned to fiery crystals.

"What sort of resemblance?"

"His general countenance. He appeared to have foreign blood, however. Hence my curiosity on whether an uncle or cousin had traveled extensively or lived abroad."

"You have investigated this scoundrel's lies on the basis of a general resemblance to a general countenance. I think you are bored. You should find an avocation to occupy your time."

"I am not on this errand merely because of generalities. It was the boy's eyes. They were similar to Mardenford's in an essential way."

Her face turned to stone. It was a lovely, delicate carving, despite her anger. "Oh, his *eyes*. That explains it. After all, you can see everything if you look into someone's eyes, can't you? You have the insight of a god."

Her quiet voice dripped with sarcasm. His own anger rose in response. "I can see enough."

She bit back laughter. Dark amusement tinged her fury.

Her ridicule stoked his own fire. *Laugh if you want, but with one touch of my hand your granite walls crumble for me.* "I think there is a good chance this boy is related to your husband's family. If so, do you want him left in the gutter?"

"I am sympathetic to all poor children. If this one has come to your attention and you wish to be his benefactor, I applaud you and will even help. However, I am sure he is no relation. He is a criminal's creation, to attempt to extort money from a good man."

"If you are so sure, then prove me wrong. See the boy. If you perceive no resemblance, I will drop the matter. Gladly. I will be grateful to have my suspicions put to rest."

She rose. Her posture straightened until she became a rigid column of indignation. "I will not see him for that purpose. I will not humor this dangerous intrusion into the life of a family I hold dear. In taking that prosecution, you were supposed to help them, not allow a scoundrel's lies to reach out from the grave. Now, you must excuse me. I have a dinner engagement for which to prepare."

She did not wait for him to take his leave. Turning on her heel, she strode to the door. That last kiss might have occurred a year ago. Or in his dreams.

She opened the door, then turned to him with an anger that filled the room. If she were clutching one of her famous parasols, he did not doubt she would hurry back and thrash him with it.

"You are so content that you see *enough* by looking into a person's eyes? Believe me, Mr. Knightridge, you cannot even see what is right in front of your nose."

CHAPTER SIX

~~~

There was nothing else for it. She had to see the man.

Nathaniel Knightridge had ruined her sleep and absorbed her thoughts for three days now. If she did not confront him, she would have no peace.

Charlotte stepped down from her coach. She surveyed the facade of the building where Nathaniel had his legal chambers. She hid her jumbled emotions under her own facade, one of calm confidence.

It was not what he might or might not know about her scandalous behavior that preoccupied her now. Their last meeting had proven that he did not know for certain that she had been at that party.

But he had wondered. She had seen the surprise and suspicion in his eyes as he scrutinized her on the sofa.

There had been something else in his eyes too.

For an instant, as he weighed the possibility, she

had also seen his shock. This man might attend Lyndale's parties, but the notion that *she* did had appalled him enough that it had killed his desire.

She swallowed the sour bile of her disappointment. When he had reached out to her, she had concluded he knew everything. She had thought, for a short while as they embraced and kissed, that he was glad that they could claim again what they had shared.

She would not think about it anymore. It no longer mattered what he knew or did not know, what he thought or did not think, about that party.

What did matter now, what had sickened her these last three days, was the evidence that Knightridge was investigating Mardenford's family and looking for evidence of some lost boy.

There was no lost boy, or any other secret. However, if he poked around and asked questions, it would be worse than if Finley told lies in court. Nathaniel Knightridge was no criminal and his suspicions would carry weight if they became known. There was nothing logical about gossip either. It speculated and assumed. It gained substance through repetition and destroyed reputations without cause. Without a factual rebuttal, it would soon encompass every man in Mardenford's family, not only distant relatives.

She made her way to the chambers of Mr. Knightridge. A clerk looked up from his scrivener's podium as she entered. The young man assessed her card quickly, then his gaze drifted quickly over her midnight blue cloak and ice blue skirt to ascertain their value and the card's reliability. He scurried into the next chamber.

A few moments later he returned and escorted her into a large, airy chamber with many glass-enclosed bookcases and a dark, tidy desk. Nathaniel rose from his chair and gestured the clerk away.

Nathaniel's gaze swept her from head to toe much as the clerk's had. Only this time the examination was slow and bold, and that of a man looking over a woman who had granted him liberties.

His attention settled on her hand, which held the handle of a parasol. "Weapon at the ready, I see."

She was in no mood for levity. She placed the parasol down flat on his desk. It landed harder than she intended, with a decided *thwack*.

"I will be plain, Mr. Knightridge. Our last meeting destroyed my peace of mind. It was unfair and ungenerous of you to call on me with such ulterior motives."

"It was only a kiss, Lady M."

"I am not speaking of a silly kiss, but of your accusations regarding Mardenford's family."

His lids lowered. "If my kisses are silly, you should do a better job of refusing them."

"I will, you can be sure of that. I only need to think of how you so quickly take up this criminal's quest to make me reject even the playful flirtation of the last two weeks."

"I can see you are inexperienced in playful flirtations. The phrase implies both more pleasure and more resistance than I have enjoyed."

Her pride reeled from the slap of the insult. Her face warmed. Her throat tightened and burned.

She turned away and battled the stupid impulse to cry. She had insulted him first, after all.

In the past his words would not have affected her in the least. She would have parried the thrust and lunged in turn. This time, for some reason, his scorn pierced her like a flaming sword.

"Please accept my apologies. That was inexcusable." The words flowed on a soothing voice close behind her. "However, you should not goad me. It provokes bad behavior in me, as you learned long ago."

It embarrassed her that he had seen her close to tears about such a little thing. His apology enabled her to collect herself.

She turned to find him watching her carefully, as if he feared a scene. She summoned enough composure so he would be reassured that she would not act foolishly.

She arched her eyebrows to let him know he stood too closely. With a vague smile, he retreated to a position near his office window. As if he accepted she was back in true form, he became the man she knew well—Nathaniel Knightridge, confident, self-possessed, and provocative.

"Now, as to the other matter you addressed, I have accused no one. I merely asked a few questions."

"You asked, with no thought to the damage just

asking can do. You are no John Finley and your interest will give credence to that rogue's blackmailing
lies."

"I promise you that I have been discreet in all inquiries."

"In such matters as these there can never be
enough discretion. However, your statement implies
you have inquired of others besides me. What have
you learned?"

He hesitated. She glared a warning that if he did
not satisfy her, there might be a scene after all.

"I have learned that there is an uncle on the distaff
side who spent time in India a dozen years ago. Also
a second cousin who, as a member of the navy, has
traveled widely."

"The cousin would be Peter. I have met him and
he is very religious. I find the idea that he fathered
bastard children difficult to believe. As for the uncle,
I do not know him. Does this boy look to have Indian
blood?"

"I would say Mediterranean. Of course, any man
in the family might have had a liaison with a gypsy or
immigrant right here in Britain."

He was being very smooth and most careful.

He was dissembling.

Her ill ease crystallized. Suddenly Knightridge
represented real danger.

"You have inquired about relatives, but you really
think James might be his father, don't you?"

He rested his shoulder against the window
frame and gazed out for a spell. When he turned his

attention back to her, his expression was serious, and honest.

"I do not know what to think, since my inquiries have been very restrained. The boy's apparent age suggests his birth occurred within a year of your brother-in-law's grand tour eleven years ago."

"My husband was also on that grand tour. Do not be delicate for my sake, Mr. Knightridge. Surely you have considered that Philip might have fathered this lost boy."

"I considered it. However, the resemblance is to James. Finley did approach your brother-in-law, and great pains were taken to make sure that Finley would not tell his story in court. While I do not doubt James's devotion to his brother's reputation, I hardly think finding the illegitimate child of a dead man warrants either blackmail or your brother-in-law's distress." He paused hard and long. "And, since we are not being delicate, I weighed that Philip fathered no children in his marriage."

Her face warmed. "Due to his illness, no doubt you assume."

"Yes."

"Let us speak frankly or my visit here is wasted. You assume that was due to his illness, and so do I. The whole world says so on its kinder days. But one cannot be certain."

Her bluntness surprised him. His face colored a little. "Not certain, but all evidence indicates this has nothing to do with your late husband. I would never have approached you for information if I thought it did. Do you think my assessment is wrong?"

"I think you are wrong about the whole matter, from beginning to end. However, on this one point I am sure you are correct. That boy is not Philip's child. Nor is he James's child, however. I am sure of that too. I know James very well and it is not in his character."

"I would say that such things are in most men's characters. A youthful passion, a bastard child—it is not a new story, or even an interesting one. The attempts to silence Finley were in excess of the notoriety that could result. It would not have been a very big scandal, even in these days."

He was correct. Revelations of a bastard son would not cause a big scandal. That truth began to settle her emotions. An oasis of calm formed and attempted to spread.

Something in Nathaniel's expression thwarted her heart's quest for peace. His gaze had turned inward, as if his own words had provoked new and compelling thoughts.

He glanced at her, then dismissed his distraction with a half smile.

He strolled forward and faced her across the desk. "Let us say that this boy is indeed related by blood to Mardenford in some way. He may have no legal rights but he deserves a moral justice. The boy is in the gutter, and will die there if he is not helped. I hope you can understand my interest, in that light."

She realized this had little to do with Mardenford

or scandal or even Finley. Nathaniel was thinking of the boy and nothing else. If finding this boy's family meant creating scandal, this man would think it a fair cost.

"This is really about your guilt over Harry Binchley, isn't it? You think that if you do not help this lost boy get found, one day you will be drinking too much brandy and waiting for another young life to end."

His expression hardened. He looked away, but she recognized the deep fire in his eyes.

She understood his desire to help this boy. She empathized with his bleeding conscience more than she wanted to. Her need to protect her own was stronger, however. And right now her defensive instincts were screaming.

She feared what had distracted this lawyer during his intense contemplation at the window. She had read his mind while he considered the other possible explanations for this claim of a lost boy.

The worst one would bring an insurmountable scandal to Mardenford. It would also have devastating consequences on Ambrose's life.

"Mr. Knightridge, I feel that I must lay this matter to rest and return Finley's lies to his grave. I came here today to tell you that I will see the boy."

"That is very good of you. I will make arrangements for you to meet him in a day or so."

"Today. Let us do it now."

"Finley's lair was deep in St. Giles rookery. It would be more prudent if I found the boy and brought him to you."

"I will not make this a formal meeting, nor allow the matter to continue even one more day. If the boy is in this lair, and the lair is in the rookery, let us go there now. It will not be the first time I have ventured into such a neighborhood. With you as my escort I am sure I will be safe."

She was not stupid. Whatever else he thought of Lady M., Nathaniel knew she was very astute. Irritating, but smart. Her perceptions could be discomforting, mostly because they were often correct.

They had not really spoken frankly of what this lost boy might mean. They had not put the worst possibility into words. She knew the danger, however. He did not doubt that she had seen it all, even without knowing exactly what Finley had said that day.

Born better than you . . . Born to be a lord.

Those words had not implied there was an unknown bastard at large, but an unknown son of legitimate birth, who should one day have the title.

Not Philip's son. It was not only Philip's illness and lack of progeny that convinced Nathaniel it had not been Philip, if indeed it had been either of them. For all his blandness, the last Baron Mardenford had exuded a quiet strength of character. Philip also would never have been so stupid as to contract a secret marriage, since he expected to inherit the title. James, on the other hand, was a vague, less distinct man who as the second son could afford to be reckless.

He realized there was another reason he was certain

it had not been Philip. Charlotte had married the man. She would not have missed such a flaw in him. She would never tie herself to a man capable of the deceptions and dishonor implied by the worst explanation for Finley's ambiguous accusations.

As Nathaniel joined Charlotte in her carriage, he admired her confidence in how this outing would conclude. He envied Mardenford's family the loyalty they had in their dowager baroness. He did not doubt that she would fight like a lioness to protect those she loved.

He hoped that by day's end she would not have cause to.

She toyed with a little ribbon on her parasol's hilt. He watched her slender, delicate fingers, so elegantly sheathed in snug lambskin gloves, stroke and smooth the tiny strip of silk. He began imagining that feathery touch gliding over his naked skin.

He forced himself to look away from those seductive fingers, and at her face. Beneath her determined and thoughtful expression he perceived the soft vulnerability that made her so similar to the other woman who occupied his thoughts.

Actually, right now, in the dull light coming through the carriage window, her eyes, her mouth, her chin . . .

For an instant his sensibility was *almost* certain, despite how his rational mind rejected the possibility out of hand.

"Mardenford is lucky to have you as his hostess. His son is lucky to have your love."

"I am the one who is lucky. Ambrose is like a son to me, and James like a brother. It is good to have such a family, and a place where one is at home."

He realized that she did not know that Mardenford was in love with her. She did not see that this brother wanted her in a way the law permitted no brother, even one through marriage.

"You were hardly without family before. The bond of the Duclaircs is famous."

"I know my good fortune in the loyalty and love of my brothers and sister. This is different, however. Peaceful. I grew up in a family full of high drama. When I was a girl, there were scandals and heart-wrenching sorrows and big secrets. They thought that I was too young to know, but I knew everything. I love my brothers and sister, but that world was a stormy sea, throwing my little boat hither and fro. In comparison, my husband's family was the most placid lake."

"I expect the contrast had an appeal."

She smiled with a girlish chagrin. The way her lower lip quivered had his heart humming with recognition and excitement.

Damn, the similarities were undeniable and alarming. He had spent three days tossing them over in his mind, convincing himself he was imagining things. But now . . .

"Oh, yes, the quiet, the stability, had enormous appeal. It first attracted the coward in me. Later I appreciated that there was more there than the perfect reflection of a perfect order on that unrippled surface.

The lake was placid, but that does not mean it was shallow."

Her expression became reflective and private, just as it had the afternoon in her drawing room when the memories overcame her. She was not only speaking of the world into which she had married. She was also referring to her husband, and her marriage.

A profound empathy entered him, just as it had at the party. The woman that night had not spoken much, but her whispers had alluded to another life and another time and an old love.

An intimacy wrapped them, as it had in her salon. She did not look at him this time, so he was not sure she experienced it too. He did not reach for her again, although he wanted to.

He was glad she had found that quiet lake as a girl. He knew something about the waves that had buffeted her little boat, and could imagine how they seemed to threaten her.

In setting her anchor in that lake, she had found safety. She alone of the Duclaircs had remained untouched by scandal. She alone was received in all the best houses. Such things mattered to most people, especially in the world to which she had been born.

He made a decision. He had no stomach for this investigation, and would not have pursued it at all except for the way those boy's eyes haunted him. If Charlotte saw no resemblance, that would be the end of it.

If she *truly* saw none, that was. He would know if she lied.

———

Nathaniel stepped out of the carriage and scowled at the old brick house with broken, chipped shutters. A lot of noise came from within. An inebriated woman sat at an open window right in front of them, grinning in sodden, private mirth.

"It is a flash house," he muttered. He shot Charlotte a glare of exasperation. "I *told* you I should bring the boy to you."

"I am aware of what you *told* me. Is it likely he is in here?"

Nathaniel had paid a costermonger a guinea for the location of this house. According to the informant, Finley had bought stolen property here, and had a partnership with the bawd whose women used the upper floors.

Charlotte had been in St. Giles rookery before, but she had never entered a flash house. The government insisted they did not exist, but everyone knew they did. A combination of gin house, brothel, hideout, and cheap lodgings, there were hundreds of them in London, all little centers of crime that flourished with impunity in neighborhoods like this.

Nathaniel looked up and down Bainbridge Street. Charlotte assumed that with his height he could see more than she could. From her vantage point at the carriage window it was a sea of people in poor clothing, making so much noise it was a wonder the din in the house could be heard.

His survey did not improve his humor. "I cannot leave you out here with only your coachman to watch both you and the horses, and I cannot bring you in. I will take you home and then I will—"

"Mr. Knightridge, do you really think I will come to physical harm in that house? With a man of your size and strength beside me? In the middle of the day?"

"It is impossible to say. It would only take four drunken men with knives to cut me down."

"Dear me, I have indeed been negligent with my own welfare. When I insisted on coming, I just assumed it would take at least *six* drunken men with knives to—"

"I spoke conservatively, to leave a margin of safety on your behalf."

Despite the sparring, he appeared truly indecisive on how to proceed. She found that rather charming.

"I have been on this street before, Mr. Knightridge, in the interests of certain charitable endeavors. I have witnessed most of what occurs in that house, only not all in one place. While I believe you are truly concerned for my safety, I suspect your hesitation has more to do with my seeing indelicate things. Since we cannot stand here all afternoon, let us be done with this and see if the boy is in there."

Face stern, not liking it one bit, muttering things that sounded like "infernal woman" and "stubborn, troublemaking harridan," Nathaniel helped her down and guided her to the door with a very firm grasp on her arm.

They walked in just behind two men who pushed by and barged ahead of them. Stale air laden with smells both human and alcoholic greeted them in the dark, filthy entry.

The noise came from the second level. Arm hovering behind her in protection, Nathaniel brought her up the tread-worn stairs and they peered in.

The room served as the gin house. A crowd filled it, sitting on old chairs and a long table and even the floor. A woman propped in a corner had gone unconscious, and from the looks of her dishabille had been trifled with in her stupor.

There were young children here, drinking like the adults. Several boys no more than fifteen also huddled in a corner with their gin cups, gambling amongst themselves with dice.

Nathaniel caught the eye of one and held up a shilling.

The boy casually left his friends and walked over to the doorway. He assessed their garments, lingering a moment on the reticule Charlotte had tucked firmly under her arm.

"Are you Finley's boys?" Nathaniel asked.

"Old John's dead. There ain't no Finley's boys no more, and we n'er were." He cocked his head toward the others. "We're our own gang."

"Where would I find the boys who used to be with Old John?"

"There's some 'ere. Up above." He grinned salaciously. "They be busy, though."

Nathaniel glanced at the ceiling. His mouth's line turned hard and flat. "I doubt any of the ones above are whom we want. The boy we seek is about ten years of age."

The youth grinned again. "Lot you know. Had me first 'fore I was ten."

"This one is very dark in eyes and hair. Like a foreigner. Have you seen him here?"

"I know 'im. Seen 'im with Finley sometimes. Not up there or here a'tall. Not for days."

Nathaniel was only too glad to hand over the shilling. He began moving Charlotte back toward the stairs.

"That one may be at the inn," the youth said to their backs. "Hear tell the young'uns stayed there."

"What inn?"

"Not a real inn. We cud show ye. Cost three o' these." He held up the shilling. "Have to walk, though. The lane is narrow."

Nathaniel smiled, but his eyes could have melted steel. "I am not entering a dark alley with your gang, boy. Only you. The others stay here. You can share the money with them later. Try anything, put this lady in any danger, and I will break you in two."

Finley's lair was on a skinny lane nearby that stunk of manure and waste and rot. The old half-timbered structure really might have been an inn centuries ago; and in a different setting and with a coat of whitewash it would have been picturesque. Its roof was pitched high and its base tilted down at one end, where the ground had settled over the ages and split its foundations.

Nathaniel paid the boy and sent him off. He insisted on keeping Charlotte close as they entered. He had been alert and attentive while he guided her through the fetid neighborhood behind their guide. His arm remained behind her back the whole way, as if he feared she might get snatched by someone passing amidst the bumping crowd that flowed along the lanes.

"It is used for storage," he said as they stepped in off the street. He blew dust off a wooden box so the lettering showed. "Wine from France. No tariff stamps, so it must have been smuggled."

"It is a wonder it hasn't all been stolen. The neighbors must know Finley is dead."

"Perhaps they fear he will reach out from the grave."

They followed a narrow path between the boxes, looking for evidence of children. Nathaniel was able to see over the stacks and he surveyed the walls.

"There is a door back there. Let us see where it leads."

It opened on wooden stairs much newer than the building. Even so, Charlotte had to accept Nathaniel's firm grasp on her arm to get down.

Blackness engulfed them at the bottom. She smelled the damp. A quick touch told her this space had been carved out of the ground, and its earthen walls plastered. Hard-packed dirt served as a floor.

Nathaniel had to duck his head to fit under the low

ceiling's timbers. "Wait here. There is a window over there, between those joists. I will open the shutters."

The dark swallowed him. Between the sounds of his boots, she heard a rustle to her left. Her skin prickled. She stepped back so she could make an escape if rats emerged at her feet.

The shutter swung. A diagonal column of light flowed into the basement from the tiny, high window. The dusty beam illuminated an astonishing array of objects.

It glanced over the side of a fine mahogany cabinet, then skimmed the surface of a table set with china. Charlotte's gaze followed its path onto a Persian carpet, until the spot where it ended on a pair of knees.

Knees?

Her eyes adjusted to the light's diffusion. She made out the form of a crouching person and a jumble of humps around it.

"Old John lived well in his lair." Nathaniel had returned to her side. His hold on her arm returned as well, this time with a squeeze of warning. His attention fixed on the humps. "Carpets and fine furniture. He probably ate with silver too. He made a little palace down here."

He stepped between her and the knees. His position also blocked the stairs.

"Come forward now," he said. "We are not going to hurt you."

Faint whispers hissed from the corner. The humps moved. The knees resisted.

"Go on now," a boy's voice said.

The shadows reassembled themselves into little people. Five children stepped into the light.

Two were girls no older than twelve, so pale and thin that their eyes looked huge. Two were young boys about eight years old. They tried to appear fierce, but they had not mastered the hardness it would take to hide their fear.

The tallest bowed his head as he whispered some words in smaller ears. This boy looked to be the oldest, maybe ten or so, and he had very dark hair.

"Where are the older ones?" Nathaniel asked.

The dark head rose. Black eyes gazed toward them. The light flowed over a long, soft face.

Time froze for two instants while Charlotte stared. Recognition sounded in her blood, quickly replaced by a familiarity less specific but more disconcerting.

Her rational mind quickly assessed both reactions. They had been evoked by the most general resemblance, one extremely vague. Had she not been anticipating something, she probably would have never seen it.

In truth, now that she looked harder, there was no true resemblance at all.

"What older ones?" the boy asked.

"The ones I saw you with outside the Old Bailey."

"Gone," a girl said. "Gone to seek their fortunes, ain't they?"

"Harry here would'n go, ain't that right, Harry? They would'n take us all, so he would'n go," a boy piped in. He gave Harry an adoring look.

"Is that your name? Harry?" Nathaniel asked.

"Is what Old John called me."

Charlotte could have done without the unfortunate coincidence. Nathaniel would be hard enough to manage without the evidence that this boy bore the same name as the defendant he had failed.

"Come up above," Nathaniel instructed. "We need to decide what to do now."

He turned to Charlotte and handed her up. They waited beyond the door while feet trudged toward them.

"You were mistaken," she took the opportunity to say. "There is no resemblance."

The two girls filed past, eating Charlotte's ensemble with their eyes. The young boys swaggered next, imitating the bravado of the streets.

Harry emerged last. He gave them both a good look, displaying the seasoned assessment of an experienced pickpocket.

The little troop arranged themselves on boxes, waiting, a motley assortment of boredom, masked fear, and challenge.

"We cannot leave them here," Charlotte whispered. "Even with Harry's protection, they will be devoured. And the girls . . ."

"For once we are of one mind, Lady M. I fear their danger is even worse than you surmise."

He stepped forward and addressed the children. "How have you been living? Who has fed you?"

Smiles and snickers replied to the question.

"There have been charitable contributions from good folk like yourselves," Harry said blandly.

The other boys giggled and gave Harry playful nudges.

"Oh, aye," a girl said. "And merchants are generous as saints to poor children."

"Saints," the other girl repeated solemnly. They both broke into peels of laughter.

"Theft is no laughing matter," Charlotte scolded.

"No, ma'm, you be right there." The first girl's eyes narrowed on Charlotte's fine mantle and parasol. "My mum always said the same thing, 'fore she died. Better to starve than be a thief, she said. So she starved."

There was no good response to that. Nathaniel came to her rescue. "Whose boxes are these?" He gestured to the stores.

"Old John's," a girl said. Her insolent tone implied she thought Nathaniel was too stupid to be borne.

"John is gone. The whole neighborhood knows that. Why would the boxes remain unstolen? The door was not even locked."

"A few been took, at night," the smallest boy said. "We let 'em, right, Harry? But they was Old John's, and now they are ours and *you* can't have them."

Nathaniel locked Harry in his gaze. "Did John work alone, with no more than children as his gang?"

Harry did not reply.

"Down below there are goods that are not English, just as this wine is French. He had partners beyond the city, didn't he? Smugglers on the coast."

"All I know is there's men who'll be comin', like they do every month," Harry said. "I expect they'll be paying right good for our watching the boxes."

"No, boy, they will not. If you know those men's faces, you best be gone when they come. It is why the others left." Nathaniel walked over to him and spoke man-to-man. "It was good of you to stay so the young ones would have protection. But you can stay no longer, nor can they."

CHAPTER
SEVEN

T he orphanges that we prefer to use are full," Mrs. Peddigrew said. "The others are places that make the streets where you found the children a preferable home."

"Returning them to the streets is obviously not a choice," Charlotte said. London was full of children such as these. One could not save them all, but once one came face-to-face with any, there was no alternative but to try one's best for them. However, this little gang could not await the attention of the charitable organizations through which she normally tried her best.

Mrs. Peddigrew was the wife of a merchant of middling means who devoted herself to helping poor orphans. Charlotte had met her through Fleur, Dante's wife. Seeking her advice had seemed the logical solution to the sudden responsibility for the children.

Now their five ragged charges were being fed in the kitchen of this modest house near St. Paul's, while the adults decided their fate in the small but pleasant sitting room.

Mrs. Peddigrew poked at the fuel in her fireplace, her thick body bending to her chore. Her cap's ribbons joined some loose brown curls dangling along her plump, rosy cheeks. "There are a few schools that would take them, of course."

Charlotte heard the unspoken implications. The schools would cost money. The children required a benefactor.

"I will pay the fees for the schools," Nathaniel said.

"We will both contribute," Charlotte said.

"Perhaps you will consider buying them new clothes, too, my lady," Mrs. Peddigrew said. "It is hard for the new ones to show up at a school looking so poor. The other children tease them, even if they were no better themselves a few months ago."

"I will see to it tomorrow."

"If you arrange the funds, we will take care of it, if you wish. We know where to buy sturdy used garments."

Mrs. Peddigrew put down the poker and settled comfortably on her stool. Her head bobbed back and forth while she thought out the rest of the plan.

"The girls can go to Mrs. Dudley's school in Middlesex. It is in the country and the air will do them good. Looking wan, they both are. The young boys will be accepted by Mr. Longhorn in Southwark.

He is full but he always manages to make room for more, good soul that he is. Now, the oldest one..." She pondered Harry's fate, and her soft face folded into worried creases.

Nathaniel frowned. "Could he not also go to Mr. Longhorn?"

"Mr. Longhorn prefers the young ones. The older boys are trouble, and it is just him and his wife. It is very hard to find a good place for a youth over eight, Mr. Knightridge. He could always be given as an apprentice or helper, of course, but..."

She did not have to finish. Everyone knew the dangers for impoverished boys sold into such service. The animals that pulled carts often received better care.

"Then he can go to a proper school for boys his age. There are many in town, and most take boarders," Nathaniel said.

"I doubt he has the necessary education for that, Mr. Knightridge."

Mrs. Peddigrew looked apologetic. Silence hung while they considered Harry's future.

"There is one possible solution," Charlotte said. "Mrs. Peddigrew, as you know, my sister-in-law, Fleur Duclairc, is establishing a school for boys up north in Durham. While the structure is built, the headmaster has taken a few students into his house already. I will ask Fleur to recommend that Harry be allowed to go there."

Nathaniel looked relieved at the solution. Mrs. Peddigrew smiled her approval.

"I was hoping you would suggest that," she said. "It was not my place to do so. Now, until that can be arranged, we need a place for young Harry to stay. All the children sleep together here, and with his age, and that of the girls, well . . ."

Another silence hung, this time with the female eyes fixed on the one male in the room.

Nathaniel nodded with resignation. "I will take him home with me until matters are arranged."

"You are too good, Mr. Knightridge," Charlotte said.

"The Lord will reward you, sir," Mrs. Peddigrew said.

Nathaniel smiled weakly.

"Did you think that you could save lost boys and bear no cost or inconvenience to yourself?" Charlotte asked.

Nathaniel stood outside her carriage, demanding that she get out too. He was refusing to close the door, and had been so bold as to order the coachman to come back in an hour.

Fifteen paces away, a motionless Harry stood amidst the jostling crowd passing on Piccadilly Street. He gazed into the gated front courtyard of Albany. With his thick dark hair and ill-fitting old garments, he looked like a young gypsy among the Saxons.

"I am not shirking my duty. I am saying you and I are in this together and you will not shirk yours,"

Nathaniel replied. "Furthermore, accusing me of seeking to bear no cost is both inaccurate and unkind. I said I would pay the fees for the schools before you did."

He offered his hand, in a commanding gesture.

The idea of entering his apartment again dismayed her. "Goodness, he merely needs shelter for a day or so. Settling him into your home does not require an army."

"I remind you that it is a bachelor's home. Nor do I have any experience with children of any age. That is why I require that you come inside and speak with Jacobs."

"Mr. Knightridge, one of the remarkable benefits of being a widow is that no man can *ever* require *anything* of me again."

He glanced toward Harry, then adopted a careful, appeasing expression. "I misspoke. I do not require it, because I have no right to. I request that you join us and help arrange things. I implore you to do so." He glanced at Harry again. *"Please."*

Nathaniel Knightridge imploring? Begging?

She rather liked that.

"Do you promise to behave as a gentleman?"

That earned her a devilish half smile. "If that is what you desire today, Lady M."

She did not miss the various entendres in his reply. She considered calling for her coachman to drive away, and the door be damned.

Just then Harry turned. The youth looked terrified at being expected to enter the imposing building.

Albany had been a royal duke's mansion before being converted to bachelor apartments at the beginning of the century.

The boy's distress touched her. Nathaniel's interest in him posed dangers to her world, but that was not poor Harry's fault. He was just a frightened child cast adrift in the world.

She held out her hand and Nathaniel helped her step from the carriage. "I do not understand why you need a woman's help. He requires a bath and clean clothes. How hard is that to explain to Jacobs?"

"If you are with us, perhaps Jacobs will not walk out, never to return."

She accepted his escort through the gate flanked by two fine shops. Harry shuffled alongside, trying to shrink to invisibility. They crossed the courtyard and aimed toward the main entrance.

"Ah, so you fear a revolt by your manservant and hope my presence will force him to accept the situation. How interesting. You present yourself as master of all you survey, but now I learn that you do not even command your very small household."

"Being master of a servant is an easy victory. It is hardly worth my effort. Now, being master of a woman of independent nature and outspoken opinion—that is a challenge worthy of a man's time. I am thinking I will seek out just such a female and see if I am up to it."

"I am sure a man of your importance has more significant wars to fight."

"I do not anticipate a war. I foresee only a few

brief skirmishes, if that. The woman I have in mind is easily disarmed with a few silly kisses."

A servant opened the door to reveal the expensive furnishings of the reception hall. Harry got one glimpse of the interior and dug in his heels.

Nathaniel placed a firm hand on his shoulder. "We will only walk through. My apartment is behind this building and much more modest-looking. Stand tall, boy. A man's worth is seen in his demeanor and carriage, not his clothing."

That was not entirely true, of course. As they passed through the ground floor of Albany, a few eyebrows rose at the boy with them. They emerged out the other side, at the walk that separated the attached blocks of garden apartments.

The less ostentatious buildings that had been constructed in the estate's gardens reassured Harry. He examined the Chinese pitch of the roof that covered the walk providing access to flanking rows of three-storied buildings. He gawked at the Asian lanterns hanging above their heads.

"Harry, have you heard of the poet Byron?" Charlotte asked. "He once lived at Albany. So have some famous leaders, like Palmerston and Canning."

"I heard of Byron," he said. His brow furrowed as if he dug for memories of when and how. "Never heard of t'others, though."

"Have you read Byron?" Nathaniel asked. His attention focused on the boy's face.

"Nah. My mum read long poems to me when I was little, though. Byron sometimes, I think."

"Do you know how to read yourself, Harry?" Charlotte asked.

"*Course*. Well . . . some."

Nathaniel stopped them all on the walk outside the door that led to his apartment. Charlotte tried to quell her discomfort at entering the sitting room where she had lost control in an extraordinary manner. One knowing glance from Nathaniel and she feared she would blush and stammer like a schoolgirl.

Fortunately, Nathaniel's attention remained on Harry.

"Before we go in, I want to explain what is going to happen," Nathaniel said. "My man's name is Jacobs. He will see that you get washed and will find some clean clothes for you. You will stay here until Lady Mardenford arranges for you to go to a school in Durham. You will be treated well here, and later there. However, I will brook no trouble from you. I want your word of honor that you will behave properly."

Harry grinned as if Nathaniel was the town's biggest fool.

"M'word of honor, eh?"

"Yes."

Harry chuckled. "It's yours, then, for what it's worth."

"You should treat it like it is worth your life, boy. It is the only thing of true value that you own."

"Of course, sir. I will prepare a bath at once." Jacobs's nose quivered just enough to punctuate his statement in a way his deferential tone avoided. Displeasure flexed the soft skin of his cherubic face.

"Also, he needs clean garments," Charlotte added. She had been the one to request the bath be prepared. "He cannot remain in these while he stays here."

"Stays *here*?"

Charlotte recognized the signs of discontent. If she were not present, Jacobs would be ever-so-politely indicating to Nathaniel how these requests were an imposition.

Like all experienced servants with long histories of good references, Jacobs probably had a clear sense of his own entitlements. Those rights, in proper English fashion, relied upon long tradition and precedents. Being asked to care for a youth who was not even a relative exceeded his understanding of his duties.

"I have some old ones that will do, if they must," he said very flatly. "We could put a cot in the kitchen, I *suppose*."

She gave Jacobs a thankful smile. "You are very good to accommodate me. Tomorrow Mrs. Peddigrew will send over garments bought for Harry, so your old ones will not be needed more than this evening. I know this is an extraordinary situation, and I am very grateful that you are willing to help me."

Jacobs softened. His lips folded into the smallest smile. He cast a skeptical but resigned glance at Harry, who was eyeing a silver snuffbox set near the table clock.

"Go with Jacobs now," Nathaniel said. "Harry has

given his word that there will be no trouble, Jacobs. Haven't you, Harry?"

Harry shrugged agreement. Jacobs beckoned. Servant and boy left, giving each other looks that said neither thought the relationship promising.

"Thank you," Nathaniel said.

"I am delighted that I could oblige you." She lifted her parasol. "I will return home and write to Fleur at Laclere Park. I am sure she will send the reference, so you should anticipate taking Harry north two days hence."

"You cannot leave yet."

She raised her eyebrows.

"If you leave, you will be standing in Piccadilly Street for half an hour," he explained. "Remember? Your coach left and will call for you."

Standing on the street would be more comfortable than staying here. Being alone in this room with Nathaniel unnerved her.

"Giving that order was presumptuous of you."

"One word from you and the coach would have stayed." He gestured to the fireplace. "Please, sit. I would like to speak with you of Harry's future."

She refused his offer to take her mantle. Bundled and on guard, her parasol at the ready, she perched on the cane-backed settee near the fire.

He took his place in the green chair. They faced each other just as they had the last time she was there. Only a lot had changed since that afternoon. He did not examine her with annoyance this time. His dark gaze carried other thoughts. He projected a power designed to create a frightening excitement in her.

She reacted, to her dismay. Her heartbeat quickened and her instincts waited.

She moved her gaze from spot to spot in the room. She avoided looking at him. She also averted her eyes from the sofa at the other end of the chamber.

Her discomfort grew. The clock gently ticked, very slowly.

"You do not have to be worried," he said. "I promised to be a gentleman."

She finally looked at him. "I am not worried in the least. I am contemplating the duties awaiting my attention, and regretting the inconvenience of this delay."

"What you are truly contemplating is written on your face. Let us stop dissembling with each other. We want each other, unexpected though the desire may be. A wall has crumbled. It is hopeless to pretend our passion in this room did not happen, or that we do not both want it to happen again."

His bluntness surprised her. His expression—so knowing, so confident in the rights she had surrendered to him—left her dumb.

Worried did not describe her reaction. Her senses were too aware of the sensual pull Nathaniel exerted to describe her inner agitation as mere worry.

She dropped her gaze to the carpet to break the spell, but she only achieved enough control to make her reaction more confusing. The unanticipated part of this desire had left her at a disadvantage from the start.

"I do not even *like* you, Nathaniel," she blurted.

He laughed. "That is the hell of it, isn't it? However, today it is for the best. If you did like me, I would be breaking my promise right now, and following my inclinations to lure you to my bed."

Dear heavens, she wanted him to lure her. That was the true hell of it.

She groped for a path to safety. Her heart knew where to find it. "You wanted to speak of Harry's future."

His smile accepted her retreat. The wall may have tumbled, but they would not frolic amidst its ruins today.

"There really is nothing more to discuss," she said. "He has found a benefactor in you. He will go to Durham and be educated. If he shows the ability, he will have a profession eventually. He will not die in the gutter, thanks to your interest and generosity. I daresay if all men of style and substance sponsored the future of one Harry, the disgrace of these poor, abandoned children would go away."

He let her finish her little speech, but wore an irritating, vaguely amused expression that said he knew her game too well. "That is not the future I meant. To be more accurate, I want to speak of what *I* should do in the future regarding Harry."

"Take him to the school, then do whatever you choose. It would be kind if you inquired about his progress so he knows he is not forgotten. You might visit if you are so inclined. Of course, you have no true oblig—"

"You saw the similarity. You recognized the resemblance."

"That is *not* true."

"I watched your face when you first saw him. I observed your astonishment."

"It was dark. Whatever you saw, you misunderstood." She turned her attention to the fire, to emphasize that this conversation was over.

"Look at me," he commanded.

She refused.

"Damn it, look at me. Will you lie to yourself as well as me? Look me right in the eyes and say that you saw absolutely no resemblance. I do not think you can, because I know that you did see it."

She did not care what he thought *he* knew. *She* knew Harry was no relation to Mardenford.

His demand, his challenge, angered her so much that she trembled. This man thought he could see into her soul if he looked into her eyes? This puffed-up, conceited tower of overweening pride believed she was so mesmerized by his light that she would not speak her mind while under his probing scrutiny?

Teeth gritting, she locked her gaze on his.

I saw absolutely no resemblance.

The words choked in her throat.

She saw in his eyes that he had indeed seen her initial reaction to Harry. He had noticed that fleeting moment of recognition.

It had been a mistake to ever meet him on that

wall, let alone to tear it down. Their intimacies had exposed her soul to him in ways that would endanger people she loved.

"It was very brief, and it was an illusion," she said firmly. "You described this boy as having Mediterranean blood. I saw the dark hair and eyes and knew he was the one. In that light, the shape of his face— for a moment *only,* for the *briefest* instant, there seemed to be some resemblance. It passed at once."

"It did not pass. It became obscured by details, but I still see it."

"Oh, tosh! I demand that you describe this similarity that you still claim to see."

"It is not in the features so much as the essence. It is in the light in his eyes and the countenance of his face when he is afraid, and when he is happy. I have seen them in Mardenford too, those expressions."

A flare of heat burst in her head. She wanted to break something. She rapped the tip of her parasol on the carpet to relieve her agitation.

"You are insufferably conceited. The great Nathaniel Knightridge can never err, to your mind. It is ignoble for you to jeopardize the reputations of that family on such vague evidence."

She was halfway to the door before he was on his feet. "Do not see me out. I will write after I hear from Fleur about the school. Take the boy to Durham, give him hope and a future, but cease this meddling or I will do everything I can to make you regret it."

CHAPTER EIGHT

Y ou think we are here now?"

Nathaniel looked over from the book he was reading. Harry was pointing to a spot on the map.

"Yes, we are about that far on the road, and should cross into County Durham very soon."

Harry wanted to treat the carriage journey as an adventure, but the long hours on the road between inns quickly bored him. To help the boy pass the time, Nathaniel had given him his pocket map and showed how the pages were organized and how to interpret the legend.

Harry flipped to the next page and its rectangular section. "That is the sea, close by, running along there." Using his finger, he measured from the mail road east, then moved his finger to the scale on the legend. "Not so close, after all."

Nathaniel watched the dark head bent over the

map. "The school will have atlases. Those are big books filled with maps."

Harry seemed happy enough with the pocket map for now.

The boy had not talked much, and Nathaniel did not mind. He had no idea how to talk to children. As the youngest among his brothers, he had never learned.

The best he had been able to do with Harry was attempt some inquiries about the boy's past the first night after dinner. Other than descriptions of his time with Old John, several years at least from what Nathaniel could glean, the conversation had been circular, resented, and not very informative.

Thus far all he knew was that the mother may have been named Bella and that she had dark hair. When Nathaniel had probed for more, Harry had turned sullen and rude.

"Do you think this school ever visits the sea? It ain't *too* far," Harry said.

"Possibly. I will ask Mr. Avlon." Mr. Avlon was the headmaster of Fleur Duclairc's new school for the sons of miners. This large charitable endeavor was under way on some property she owned in Durham. According to Charlotte, Mr. Avlon currently lived in the estate house with a few boys who were beginning their studies while the school building was constructed.

A letter of reference from Fleur was tucked in Nathaniel's valise. It had come the afternoon after Harry entered his home, sent from Charlotte by messenger. No note from Lady M. had accompanied the document.

Harry still ran his finger down the engraved coast on the map.

"Have you seen the sea before, Harry?"

Harry nodded. "Lived there."

Nathaniel closed his book. "Was this when you were a little child?"

"Not so little."

"Was it a village?"

"There were boats and all, and houses." He spoke in a distracted tone. "I went out on a boat once. Was scared at first, but then not. I could see all the houses from out there, all at once. Not such a big village. The boat was for catching fish. They all were, but you could see the big ships goin' out to sea."

He was describing a fishing village near a trading route. "Is that where your mother lived? In this village?"

Harry's gaze never left the map. His finger continued to trace, but his body went very still, as if nothing but that finger moved, not even his lungs to breathe.

"I would like you to tell me what you remember. If there are relatives, we can find them. There might be a family looking for you."

The finger stopped. Nathaniel could not see his eyes, but the face had gotten tight.

"No family," Harry muttered. "Just Old John and t'others, and he's gone and t'others are back there and I'm here."

He sounded close to crying. Nathaniel had no idea how to deal with that.

Of course the boy would get homesick. That

basement had been a thief's den and the children had picked pockets for Old John, but it had been all the home and family they knew.

He hoped the younger ones had found more sympathetic guardians in Mrs. Dudley and Mr. Longhorn than Harry had found in Mr. Knightridge.

"Perhaps in the village someone knows of your other family. Your mother's people."

The silence lasted longer this time. Finally, Harry dropped the map to the floor and swung his legs so he could lie curled on his side with his back to Nathaniel.

Nathaniel opened his book again. He did not read, however. A few sniffs suggested the boy was weeping. He looked over at the huddled body and hiding face. What was it like to be so young and have no place in the world, no home?

A muffled sob tore out of the child. Nathaniel leaned over and placed a hand on the boy's shoulder. He doubted it would give much comfort but it would not be right to ignore this sorrow.

"The old woman might know," Harry said, his voice rough with tears. "Jenny might."

•

"We still might be able to save him, sir. Yes, we might."

Mr. Avlon issued his optimistic appraisal while he and Nathaniel drank coffee in the estate house's drawing room.

A Quaker, the youthful Mr. Avlon dressed plainly

and wore his hair in an old-fashioned blond queue.
His enthusiasm for his new position, and his belief in
Fleur Duclairc's grand vision, had been apparent earlier when he showed Nathaniel and Harry the
grounds and schoolroom. Now Mrs. Avlon was settling Harry into his bedroom and Mr. Avlon spoke
frankly.

"He has been in Satan's clutches, but we have him
now. We will see what education he has had and start
from there. It is astonishing how fast they learn if
they have been deprived. It is like pouring water into
sand, they absorb so quickly."

"Do you have outings of any distance? Say, to the
sea?"

Mr. Avlon blinked. "The sea?"

"I promised to ask."

Mr. Avlon chuckled. "Not so close, but who
knows, perhaps so. The study of nature at the sea
might be a good outing."

Nathaniel drank more coffee. He should probably
be asking other questions, but he had no idea what
they might be.

"We do not use the rod overmuch," Mr. Avlon
said. "With a boy like this, others would want to beat
the sin out of him. But, no, I do not hold with that. He
would likely run away, and be lost to God forever. I
cannot promise that he will not disappear anyway, of
course."

"Ask for his word that he will not run away or mis-
behave. If he gives his word, he will keep it."

Mr. Avlon raised his eyebrows. "Indeed? Thou

have brought me an unusual child, Mr. Knightridge. A boy raised by a criminal, a boy whom I think we can assume is a criminal himself, but who keeps his word."

It had been most unusual. Harry had given no trouble. No snuffboxes or coin had gone missing at Albany.

Now this unusual boy would be cared for by Mr. and Mrs. Avlon. He would be educated and, from the looks of things, even loved. He would have another family of sorts, and not be lost to the streets.

Nathaniel realized that his responsibility for Harry had ended. Charlotte had been right. He could inquire or visit, but he had no obligations to this boy.

He should get in his carriage and ride away from the mystery Harry presented. If he did, Charlotte might look kindly on him again. If he did not, she would never have another civil word for him. A new wall would stand between them, never to be breached.

He did not want that. It startled him to admit how much it mattered.

He really did not know anything for certain about Harry. He had nothing more than a criminal's words and his own instincts urging him to learn more. His mind said it was not enough, that Charlotte was right and he might jeopardize a family's reputation on an investigation built on lies.

His soul, however, *knew* there was more to Old John's words than lies.

And his heart—well, his heart was torn. Part of it

wanted to help this boy who had felt so alone in the carriage. But another part of it, too much, wanted to give Charlotte the gift of silence.

Sounds suddenly poured through the house. Young male voices could be heard beyond the drawing room door, laughing and talking.

"Those are the other students," Mr. Avlon said. "They have come from the construction site. The boys help there in the afternoons. For the rest of their lives they can point to the school and say 'I helped build that.'"

"You are giving them pride and accomplishment along with ciphering and letters. I can see that Mrs. Duclairc chose her headmaster well."

Mr. Avlon blushed. "It is her vision, her curriculum. We are of one mind where these boys are concerned, however. The primitives in America and Africa care for their society's children better than we care for ours. Until all of Britain's children are safe and fed and educated, we cannot claim to be truly civilized." He shook his head. "No one wants responsibility for poor children. No one wants to stand up and say 'I will be thy voice and take up thy cause.' Thank God for good women like Mrs. Duclairc."

Nathaniel set down his cup. He rose and walked to the front window. In the distance he could see carts and the low walls of the school being built.

A woman with no legal voice was investing her fortune in the cause of poor children. For a lawyer to lend another hour to the cause of one lost boy was a small thing.

"Mr. Avlon, before I leave, I would like to spend some time with Harry alone. Perhaps before supper. In the schoolroom, if you would permit."

"Certainly. Will thou require anything of us?"

"Only privacy, and a good county atlas."

Upon his return to London, Nathaniel called on Lady Mardenford. He had learned much from Harry and wanted to share it with her.

He was not received. Lady M. had retreated to the country, he was informed. She had gone down to her brother's estate in Sussex.

He left her door cursing under his breath. She had fled so she would not have to see him. This was her way of announcing their brief alliance was over.

His reaction to her abrupt departure got darker as he dealt with his affairs that evening. It was not only the boy's situation that she was avoiding by going down to Laclere Park. She was also running away from the man she desired but did not like very much.

He decided that he was not willing to accept that.

Before dawn the next day he called for his horse and rode out of the dark city. He did not contemplate his decision much. He just did it.

There would probably be a row when they spoke. He preferred her barbs to silence, however. He might be a man she disliked, but he would be damned before he was a man she dismissed.

The rambling Gothic mansion at Laclere Park appeared quiet when he approached that afternoon. The servant who opened the door did not even want to take his card.

"The viscount is not receiving, sir."

He had not realized Laclere had come down too. "I am calling on Lady Mardenford, not her brother."

"The entire family is in seclusion." His tone implied something serious had happened.

Nathaniel immediately felt foolish. She had come here for reasons totally removed from her dealings with him. She had not run away. She had been called here.

It had been stupid to think her decisions revolved around him. He occupied no more than a small, irritating corner in her life.

"My apologies. I hope nothing is amiss. Please give the family my good—"

"Who is that?" a man's voice asked. Nathaniel glimpsed Laclere's tall form and dark hair at a door leading off the reception hall.

The viscount walked toward them, brow furrowed over his blue eyes. "Is that you there, Knightridge?"

"I have intruded badly, it seems. I will—"

"You must come in. I am at wits' end with him, and Hampton rarely talks, so he is no help at all."

Laclere was not making sense. He also looked haggard and tired. His bright eyes had dulled and the furrow between his eyebrows dug deeply. He turned and walked away.

Perplexed, Nathaniel followed him into the library.

Julian Hampton, Penelope's lover, sat on one side

of a table, and Dante on the other. A chessboard waited between them. From Hampton's patient but bored expression, it seemed a long time had elapsed between moves.

That was probably because Dante's sight was on nothing in the room, but instead on his own soul. His brown hair was mussed, his cravat askew, his face tight and his body tense. Dante Duclairc, so recently the handsome and elegant curse of more husbands than could be counted, looked like hell.

He also reeked of fear.

"Look who has turned up," Laclere announced with forced enthusiasm.

Alertness entered Dante's eyes. So did extreme annoyance. "I don't need another damned nurse-maid."

They were old friends and Nathaniel had never seen Dante either rude or angry before.

"He is not himself," Laclere muttered. "Do not take offense."

"Why is he not himself?"

"Fleur is above, lying in."

Hell.

"I will leave. I am intruding worse than I feared."

"Will you let him go mad? Distract him. At least take over in getting him drunk. I am half-foxed from trying, but the spirits have no affect on him yet."

Heartily wishing he were back in London, Nathaniel moved a chair to the chess table. Laclere sat on a nearby sofa.

Dante shot a piercing glare at his brother. "*He*

won't let me go above and ask questions, Knightridge. I think I should be able to."

"I think so too."

"You are supposed to be helping, Knightridge," Laclere said.

"I am left to just wait in ignorance," Dante said.

"That is not true," Hampton said. "Pen and Charl take turns coming down and reporting."

"Only every hour or so. Nor do they tell me anything useful. Maybe it will be Charl next time, though. When she sees Knightridge here, that should at least make for some good theater. Anything is better than this damned waiting."

Laclere and Hampton chuckled at the idea of Charlotte and Nathaniel engaging in their typical war of words. Nathaniel forced a smile.

If Charlotte came down, he was doomed. When she saw he had invaded on this most private of family affairs, she would give no quarter. She would hang him high and leave him twisting in the wind.

A long, silent hour passed. Nathaniel took Hampton's place at the chessboard and managed to engage part of Dante's attention in a match.

He trained his hearing on the house, listening for sounds of a woman coming. Finally an approach was heard. Dante's gaze snapped to the door.

Nathaniel's did not. He focused on the chessboard and hoped like hell the messenger would be Penelope.

The door opened to the faint swish of petticoats.

The men all stood. Dante rose so abruptly that his clumsy movement caused chess pieces to fall.

"What news, Charl?" Dante said.

Nathaniel inwardly groaned.

She came over to Dante, her face a mask of happy optimism. She gave her brother a kiss. "All is well. The midwife has no concerns, and Dr. Wheeler is confident. It will be some time yet, but you are not to worry in the least."

Dante appeared reassured, for about five seconds. His gaze turned inward again.

Charlotte watched him carefully. Then she acknowledged Nathaniel's presence. "Mr. Knightridge, how extraordinary to see you."

"I was nearby in the county, and decided to call. It was an unfortunate impulse."

She glanced at her brother. "Your journey to Durham was successful, I trust. Dante, Mr. Knightridge brought a boy to the school. Fleur wrote the recommendation."

That got Dante's attention. Charlotte explained Harry's situation, with no reference to Old John's lies. Dante quizzed Nathaniel on the progress of the school. Taking up Charlotte's cue, Nathaniel described matters in lengthy, elaborate detail.

When the topic waned, Charlotte excused herself. "I should return to Fleur. Perhaps you would walk with me to the stairs, Mr. Knightridge, so I can learn more about the journey north."

Expecting the worst, he left the library with her.

He prepared for the wrath he would face once the door closed on their departure.

Instead she sank back against the door and closed her eyes. The mask dropped at once. Exhausted worry dragged her expression.

"You are not well. Let me call Laclere and—"

"I am fine." She composed herself and straightened. "It is very hard to come down, hour after hour, with no news of progress. Pen and I take turns and dread the clock's chimes."

Nathaniel was at a loss for what to say. He had never felt so useless. "Surely Mrs. Duclairc will be fine. Such things are lengthy many times, are they not?"

She walked toward the stairs and he fell into step beside her. "She is getting weak," she said softly. "She is serene. I cannot bear seeing my brother's fear, however. Poor Dante."

"My intrusion is even more inexcusable than I thought. I cannot blame you if you are angry with me. There is no need to upbraid me, although I will not offer any defense if you do."

She stopped walking.

"I am not angry. Quite the opposite. When the door opened and I saw you in the library, I was relieved that Laclere had sent to London for some friends to hold the vigil with Dante. It sounds as if you did not arrive at Laclere's request, however."

"No."

She cocked her head and raised her eyebrows a fraction. "I hope that you will stay all the same. When this is...over, you can explain why you did call. I daresay I will need the distraction."

"How did you ever bear this four times?" Dante asked.

"I have no idea." Laclere did not raise his eyes from the book he had taken to the sofa. The others had arrayed themselves on chairs and seats. All pretended to be reading.

"Does it get easier with experience?"

"Not in the least."

"Hell."

Neither Charlotte nor Penelope had been down in a long time. Night had fallen. Nathaniel could not ignore the gathering dread that was permeating the house.

"It has been a long while," Dante said.

"Not so long. Not too long." Vergil looked up from his book and emphasized the last words.

Nathaniel did not believe him, and doubted Dante did either. It had been four hours since the door closed on Charlotte. Four hours of waiting. Four hours of hell.

He barely knew Fleur Monley, who had married Dante last year. He was sick with worry anyway.

They each had a glass. A good deal of brandy had been imbibed in the silence.

Dante grit his teeth and hurled his book against the wall.

Laclere did not even glance up.

"How long do *you* wait before *you* get worried?" Dante demanded.

"There is no clock to these things. I try not to get worried until I have cause to."

"Have you ever had cause to?"

Laclere hesitated. "Yes. With Edmund."

"I do not see why we can't go up above," Dante said resentfully.

"No one is forcing us to stay down here."

"I was told I could not be with her."

"Oh, you mean up above *in the birthing room*. I have no desire to go there. Nor do Hampton or Knightridge. I am correct, am I not, gentlemen?"

"Not all of you. *Us*. Husbands."

"You cannot because there is a midwife with very strong arms and a field marshal's demeanor who says you cannot," Hampton said.

"He is right, Dante," Laclere said. "Mrs. Brown and her sisters in trade insist that husbands are unbearable nuisances and also pitifully weak. We are worthless, in short."

"Well, damn it, if I am paying her fee, I should have some say in things."

"You think so, do you?"

"Yes, I do."

"As a man, you should command. As master, you should at least be kept informed."

"Damned right."

"Knightridge, pour him more brandy."

Dante slammed his fist down on the table. "I am

going up to see what is happening. Wheeler is in there. He will let me in."

He strode from the library. Laclere sighed.

"Knightridge, follow him, will you? He will only resent my presence. After the midwife cuts him into shreds, carry the pieces back to us."

Dante took the stairs two at a time. Nathaniel climbed in his wake. They approached the chamber where Fleur was being kept.

A blond man lounged in a chair near a window at the end of the corridor, reading a newspaper by the light of a lamp on a nearby table.

He looked up with a welcoming smile and pushed his spectacles up his nose. "Thank goodness you are here, Duclairc. Your company will help pass the time."

"What in hell are you doing out here, Wheeler?" Dante demanded.

"Waiting." He pointed to the newspaper. "It says that the shares in the Hartlepool line have risen again. Since you will be so rich, I should increase my fees."

"I do not see why I should pay you any fee. I brought Fleur down to Laclere Park so you could attend, and all you are doing is reading newspapers."

"There is nothing else to do. Not for anyone. The viscountess is in there copying music, the countess and the baroness are reading books, and your own wife is knitting gray socks."

Just then a gasping moan penetrated the door.

Wheeler smiled weakly. "Between the labor pains, that is."

"Things are progressing normally, then?" Nathaniel asked, trying to make it a statement more than a question.

"Certainly." There had been the slightest hesitation before the reply was given.

Another groan, more frantic, passed through the door.

Dante's face drained of color. "What is happening, Wheeler?"

Wheeler's smile fell to something less confident. "The pains came quickly earlier, exhausting her, but have now slowed. She is tired and has lost the strength to aid nature. All will be well, but it will be longer now. It is not unusual with the first children of more mature women. In such cases, one can only wait." He paused, then added very gently, "However, if we wait too much longer, I will send for the surgeon and consider allowing instruments."

In other words, things were not really progressing normally at all, Nathaniel thought. Charlotte had intimated as much.

"I am going in," Dante said.

"Duclairc, it is not done," Nathaniel said.

"You will not be welcomed. I am barely tolerated," Wheeler warned.

"I am going in, damn it." He turned the door handle and made good on his word.

Nathaniel caught a glimpse of the chamber over Dante's shoulder.

Bianca, Vicountess Laclere, was not copying music. That chore had been abandoned. She sat beside Fleur, wiping her face. The midwife was coaxing Fleur to push with the pains. Fleur looked as spent as someone who had run thirty miles.

Charlotte sat on the other side of the bed, holding Fleur's hand, whispering something. Like all the women, she wore an apron over her dress.

She looked up just before the door closed behind Dante and Wheeler. Her gaze met Nathaniel's. He saw the helpless fear in her eyes and his heart clenched.

Dante's entry brought all of their attention on the doorway. Dr. Wheeler slipped in with him.

Charlotte caught a glimpse of Nathaniel before the door closed. She wanted to run out there to him, and beg him to hold her and take her away. She wanted to lose herself in sensations that spoke of living and hope.

"Dante," Fleur said with surprise.

The midwife frowned deeply and rose to confront the intruder.

"Let her see him," Charlotte cried. "She will be better for it."

Charlotte was exhausted and scared. She knew the midwife was worried, and Bianca's eyes had glazed with concern many hours ago. Fleur was getting dangerously weak, and it was as if they assisted in her slow death, not the bringing forth of life. The last few hours had been so tense that the air had turned heavy with a horrible anticipation.

Wheeler stepped forward and with a calming gesture told Mrs. Brown to retreat. Bianca moved out of the way and Dante came to Fleur's side.

"You are not supposed to be here, Dante." She managed a smile but it looked sleepy.

"I wanted to see you, darling."

"Mrs. Brown says the child would be born by now if I would put my back into it."

He glanced over for confirmation. Charlotte nodded.

Another pain racked Fleur. She tried to raise herself up to push. Charlotte and Dante tried to help but before the contraction stopped she collapsed back.

"I am stupidly weak," she muttered.

"After hours of this, even Laclere would be weak," Charlotte said.

"You can use my strength, darling." Dante bent to remove his shoes. "I will sit behind you and support you. Perhaps that will help."

Mrs. Brown objected. Bianca appeared stunned.

Wheeler considered the matter. "Mrs. Brown, it may help if she is more upright, since she tries to rise anyway," he said. "She is a woman who might have done better in one of the old birthing chairs."

"It cannot hurt to try," Charlotte said. She was desperate for anything that might break the deadly impasse of the last few hours.

Dante did not wait for permission. He sat Fleur up

and climbed in behind her. She sank back against his chest.

Another contraction started. Charlotte cringed as she saw it tense through Fleur's weak body. A guttural groan sounded in the room as Fleur leveraged her body into it.

"Did that help?" Dante asked softly.

"Just having you here helps. But, yes, I was not useless that time."

Wheeler felt her swollen belly. Mrs. Brown peered beneath the sheet covering Fleur's bent legs. Midwife and physician looked at each other with wordless communication.

"You may stay, Mr. Duclairc," Mrs. Brown decreed.

Dante held Fleur as the pains came. Charlotte moved back in the room, useless now that Dante was here. Pen joined her and clutched her shoulder.

Soon there was little rest between the pains. Mrs. Brown disappeared behind the sheet. Wheeler stood behind her and watched.

Bianca mopped Fleur's face with cool water, and then began wiping Dante's too. "It will not be long now," she reassured.

It was not long at all. Fleur knew. A joyful note entered her cries of effort. A new determination lit her eyes. Charlotte silently urged her on and prayed it would be over soon, and safely.

Wheeler announced the baby was coming. With a triumphant, agonized cry, Fleur collapsed against Dante.

"A boy," the invisible Mrs. Brown announced.

A cry of grateful relief escaped Charlotte before she could catch it. Her body went limp and she hugged Pen for support. She watched through filming eyes as the baby was cleaned and wrapped. Dante's embrace encompassed Fleur, and supported her arms when the child was given to her.

Husband and wife looked at the little babe, then at each other.

Their expressions stunned Charlotte. Their naked love overwhelmed her emotions. She knew they loved each other, but now she glimpsed the depths normally shown only to each other.

Her brother's eyes fully revealed his adoration and desire and his promise of endless passion.

She had never seen anything like it in her life.

Not in her entire life.

Something shattered in her. Her tears flowed so violently that the sobs hurt her body. She could not control them and finally gave up the effort.

She cried out her happiness and relief into Pen's shoulder, but grief and disgraceful envy poured out too.

CHAPTER
NINE

~

The weeping sickened Nathaniel. He stared at the door, sure a tragedy had just transpired on its other side.

It was time for him to slip away and leave this family to its grief.

He had taken two steps when the door opened. Penelope came out, supporting Charlotte in her embrace. Charlotte gasped for breath between her violent sobs.

Penelope pulled the door closed. She looked over at Nathaniel with a helpless expression.

Acknowledged, he had to say something. "I am so sorry. I will never forgive myself for—"

"All is well, I assure you. Wonderfully so. A male child has been born, and it looks as if Fleur will be fine too."

Charlotte let loose with another outpouring, smothering the sounds in her sister's shoulder.

Penelope patted her head. "She is very tired. She has been here with Fleur from the start. I am sure the strain has undone her, that is all."

Charlotte appeared ignorant of his presence, for which he was grateful.

"Mr. Knightridge, do you think you could sit with her? I would like to go down and tell Laclere and Julian. If they heard this weeping—"

"Of course. I would have offered, but I did not think..." He did not think Charlotte would appreciate his aid, was what he did not think.

He went to them and Penelope eased Charlotte's body into his arms.

"I will return soon," she promised. She hurried to the stairs.

Nathaniel looked down at the dark hair on the head pressed to his frock coat. "There is no need to hurry. I will take care of her," he said, even though Pen was gone.

Charlotte did not seem to realize she had been transferred. Whatever caused these soul-wrenching sobs, it made the embrace that held her irrelevant.

He could not say the same for himself. She felt very small in his arms, and very weak. He would never have thought Charlotte would break down so completely, for any reason. She cried her eyes out in a way he had never seen a woman do before.

He wished he could think of a way to offer more comfort. Instead he stood there, not daring to move, while her tears stained his coat.

Eventually she began calming down. From the

way she tried to stifle the sobs, he guessed that she had realized who held her. She stiffened, as if embarrassed. She battled mightily to collect herself.

"Come and sit." He turned her in his arms, guided her to the chair where Dr. Wheeler had been, and set her down.

She withdrew a handkerchief from her apron pocket and wiped her eyes. She composed herself with several deep breaths.

"You poor man. Pen should not have thrust me on you."

"I did not mind." He had been glad to hold her. Her vulnerability had touched him. "I am just relieved the reason for your tears was not the one I first feared."

She gazed down at the handkerchief crushed in her little fist. She still seemed very fragile.

He dropped to one knee beside her chair. "Do you want me to call for your maid? Perhaps you should rest in your room."

She shook her head. "I am tired, that is true, but my loss of composure was not because of that."

Her gaze remained on her hands and lap. A considering expression entered her eyes, as if she assessed an object far in the distance, trying to identify its form.

"I only understand part of what caused this emotion," she said. "Mostly I reacted to a happiness that was too sweet and beautiful to be borne. As for the rest of what I experienced, it was not worthy of me, and I am not sure that I ever want to understand it."

He placed his hand over her fist. "There is no shame in being human. We cannot summon or reject emotions at will."

Her gaze rose to meet his. No armor protected her. No veil obscured what he saw. She still trembled with the helplessness he had held in his arms, and her soul was in her eyes.

Passion did not interfere with his perceptions this time. He gazed into her tremoring depths and every layer was familiar to him.

He had seen them before, after all.

He was sure now.

Joyful voices came up the stairs. Charlotte glanced in their direction. Nathaniel released her hand and stood. Laclere, Hampton, and Penelope arrived on the landing.

Penelope came over and gave her sister a critical examination. "You are yourself again, I see. Come, we are going to cajole Mrs. Brown into letting us see the baby."

"I do not trust myself to enter again. If I create another scene, it will disturb the child. I think that I will take a turn outside. It is not too cold and I need some air," Charlotte said.

"And it is past time that I take my leave," Nathaniel said. "I have intruded too long."

"You cannot go now," Penelope said. "It is too dark. I have told the housekeeper to prepare a room for you."

"Yes, you must stay," Charlotte said. "You have not yet told me the reason for your visit, and I want to learn all about your journey to Durham." She rose and walked to the stairs leading to the upper floor.

He watched her ascend out of sight, wishing now that there were nothing notable to report.

Laclere was at the bedroom door, holding negotiations with his wife and Mrs. Brown. He turned to the rest of them. "We get to peek, no more. Fleur has fallen asleep."

Penelope hurried over with Julian in tow. Nathaniel waited until they dipped into the chamber, then aimed for the stairs to make himself scarce.

"You do not care for babies?" Laclere asked.

Nathaniel turned. Laclere was still in the doorway.

"It is a family time, Laclere. I will go below."

"We do not stand on ceremony here, Knightridge. It is true that Charl cannot stand the sight of you, but the rest of us count you as an honored friend. If you suffered in hell with Dante down there, you should at least glimpse his heaven. Come and see his son."

Feeling a little coerced, but also a little curious, Nathaniel moved closer and peered into the chamber, past Laclere and over Hampton's shoulder.

Fleur lay under crisply clean bedclothes. She looked like a dozing angel, peaceful and happy, with her long dark hair streaming over the pillow.

Dante sat on the far side of the bed, holding a little wrapped bundle. He had it angled so the baby's pink face could be seen by the audience that had intruded. Dante did not look at them, however. His gaze was on his wife.

Nathaniel's chest tightened at the image the new

family presented. He understood what Charlotte had meant, about a beauty and sweetness not to be borne. No one could view this and not be moved.

There was a hollow spot within his joy, however. An empty corner in his heart recognized and resented its deprivation as he glimpsed the love and intimacy in that chamber.

He wondered if it had been a similar emotion that Charlotte had experienced and did not want to understand.

The crisp air felt good after so many hours in that chamber. Charlotte inhaled the clarifying cold as she strolled near the stone wall that edged the terrace outside Laclere Park's drawing room.

She hoped Nathaniel would join her. If he did, she suspected they would have an argument.

He had not ridden here from London on a social call. Something must have happened concerning Harry that he wanted to tell her. If the discovery had been impressive enough to bring him all this way, she suspected it would be news she would not like to hear.

She could use a good argument right now. It would distract her from reflections on what had happened up in that chamber. What she had felt.

She thought she had reconciled herself to being childless, but this birth had reopened that wound. It might not have been any lack in her, of course.

Philip's illness might have played a role the way everyone pretended to assume.

She feared not, however. Her heart had accepted that barrenness might follow her into another marriage should she ever have the inclination to wed again. She thought she had found peace with that. Today, however, she had mourned her unborn children as she never had before.

It was not seeing Fleur's newborn that had truly undone her, however. Her love for Ambrose had responded to that grief, comforting her, reminding her that she was not really childless in the ways that matter. No, the envy had not been uncontrollable because of the babe. Rather she had been devestated by what she discovered as she watched her brother and Fleur.

She had always been confident that she and Philip had been in love. Not soul-searing love, perhaps. Not highly dramatic passion. But a love just as worthwhile, and, she had always believed, better in the long term. Not dangerous and tumultuous, but peaceful. Contented. Comfortable.

Now she suspected that it had not been love after all. Philip had never looked at her the way Dante did Fleur today. Not even in their most private moments together.

Had he loved her? Really loved her? Or had it been a happy, pleasant affection? Philip had been amiable and polite and . . . passive. Maybe he did not even have it in him to really fall in love.

Maybe she did not either.

A sense of loss shadowed her. A picture that she

had painted in her mind had been torn, and she was sorry to see it ruined. She suspected that she would begin reassessing all of the images now, and learning that her life had not been quite what she thought.

She would have preferred to be spared that. Already it was making her feel old and worn and . . . stupid.

"You appear deep in thought."

She turned at the address. Nathaniel stood near the house. The light from the drawing room backed his tall, dark form.

"Too deep, I am concluding," she said. "Strange how something as commonplace as the birth of a child can encourage introspection."

"A commonplace event, but also a momentous one. It is not surprising that you dwell on it, since you played such an important role."

"It is not the happy event of my nephew's birth that I contemplate, I am ashamed to say. My thoughts are self-absorbed."

"Do you wish to be left with them, or do you require some distraction, as you foresaw earlier today?"

"Distraction would be welcome."

He approached, giving off a magnetic aura that almost had her meeting him halfway. He stood near her differently too. A little closer than in the past. More at ease and familiar, as if what had transpired outside Fleur's chamber had toppled yet another wall.

He fingered the hem of her mantle. "Are you warm in that?"

"Warm enough." Warm enough to stay out here. She did not want to return to the house just yet. Her heart was still accommodating what she had experienced today.

"Let us walk in the park," she suggested. "Laclere will want to celebrate, and I would prefer to avoid him for a short while more."

"There is very little moon. I do not want you stumbling and hurting yourself."

"I know every inch on the path we will take. I often walked it alone in the dark when I was a girl." That was its appeal tonight. She might recapture that girl's courage and honesty if she again trod her path.

They slipped down the stone stairs and ambled through the garden and out to the broad lawn dotted with trees. They strolled along the left side near the edge of the woods that were home to the estate's historic ruins.

The stars shone brightly out here, away from the house. They glinted in the velvet blanket of the night.

His warmth at her side, his presence and energy, comforted her, just as it had earlier. Comforting, but not *comfortable*. This man never left her at peace. Her instincts always did a nervous jig when he was nearby. The intrusive stimulation could be annoying, mostly because she possessed no control over it. She had resented the disturbance in the past. It had provoked the impulse to put him in his place, which was distant enough to spare her the sensation.

She understood the reason for that agitation now, and comprehension only made it worse. The silence did not help. Their quiet walk created a tension that demanded release, and not with words.

She sought relief in words anyway. "You came down from London to tell me something, didn't you?"

"Yes, that was one reason."

The other reason was in his tone and in the night. It pulled at her like a tightening tether.

"Your news must be important."

"It seemed so yesterday, but it appears insignificant now."

She could not imagine how one day would render important news insignficant. She suspected he was trying to be kind after seeing her in emotional shambles. "Since you made the journey, you may as well tell me. You are supposed to be distracting me, remember?"

"I will reveal all, if you insist," he said. "First, however..."

His hand took her arm. He pulled her into an embrace as encompassing as the one outside Fleur's chamber.

The goal was not comfort this time. His kiss created clamorous pleasures that aroused her whole body. A silent moan of relief sounded in her heart as he took command of her passion, calling it forth with nips on her lips and the firm press of his mouth and, finally, with the intrusive sweep of his tongue.

His ravishing mouth sought her ear, then her neck. The kisses produced delicious excitements. He held her so close that she could feel his strength pressed to her breasts and hips. She encircled his neck with her arms so she would be closer still.

"I wish it were summer, and not so cold. Or that we were in London, and not your brother's home," he muttered. His mouth and breath made her neck tingle.

He kissed her again, releasing a passion that made her senses spin. She did not care that it was cold, and wished he did not either. They could go into the woods, and—

He broke the kiss and just held her. She huddled against him, her face pressed to his coat, once more collecting herself, *finding* herself, on this emotionally astonishing day.

His hand eased her head up. He looked into her eyes, as if he could see everything despite the dark. "You and I have much to discuss, Charlotte, and my journey to Durham is the least of it."

She was not sure she wanted to discuss anything at all. They never seemed of one mind when they did. She rather wished they could just abandon themselves to this madness and live in it forever, separate from the world.

Impossible, of course. His words reminded her just how impossible.

"That journey may be the least of it, but it may also be a good place to start," she said.

Their desire and that journey were not completely separate, after all. She wished they were, oh, how she did, but they were not.

He tucked her arm in his, and they began retracing

their steps. She waited for him to broach the subject, but her blood was still humming with excitement.

"Harry told me his story. He revealed a few details on our journey north. I then learned more from him before I left Durham."

Her heart sank. She had feared this was what he would say. The effects of their passion lingered, however, and made her truly wish she had been wrong.

"Am I going to hate you for discovering this information?"

"It does not concern Mardenford, if that is what you mean. Harry only spoke of his own history."

That did not mean it did not concern Mardenford. "What did you learn?"

The night wrapped them, preserving their intimacy. The lights of the house waited, however, and grew brighter with each step.

"He remembers living in a village on the coast, one near a major trade route. His mother lived with him there. He also remembers his journey to London with her. And, I fear, he also remembers her suicide."

Her emotions were raw and this revelation caused a pang of the worst sadness. Poor Harry. She knew too well the kind of guilt and confusion a child experienced when a loved one died that way. She had been not much older than Harry when her oldest brother took his own life. There were nights even now when the sorrow returned because her thoughts turned to that old tragedy.

"Does he know she did it? You said you feared he remembered..."

"He calls it an accident, but I think he suspects. They had been in London some time. One day she dressed in her best clothes and took him to the quay near the Thames. She chose a spot a few streets away from the river, and told him to stay there until she returned. He waited a long time, he says. Then a commotion came from the river and people rushed there. He followed the crowd and saw her body being pulled from the river."

"Oh, dear heavens. That poor child."

"Shocked and frightened, he ran away, and got lost in the city. Finley found him. This is my description of his story. His own memories were scattered and often vague. He did not want to speak of seeing his mother's body, and cried violently when he finally did."

She pictured that. She saw Nathaniel holding the boy as he had just held her outside Fleur's chamber. She did not doubt he had done so. He had forged a bond with the boy.

"How long ago did this happen?"

"I calculate he was with Finley at least four years. He thinks his mother's name was Bella, although as a child he never called her by name. He thinks she called him Harry, so that may be his real name."

The air between them was as heavy as when they walked away from the house. The sensual tension remained, but a new one had joined it.

"What are you going to do about this?" she asked.

"What do you want me to do?"

She did not know. That was a lie. She did know.

She wanted him to kiss her again and forget about Harry. God help her, that was the impulse in her heart. She wanted him to forget he had ever met Harry, because if he did not, she feared this investigation would always stand between them, in all its horrible possibility for shocking discoveries, and kissing him would become a betrayal of her other family, and of her love for little Ambrose.

It was an unworthy reaction. The second in one day. Unworthy and selfish. Normally she acted as a champion for the poor. She supported endeavors to aid them, and she personally worked for some that helped children.

Her reactions to young Harry embarrassed her. It was not the boy but the danger he represented that made her like this. It excited her that he had found a benefactor, that one more child had been saved. She just heartily wished this particular child's benefactor were not Nathaniel Knightridge, and that Nathaniel had not taken up Harry's cause for the reasons he did.

Now Nathaniel was asking what he should do. For some reason he was giving her a chance to demand his retreat. She could not fathom why, with these new clues in hand, he would suddenly be willing to do that, let alone at her request. He had to know the risks to her world that hid in Harry's mystery. To Mardenford and to Ambrose, and maybe even to her. Nathaniel was brilliant, and if she had seen the worst possibilities, he undoubtedly had as well.

She weighed her answer. The words that called a retreat formed in her mind. They tempted her to the point of anguish, but she could not speak them. She could not sacrifice a child to protect her little world, even if her heart cried that she should.

"I do not think you should consider what I want you to do. You must do what you believe is the right thing. There is really no other course for a man of honor, is there?"

A tenseness left him, as if he had feared she would ask him to be other than he was born to be. She knew that she might forever regret not doing just that.

"From his story, I think that I have surmised where this village was situated. The general area of the coast, at least. It was not far from here, actually. The journey to London was not a long one, and his memories of watching the big ships going out to sea were vivid. He spoke of an old woman with whom they lived, probably as boarders."

"Do you intend to seek out this village, and this old woman?"

"I have considered it. She may be someone who knows more about his family. He is very alone in the world. Even the care of Mr. Avlon and that school cannot fill that hole. If there is a chance he can be reunited with family, it is worth a day or so of my time."

"Do you expect that family to be Mardenford's?" She wanted to know what he anticipated. She wanted to know if this would be their last friendly stroll, and if they had just shared their final indiscreet kiss.

"I think that is unlikely. There is a sad predictability to his tale. A poor woman goes to London, hoping to better her life, only to be crushed by the city's harshness. She despairs and takes her own life. I think that Finley found a boy whose grief had obliterated his memory, and created a history to fill the void."

She knew Nathaniel very well, she realized. Too well. Their intimacies had stripped him of certain defenses as much as they had deprived her.

Right now, she knew he was appeasing her. She heard the smooth lawyer talking.

"You are implying that the potential for scandal is gone, but you know it is not. You still think there was a reason Finley fixed his sights on Mardenford."

He sighed. The sound carried a touch of the old exasperation that marked their exchanges. "If there was, Harry did not give that reason to me. I am saying to you that I am not looking for such a connection, but only evidence of this boy's family. I do not anticipate it will be the one I first suspected."

"And if it is?"

He did not reply. Which was answer enough. But then, she had already told him to do what he thought was right.

"When do you intend to visit these villages?"

"Soon."

"If you find that old woman, I want to know what she says."

"I will report at once. However, if you desire immediate satisfaction, and word-for-word accuracy, you will have to be there to hear it yourself. You have been so vexed about this whole inquiry that I think you should come with me."

"Do you indeed, sir?"

"Yes, I do, madam."

She could not deny that she wanted to hear for herself what this old woman said. She did not think Nathaniel would lie to her, but she wanted the finality of being present when Nathaniel's suspicions were laid to rest.

She wanted to look in his eyes at that moment and see that he accepted he had been wrong, and that this quest for truth and moral justice was now over.

"If you join me, we can bring the petitions," he said. "We will even hold meetings at the larger towns en route, so you can present your cause to assemblies. It should not take long to arrange a few before we leave."

"Mr. Knightridge, are you bribing me to accompanying you?"

"I am indicating that such a journey would be useful to you."

"I admit that there would be some pleasure in seeing you proven wrong about Mardenford."

"Giving you pleasure is my only goal." They had reached the terrace, and it was as if the ebbing privacy had altered the mood. He spoke in a low, teasing tone, one flecked with innuendo.

"That sounds as if your intentions in cajoling me to this journey are not entirely honorable, Mr. Knightridge."

He guided her up the stone steps to the terrace. "Actually, your honor and your reputation are foremost in my mind of late. I intend to scold you at length to be more careful with both."

"There is no need. Rest assured I will be bringing my abigail on this journey."

They approached the doors to the drawing room. Inside they could see the family celebrating in the lamplight, laughing with the high spirits that were ending the day.

Nathaniel opened the door. Laclere saw them and glanced a question at Bianca.

"It is not your future behavior that requires scolding, Lady M., but past lapses." Nathaniel spoke lowly amidst the greetings sent their way.

Laclere approached with two glasses of champagne, trying to hide his curiosity about why they had been out in the dark together.

She held out her hand for her glass. "I cannot imagine to what you refer, Mr. Knightridge," she whispered. She raised the glass to her lips and sipped.

"Can't you?" He accepted his own champagne. He turned his head so that his low tone reached only her ears. "I am speaking of your attendance at Lyndale's party. As I said, we have much to discuss."

Shock made her gag. Her champagne sprayed, showering Laclere's coat.

CHAPTER
TEN

The assembly was not going well.

Nathaniel had sensed trouble from the start, when he examined the townspeople as they arrived.

It was much like interpreting the predispositions of the members of a jury. People usually wore their prejudices on their faces, and some of these faces had come not to listen but to reject whatever Lady Mardenford had to say.

Now he sat in a corner near where Charlotte spoke, and bided his time. This was her performance, not his. She was doing a splendid job. If not for some disruptive listeners, it would have been a success.

He just wanted it to end so that he could get her alone and have a conversation that was long overdue.

He saw Charlotte glance furiously at the man in the first row who taunted her as she finished her speech. This prosperous, plump merchant with sparse hair and a high starched collar had begun shaking his head as soon as she opened her mouth. His none-too-quiet chorus of *Goodness me*'s and *Oh dear*'s had now given way to forthright mockery.

"We are a nation of law," she intoned, aiming her voice above his. She spoke to the packed drawing room that the reform-minded widow Mrs. Darby had made available in New Shoreham. At least fifty people sat shoulder-to-shoulder on sofas and settees and chairs.

"It is past time for the civil government to have the authority in divorces. It is past time for the laws to allow unions to be thoroughly severed when cruelty, adultery, or abandonment is proven, and for women to retain rights to their children when such independence is granted."

"Cruelty," her pompous merchant scoffed. "Living the good life off a man's hard work does not sound like cruelty to me." He nudged the man to his right and sought agreement. A tittering of giggles snuck through the chamber.

Charlotte's color rose. Nathaniel hoped she knew better than to engage with this fool.

The man grinned nastily. "I think a better law would be to have the widows of this land forced to marry again. Then Mrs. Darby could not be instigating trouble like this, because there would be a man at the reins."

"You are a dull-witted fool, George Taylor." Little, birdlike Mrs. Darby spoke from her chair in the back of the room. "You always were, and your aging mind is not getting any sharper. You know my late husband's name would have been on that petition before mine."

"I believe I spoke of a *man* at the reins, Mrs. Darby," Mr. Taylor muttered.

The men near him snickered, and his words were carried to other ears. Mouths gaped, but the eyes above them sparkled with the hopes of more theatrics.

"Then again," he confided to his neighbor, "considering his marital situation, maybe Darby would have signed first."

A buzz passed the insults to Mrs. Darby. She bolted to her feet. Only the restraining hands of two lady friends kept her from marching forward and visiting her wrath right on Mr. Taylor's head.

Nathaniel rather wished those friends had been less quick. Taylor was unforgivably rude and was due a thrashing.

Unfortunately, it appeared Charlotte was thinking the same thing. She fingered the handle of her parasol in an alarming manner.

Emboldened by the dissent, a woman spoke from the middle of the group. "Make it easier, and men will be divorcing wives whenever a young chit catches their eyes."

Mumbles and nods greeted that.

"Not so," Charlotte countered. "There will still need to be proofs and cause in the civil courts. Only, women will also be able to show their proofs and their cause too."

"Oh, yes," her front-row tormentor sighed. *"He*

*hasn't bought me a new bonnet in a year, your honor.
He is so cruel.*" His voice rose to a squeak as he imitated a whining woman.

The audience loved it.

"He keeps a woman in Lewes and has got two children on her, your honor," a solid-looking woman of middle years responded, using the same inflections he had. Her glare pierced the back of Mr. Taylor's head.

"He has the presumption to expect me to warm his bed every six months or so whether I want to or not, your honor," Mr. Taylor snapped back, with a vicious edge to his high-pitched voice.

The group laughed and waited for more.

Charlotte's eyes widened. She looked too stunned to enforce order. The horses were breaking down the corral of polite social discourse. After the stampede, nothing she had said would be remembered.

She tried to pretend the bickering did not exist. "All such evidence would be—"

"It should remain with the Church," a small, tidy man announced. "What the Lord has joined, let no man—"

"Sounds like if the Lord did more joining, old George here wouldn't be going to Lewes," another man quipped.

Matters dissolved quickly after that. The polite group of fifty townspeople, a gathering of which Mrs. Darby had been so proud just an hour ago, kept blurting rude, revealing, and sometimes scandalous details about each other.

Nathaniel watched as Charlotte tried without success to herd them back to matters at hand. Unfortunately, they were having such a good gallop that all thoughts of her petition were gone.

George Taylor was in the midst of it all, waxing eloquent and witty. Charlotte's gaze fixed on him and her eyes narrowed. Her face tightened in a way Nathaniel knew all too well.

He sighed and rose to his feet.

She would probably resent his interference. That was preferable, however, to having her family read in the newspapers that Lady Mardenford had instigated a riot when she pounded George Taylor into the ground with her parasol.

Charlotte watched helplessly as the gathering turned into a rout. She knew this was an emotional topic but she had not expected the assembly to take this turn.

Try as she might, she could not garner their attention. The situation had become hopeless and that idiot George Taylor was in rare form now, raving about women as harpies, leeches, and jezebels.

She had spotted him as trouble from the first, what with his florid, smug face and contented smirk. He had ruined her speech and was now helping to ruin her meeting. If he did not restrain himself soon, by Lucifer, she was of a mind to give him a good—

From the corner of her eye, she saw Nathaniel stand. As soon as he rose to his feet, half the eyes in the room turned to him.

The female ones.

Women young and old, gentry and common, slowly took in his tall, lean form and broad shoulders, his dark golden hair and his classically handsome face. Silly little smiles played on most of the female mouths.

He walked forward and the men noticed him too. He took a position right in front of Mr. Taylor. He gazed down, hard.

There was no mistaking the message he was giving.

The giggling and joking bled away. The room hushed.

Mr. Taylor tried meeting the challenge with expressions of bravado and indignation, but soon he was squirming.

"Do you have a sister of whom you are fond, sir?" Nathaniel asked. The query was conversational, almost gentle, but you could hear it clearly in the suddenly silent room.

He got a nod in response.

"And if this sister were dependent upon her husband for her very bread, and if she did not have a prosperous brother such as yourself to turn to in need, and if this husband beat her, hurt her cruelly, what would your reaction be to her situation?"

Mr. Taylor's plump face turned very red.

"Would you not want her to have recourse, short of abandoning her children and being forced into an independence that entails poverty and degradation? Would you have her remain in a marriage that means her suffering in a way that you, a man, never have?" He gestured toward Charlotte. "Lady Mardenford has seen much that you have not, sir. She was blessed with a good husband and a secure life, but she knows her blessings are not shared by all. It is not for herself that she takes up this cause, but for the women in bad unions, whose very lives are endangered due to their lack of protection under the law."

He spoke quietly, but people angled to catch every word. Finally, he turned his attention away from a chagrined Mr. Taylor and began addressing the assembly at large.

He was magnificent. Mesmerizing. The same powers of oration that won his clients the advantage in court now held the attention of her assembly. The commanding presence and magnetic aura that made juries want to lie at his feet now seduced every man and woman to conclude that the petition deserved some consideration.

Charlotte just watched, as impressed as the others. She knew by heart the points that he made. She had just itemized them herself, but they all sounded new and *important* as they flowed from his mouth.

He finished on a quiet note, not the dramatic flourish she expected. Smiling almost boyishly, as if he did not know how to exit the stage, he gestured toward the petitions and shrugged.

Charlotte was sure she heard several woman audibly sigh.

Bodies began shifting as he retreated to her side.

"You were wonderful," she said. "Thank you. I believe your oratory gifts saved the day."

"I merely summed up your excellent speech." He dismissed her admiration as if it embarrassed him. He checked his pocket watch. "It would be best if you left for a half hour and allowed Mrs. Darby to see to the rest. There will be those who are too timid to approach the table if the widow of a baron attends it."

She had not thought of that. "I will take a turn and visit the churchyard. Mrs. Darby says it has a lovely garden."

"I will join you."

She had thought he would stay to lure some of those sighing women to pen their signatures. She had rather counted on it for reasons that had nothing to do with her petition. Instead he called for her wrap and escorted her into the sun.

They trod the paving stones of the commercial street, heading for the spire down the way. Signs for grocers and haberdashers, for a silversmith and two taverns, swung over their heads. The windowpanes formed colored quilts of shops' goods.

"Your journey here went well?" he asked.

"It was pleasant and uneventful. We traveled at a leisurely pace."

It was their first chance to speak privately all day. He had ridden down from London and arrived just this morning. She and her lady's maid had traveled by her coach from Laclere Park yesterday.

The arrangements for this tour of western Sussex's coastal region had all been his, communicated to her from London by post. He had planned the route they would take once they left New Shoreham this afternoon, and the towns they would visit. He had located the inns where they would stay, and the fishing villages they would investigate. He had even had the petitions prepared.

It had all been managed with precision and with no effort on her part. She was able to remain at Laclere Park and spend the last few days with her sister and brothers, making sure that Fleur regained her strength.

Which meant that until Nathaniel walked into Mrs. Darby's drawing room today, Charlotte had not seen him since he departed Laclere Park the morning after Fleur had given birth.

She had thought about him, however. He had thoroughly intruded on her emotions, making a jumble of them. Anticipating his arrival this morning had caused a building nervousness. The notion of spending several days in his company did nothing to quell her churning stomach now.

At some point on this journey he would again raise the matter of her behavior at that party. She did not think that she would like hearing what he intended to say.

As for herself, there was not much that she *could* say.

That conversation now hung in the air waiting for its moment. It crackled between them as they walked down the lane of shops.

She felt his attention and caught him looking at

her with a sidelong gaze. His eyes reflected a subtle, new familiarity, and she felt herself flushing. She turned her own attention to the passing stores.

That same *knowing* had been in his eyes that last night at Laclere Park, while they joined the celebration and spoke of commonplace things.

It had penetrated her the next day as he bid adieu.

It was present when he greeted her this morning, and right now, as they strolled silently toward the churchyard, it affected his whole presence.

His awareness of what she had done, and what they had shared, drenched the mood between them.

She should have known it would be visible. Palpable. She should have guessed that when it wasn't, that meant he did not know she had been with him that night, or at least was not sure.

He was sure now. For some reason, he had become sure that day at Laclere Park.

They crossed the lane and aimed for the gate of the churchyard.

"Mrs. Duclairc is well?" he asked. "The boy is healthy?"

"Both are flourishing. They will name the child Vergil, after my brother. Laclere was so moved when Dante told him, he had to leave the room. Dante says you helped save his sanity, so I think you have a friend for life now."

He opened the gate and stood aside for her. As she passed him she saw a vague smile toy with his lips.

"What is amusing?" she asked.

He closed the gate and fell into step again as they

strolled through the plantings. "I think that you exaggerate his new devotion to our friendship. I suspect that either he or Laclere would call me out if they knew about that party."

Her heart flipped. She glanced around, hoping to see evidence this topic could be delayed. Unfortunately, no one else was visiting the churchyard today. They were alone in the garden.

He aimed their walk to a far corner. The little internal jig that his presence always provoked turned into a dervish's spin.

She cleared her throat. "It isn't as if Dante hasn't... and as for Laclere, I have cause to think... that is, I do not believe either would be so hypocritical as to call you out."

His eyes were very bright now. The vague smile expanded into an expression dark and sardonic. "Yes, Dante attended Lyndale's parties, and Laclere was no saint, despite what everyone assumed. However, I do not think they would agree that their own behavior excuses mine toward you."

"I am not a child. It is no longer their concern."

"You are their little sister. In their minds, you will always need protection."

They had reached the end of the path. He stopped and faced her. The branches of a fruit tree formed a canopy over their heads. The spindly lines were swollen and red, impatient for the warmth that would allow them to bud.

"I could always plead ignorance, I suppose." He

speared her with that new look. "You, however, cannot."

A weak smile quivered on her lips, but died. She had never been at such a disadvantage in her life.

He gazed down at her with an indescribable expression. One that mixed amusement, dismay, and anger.

"Whatever were you *thinking,* Charlotte?"

Whatever were you thinking, Charlotte?

She looked away. She considered his question at length. What *had* she been thinking?

She summoned the memories of that week, and the mood that had led her to that party. She had plunged headlong into the preparations, delighting in the secrecy and the madness of what she plotted. She had been heady from her own audacity. Once she made the decision, it became an exciting, enlivening adventure.

It was not those thoughts that explained her behavior, however. Other, less pleasant ones had spurred the impulse that sent her, masked and anonymous, to that party.

"I was thinking that my life was very dull," she said. "I had been to a dinner party and Lyndale was seated beside me. He asked when I intended to drop the mourning. That shocked me. I have not been mourning all this time. But his words held up a looking glass. I saw what he saw. I realized that while I had not been in protracted mourning, I had not really been living either."

She looked back at him. She could not fathom his reaction from his eyes. Her explanation sounded very thin to her own ears.

She tried again. "Six years had passed. Six years in which nothing of significance had happened in my life. All around me there was drama, but I was in the wings, watching. Even Penelope—God forgive me, she suffered so, but at least she was finally experiencing something besides the vacant, bland, seamless movement of time. There is such a thing as being too comfortable, don't you think?"

"I suppose there is."

"I had only experienced one true emotion during that time. It stirred me so profoundly that it made my heart and soul appear a wasteland in comparison. That was my growing love for little Ambrose. I wondered at it. Savored it. That love reminded me that I was alive, but mostly dormant. And suddenly, one day I woke up and it was not enough, none of it was. Not my station, nor my family, nor my memories."

She could not go on. There were no words for the desperation that gripped her that day. She could not convey the horrible restlessness, as if her life had become a casket entombing her before her time. She could never tell this man about the night she gazed in the looking glass and finally saw what was there—a pretty woman, no longer so young, for whom time was moving fast.

Whom life was passing by.

Sadness slid through her. And disappointment. She began walking back to Mrs. Darby's.

He caught her arm and stopped her. "Charl—"

"No. Let me go. You are demanding an explanation that I cannot put into words. You were the last person I thought would chastise me. I thought you understood. I thought you just *knew*. I did not go to that party intending to . . . I wanted to be shocking and daring, that is true. I ached to shake up my boring soul by doing something reckless and outrageous. But I only intended to see what all the whispers were about, not to participate." She glared back at him. "I thought you understood *that* too."

"I am not seeking to chastise, but to learn where your mind was."

"My mind? It was half mad, in ways I suspect a man's never is." She jerked her arm. "Let me go, Nathaniel. Please. It was my hope that you would never discover it had been me. I suppose I knew it would be ruined if you did."

"I will let you go if you want, after I ask one question."

Sick at heart, and resentful at the humiliation making her feel like the biggest fool ever born, she faced him.

"Ask your question, Nathaniel."

His eyes burned. With what? Anger? She could not tell. His expression was crisp, however. Chiseled and set.

"Why me?"

Her heart fell even lower. "Oh, *that* question."

"I think it is a good one."

It certainly was. She had asked it of herself a hundred times since that night.

"I wish I could say something arch, such as you were the first man available, but that would be dishonest."

"I am relieved to hear it."

Dishonest, but easier. "At first I felt safe with you. I knew you, even if you did not know me. And because you did not know me, it was a different you from the one I knew. And then . . . I said so little, but I felt that you comprehended the volumes that remained unspoken, and then . . ." How to put it in words? How to explain that he might as well have been wearing a mask too. The emotions were that startling and unexpected. That new.

She was grateful when he did not press her for more. He simply continued to gaze with that invasive speculation, that binding familiarity.

His eyes did not comfort or absorb her, however. That look only increased the awkwardness and her embarrassment. She had left that party thinking that every word she had just spoken in this garden would have been unnecessary with him.

Apparently not. Her memories of that night were fantasies, created to appease her conscience. This man was appalled, and trying valiantly not to show it.

"You think badly of me. You were shocked to realize it was me."

"I was shocked, but I do not think badly of you. If I have implied that, I am sorry. I am not secure in what I think. I have not been able to move beyond the realization that I have compromised you in the worst way."

"You had good reason to believe I was a woman beyond compromise. You cannot compromise someone if you don't even know who she is."

"Normally I would agree. We found a way for me to do it, all the same. Furthermore, I *do* know who she is now and my honor commands that I find some solution to the dilemma."

"That is the reason for this interrogation?" A different kind of disappointment spread. A distinctly annoyed one.

Here she was, close to tears over the death of a transcendent dream, and he was plodding along, seeking to find a path back to dull respectability.

"Put your mind at rest. I do not hold you responsible. You have no obligations to my reputation."

"I disagree. Eventually it will come out. Lyndale knows, I am sure." He began strolling slowly, as if stepping through his thoughts. He moved back and forth beneath the tree.

"Did he tell you it was I in that mask?"

"No, but he knows. I can tell. He knows it was you and he knows you and I—well, he knows. You are aware of how tactless he is. Someday he will be talking about something else entirely, and in a flood of wit, out it will come."

"I am sure he will be discreet."

Nathaniel shot her a glance of supreme skepticism.

Since Lyndale was not celebrated for discretion, she had no words to defend him.

"So, here we are, Charlotte. Your situation is dangerous."

"I disagree. It would not ruin me, not totally, even if it became known."

"Nonsense. Your position would be damaged beyond redemption. I have contemplated this for several days and concluded there is only one way to rectify my behavior—"

"Don't you mean our behavior? It is very good of you to take all the blame yourself, but—"

He stopped walking and raised a hand to silence her. "Lady M., I must ask that for once you restrain from interrupting and contradicting me. In the best of circumstances it is—just allow me a few sentences in peace, if you will."

"Of course, Mr. Knightridge."

He inhaled audibly and found his stride again. "The course is clear, I think you will agree."

She watched him stroll, to and fro, much as he did in a courtroom. Too relaxed for pacing. Too deliberate for meandering. This was a way of declaring dominance of a territory.

"There is only one thing to do. We should wed at once. If we are married when gossip spreads, it will not affect you nearly as much. I procured the special license before I left London."

She stared at him. He spoke as if she had been anticipating such a suggestion. He threw out the notion of marriage as calmly as if he were announcing which route they would take back to London.

He stopped moving and gazed at the church. "We may as well do it here, before we leave. I will speak with the vicar."

"I think that we should first—"

"I will arrange it for tomorrow morning."

"There is no reason to be hasty. After all—"

"It will not even delay our progress much."

"Mr. Knightridge."

He looked over, startled by her sharp tone.

"Mr. Knightridge—Nathaniel—you are very good to want to rectify matters, and to be so protective of my reputation. This is very noble of you. However..."

He cocked his head when the pause lengthened. "However?"

She sighed. It seemed to her that the *however* was obvious. "We do not *like* each other, Nathaniel."

"So you keep reminding me. *However,* recent evidence indicates we like each other well enough."

"That was only because you did not know who I was that night."

"I have known who you were *since* that night."

"I see. You are not referring to our big indiscretion but to our more recent, smaller ones." Her mind groped for a rationalization. "I will admit those are harder to explain."

"Not at all. As I said, a wall crumbled. My soul recognized you even if my brain insisted on being blind. I wondered, you know. Every time we kissed, my instincts kept suggesting the possibility, but my mind said, *Impossible. Charlotte Mardenford does not attend such parties and have casual liaisons with you, of all men.* You might have told me. At least our sudden impulse toward little indiscretions would have made some sense."

An edge of anger entered the last sentences. It held her response in check. Dismissing that desire as no more than silly kisses and flirtations would not be wise today.

"Despite the intimacies between us, it would be rash to marry. There is no need, and there is still much that divides us. Even this proposal was marked by contention. You cannot really want this. You merely feel obligated. That reflects well on your honor, but I am not a young girl who requires marriage to save her reputation. Therefore, I decline."

His expression hardened. He paced toward her until he was mere inches away. He looked down.

"It was an orgy, Charlotte. We were not alone in that chamber. If it is learned you were there, you will be ridiculed and scorned. If it is discovered that you were there *with me,* whom the world knows you *do not like,* it will be thought that you are not only promiscuous, but coldly so."

Is that what he thought? That she was a scandalous lady of sin? She suspected it was.

"I do not think it will be learned I was there. Even you did not know it until now. Lyndale is a better man than you say, and he will not betray me. Nor will you."

His gaze warmed. Suddenly she was looking into the eyes that had captivated her that night. Her soul responded with an ache of yearning. They may not like each other, and he might be a threat to other memories and securities, but that night had forged a unity. That bond could pull at her now whenever he acknowledged it existed.

"I have tried to deal fairly with you," he said.

"I appreciate it. I truly do."

"Your rejection leaves me only one recourse, and that is to seduce you."

"That is an odd conclusion to this conversation. I would not say that is the *only* recourse."

"I see no other."

"Restraint? Gracious retreat? Friendship?"

"I am not inclined to be restrained with you. Nor have you demanded it from me of late."

That was true, but things were different now. If she allowed further liberties, if she succumbed to a seduction, it might destroy what little remained of her memories of that night. They might be fantasies, but they were beautiful ones and very dear to her. If she permitted another indiscretion now that she knew he knew, she might be forced to learn for certain that she had been a promiscuous fool.

He crooked a finger under her chin and tilted her face up. "I look at you now and all I see are the eyes gazing up at me while I held you that night."

She felt her face warming. "I suppose that could be inconvenient until it passed. Surely it is only a small problem, however."

"A *small* problem? You do not know men well."
He glossed the backs of his fingertips over her cheek.
His touch made her light-headed. "I must have you at
least one more time, Charlotte. Otherwise I will
never know."

A creak at the gate penetrated her swimming
senses. Voices broke the silence of the yard. He
glanced over at the sounds. His hand left her face.

"You will never know what, Nathaniel?"

They began retracing their path through the garden. He looked to the intruders but his eyes were
hooded, as if he really looked inside himself. "I will
just never know."

CHAPTER ELEVEN

~~~

He had to know, that was all there was to it.

Had he imagined the best of that night? Had he merely been besotted by the mood, the lighting, the mystery?

If so, he would let reality demolish the illusions. He was not inclined to live his life nostalgic over an experience that had been a fraud.

Evidence indicated that Charlotte had used him badly. Played him for a fool, to be frank about it. She may not have intended to. Unhappiness may have driven her to take impulsive risks, but she had still deceived him.

And yet . . . well, he had to know.

She was on her guard as they continued their little journey. She kept her abigail close and even insisted the maid share her chamber at inns. She managed never to be alone with him, as if she feared he would commence a seduction at the least provocation.

She averted her eyes, trying to deny the intimacies that bound them. She retreated into the contentious exchanges that had marked their conversations in the past.

He found that charming, and wondered if she suspected how hopeless her efforts were.

Their tour improved after New Shoreham. The assemblies went smoothly and the petitions gathered signatures. Charlotte performed alone. Nathaniel's interference was not needed in the three towns they visited over the next days.

The true reason for the tour was less successful. Whenever they stopped at fishing villages on the coast, Nathaniel sought out an old woman called Jenny. He found four, but none of them had any knowledge of Harry or his mother.

"I fear we will not find her," Charlotte said on the fifth afternoon. She had just completed her speech and was retreating from the room while townspeople surrounded the petition table. On passing him, she saw that he was perusing a map of the coast, circling the villages to be visited during the next few days.

"We will then return to London, with you relieved at our failure, and with me content I did my best for the boy."

"I hope you understand that I do not want Harry left rootless."

He understood that.

He did not blame her for hoping no Jenny would be found. He trusted that she did not blame him for looking, despite the potential danger in this search. It was an unlikely danger, he was concluding, but it was still there.

This was one of the things that still "much divided" them, as she had said in response to his proposal.

He had not truly believed she would agree to marriage, but had procured the license anyway. It was a way to assuage his discomfort at discovering just who his mystery goddess had been.

It had not been dutiful resignation that affected him when he finally held the license in his hand, however. His reaction had been lighthearted. Cautiously delighted. Her quick refusal had angered him.

Which was why he had to know.

"Is it your intention to stay here and visit those villages tomorrow?" she asked, angling her head to study the map.

"I have made other arrangements for our lodgings tonight. We should depart as soon as the petitions are completed."

"Those villages are not far from here. We could avoid the extra time on the road if we remained at our current inn."

Her color had risen a little. She kept her gaze on the map.

She suspected he was up to no good. Perhaps his restraint these last days had confused her. Or maybe she felt the anticipation coiling tighter in him with each passing hour.

"We will take lodgings tonight that are more spacious for you, and less rustic. I assumed that after five nights you would like more conveniences than this town's inn affords."

She glanced askance at him. He smiled innocently.

Half-convinced, but still on guard, she left to pack with her abigail.

He rode with her in the carriage again.

He had done that every day. There was plenty of room, so she could hardly refuse. With her maid Nancy sitting beside her, there was no chance of small indiscretions, let alone a big one. He did not even require conversation, since he normally read a book.

Unfortunately, she could not ignore him if he sat right there, facing her, their knees almost touching. She had too much time to notice he was so handsome that it was unnatural. The light from the window revealed how his hair contained many colors, from lightest blond to deepest bronze. His skin was not as pale as one would expect with that hair. Like his eyes, it revealed the influence on his breeding of his mother, who had not been fair at all.

She saw all the details, even though she did not want to. He was just *there,* compelling her to look and notice and study. His presence filled the small space so completely, she half expected the carriage walls to bulge to accommodate him. His physical command was the least of it. That energy that so unnerved her poured out, flooding everything.

She suspected that he knew his company made her uncomfortable, and that he intended as much. He wanted to remind her with his proximity of that conversation in the churchyard and how it had ended. He wanted her worrying about when the seduction he threatened would take place.

If that was his goal, it was working. She was very worried. She could not read her own book at all. Her condition both excited and vexed her.

Eventually the vexation won out.

"The day is very fair," she observed. The carriage rolled through a countryside painted in the muted tones of late winter. "I believe the weather is starting to break in earnest."

"It appears so," he said.

"Will we be going far today?"

"An hour at most. We are almost there."

"Such a short distance? I am surprised you did not choose to ride ahead on your horse. Since the day is so fair, that is."

"I need to give the coachman directions."

"You could have done so in advance, if you wanted to ride. You still could."

"I did not say I wanted to ride. It appears that you think I should, however."

That was just the sort of response that Nathaniel Knightridge had always given her. He had an annoying habit of thinking he saw when she dissembled, and letting her know it. It was very disconcerting to have a man not only assume that he perceived her intentions, but point them out so baldly. That he was often correct only increased the irritation.

"I only thought that your horse could use a good gallop, and that you might enjoy that too, since the day is so fair."

He gave her a look that said he saw her game. It also communicated much more, and her heart began a slow, heavy beating. "Would you prefer if I rode? Is my intrusion unsettling you?"

"Not at all. I barely know you are here. I simply did not want you to think that you had any obligation to help me pass the time. I would understand if you preferred to ride ahead, since—"

"Since the day is so fair."

She glimpsed amusement in his eyes. Oh, yes, he was enjoying this. He kept barging into her carriage for one reason only, and that was to exude his power and tease her with the anticipation and memories of their kisses and more.

At the inns and meetings, in the towns and villages, she could avoid him or dilute his effect with distractions. Not in this carriage, however.

She did not like playing the mouse to his cat. If Nancy were not here knitting at her side, she would tell him so very frankly. She was of half a mind to anyway.

"I know why you did not ride that horse, Mr. Knightridge. You are not the only one who can see matters very clearly."

"Good. Then we are of one mind in seeing matters, if nothing else."

His amusement deepened. He looked pointedly at Nancy, and smiled at her predicament.

He angled to look out the window, then called up to the coachman. "There is a lane on the right, past the next crossroad, where you must turn."

The carriage followed the lane for a quarter mile through some woods. Charlotte peered out the window, curious at the route that was unexpectedly taking them north.

The lane curved to the left, and the woods fell away. In the distance on a little hill there perched a rough-stone manor house of good size but simple design.

Its appearance startled her. Nathaniel was not taking her to another town and another inn, as she had thought.

She called to her coachman to stop. She narrowed her eyes at Nathaniel. He returned the most placid expression.

She glanced furiously at Nancy, who had suddenly become an inconvenient hindrance to conversation.

"Mr. Knightridge, I would like to step out for a moment, to take some air."

"Because the day is so fair?"

She glared at him.

He helped her down onto the lane. She paced ahead twenty yards, and heard him follow.

She turned on him and gestured to the house. "What is this place?"

"Elmcrest is a family property. It is not used much, but there will be enough staff to see to your comfort."

The level of staff was not her concern. "Do they expect us?"

"I wrote to tell the housekeeper that we would visit for a day or so. The rest of the villages are an easy carriage ride from here."

She gazed at that house. It had numerous chambers, which meant that Nancy would be sent to her own. "I would prefer to use inns."

"I would not. You brought your maid, but I did not bring Jacobs. I grow weary of inns and their servants."

"So it is your own comfort that you seek."

"And yours. You will be more at ease if you do not have to use a different bed every night. You will have more privacy here, and service that is worthy of your station."

He might as well have said *I would prefer to seduce you here than at an inn. The beds are better, and it will be more discreet.*

"You do not have to look so worried, Charlotte. I would never importune you."

"You have once before."

"I think true importuning requires a little more resistance than I met that day, don't you? If you are so afraid of me, tell your coachman to drive on. There will be another town and inn down the road. I, however, am staying here and will be going to those villages from this house."

I am not afraid of you. Except she was. Being with him in that house would make her vulnerable. He was up to no good with this plan. Even a schoolgirl could see that.

Already their isolation affected her. She did not like the confusion that quickened her heart. She wanted to think a very long time before she agreed to further intimacies, but she felt time running out.

He might have to know, but she was almost certain she did not want to.

"You are not being fair," she said. "I should not have to decide now. I should not have to choose whether to risk the memories here, while I stand by the side of a road."

"All you have to decide now is whether you enter that house, where servants await you with hot baths, good food, and quality linens, or whether you spend another night in a drafty inn on old muslin and a sagging mattress. I have no reason to interpret your decision as meaning more."

He was good with words, she had to give him that. With a few careful sentences he had made her resistance look childish and silly.

Determined to be neither, she trod back to her carriage. He was right. She agreed to nothing by staying at this house.

He handed her into the carriage but did not join her there. Instead he unleashed his horse and mounted it.

"I think I will ride ahead," he said. "Since the day is so fair."

She faced him through the window opening.

"Sometimes I really do not like you, Mr. Knight-ridge."

He laughed. "And sometimes you really do, Lady M."

"It came to the family through an uncle, my mother's brother," Nathaniel said. They were strolling through the ground level of the house. Charlotte had decided to do so immediately upon coming down after the housekeeper settled her into a bedchamber.

She walked beside him so slowly that it made his paces awkward. She studied every detail of the drawing room and library, of the morning room and hall. She was prolonging this, as if she intended to fill the whole afternoon with this tour.

"It is not that far from London, and the prospects from the windows are lovely," she said, peering out one in the dining room. "There are horses back there, on that hill. Is this a farm?"

"Horses are bred here, by my eldest brother. He does not visit much, however."

"It is his property, then?"

"Its actual owner is not clear."

"I did not think any land in England had an un-clear owner."

"Contested property does. My uncle left it to someone, but his will was interpreted to be ambiguous, as such things can be. So my father holds it and awaits developments at Chancery."

She strolled along to the next window. A tree diffused the light coming through this one. The way it illuminated her face captivated him. It created the *sfumato* seen in old Venetian paintings, with the hazy atmosphere softening all the features on her face, making her appear ethereal.

"To whom did your uncle bequeath the land?"

"Me." He knew she had guessed. It was in her thoughtful countenance. Her mind often jumped ahead like that, reaching the correct conclusion before most would, seeing the whole landscape no matter how small the window from which she viewed it.

She turned to him, her brow puckered with concern. "You inherited this property and your father has interfered with your receiving it? That astonishes me."

"He did it as a punishment. He had plans for me that I did not accept, and I had plans that he did not like. Contesting my uncle's will over this property was his way of persuading me his way was best. Even when I compromised, it was not enough."

"What compromise did you offer?"

"I agreed that I would not become an actor."

Her expression lightened. Delight glinted in her eyes. "Oh my, Nathaniel. Did you really intend such a thing?"

"I had it all planned. I attended university to appease him first, and even took my degree. After that, however, I intended to trod the boards. When I informed him, he almost suffered apoplexy."

She giggled and pressed her hand to her mouth. "I am picturing it. What a delicious scandal that would have been. Norriston is so upright too. So very *important* in the government and society. It was kind of you to change your mind."

"It was a great sacrifice. I felt very noble. I expected that whatever I chose to do after that to be welcomed, because anything was better than the theater. I was wrong, of course. Men like my father are not merely interested in avoiding the worst and achieving better. They want to ensure the best."

She crinkled her nose in the most adorable way. "He does not like that you are a lawyer, you mean."

"If I had become a barrister, and spent my years milking families of the value of their contested estates, he might have grudgingly approved. Common Pleas is tainted by trade, of course. And the Old Bailey..."

"Yes." She moved on, and he fell in step. "When did you realize a courtroom was a stage, and you could still be an actor?"

She was very perceptive. Very smart. "The first time I performed, and saw my effect on the audience. I had been trained in rhetoric for the church. I argued that first case as if I were a preacher. Actors, preachers, lawyers—we all use spoken words to persuade. There I was, preaching, and I realized it might be more effective if I ceased using a pulpit and treated that court as a stage."

She looked over at him as they passed back into the drawing room. "You would have been a magnificent actor or clergyman. I imagine your father wanted the latter role for you."

"He still does. And this—" He gestured to the walls and ceiling and beyond. "This and much more waits for me if I agree."

She sat on a chair. Her gaze followed the path his arm had made. "How much more?"

He took another chair, which was positioned where he could see her completely. "It keeps increasing, as we both age and time for it runs out. He wants a bishop in the family."

She appeared very serious as she calculated and weighed the situation. "Is this property very large? Are there farms and rents attached?"

"It is more than respectable."

"Have you fought Norriston in Chancery for it?"

"No. The matter just sits there, neither bleeding the estate nor progressing, as such things can for decades."

"So you live at Albany, instead of a town house. You make your own way, instead of enjoying the fruits of your birth. It is a high price you pay for your pride and independence."

"I do not make my own way entirely. Norriston is not that stubborn. There is a small allowance, and I also have a portion from my mother."

She kept gazing around the chamber, at the walls and windows and moldings, taking measurements for her thoughts.

Finally she turned her attention to him.

"Why did you bring me here?"

"I think you know why, Charlotte."

She flushed slightly, but her thoughtful demeanor

did not alter. "I speak of your original intention in arranging this visit. You offered marriage three days ago. If I had accepted, I would have come here as your bride. What did you intend to show me in bringing me to this house? That I had married a man who could not be bought? Or that I had married a man who could give me wealth if I wanted it?"

Oh, yes, she was smart. It would help sometimes if she were not. "I intended to explain my situation and hear your thoughts on it. Since you refused, that conversation became unnecessary, although we seem to be having it anyway."

"When you marry, you will reconsider?"

"The responsibilities of a wife might require it, I suppose."

"Responsibilities do that, don't they? No wonder men like Dante and Lyndale were tempted to live their whole lives without any. I am curious, however. Is it the boy in you that resists your father and rebels at his command? As I said, you would make a magnificent clergyman, and I think you know it."

He thought about his answer. He realized that it mattered to him what she thought of his decision. "It is not the rebellious boy, but the honest man, I hope. I do not belong in the church; this I know. If I am going to play a role, let it be clear that I am an actor on a stage."

She accepted that with little reaction. She rose, and he did as well.

"I will retire and see how my maid is progressing

with unpacking. Perhaps I will have that bath you spoke of."

She walked to the door, but stopped. Once more she surveyed the chamber.

"I despise blackmail. It is a curse from which my family suffered most cruelly, and I loathe the people who engage in it. Norriston is doing something very similar. He is trying to extort something valuable from you. It is disgraceful for a father to do such a thing, although it is common enough."

Her words seethed with a vehemence that surprised him. That which still divided them suddenly intruded. Finley, Mardenford, Harry—all of it had begun with a blackmail threat. He had not realized she had experienced its devastation before, but her anger and speech implied that she had.

"If I had accepted your proposal and come here as your bride, I would not have asked you to be a hypocrite for my sake, Nathaniel." She opened the door. "Instead I might have urged you to tell Norriston to go to hell."

She could not decide what to wear. The one dinner dress that she had packed, with its ivory silk and ecru lace and sloping décolleté from shoulder to breast, showed a lot of skin. She did not want him thinking she was luring him. There was nothing worse than a tease.

Unfortunately, the other dresses were not suitable for a country house. They had been brought on the assumption she would stay at inns. The ivory dress had only come on the chance some notable in some town invited her to a proper dinner, as indeed several had.

She eyed all the options, and knew it would have to be the dinner dress, skin and all. It would look odd, almost rude, to sit in that dining room in anything else. It would also prove what a coward she was.

Nancy set to dressing her hair. Charlotte kept insisting the style be made more sedate. Nancy wanted to do a bit of painting. Charlotte refused.

All the while her mind hopped from thought to thought, but her nervousness and indecision about Nathaniel flowed like a racing current beneath it all.

Mostly she considered what she had learned today. She had been indifferent to Norriston in the past. He was a presence one could not ignore in society, tall and imposing, a bit severe but temperate in demeanor. It was not hard to see him in Nathaniel, although Nathaniel was more amiable and quicker to smile.

Now she decided she did not like Norriston at all. It was not fair that he coerced his son by withholding this property, and whatever else was involved. While it was true that younger sons of peers often entered the church, and while it was also true that most of them had no business doing so if one examined their beliefs and constitutions, that did not mean that all younger sons should strike that bargain without thought.

She found it admirable that Nathaniel did not want to live a lie. If more men were that honest, the church might not be in the doldrums that begged for the winds of reform.

It was a lovely property that he sacrificed too. The house was not distinguished, but it was large and very comfortable. The land was beautiful. The entire setting evoked peace. It had to tempt him. One word, one shift in where he performed, and it would be his. And more, he said. Probably much more, if Norriston had been increasing the bribe for almost a decade.

Nancy finished with a final tweak of a curl, and fastened a simple necklace. Charlotte examined the results in the looking glass. She appeared elegant in an appropriately restrained way. There was nothing in the image she faced that would entrance a normal man, let alone Nathaniel Knightridge.

I have to know.

Well, he would have to survive not knowing. The last few hours had convinced her there was more to lose than win in any affair. Not only her memories of that night were at risk, but other, older ones, which had nothing to do with Nathaniel, also cringed on the edges of her heart.

Lyndale's party had not threatened those memories in the least. The entire episode had been removed from her real life, both past and present. It had been an experience in a separate realm of existence.

That would not be true next time.

She had begun to doubt the old memories. The pictures had sharpened again, so her mind could examine them. She resisted doing so. She did not want any proof they were the forgeries that she feared.

She accepted her silk shawl from Nancy and left the bedchamber. If Nathaniel made advances, if he embarked on his grand seduction, she would explain all that to him. She would make him understand that sometimes it is better not to know.

He paced, waiting for her to come down from her chamber. There was nothing casual about the way he moved. He trod a distinct path in the drawing room, back and forth, his strides determined and clear.

He resented his impatience and the agitation it caused. Images assaulted him, of Charlotte in his arms, of her warmth, her skin, her passion . . .

He kept insanity at bay by contemplating their recent conversations. She had alluded to blackmail hurting her family. Not her husband's family. Her oldest brother had died young. There were whispers even now that it had been suicide.

He strode out the calculations. Charlotte would have been a girl. Fifteen, perhaps. His jaw tightened as he imagined the grief such a loss would have caused her. If she knew the reasons—he remembered Harry's misery as the boy described seeing his mother's body dragged from the river. Not only sorrow twisted the boy's face, but also pain from the abandonment. Questions of why. Doubts about love.

Small wonder Charlotte had found Mardenford's quiet lake so appealing. Of course she would despise Finley. She would hate any suggestion his blackmail had been based on fact, and that there might be secrets hidden in her adopted family as well, waiting to ruin her peace.

It was astonishing she had spoken to him again after he revealed his suspicions. He realized that she had only in an attempt to defeat and divert him, and to protect those she loved.

That was not the only conversation that kept returning to his brain as he paced. The other, out on the road, repeated again and again. *I should not have to choose whether to risk those memories here.* He did not think she only meant memories about their prior passion.

It was all tied together. Much still divided them, she had said. The chasm had actually deepened these last weeks, even as little indiscretions temporarily built bridges. Bridges made of air, perhaps. Maybe they could find common ground only if they met as strangers.

He found himself thinking that he did not want to know after all.

A sound penetrated his focused thoughts. He pivoted in mid-stride. Charlotte stood near the door.

"You are making a valley in the carpet," she said. "Are you practicing a defense that is imminent?"

"Yes." *No. I am thinking about you, and all that I don't know and the little I do, and trying not to want you too much.*

She looked so beautiful that he ached. The ivory and ecru of her dress enhanced her pale skin. Her shawl did not cover that skin well, despite the way she kept it high. Her lips looked very red. Not paint.

The color had gathered in them due to the way she kept nipping the lower one.

That was the only sign she was nervous. Her bearing was proud and straight, her gaze level and distant. This was Lady M., with whom he had so often engaged in a battle of wits. This was the baron's widow, whose intelligence and self-possession impressed society, and whose impeccable behavior had overcome the taints on her family name caused by other members' less conventional lives.

He offered his arm. "They await us. Dinner was announced a while ago."

"I dallied too long."

"I did not mind waiting, since the result is so beautiful."

She smiled weakly. They both knew she had not dallied for that. Half the time would have turned her out just as well.

She did not have to come down at all. She could have sent word she was tired, or ill, and taken her meal in her chamber.

But she had come down and now her hand was tucked around his arm. His deep contemplations seemed distant as he escorted her to the dining room. The gentle touch of her hand urged him to forget everything except the long night stretching in front of them.

Charlotte watched how the servants attended them at dinner. She noted the familiar smiles Nathaniel gave them, and the special care they took.

It had been thus since they arrived. The house-keeper had been overjoyed to see him. The sleepy house had come alive with his entry.

"They are happy you are here," she said after finishing her meal. An excellent meal. She judged it had taken many hours to prepare. "They treat you as the master of the property. I suspect your brother is not greeted so warmly nor fed so well when he arrives to see his horses."

"I often visited with my uncle when I was a boy. I was his favorite. Mostly, I think, because he also was the youngest of a large brood, and guessed how number five is something of an invisible addition."

"I cannot imagine your ever being invisible."

"I exploited the situation. I was fully grown before my father had any idea who I was."

She had to laugh. She pictured that meeting, with a startled Earl of Norriston facing a son equal in height and force of will, being informed that son would become an actor.

"And your mother? Did she not know you either?"

"That was different. As the youngest, I had her attention in ways the others never enjoyed. In that I was blessed."

She should have been able to understand that, but she did not. She had also been the youngest, but she had not enjoyed a similar attention. She had been not so much invisible as much as an afterthought. As a child she had been a potted palm in the room while her mother plotted the future of the family.

That had been part of Mardenford's appeal. His

attention had disarmed her. A cool peace surrounded her when he came to call. She was at the center of someone's attention for what seemed the first time in her life. Finally, what she said was heard and not lost in the noise of others' opinions and views.

Not only heard, but respected as the words of an intelligent woman and not those of a little sister.

She had found her voice and her character in her marriage. She had forgotten how much. Now images of that quick blooming sped through her head.

It appeared that the sharpened memories did not harbor only disappointments. The truth might reveal value she had not counted too.

She blinked, and realized she had been lost in a brief reverie. Nathaniel was watching her, permitting it, just as he had in her sitting room that day.

His gaze held the same patient understanding.

"Tell me about him. I did not know him well."

The overture stunned her. He appeared truly interested, and that surprised her more. She looked at her plate, trying to think of what to say, and how.

"I am sorry, Charlotte. You said you no longer mourned him. I thought—"

"Do not apologize. I just . . ." A year ago she would have spoken freely. Everyone always commented on how she could talk about her husband and marriage with ease, how one did not have to be cautious around her in making reference to him.

"I was happy," she said firmly. "He was a good man. Generous and caring and kind." And affectionate, in his way. Her own love had been quiet too.

There had been no tumult in her emotions. *He was a good man, but he was nothing at all like you.*

"I want to know something. It is important to me to know it, so I hope you will tell me honestly."

"What is that?"

"When I kiss you, do you feel that you betray him in any way?"

Her pulse quickened, but everything else in the chamber went still. The question did not shock her as much as it should have. It had been waiting on the edges of her confusion as she contemplated memories old and new.

"No. That frightens me. I think that is what undid me at that party. How he was not there with me, and I was alone. Truly alone as I had never been in years. And when you spoke to me . . ."

Are you realizing that you do not belong here? That was what the voice behind her in the shadows had said. *Sit here. No one will approach you, I promise.*

What followed could be seen as a betrayal, if she thought about it long enough. Not the acts, but the emotions. The passion and the intimacy. What kind of woman shared that transforming bond with a man anonymously, when she had not done so with her husband?

If indeed it had been shared at all.

She felt helpless. "I do not know what to make of what happened between you and me. I think if I ever do, the conclusions will not be flattering to me."

He took her hand and kissed it. "There is nothing in my memory or my thoughts about that night that is not flattering to you. Are you convincing yourself to feel guilty for not feeling guilty? If you have decided to live the life of the moment, and not the past, that is a good thing. It is why you went there that night, you said."

"Perhaps it had nothing to do with the past, or even the present. Maybe it was appropriate that I was masked, made anonymous, because it was not really me there."

He looked down at the hand he held. His thumb caressed its back. "It was you. Unless you tell me that you never think of it, that it made no difference in the days ahead, and that you reject the memories and regret the passion, it was you."

She could not say that. It had made a difference. The old ennui was dead. She saw the world differently. She noticed colors and lighting, and felt the cold of the air and the warmth of the sun, as if her senses had been revitalized. All of them. Those of the body, but also the more primeval ones of the heart and soul.

He raised her hand and kissed it. "We both went there alone, two people who had loved others long ago, and we shared something very unusual. The only question is whether the intensity was born of the mystery, or whether it can happen again. I have to know. Don't you?"

She had not expected such a question. He was not seducing her at all, but requiring a deliberate choice.

The sensual lure remained, however. The firm hold of his hand, masculine and firm and strong, excited her. She had been waiting, waiting . . . now waiting became anticipation, making her vibrate.

It was his gaze that undid her, however. It claimed her more completely than his hand. The stark familiarity in his dark eyes, their fathoms of comprehension and desire, drew her in. The most potent memory from that night became real again. Not one of pleasure, but of a trust born of knowing another so thoroughly, so instinctively, that her own soul could hide nothing in response.

They might never find common ground except in this bond, but she could not deny its power. Only the biggest coward would reject what might be waiting.

"Yes, I have to know too."

CHAPTER
TWELVE

S he rose to retire at once. She could not bear to be in his presence, trembling and breathless, while servants waited nearby. She could not make polite conversation now and pretend she had not just given him an astonishing agreement.

The fire in his eyes as he watched her leave almost had her swooning. Feeling so alive it was unearthly, she hurried to her chamber.

Nancy was surprised by her early return. With wordless gestures, she had Nancy undress her and prepare her for bed. Then she sent her maid away, with instructions not to wake her in the morning or return until called.

Gowned in a bed dress of fine white cotton, she realized that she now had hours to wait. Nathaniel would not come here while the servants were about.

She tried to make some plans about the petitions. Her eyes read the notes she made on her paper, but her mind did not see them at all. It pictured Nathaniel down below, waiting too. His expectation flowed to her through the walls and space, arousing her despite his distance.

She did not know how long she sat at the small writing desk, with the phantom sensations building until she neither saw nor felt anything else. She sensed the house quieting, though. The stillness of night crept over it until empty silence stretched.

She went to her bed and lay down. She did not look at the clock. Its ticks did not matter. She was already captivated by his power and he was not even in the room.

He drew her into memories so vivid they became her world, and she did not even notice how they blended into dreams.

The touch, when it came, was no intrusion to that deep reverie. A vague consciousness returned to her, and with it an intuitive awareness that it was Nathaniel's hand on her arm. Her most basic sense had absorbed his presence near her some time ago. With the gentlest guidance, he pulled her back to the world.

A dark world. No light leaked through the window drapes. Only the small lamp she had left burning near her bed gave any illumination.

He stood beside her, looking down. No urgency marked his expression or manner. He appeared prepared to wait forever for her to open her eyes.

It took a few moments for her to fully waken. During that brief lull of luxurious relaxation, before her body found its own alertness, she languidly admired how handsome he appeared in the lamp's glow with his dark coats and high boots and his hair falling carelessly across his brow. His eyes held a compelling expression, with nuances of both warmth and severity.

His fingertips brushed her cheek, then gently closed on a lock of her hair. He lifted it while his touch slid down its length. "I was torn between waking you or watching you. You were smiling in your dream, and appeared like a girl."

She began to rise. He shook his head. "Stay there."

He began undressing. She watched, fascinated by the distracted male movements. The way he shrugged off his frock coat and stripped away his cravat created a domestic mood that was in marked contrast to the frantic, mutual disrobing of the last time.

She knew then that it would be different. It had to be. They were alone and this was no impulse, no unexpected crescendo of passion. The methodical way he dealt with his garments said as much.

She had never watched a man undress before. The emergence of his true form, the expression that said his thoughts were on the purpose, not the process—all of it captivated her. Her breath caught when he slid off his shirt to reveal his lean, athletic torso. She had held that body in her arms, but she had not simply looked as she did now, stirred by his beauty alone, without so much as a touch between them.

He rested his hips against the bed's high edge. The muscles of his back corded and stretched as he bent to remove his boots.

His lower garments loosened. He stood and they dropped. Her eyes filled while he stepped out. He had a magnificent form, broad shouldered and wonderfully proportioned. Tight, hard lines delineated his muscles and lured her gaze down the taper of his back to the firm swells of his buttocks. The lamp washed his body in a soft, golden light.

He turned, his expression still lacking any interest in his actions. Their gazes locked and it was clear his thoughts had been absorbed by her. His arousal made that very evident too, but she was halfway to ecstasy herself already. Seeing his erection caused the most delicious thrill to tremble between her legs.

He lifted the sheet and joined her in the bed. She ached to hold him, but he braced his weight on one arm and looked down at her.

His masculinity became a palpable force, altering the energy he exuded, imbuing it with sensual danger. A primitive chime of vulnerability rang in her instincts. It was a reaction as old as time, holding the potential for both excitement and fear.

The bedclothes bunched at his waist, and she let her gaze linger on his shoulders and chest. She wanted to touch those muscles and skim her hand along the shadows created by the light that his body partially blocked.

He dipped down to kiss her lips. Desire pulsed in the soft joining of their mouths.

He rose up again. His palm and gaze lowered to her neck, then to the ribbons of her nightdress. His fingers started loosening them. Her breasts tingled from the proximity of his touch.

"I have been half mad the last week," he said. "Unable to think clearly. When I realized for certain it had been you . . ."

"When did you?"

"Outside Fleur's chamber that day. You are better than most at hiding yourself from the world, but that day you could not. Even conceited, irritating men sometimes see what is right in front of them."

She smiled at his reminder of her barbs. They seemed distant history right now.

Her nightdress gaped at her neck now, and his hand was finishing its work lower. The fabric moved subtly over her erect nipples, causing a delicate caress that proved how sensitive her body had become.

All of her body. From her face down to her toes, she waited, taut with anticipation and enthralled by the smallest sensation. She could not bear the separation even though the waiting was exquisite torture. She moved her hand and slid it up the strong arm braced beside her.

He pushed the edges of her nightdress aside, revealing her breasts. His fingertips and gaze slowly moved around their swells. She grit her teeth to hold in the impulse to moan.

"You did not speak much the last time, Charlotte. Do you intend to be silent again?"

"It may be wise, don't you think? Our conversations are so often quarrelsome."

"Only because you take pleasure in challenging me."

"And you me."

"Perhaps we both only sought to deny what brings us to this bed. I have found your willfulness more charming than challenging since we have shared indiscretions."

"Then perhaps I will speak, if I am so moved."

He dipped low and kissed one nipple. A shimmer of pleasure eddied through her skin. "I will have to remember to move you to speak in pleasing ways."

"What kind of speech would be pleasing, Nathaniel?" She doubted it would matter. Speech required breath, and she was losing hers.

"Let me think." He peeled the dress off her shoulders, and lifted her so he could slide it down her arms. "I think I would be partial to *Do not stop, because I am in heaven.*"

She laughed, but most of her attention centered on the way he pushed away the bedclothes. "I can see how you might prefer that to contradictions."

He slipped the dress lower, and gently tapped her hip. "Up."

She raised her hips so the dress could continue its path, exposing her naked body.

"Then there is *Just like that, right there, it feels very good,*" he said. "I am sure I would welcome discourse of that nature."

"That sounds like instruction and command. I would not expect you to welcome that at all."

He smiled vaguely as he bent to pull the billowing fabric down her legs and over her feet. "There will be no mistaking who is commanding, pretty lady."

His caress and gaze proved that. Both took possession of her body in a masterful way. Both moved without restriction, freely taking what she had offered.

That chime sounded in her instincts again.

He eased atop her. The sudden contact, so full and complete, made their playful talk a game now ended. Braced on his arms, he filled her sight, and his weight and strength lined her smallness, dominating and overwhelming her. That intuitive fear spoke like a soft voice, pointing out her helplessness.

"Or if you prefer, you need not say anything at all," he said. "I do not need words to know you."

He had said something similar that night. The repetition now startled her.

She bit her lower lip and placed a hand flat against his chest. "Do you say that to everyone?"

"Only once before, with a woman I met at a party, who in donning a mask became free to reveal more than she hid."

She gazed directly into his eyes for the first time since he had arrived.

She had feared what she would see or not see if she did that. Now the most beautiful reassurance waited for her. Suddenly they were back in a dark corner of a salon, and the laughter and movements of others were dimming into obscurity. An intimacy deep and profound instantly built between them that made the world irrelevant. No judgment showed in his eyes. No questions. Only an acceptance and comprehension that made her tremble, and deep fires of desire that burned only for her. She might be a stranger, but the things that mattered were understood.

She responded the same way she had that night, with a soul so grateful and relieved that she wanted to weep. The chimes died and the instinctive fear retreated. Trust drenched her, a trust complete and certain.

He kissed her. She could not mistake that it was different from that night, even if much else was the same. Their mutual awareness was starkly alive. They were not strangers. Nathaniel Knightridge was in bed with Charlotte Mardenford.

If not for the trust, that might have made her shy in her response. Instead she discovered that she liked the fact that he knew it was she in his arms. It added layers of history and familiarity to the knowing.

The kiss deepened, increasing the tense anticipation that had kept her alert and aroused the last days. Like a string stretched too far, it snapped. Sensations of bliss trickled through her body, tantalizing her with streams of pleasure. He lowered and embraced her, his firm hands sliding beneath her body to hold her, his breath teasing her neck and ear and skin as his mouth pressed other spots of excitement.

Just holding him sent her senses spinning, then

narrowing on the feel of his skin beneath her finger-tips. Each touch and moment was real, perfectly alive. Already dampness slicked her thighs and passion had her half-crazed. She felt the hardness of his erection pressing her thigh and parted her legs to bring him closer.

She waited for him to move, to join, to quickly succumb to the onslaught of desire just as they had the first time. Instead he rose and looked down.

"It does not have to be fast tonight. No one can see us, Charlotte." He did not wait for a response, but shifted a little lower and flicked his tongue on her right nipple.

She closed her eyes to attempt to contain what that did to her. She failed. Her whole body trembled. It became a wonderful torture, one that she did not want to end but that created cravings for more. "Yes," she heard herself whispering. "Just like that. It feels wonderful."

He paused. She opened her eyes to see him looking at her, pleased that she had spoken. He turned his attention to her other breast and with licks and nips made her insistent hunger even more intense. When he began drawing on the tip, sighs sounded in her head and breath. His fingertips caressed her other breast, multiplying the sensations, and rational thought escaped her mind's grasp. She arched, swaying into it, offering her swollen breasts in a begging movement that knew no shame.

Instead he stopped and looked down with an expression chiseled and hard. The sensual energy she had sensed at the beginning poured off him, exciting her more. He caressed down her body and shifted off her so her legs were free.

Suddenly her pose felt vulnerable and scandalous. She began to close her legs. His hand had reached her hips and with a firm hold on one leg he stopped her.

He touched her down there and she was lost. Nothing else mattered, no kiss or embrace. Only the incredible pleasure and crying need commanded by that touch existed. She floated in it, awed by the pleasure lapping through her and the way it affected every inch of her body.

Then it changed. Not floating, but climbing. Reaching. Frantic impatience trembled within the pleasure. The sensations became excruciating and desperate. Nothing but yearning lived in her head, no other sights or thoughts. She dimly knew she was crying out, giving voice to the silent screams of pleasure racking her.

Nathaniel's face was close to hers, saying something, praising her. She barely heard. She had reached an unbearable place. She either had to stop him or jump off a cliff.

She clawed at his shoulders and jumped.

For an instant only bliss existed, pouring through her in a beautiful shock. Then awareness returned, still trembling and vague. Lips brushed her cheek and he moved back into her arms, his body pressed against hers. Her climax had not eliminated the need. Again she shifted, to bring his hardness closer. This time he entered, filling her, giving the final completion that she wanted.

She kissed him hard. His own kiss spoke of much more to come. He withdrew and reentered. The intimacy moved her so deeply, she could barely contain it.

They joined slowly, savoring the sensation, gazes locked in acknowledgment of the power. She could have stayed like that forever, holding him, feeling him in her while she drifted in sated, stunned emotions. He could not. She knew he was going where she had just been from the light in his eyes and the severity of his face. She did not mind at all when the thrusts came harder and faster.

A new trembling woke where they joined, surprising her. He fanned the fire until she was burning again. It was different this time, and focused on him and that fullness. A wildness broke in her, more primitive than her last quest for completion. She wanted him more, harder, *there*. She abandoned all sense and shame, crying, pleading, urging him.

The end was violent, a ravishing that she welcomed. In the midst of it a glorious tremor began where they were joined. Like a plucked harp string, it centered in that flesh, but its vibrations throbbed through her entire being in an amazing release that joined the masculine tremor she held in her arms.

Jesus.

His heart slowed to something like normal. His head cleared of the cloud that had followed the lightning. Sanity returned. So did awareness that he was a dead weight atop Charlotte, and probably smothering her.

He braced up on his forearms and looked down through strands of damp hair. Her eyes were closed but a gentle smile softened her lips. She appeared contented enough. And very young with that dreamy expression. He trusted that meant that somewhere in the turbulent chaos at the end, she had found fulfillment.

He rolled off her, away from the light so he could see her in its faint glow. His movement made her stir. She dragged up the sheet to cover their nakedness. They lay side by side, looking at the ceiling, their breathing still deep.

"You near killed me, Lady M. I may sleep for two days."

"And I may not walk for a week, Mr. Knightridge."

He looked over at her. "Did I hurt you?"

"Let us just say that I am aware you visited a long time." She smiled impishly, and he was reassured.

"The hospitality was so inviting and enthusiastic that I completely forgot my manners. Are apologies in order?" *Enthusiastic* was an understatement. He had not been urged on like that since he rowed against Cambridge at university.

She giggled. "An apology is not necessary."

He took her hand and raised it to his lips. "An expression of gratitude is, however." He arranged pillows to his satisfaction and pulled up the coverlet. "I believe that we may have finally achieved a right understanding on something."

"Once more without words."

Yes, once more. He'd had to know, and now he did. He just did not know what to do about it.

It appeared she did not either. She tucked the covers about her more neatly. She kept sneaking glances at him.

"Are you embarrassed, Charlotte?"

"No, not at all. Well, I could be if I thought much about . . . but, no. Why do you ask?"

"You appear unsettled."

"I am just wondering . . ." Her voice drifted off as she glanced at him, the door, the lamp, the bed.

"Do you want me to leave?"

"No . . . that is . . . were you thinking to . . ." Blushing, she groped along incoherently.

Charlotte Mardenford was at a loss for words. He never thought he would see it. He could not resist the impulse to let her flounder through a few more broken phrases.

"You have never actually slept in a bed with a man before, have you?" He knew many women hadn't. Their husbands visited, poured seed in the vessel, and left.

Her weak smile said he was right. It was one more thing he had learned tonight about her marriage. If not for the insights it gave him on her, it would in sum be more than he wanted to know.

"I am thinking I will stay awhile." He did not wait

for her permission, but made himself comfortable
and drew her into his arms.

She tried to act sophisticated, but he suspected
this was the most astonishing thing he had done all
night. He reached over and gutted the lamp. The silence and dark quickly had him drifting into languid
repose.

"What if you are found here?"

"The door is locked, and I will leave at dawn
anyway."

She snuggled in. Her head fit perfectly on his
shoulder.

"It was very nice," she said quietly. "I am glad I
was not a coward."

He pressed his lips to her crown. It had been nice.
Amazing, actually. There had been no doubt that they
were in that intensity together, but her words touched
him. She intended her admission to explain that her
misgivings had been unfounded. She wanted to reassure him. There was no winning or losing tonight, in
this bed.

One chamber of his mind jumped to the days
ahead. There might be winning and losing then.

He shut the door on that room. He would not examine its furnishings too closely right now, with his
sated body hovering on the edges of sleep—

"Do you snore, Nathaniel?"

"I would not know. Wake me if I do."

Holding her body created a peaceful intimacy.
The night had left him very contented and he began
to drift—

"Do you really plan to sleep for two days?"

"More likely two hours. Then I will wake and ravish you again."

"Oh."

The silence pulsed, then flowed. Dreams beckoned—

"Nathaniel, if you snore, one of your other lovers would have told you by now. If it is customary for a man to sleep in his lover's bed all night, you would indeed know if you snore."

"You will have to ask your brothers if it is customary. It is not customary for me, so I would not know if I snore."

"It isn't? Why not? This is very pleasant."

That he had decided to stay tonight, without even realizing it was unusual, begged for some reflection. He was too drowsy to engage in mental inquiry now, especially since he suspected the conclusions would further complicate consideration on what to do about all this.

"I have not made it customary because there are rumors regarding what happens if a man remains after the passion is over."

"Rumors? What sort of rumors?"

"You will find them astounding. It is said by men who know, that after sexual relations women want to talk all night. It is said that a man who stays will get no sleep at all. Can you believe it?"

Silence hung for a five count. Then her little fist gave his ribs a little punch.

He laughed to himself and held her closer. At least it hadn't been a parasol.

He did not snore. Nor did he wake in two hours and ravish her again. She knew, because she did not sleep for a long time. She lay in his embrace trying to herd scattered thoughts and reactions into order.

It was impossible to do. The intimacy dulled her mind. Comfort soothed the nibbling concerns. She knew only that her emotions had not been an illusion, and she had not built a fantasy on that first night. The sensations and bond had been repeated now. They were real.

She wondered if that reality existed only in silence, though, and in passion. They could not spend their lives alone in bed. A world waited outside these walls. Soon they would walk forth and enter it again, and their paths might once more leave them facing each other across a chasm.

The rhythms of Nathaniel's breaths in her ear finally lulled her toward sleep. As she sank away, a waking dream came to her, of little Ambrose laughing as he rolled a ball toward her. She would not be there for his visit again tomorrow. They had been parted a long time.

She rolled the ball back. Ambrose held out his arms for it. Before it arrived, however, a man's hand reached down and took it. Puzzled, Ambrose came to her embrace and snuggled close. Together they watched that hand carry the ball out the door.

She woke at first light. The faintest silver glow etched the outlines of the furnishings in the chamber.

She had moved in her sleep, and Nathaniel had with her. She lay on her side with his body close behind and his arm around her waist.

She looked down at the hand lying on her stomach. There had been a dream last night . . . not a frightening one, but it had disturbed her. She could not remember it now, but . . .

His hand flexed and he held her more firmly. His breaths no longer marked out time. He was awake.

She felt him rise slightly behind her. His chest pressed her back and his lips kissed her cheek.

"Dawn comes," he said.

"You must go." The idea saddened her. She feared an end might come if he left. She could have lived forever on the memory of one scandalous night, but she knew the memories of two nights might bring pain. "I wish you did not have to."

He kissed her shoulder. His hand moved in a firm caress over her hip. Excitement glistened through her, making her wish he had not slept so soundly.

"The house is still quiet. I can delay a short while." He gently palmed her nipples. They hardened at once.

There was no ravishing this time, but instead a slow, luscious blossoming of pleasure. She noticed every nuance of the sensations, every inch of every caress. With him behind her she could not even kiss him in turn. She could only accept the pleasure he gave.

She felt his erection pressing between her thighs, and realized what he was going to do. He felt very deep after he entered her. Very tight. She did not become crazed this time. Even her climax was lazy and quiet, breaking as softly as the dawn itself, sparkling through her with a lovely, sweet tremor. The closeness of their sleeping embraces deepened the pleasure. The approaching return to their normal lives added poignancy.

She did not watch him dress afterward. She kept her gaze on his face, so the movements were a blur.

His parting kiss was sweet. His last look was warm. After he slipped out the door, she was left with her thoughts, wondering if dreams could ever outlast the night.

CHAPTER THIRTEEN

~~

Charlotte came down from her chamber late. She entered the morning room just before noon. Nathaniel looked up from the letter he was scribbling to see she wore a carriage ensemble and carried a parasol.

The scent of lavender entered with her. He guessed she had called for another bath. He pictured her in it, hair bound up and skin slick and rosy. He wished he had been there.

"I apologize for the delay." She propped the parasol on a chair. "It is only noon, however. We should still have time for one of the villages today."

The mood of the morning's passion had not left him yet. He drew her to him and kissed her. Sounds outside the chamber forced him to release her quickly.

"It looks to rain. I think we will put off visits to villages today, Charlotte."

"Can we do them all tomorrow? I should return to London soon."

As should he. There were affairs waiting attention that could not be ignored forever. Right now he wished they could be.

The door opened a crack, then closed.

"We are delaying some servant's duties in this chamber," he said. "Take a turn outside with me."

They strolled through the garden and beyond to the field. The day was warm but the air carried a heavy damp. No clouds showed in the soft, gray, hazy sky.

"I have decided that it is not worth the effort to visit those last villages," he said. "This has been a fool's errand on my part, and there is no reason to prolong it."

She trod on in silence. At the base of the next hill, she stopped and faced him.

"Nathaniel, it would be a sad thing if last night started our lying to each other. You do not really believe this has been a fool's errand because, while there is much that you are, a fool you are not."

Nor was she, unfortunately. An arrow of the old exasperation poked at him. If he was willing to retreat, she might allow him to do so gracefully.

"We have visited ten villages to no avail. If we visit three more we will only further waste our time."

"I will not consider it a waste of time. Oh, I do not believe you will find Harry's family in one of them, or even information on where that family can be found. But that is not why you seek out that old woman. Not really. Therefore, I believe that you should look for her still, and hear what she has to say, and whether it supports your suspicion that Harry has Mardenford blood."

"What does it matter, Charlotte? If Harry is an illegitimate son of any man in that family, finding the truth will not make a difference."

She looked him in the eyes so directly it was disconcerting. The cool, even light allowed his tiny reflections to show in each dark pool of her irises.

"Is this the gesture of gratitude you referred to last night?" she asked.

Hell, he didn't know. He just wanted to put all of this away and stay in this house with her for a few days.

Her expression softened to the warmest, gentlest countenance she had ever shown him. "Nathaniel, I am without defenses today. I am incapable of dissembling, and you are doing a poor job of it as well. If an illegitimate son is abandoned, it is the way of the world. As you once said, it is a moral injustice but there is no legal claim."

"Exactly. Which is why there is no real purpose to vis—"

"That is why I know that if you pursued this, it was because you feared Harry is more than a lost bastard."

Damn. *Now* she decided to baldly state it. Now, when he had just spent hours convincing himself to walk away.

Her brow puckered over earnest, concerned eyes.

"You think Harry may be a son of a secret marriage. You think he may be my brother-in-law's legal, first-born child. There is no other explanation for your interest. There never was."

He crossed his arms and gazed up the hill. A full-bellied mare walked along its crest.

"Has anyone ever told you that sometimes you are too clever by half, Lady M.?"

She laid her hand on his arm. "Do not be angry with me. I want badly to grab this offer that you make. It would be easy to accept, because I know you are wrong. However, if you do not complete what you started, you will never know the truth as surely as I do. You will always think you did not do your best for that boy who is alone and lost. Questions will always be there."

There, between us. She did not say it, but it was in her tone and eyes.

"And if I am right, Charlotte? If the truth is the worst that I first suspected?"

He wanted her to say it would not matter. He wanted to hear that this passion could not be destroyed by truth. In the pause that followed, however, he knew that she was picturing the devastation to Mardenford and the child she loved so deeply. Nathaniel Knightridge was no more than a shadow on that vision.

"If you ask that question, Nathaniel, it proves you are not convinced that I have nothing to fear. Let us do what we can to prove your worst suspicion is wrong. Otherwise it will not die. Not my fear, and not your questions."

They made the short journey to the village as if the quest did not matter. However, Charlotte could tell that Nathaniel was not pleased. Beneath their banter she heard the echoes of old arguments. In his eyes she saw lights of concern.

When they arrived at the coast, he wore a stern expression as he entered the village tavern to seek information. He resented that she had forced the inquiry on him.

The difference when he emerged was indescribable. His mood had visibly lightened. The day remained overcast, but not his countenance. He approached the carriage with a spry step.

"No Jenny here," he announced with satisfaction. He immediately climbed back in.

Charlotte did not share his glee. She wanted the woman found. That he did not only emphasized that he still thought Jenny would tell a story that would support his worst suspicions.

She was flattered that he wanted to protect her now. She was not pleased that he thought he owed her lies. Worse, whatever truce he made with his conscience would not last. If he suspected Harry was legitimate, this man could no more ignore the injustice than he could agree to become a bishop.

If they would just find the old woman, all this

would end. Jenny would show Finley's blackmail for what it was—a bold deception built on air.

As soon as the carriage left the village, Nathaniel pulled her onto his lap. "Duty finished. Now we can play."

His kiss let her know what game he intended.

She stopped thinking about Jenny.

Amidst kisses and smiles, he had her dress unfastened and stays loose in moments. Cool air fluttered over her naked skin, tantalizing her, hinting at the human caresses that would follow.

He rearranged her so she straddled his legs. Billows of skirt and petticoats mounded between them, up to his nose. They laughed while he fought them into submission. She circled his neck with an embrace and hung on him as the carriage rocked them down the road.

His kisses lured, claimed, scorched. His fingertips whisked both her nipples like an erotic breeze. Both his hands were free, and they did wicked things to her, increasing her sensitivity until a very impatient hunger cracked her control.

Feeling very bold, she reached down between them and closed her hand on his erection. She enjoyed seeing what that did to him, how his jaw tensed and the sensations so obviously consumed his attention. She slid her fingertips up the hard length, and found the tip through his garments. She rubbed playfully, then more deliberately as she saw her effect. It became a challenge, to see if she could madden him as much as he did her.

She released her other hand's hold on his shoulder so she could loosen his trousers. He did not help, but only steadied her body while the swaying carriage jostled them and she fumbled with the garments. She freed his phallus and circled her palm around its hardness. Looking down, she caressed and fingered the sensitive end.

He let her, accepting as she had done, permitting this brief command. *Just like that, right there, it feels very good.* He did not say it, but in a hundred ways he really did. A heady thrill slid through her again and again, descending until her vulva pulsed a hollow ache. Creating this desire aroused her as well as him.

Suddenly his hands burrowed under her petticoats and grasped her bottom. His eyes opened to reveal ferocious lights. He lifted her and shifted forward and brought her down firmly so that they were joined.

She was the one who had to move, but his grasp on her hips guided her. What had started playfully ended hard. With consuming kisses and powerful thrusts, their frenzy filled the carriage.

"Who was she?"

Charlotte asked the question that night as their hot bodies cooled in the aftermath of another astonishing passion.

It took Nathaniel a moment to comprehend the question. His mind was preoccupied with calculating how this affair could continue once they returned to London.

He set those thoughts aside. Charlotte could startle him at the least expected moments.

"She?"

"The woman you loved long ago." She turned in his arms and looked down at him. "The first night here, when you were cajoling me to this affair, you said we had both loved long ago."

"How indiscreet of me."

He pretended the conversation was completed, but knew she would not accept that. She waited.

"I was very young and in love the way very young men can be," he said. "I believed my affections were returned. They were not, as I learned. It is a common story."

"Not so common. Nor would its predictability ease the pain."

She appeared concerned. That touched him. She was not asking out of idle curiosity. She was not building a jealousy on the past either.

"How did you learn she did not return the affection? I cannot believe a girl would not fall in love with you. You look like the hero in a book or painting, and did even when you were younger. We all thought so."

"If you thought so, why did you avoid dancing with me at the balls during your season? As I remember it, I had one turn. Not even a waltz."

Her lids lowered. "I was spoken for, from the first. Everyone knew that." She looked at him again. "So, how did you learn the truth?"

She was not to be distracted. Of course not.

"My father arranged that she should visit us. Here at Elmcrest."

"Ah. He is ruthless, isn't he?"

"He was more aware of the things that move a woman's heart than I was at that age."

"So she saw all this, and learned of the *and more,* and did not understand, I assume."

"I was hard-pressed to explain it in ways she would comprehend. She only saw that with one word I could offer her fashionable wealth and not merely fashionable comfort. She thought that if I loved her, I would compromise. I thought that if she loved me, she would not ask it." He shrugged. "Such are the simple ways youth sees the world."

She drew a little pattern on his chest with her fingertip, reminding him how her hands had inflamed him today. This night's passion had been different from last's. The eroticism had contained a mutual aggression that hinted at bold developments to come.

"You said marriage would demand consideration of compromise," she reminded him.

"I am no longer so young, and the world is no longer so simple to me."

He realized as soon as he said it that he was not speaking the entire truth. Not only experience would make him consider it. The different woman involved would too. Charlotte would never have asked it of him so that she could buy more gowns or someday be a bishop's wife. Even if she had been poor, she would not have done that for those reasons.

He knew that as surely as he knew anything. He

had never in his life been as sure he knew the character of a woman as he did this one's.

"I assume she married someone else."

"Eventually. We had been discreet, so our alliance did not affect her. Still, having almost had the son of a peer, she could not settle for less. She waited until she found another one who suited her better." He tapped her nose. "As I said, it was long ago, and it was not a love like you had. I have no memories and no regrets."

Her expression softened and turned private, as if his words had called forth those memories. He began cursing himself for a lack of tact.

"I suppose one cannot have one without the other, memories and regrets, that is," she said, coming out of the distraction as quickly as she had entered it. "The trick, I am concluding, is to respect both, but to let neither own you."

She kissed him in a way that suggested she was proving neither owned her now. The declaration was unnecessary. It was not the past that might fracture this fragile contentment they had found in each other, but the future.

Charlotte waited in the carriage, as she always did in the villages. Nathaniel strode into the second tavern located in this one, his blond hair ducking below the low header of the ancient doorway.

They had already been to another village, with no Jenny found. They would visit one more before they were done. Tomorrow they would begin the journey back to London.

She tried to picture how this affair would change then. She attempted to try it on, much as one did a new dinner dress. Would this passion survive the daily living in town? Would the suffocating need for discretion, and its tiresome lies and games, annoy them both?

They had not even spoken of what would happen in the days ahead. Nor had she given it much thought. She now did, and hoped that they could find a way to be together at least on occasion. She did not expect the astonishing intensity of the last few days to continue, but having found some common ground, she trusted they would not quickly relinquish it.

The fishing village had a picturesque quality, with some very old houses facing the lanes that tumbled down a low slope toward the sea. A few had been painted red and yellow, as if a fisherman had visited the Mediterranean a decade ago and brought back a new fashion. A breeze carried the scents of fish and salt to her. She could see the water's expanse, and make out the tall masts of ships aiming in a diagonal line toward the horizon.

Nathaniel did not return quickly. When the door finally opened and he stepped over the threshold, she knew he had learned something. His countenance was serious and thoughtful.

"There is a woman named Jenny Thresher here." He spoke through the window. "She takes in boarders." He gazed down the lane. "That should be her place down there, with the white door."

"Let us visit at once."

He handed her down and they walked up the lane. "You do not seem pleased to find another Jenny," she said, glancing at his firm, straight mouth. "You think this is the one, don't you?"

He shot her the same look he had yesterday, when he told her she could be too clever by half. "The tavern owner remembered a young boy from some years ago. However, this Jenny is not old, he says, so that may be a coincidence."

They presented themselves at the white door. The house was old and modest but well kept. White curtains showed at all the windows.

A serving girl brought them to a tiny sitting room. Its furnishings, with too many chairs, suggested this functioned as a common room for the guests.

They waited as the girl's steps sounded on the stairs and across their heads. Then more steps retraced the path.

An expectation built in Charlotte. She tried not to succumb to the certainty they had found the right Jenny, but her heart beat with the excitement of running the fox to ground.

Nathaniel did not appear to share contentment in the victory. "I will introduce you as Mrs. Duclairc," he said. "We will keep Mardenford out of this, unless Jenny says the name."

Jenny was not really old. As soon as the woman

entered the sitting room, Charlotte understood the confusion, however. This Jenny had the gray hair and mature form that would have a child thinking her old, but her face and bearing suggested she was at most forty-five.

They sat on some of the many chairs, and Nathaniel explained their visit.

Mrs. Thresher shook her head. "I have had no boy named Harry living here at any time."

"That may not be his name. He would have been between six and eight, I think. Dark hair and eyes, and the appearance of foreign blood. He would have been here with his mother."

Jenny's eyes widened. "You are describing Joseph. José was his name. You have met him?"

José. Charlotte saw how that became Harry in the rookery. A child says his name is José, and an old thief hears Harry.

"We know of the boy. He is safe and healthy," Nathaniel said. "We hope you may know of his mother's family, so the boy can be returned to them."

Jenny thought that over, shaking her head all the while. "It was a bad business from the start. I tried to tell her, gently, mind you, but she would not hear. I know nothing of her family, or even much about her. She took chambers here for herself and the boy soon after she arrived in Britain. She came in through Southampton, and we are the first village with a place like mine if you travel east from there. She paid with links from a gold chain."

"You said his name is José. They are Spanish?" Nathaniel asked.

"From Cádiz. She spoke of war, and finally getting passage to leave. She came here to find the boy's father." Her mouth pursed. "Her husband, she said. Well, it isn't for me to judge. If a woman with a bastard wants to say her husband is gone or dead, that is not my concern. I did try to explain that this 'husband' would not welcome her demands, however. When the letters never were answered, I tried to make her see that."

"Did she mention the name of this man?" Charlotte asked.

"Never. She was very mysterious about it. She let me know he was of good birth, like herself. She had expectations for service that exceeded the normal, if you know what I mean." She shrugged. "I believed her own birth was high. She possessed that air that says so. She spoke English well, and could read and write it too. And she was paying for things with those gold links, wasn't she?"

"How long was she here?" Nathaniel asked.

"About a year. All the while writing letters and waiting for someone or something. She grew subdued toward the end, however. Very melancholy, as if she was beginning to understand that she had been seduced and abandoned like a farm girl, no matter what her birth. Her worry was for the boy, of course. Not much future for a Spanish bastard in England, is there?"

Charlotte did not know what to think of this story.

They had learned much, but really had not learned anything at all. They only had Harry's own memories confirmed.

"Why did she leave?" she asked.

"I do not know. One day she took the boy and two valises and was gone. She left what would not fit in the bags, saying she would send for it. I never expected to hear from her, and did not. Paid a man to take her back to Southampton, I expect. I assumed she had gone home."

"Since we found the boy in London, it appears not," Nathaniel said.

An empty silence claimed the chamber. Three people slowly chewed the few details of the story.

"What name did she use?" Nathaniel asked.

"A false name, to be sure," Jenny said with a very knowing smile. "She called herself Mrs. Marden."

A silent quake vibrated through the room. Charlotte stared at Jenny, who did not appear to notice how her words made the world shake. Charlotte's heart thickened. She looked at Nathaniel, desperate for reassurance that this false name did not herald a terrible disaster.

Nathaniel's face had fallen. "Mrs. Thresher, I must ask again whether she ever spoke of the boy's father. It is very important that you try to remember."

Her brow puckered and her lids lowered, as if she sorted through all the memories. "She said nothing to me. I was a servant to her mind, of course. However, sometimes she would read to the boy, and I would hear them in here. She always read in English, using those books there, and told him he must learn it well, that he would have to be English."

Charlotte did not care what that woman had read or not read. Her shock was threatening to become a panic.

Nathaniel rose and walked over to the shelf. His finger touched one. "Byron."

"She did enjoy that, now that you mention it, but she read to him from all of them, and from the Bible."

"Did you hear anything else by accident as you went about your duties in the house?"

"Well, she kept giving the boy airs, teaching him to be proud like she was. It caused a bit of trouble in the village one day with some other children. Seems little Joseph got into a scrap with some others, and he began yelling at them. Kept shouting the same word over and over while he faced them down. A fishwife who heard it later told me he had been shouting "Bow, bow!" Everyone thought he was imitating a dog, but I suspect he meant they should kneel to him. Quite the little king he could be for a homeless bastard."

Oh God, oh God. Charlotte thought she would burst from the expanding horror. This Spanish woman had come to Britain after Philip died, after James had inherited the title. She had come with her son to claim the boy's place in the household of his father, the new baron. *James, how could you?*

Nathaniel still stood near the shelf of books. She turned to him, frantic.

His gaze met hers. Warmth waited for her in it,

but also resignation and sadness. *You should have let me compromise while I still had the chance*, his eyes seemed to communicate. *For you I would have done it.*

She wished she had let him. Oh, heavens, how she did. She cursed herself for her stubborn trust in Mardenford. She hated herself, and her willfulness, and even the hunger for passion that had lured her into trying to remove this final barrier between them.

"If you have the boy, where is his mother?" Jenny asked, her head cocking as if the omission of this fact just dawned on her.

"She took the boy to London. We have reason to believe she is dead five years now."

Jenny clucked her tongue. "Was running out of those links, she was. If she wasn't going home, she should have stayed here. The parish would have seen to her. We all would have helped even if she was a foreigner. London is no place for the poor. Odd for her to go there after a year."

Yes, odd. Charlotte's chaotic thoughts allowed that to penetrate.

"Well, if you have the boy, I should give you the things she left." Jenny rose. "Not much, just a small trunk, and I've no idea what is in it. If you come with me, sir, I'll show you where it is stored."

Charlotte could only sit numbly as Jenny opened the door. When Nathaniel passed her chair, his hand gripped her shoulder gently. His presence at her side made her startle. He felt very big there, looming with strength and power of will.

"Do not allow your thoughts to run away from your rational sense," he said quietly. "We really do not know anything for certain yet."

That helped her battle the sickening shock a little, but not much. She watched him follow Jenny.

Yet. They knew nothing for certain now, but he could not ignore what had been said here today. What she, in her stupid arrogance, had demanded he hear.

CHAPTER
FOURTEEN

D inner was quiet. Carefully so.

Charlotte's distress had affected everything since leaving the village. A sword hung over them, waiting to fall. Nathaniel wondered if he could find a way to avoid that happening.

She did not eat much, and he could tell that her mind was working hard.

"You are correct. We know nothing for certain," she said after the meal was finished.

He did not welcome her speaking of it. The man who desired a woman resented that she did not wait until tomorrow to broach the subject.

He gestured for the waiting footman to leave.

"Her use of the name Marden cannot be explained away, of course," she added, after the door closed and they were alone.

"No."

She raised her gaze to his and a spark of the old

glare flickered. "So, it appears that my brother-in-law had one of those common, youthful passions after all."

"Yes." He'd be damned before he'd encourage where this was going. That particular road could wait.

Unfortunately, she did not agree. "Calling herself Mrs. Marden does not mean anything. A woman with a child would call herself Mrs. Something."

"That is true." It was also not the most provocative piece of information Jenny had given them. Charlotte had to know that. A woman too clever by half at the most vexing moments would have recognized the really dangerous information.

Harry's mother had begun training him to be an English lord. The woman thought her son was legitimate. Which meant she had been secretly married and abandoned, or badly deceived.

He pictured the two Baron Mardenfords. He saw their eyes and their characters. It had not been Philip who misled Harry's mother, he was certain of that. Philip would never be so dishonorable.

"You are unusually short-spoken tonight." She speared him with one of *those* looks. "Do you intend to pretend today did not happen?"

"For now, yes. It can wait."

"That is easy for you to say. You are not the one whose life might be ruined."

"Nor are you. Even the worst scandal about this, and the worst resolution, will not ruin your life."

Her face fell. *Not my life,* her expression said, *but my happiness will be much affected.*

Hell, he knew that. Which was why he wanted to delay this conversation.

She rose and slowly strolled down the table, skimming her fingertips along the tops of the chair backs.

"I should have let you think it was a fool's errand."

Yes, she should have. That had been his first reaction on hearing Jenny calmly describe her evidence. *Look what your willfulness has done, my love. You risked too much in trying to be sure the bridge had no flaws.*

"Well, you know the family intimately, Charlotte, and were very sure I would be proven wrong about James."

She flushed. She paused at the foot of the table. Grasping the chair's back, she faced him. She could not be farther away if she tried.

"You have to know now, don't you?"

"I have not decided." Not that it would matter. No matter what he did, he would lose something and gain little. If he retreated now as he had wanted to yesterday, he could not lie to himself. He would live with a gnawing guilt over Harry, if nothing else.

If he did not retreat, the woman facing him down the long expanse of the dining table would never forgive him.

Her eyes appeared misty. His heart clenched. She appeared very small behind the chair, and very frightened. He sensed that she saw both a possible protector and potential villain as she gazed at him.

Her lips parted.

Do not ask it of me. Not yet, not now. Let the decision wait.

She looked down at the table. He could see a faint blur of her sadness reflected in the polished surface.

He rose and went to her. She did not fight his embrace, but that sword remained poised above them.

"Kiss me," he said.

She looked up, the tears still threatening.

"Kiss me, Charlotte. There is time enough for decisions and worry in the future."

Her lips touched his, tentatively, as if she checked to see if their passion still had meaning.

He needed no more encouragement. He held her to a deep kiss intended to burn away any hesitance. She accepted and responded, but he felt confusion within the desire.

She tucked against him. She rested her cheek on his shoulder. He held her, tightly and possessively, waiting for a sign that the future did not start right now.

They shared as sweet an intimacy as he had ever known. That at least had not been ruined by this day.

Her fragility touched him. The impulse to protect at any cost spread like the primitive fire it was.

"Charl—"

Her fingertips touched his lips, stopping him. Her gaze implied a knowing of him that exceeded his own.

"I was only going to say that I am not a danger to

you." That was not what he had intended to say at all, but it seemed a fitting substitute.

She eased out of his embrace. Her glance toward the door made her separation seem inspired by discretion more than rejection, but it was not a distinction he would wager on.

"An honest man is always a danger, Nathaniel."

She drifted away, from his hold and his body and finally from the room, leaving him to wonder if her door would be locked tonight.

She spent the evening in her chamber. Nancy tried to serve her but she sent the maid away, unable to bear the intrusion on her thoughts.

The meeting with Jenny had been disastrous. And dangerous. Oh, yes, very dangerous. Nathaniel would have to know now, no matter how much he wanted to delay a decision. A grave injustice may have been done. A legal wrong. Worse, Nathaniel knew the victim, had given the boy protection and friendship, and probably felt responsible for young Harry.

She rose and paced to relieve her agitation. She saw her home, and Ambrose playing on the carpet by the fireplace while his father watched.

She had been an idiot. So sure, so trusting that Mardenford could never be reckless about a woman. And if Harry's mother thought her son was legitimate, it had been James after all. Philip would never deceive a woman thus. He would never compromise his duty that way. She knew he was honorable as certainly as she knew her own name.

But James? *James?* Dull, pleasant James? It was hard to believe. He was so . . . flat. No highs or lows, no secret valleys or lofty dreams. His life lacked drama, and his character was devoid of solidity. A scandal of this nature would become a ruinous tempest merely because society would be so utterly amazed.

Perhaps his want of distinction had been his downfall. She could picture him, young and unformed, a watercolor sketch traveling in a world of rich oil paintings on that grand tour. He would have been overwhelmed by the deep colors and theatrical lighting and dynamic compositions.

She saw him beside Philip, watching a fire dance on the Spanish coast, and women, exotic women, spinning around the flames in the night.

A sickening heaviness filled her stomach. Yes, he could have done it. Dull, placid James could have fallen in love and made an impulsive marriage if passion gave him the illusion of notability. Sensual excitement had a way of making one feel fearless and special. She certainly could attest to that.

If he had married on those travels, would it even be legal? Was there any proof? How big was the danger?

Big enough, if Nathaniel Knightridge investigated.

She muttered a curse so tightly that her teeth clenched. She damned her stupidity. He had offered to remain ignorant, for her. For the passion. But she had been so very, very sure she was right. And she had hoped . . . she had hoped they might clear the way for possibly knowing more than a passing affair.

Now there would probably be nothing more. Soon there might be nothing at all.

An unworthy thought entered her head. A truly sinful one. Could she dissuade him? Buy him off, at least for a while?

Possibly. Maybe. Not forever, but until his desire began waning. He had already offered once, and had come close again as they embraced in the dining room. She might strike a bargain with him. *I am yours as long as you leave Mardenford and Ambrose alone.*

Her face heated. It would be a type of whoring. With another man she might have seriously considered it, however, and armored herself against self-loathing with thoughts of little Ambrose safe from stain and displacement.

With Nathaniel, it would change every memory and turn a beautiful passion into something cynical and base.

She let down her hair and brushed it slowly. *There is time enough for that decision and that worry.* He knew it could not be avoided but he wanted to delay whatever it would mean. He waited in this house for the night to bring its silence and discretion, wondering if a new wall had been built already, one so high and thick that they could not reach each other.

That wall would be there very soon. Tomorrow, or

the next day. Her heart cried at the certainty. She tasted the worry and unhappiness. Her eyes misted as she felt the loss.

Not yet, however. Not tonight, unless she insisted on laying the stones of that wall right now.

She realized she would not. She could not. She wanted the beauty and intimacy tonight. She wanted her fill of the pleasure and excitement while she could still have them without guilt or compromise.

A visceral arousal stirred in her, like a deep, erotic purr. There was time enough for decisions and worries, and duties and even honesty.

She added fuel to the fireplace. She did not lock her door.

He paused outside the bedchamber. The house was silent. Someone had left a window open somewhere, and the slight draft carried scents of earliest spring.

No sound came from within the chamber either. He gazed at the dark line of the latch, wondering if it would move.

She had blocked his retreat from Harry's cause yesterday, and again tonight at supper. She feared the truth, but would not allow him to ignore it. Three times now she had refused his gift of silence.

He should be grateful that she did not use his passion in that way. He was glad she did not ask him to be other than he was. He understood the implications, however. She might insist he be who he was, but she might also barricade herself away from that man.

There was only one way to find out if she already had.

He slowly guided the handle down. It met no resistance. The door opened silently. He stepped in and closed it.

The room was dark except for the light cast by low flames in the fireplace. He was halfway to the bed before he realized she was not in it. He glanced around, wondering if she had left completely.

A small movement drew his attention to the fireplace. A chair stood in front of it, its back to him. A small hill on its top had tilted. He heard another movement, and a small, pretty foot appeared beside the chair's base.

He walked to the fireplace to see if she had fallen asleep there.

She was not asleep. She sat in the high-backed chair, regally poised with her head against its back and her lidded gaze on the flames. She sat properly, straight and tall, with her knees pressed together. Her lower legs angled more casually, making an elegant diagonal to the feet tucked around the edge of the chair.

She was naked. Starkly, beautifully so. The light from the fire moved sensuously over her skin in a fluid glow. Her dark hair tumbled around her shoulders and the ends of long waves framed her firm, high breasts.

He moved to the side of the fire so he could look at her. The contrast of her nakedness with the upholstered chair's dark pattern was very erotic. So was her boldness in waiting for him like this.

She could still appear girlish at times, but not now. Nor was the earlier vulnerability present.

"I thought you would never get here. I feared running out of fuel," she said.

"I was not sure that you wanted me to come."

"Would you have stayed away if I told you to?"

"I doubt it."

"Of course not. You would have to know."

She did not speak accusingly. She seemed unaware that she had echoed words that referred to his danger as well as their passion now.

He made no move toward her. He enjoyed watching her. "Have you been waiting long like that?"

She glanced down at her body. "Yes. It is pleasant, I discovered. I have been thinking that I would like to have a private, hidden cottage where I could live without clothing, feeling the air and warmth on all my skin. The sensation is like so many delicate feathers."

Feathers that subtly aroused. He saw that in her, and sensed it in the air. She had been sitting here a long time, the elements making her ready. His own desire had responded as soon as he stepped around the chair and it tightened with each passing moment.

"I thought if you found me like this, you would know I was glad you came. There would be no question, then."

"I have no questions at all. I can barely think."

"Is that why you are still standing there? Because you cannot think?"

He had to smile at the scold. It was so like her challenges in the past.

He was not inclined to stop the way the air and warmth enlivened her, so he walked to the bed and dragged its coverlet back to the fireplace.

He began undressing. She watched as she had the first night in this room, only this time it was very obvious she did so. She sat there like a queen while he shed his clothes.

"I do not want to speak about what we heard today. There is time enough for that later, you said."

He pulled off his shirt, and his body joined hers in being titillated by cool air and tongues of heat. "We do not have to speak of anything at all, if you want."

He needed to sit to remove his boots. He approached her chair. She looked up at him, her gaze slowly ambling up his chest with a frankness that made fires blaze in his head.

"Lie there." He pointed to the coverlet on the carpet, not thinking of boots at all.

She slid off the chair, onto her knees. Her naked body crawled the few feet to the coverlet, her hair dangling, her curves moving. He blinked hard to control the ferocity of his reaction.

She laid on her side, facing him. The fire glow emphasized the elegant line curving from shoulder to waist, then up the gentle hill of her hip. That line undulated down the subtle curve of her leg.

He sat and dealt with the boots and the rest. She

watched as she had the first night here, as if she found the various fastenings of a man's wardrobe intriguing.

"I do not know if I will want silence. That might be too sad."

He shed his remaining clothes. "What do you want, Charlotte?"

"Everything. I want to be bold and daring. I want one more scandalous night." She rose and sat back on her legs, facing him in his chair. Her hair drifted down her body, looking like black silk in the flickering light. "There can be no masks anymore, not really. But you were right, and the future can wait."

Wait, but not disappear. One more night might be one last one, depending on whether they could ignore the day's events. He had come here tonight half hoping she would demand that. Seeing her like this, hearing her offer of everything, he doubted he could have refused.

It moved him that she had not tried that, even if he wished she had.

She stretched forward and swept his garments away from the floor between them. The view down her naked back and bottom as she leaned toward the chair made his mouth dry.

She began to sit back on her folded legs again, but paused. Instead she leaned farther, until she was on hands and knees, and gently kissed his leg.

He grit his teeth at his body's cataclysmic response. She crawled closer, her body moving as elegantly as a cat's. She kissed his knee.

Blood pounded in his head. He lost awareness of everything except the insinuations of that kiss and the scathing arousal that threatened to burn him up.

She moved closer and rose until she knelt right in front of him. Her gaze meandered like a caress over his body. "You look like a god sitting there. So perfect and beautiful." She reached out and skimmed her fingertips over his chest, carefully watching her hands move.

"I am feeling very human." It amazed him he could talk. "Gods are immortal, and I want you so much it is killing me."

She smiled, and a girlish delight in her effect entered the way she watched her caresses. "Do not die too soon. We have all night."

He parted his knees and pulled her closer, into an embrace and kiss.

The feel of her, the scent, the looking and the mood already had him on the edge. His mind darkened under the assault of savage impulses. She was with him, her hands all over him, her cries and kisses and passion only making him hotter.

He began to lift her to his lap. She ignored the command. Her hand closed around his erection firmly.

She stopped the devouring kisses and looked at him. Into him. Deep comprehension burned in her gaze as she understood the begging hunger that maddened him.

She glanced down. His body howled. He really would die now if she lost her nerve.

She didn't. Her head lowered. Her hair feathered his thighs. With the first moist touch of her lips his whole essence groaned and ascended to an erotic cloud of indescribable pleasure.

Charlotte studied the man stretched out naked in front of the fire. He had not moved in a while. He had fallen asleep.

She eased out of his loose embrace so she could sit and really see him. She felt quite possessive about his hewn beauty right now. She was entitled to look as much as she wanted. Nor did she feel any need to be restrained and modest. Her daring and boldness had crossed a line, she knew. Ladies were not supposed to do what she did tonight.

She did not care about that. Nor did he. She had seen in his eyes before and after some surprise, but no disrespect. It had not been as unpleasant as she expected. The control of his pleasure had stirred her in new ways.

The fire needed more fuel. She pushed to her feet to walk around him and deal with it. She made it only one step before a hold on her ankle stopped her.

"Where are you going?"

She gestured to the fireplace. "And if you intend to sleep here, I was going to get another coverlet."

"I intend to sleep in bed, when I sleep." He pulled her back down, then swung his body around and laid fuel on the fire.

"You were already sleeping," she said.

"I was finding a second life. I said you were killing me, and you did." He braced his weight on his arm and looked down at her. "I was also trying to decide just how bold you were willing to be, and how much of everything you even know about."

A long caress down her body reminded her that he might have died but she was alive and well and tortured by desire unquenched.

She glanced down. "It does not appear that you have been reborn just yet."

He looked down at his lax penis. His mouth gaped in mock surprise. "I'll be damned, you are right. How good of you to let me know, Lady M. I can always count on you to point out my failings." He laughed gently, shaking his head while he turned his attention to caressing her breast.

His hand was awakening her dozing arousal far too well. "I merely thought that we could wait until—"

"If you think about anything, let it be this." He dipped down to flick his tongue on her nipple. "And this." His caress slid down between her legs and tantalized her with another devastating flick. "And what I am going to do to you before dawn comes."

He told her what, very clearly. He described the ways he intended to possess her body in the hours ahead. She felt her face blushing.

"Unless you refuse, of course."

She swallowed hard. The way he titillated her tight nipples had her halfway to delirium, and his intentions did not sound *too* astounding.

"I did say I wanted another scandalous night. Since I have already astonished myself with my own boldness, it would be cowardly to deny you yours."

He watched his hand stroke lower. She parted her legs anxiously, and noticed that his resurrection was well under way.

"Actually, you said that you wanted *one more* scandalous night, Charlotte. So I will command this passion while I can, and be as bold as you will allow."

He was bold and commanding; she could not deny that. Less polite than in the past. Less careful. Every touch and kiss spoke demands, not requests. His aura, so exciting in its hints of danger and power, spread over her.

She did not mind. She submitted physically, even if she reserved internal corners to herself. She thrilled to the way he handled her, to the subtle domination. Her own daring had opened the gate in another wall, to an inner sanctum where sensuality became erotic. She sensed no disrespect in him, however. Tonight their passion had no link to the normal rules, just as their very first night had not.

Knowing his intentions piqued her responses. A new wildness claimed them both. She joined him in hungry kisses and impatient holds. She arched her breasts to his mouth, greedy for more pleasure. His hand rested on her inner thigh. Her body wept for the small movement that would bring his touch to the unbearably aroused flesh just inches from his hand.

He did not cooperate. Frustration made her whimper. She came close to scolding him, or begging.

Then his body moved, not his hand. He kissed down her body, leaving her embrace as he descended. She realized which scandalous part of this scandalous night would come first.

The idea provoked sensations so intense, so full of crying impatience, that her vulva trembled and throbbed. Her mind did not accept the reality so quickly. A little shocked and embarrassed, she watched his kisses lower until he nestled between her thighs. Despite her dazed senses, she thought this much more wicked, far more intimate, than what she had done to him.

His touch obliterated that thought, and all others. He kissed her thighs and mound while his fingers made her scream. When she thought she would die, he used his mouth to create a new caress with new friction. That devastated her. She cried out, again and again, into a long darkness shot with pleasure of un-bearable intensity.

She woke in the bed, alone. Dawn had broken, and the light streaming in the window turned the long night into a dream. A startling dream, in which she had given her body freely to this man. A dangerous night, in which she had almost lost herself and her will completely.

She sat up. The nest by the fire was gone. Her nightdress waited beside her, so she could don it be-fore Nancy arrived. Nothing in the chamber hinted at what had occurred. Only the images unfolding in her head spoke of it. And the echoes of the pleasure that rippled through her body.

She turned to sleep again, and saw the note. It lay on the pillow beside hers. *I have decided to ride back to London, because the day is so fair.*

Another woman might be insulted or feel abandoned, but she understood. It had been kindness, not callousness, that sent him from this bed in the dark. The journey would be awkward together. The carriage would have been full of unspoken matters that required private deliberation, not conversation.

They both knew that this chapter of their affair was over. She did not know whether they should turn the page, or if it would be wiser to simply close the book.

Nor did he, it appeared.

CHAPTER
FIFTEEN

～

Charlotte gave her wrap to the servant and sent word to James that she had arrived. While she waited for him to come down, she entered the dining room and consulted with the butler on the seating arrangements that would be used at the dinner.

She had helped James plan this party some weeks ago, but her absence from London meant she had not been available to manage its preparations. The household had been required to execute the plans without her.

Her negligence had surprised James. She had arrived in London to find a letter from him, sent to Laclere Park and then on, back to town. In it he reminded her of her promise to serve as hostess.

He entered the dining room as she finished with the butler. He had already dressed for dinner, as if in anticipation of her early arrival.

She had not seen him for almost two weeks and

much had happened in those days. She gazed at the friend and brother she knew, but also saw the youth mesmerized by that fire dance.

"You have been gone a long time," he said after she greeted him. "I would not have thought attending the birth of a nephew to take so long. I began to wonder if you had forgotten this dinner party."

"I promised to be here, and I am." She understood his annoyance. However, it reminded her how his dependence on her as his hostess was not such a good thing. He sounded as if the duty were his to demand tonight.

"Your sister returned two days before you did."

His pointed observation intruded on her examination of the dining room table, as she checked that all was in order.

"Pen had a friend leaving for the Continent and wanted to see her off. I, on the other hand, had affairs out of town and was seeing to them."

"You were not at Laclere Park?"

"Not the entire time, no." A month ago she would have explained, but rebellion and caution stopped her now. She had been investigating him, if truth be told, so it would be better that truth remain quiet.

She and Nathaniel had not spoken of what would happen now. Not that last night, and not since. Since her return to town she had received a letter from him, one of appreciation and praise that hinted at the astonishments of their passion. There had been no allusion at all to Jenny and Harry and the rest. No veiled reassurances either.

She guessed that she had not bought him off, and was glad she had not tried. She had bought a brief reprieve, however. If his memories of that night were at all like hers, it might take him a few days to emerge from the effects.

She still fought to keep her mind from dwelling on him all the time. Even now, as James quizzed her, she floated in a pleasant fog. Blissful memories beckoned.

She noticed James watching her. The smallest fires of suspicion brightened his eyes. It was almost as if he had read her mind during her contemplation of Nathaniel, and guessed not only about those nights but what had occupied the days.

She was imagining that, of course. Her guilt over deceiving him, her simmering worry over Jenny's tale, had her seeing much more than was there.

He remained expectant. He waited for her to tell him of those affairs that had delayed her return.

"There is an hour before the guests arrive," she said, walking past him. "I will go above and visit Ambrose. I have missed him badly."

"You cannot have missed him too much," he muttered at her back. "The nurse says he has been crying at night because you disappeared. He thought you abandoned him."

She did not break her stride, but guilt sickened her heart. She resented how easily James had shot that bolt and used her love of the child to express his own resentments.

His tone indicated he would not hesitate to do it again too.

Charlotte led the ladies from the dining room. It was a large party, and they broke into groups upon reaching the drawing room.

Her absence during the preparations for this night had taken a toll in the details. The household had become as dependent on her as James had. There were a few missteps as a result, and she could tell that James was not pleased.

She did her gracious best to make up for it with the ladies. Moving from group to group, she initiated spirited conversation among them.

Unfortunately, her mobility allowed one lady to corner her alone for a few private words.

"I hope you will not find me too bold, Lady Mardenford," Mrs. Powell said. "I thought that you could advise me on a distressing development."

Charlotte already knew what distressed Agnes Powell, and wished she had remained anchored to one sofa and unavailable for this tête-à-tête. Instead she guided her away from the others and slowed her steps so it might look like they merely chatted about the arrival of spring's rain.

"I fear that I have offended Sophia, and I do not know how or why," Mrs. Powell confided. "She did not invite me to her salon last week, and when I called on her yesterday I was told she was not receiving."

Charlotte rather wished the Duchess of Everdon had received Mrs. Powell, and been honest about the loss of favor. She was in no mood herself to dissemble with this young woman whose quick mind had gained her entry into Everdon's circle, but whose lack of discretion had now earned her ejection.

They approached the end of the chamber and turned so they would follow its northern wall.

"It is your misfortune that Sophia overheard your conversation with Lady Fulton several weeks ago. The one at Bianca's party, when you spoke with great freedom and wit near the garden doors. The duchess, you see, was taking some air right outside those doors."

Mrs. Powell's face flushed. Charlotte kept her voice level and calm.

"Sophia is not very tolerant of gossip, especially that which hurts her friends. Her lack of generosity on this point may be a failing, but her friends, I assure you, are grateful for the protection she wields with her station."

She sensed Mrs. Powell's growing dismay and did not mind in the least. That conversation near the garden doors had been about her sister Penelope, and had veered toward dangerous speculations of the cruelest kind.

She stopped and faced Mrs. Powell and forced a smile so that anyone watching would think they spoke of simple things. Mrs. Powell's own smile trembled, and her blue eyes reflected her horror that Charlotte knew what had been said that day.

"Do not be too distraught at losing Everdon's favor. There are ladies enough in society who will welcome you as a friend. They will be happy to whisper with you about my family and others, and about you when you are not present."

She gestured Mrs. Powell forward and they finished their turn of the room in silence.

The conversation unsettled her, and not only because of the anger that had spiked on Pen's behalf. It reminded her of how those whispers spread and grew wings, and took on a life removed from fact and truth. She knew their danger too well, and imagined them buzzing about this house, ruining the people who lived in it.

She pictured drawing rooms down through the years, where smiles would turn a little cruel as she walked by. Worse, she imagined Ambrose forever shadowed by either rumors or scandal. Each time he met a new person, that person would soon be treated to the whole story.

Hell of a thing, to be heir and then learn there was another son before you. Spanish no less. Mardenford must have lost his head.

Even if no such displacement occurred, the question would follow Ambrose forever. The inquiry itself would be public and humiliating.

Nathaniel knew that, but she doubted he really understood the cost. He was the sort of man who lived life as he chose. He did not bow to society. She suspected Ambrose would be more like his father and uncle. Like all the Mardenfords, he would want to stand shoulder-to-shoulder with the best of the best, secure in his place and free of scandal.

Right now at Albany a man was deciding whether to permit that, or whether truth had a bigger claim on his conscience.

After the last guests departed, James silently headed for the library. It was customary for Charlotte to join him there for a short while after such dinners, to assess the event's success.

She did not want to do so this time. She felt too much as she had as a girl when she anticipated a scolding from Laclere for her behavior. Only she was not a girl anymore and James had no right to scold. She was not in the mood to suffer it with grace. If he criticized, she might just put him in his place.

She did not follow. Instead she took a small lamp and walked up the stairs to the high chambers that housed the nursery.

Ambrose was whimpering when she entered. He made a low, careening drone that wrenched her heart. He had not woken the nurse, so he cried alone.

She hurried to his bedroom and picked him up. His little arms hugged her tightly. After a few deep sobs he began calming.

"Ancharl," he said contentedly, rubbing his tear-stroked face on her *gros de Naples* bodice. "Ancharl" had been one of his first words last winter, and his way of saying "Aunt Charl."

"Did you have a bad dream?"

He shook his head. "Wanna play," he said accusingly, sounding much like James in his tone.

When she had visited earlier, he had wanted her to get on the floor as she often did and join in games. Dressed as she was, the result would have been a disaster. She wished she had been less particular about her appearance now, if the child on waking in the night had still been hurt by her rebuff.

"I had to be hostess at your father's dinner, Ambrose. We cannot always play when we want. I love you even when I cannot play."

He angled his weight back so he could look at her. Her arms strained to balance him. Soon he would be too big for her to pick up and embrace.

He considered her with a skeptical inspection, as if judging whether she had meant it when she said she loved him. She wondered what James had said the last two weeks when he explained to Ambrose that they could not make their visits to Ancharl's house.

He suddenly embraced her neck and kissed her. "Wuv too."

The light shifted. They both looked over. James stood at the bedroom door.

Ambrose reached out a pudgy hand to his father. James joined them. "You should be asleep, son."

"He was awake when I came up. I think he will sleep now. Won't you, Ambrose?"

He rubbed his eyes with his fists and nodded.

He let her put him down and tuck him in. He curled on his side at once and stilled.

She enjoyed the sweetness of watching his innocence in the dark. Then James moved away and she reluctantly followed him.

"He is getting big. In a blink he will be too old for me to hug," she said as they left the nursery. "I will turn around and he will be at university, turn again and he will be on his grand tour—"

James walked beside her. She knew he wanted to say something or he would not have followed her upstairs. His bad humor was palpable, but that was not what made her speech falter.

His body had tightened, visibly flinched, when she mentioned the grand tour.

She looked at him in the lamp's glow as they descended the stairs. His face had gotten very long indeed. His eyes appeared dark in the yellow gloss, very dark. Dark and cautious. A cramp gripped her stomach and an eerie sensation overtook her.

He appeared much like Harry right now. The resemblance had emerged vaguely, like a form pressed against the back of thin silk.

The effect unsettled her enough that she had to use the banister for security. Her feet sought the last stairs awkwardly.

He peered at her as if he noticed her unrest and found it suspicious. She was imagining that, certainly. She was imagining all of it. He had not flinched, and he was not worried, and he did not find her reference to a grand tour odd at all.

"After that, I will be the old aunt whom he is obligated to visit when he is in town," she finished. "Such is the way of life, however."

"He will never think of it as an obligation. I will not allow him to grow so callous."

"All young men are somewhat callous, James. They must be, to find their paths away from those childish embraces of mothers and aunts."

They were in the reception hall now and more lamps lit the space. The fleeting resemblance to Harry was gone. It had been nothing more than the dim light and the peculiar mood between them tonight.

Her shock bled away and her stomach unclenched, but a newly born instinct in her would not completely retreat.

She asked a footman to call her carriage and send for her wrap.

"You are leaving already?" James asked.

"I am tired."

"From your journey?"

She had hoped to avoid further talk of that, but he had found a way back to the subject anyway. "Partly."

He appeared quite normal now. Normal and typical and the friend she knew, not the stranger on the stairs.

"You seemed unhappy when I mentioned a grand tour," she heard herself saying. The impulse to prod, to know, surged and spilled without enough thought.

A subtle tightness flexed his face. Undeniable this time. One of the soul as much as the countenance. She felt it as much as saw it. Hollowness spread through her chest.

"It only reminds me of the duties I avoid. I took my tour with a brother, and Ambrose has none."

"A young man does not need a brother for such things, although one is good to have," she said. "I am sure it was a special time for you and Philip. A great adventure together."

He smiled reflectively. "Yes, a great adventure."

"You never speak of it. I am sure there are wonderful stories. Do the memories pain you now that he is gone?"

"It was another life, another world. I try not to bore people."

"Memories are not boring, James. Not when they are about someone we loved."

His face fell. He shifted his weight and crossed his arms. He only relaxed when footsteps heralded the arrival of her wrap.

A series of discomforting reactions and impressions bombarded her. They swept like winds from different directions as she accepted her long mantle and James escorted her to her carriage. She could not absorb their meaning because they came in fast succession, blowing her thoughts like weightless leaves.

He closed the carriage door but put his face to the window, peering in at her. The resentful mood that had started this night poured off him, jumbling her reactions even more.

"Did you make that journey alone, Charlotte?"

His tone demanded satisfaction. Did he suspect Nathaniel had accompanied her? Had he learned of those discreet inquiries he had made here in London?

"Of course I did not journey alone. I had my abigail with me."

She called for her coachman to drive her home.

"You are not paying attention," Lyndale muttered. He had taken a post behind Nathaniel's shoulder at the faro table. "What are you thinking with such a stupid wager?"

Nathaniel glanced back at his tormentor. "I thought you had tired of the game and left."

"I only tired of the easy winnings you offered."

"Then go find a bigger challenge and stop harping like an old woman. You are intrusive and irritating."

"I am not harping, but voicing the obvious, which your own brain appears incapable of grasping. It is a friend's obligation to be intrusive when his fellow man is on the path to ruin because he is foxed."

"I am not foxed."

"Then you have no excuse. You are losing to Abernathy, Knightridge. *Abernathy*."

Nathaniel looked down the table at Abernathy's glee.

Lyndale was right. He wasn't paying attention and his play was badly off.

But then, his whole life had been off these two days since returning to town. He could not think about anything except the mystery woman who was no longer a mystery.

He had tried to distract himself tonight with the company of others, only to sit in this gaming hall saying nothing, hearing nothing. He had barely been aware that Lyndale had taken position behind him until the incessant mutters of criticism began.

He gestured for the dealer to skip him.

"Now, that is being a sensible boy," Lyndale said. His voice carried a soothing note, as if he were speaking to an imbecile.

"I am not foxed," Nathaniel repeated.

"Then perhaps you are ill."

"Not the way you mean. I know who she is."

"She?" Lyndale's face fell to that uncharacteristic blandness.

"Yes, *she.*"

"Whatever is the man mumbling about?"

"Continue to feign ignorance and I will thrash you."

"You will *try* to thrash me, you mean." He looked down seriously. "By 'she,' do you mean your friend from my last party?"

"Yes."

"You are sure?"

"Positive."

Their gazes locked in tacit acknowledgment of who that lady was.

"Astonishing, isn't it?" Lyndale said.

Lyndale did not know just how astonishing.

"So, now you know. I am therefore no longer constrained, and can tell you that I am very disappointed."

Nathaniel rose to his feet. "Speak one word against her and—"

"Against her? Why would I do that? I am disappointed in *you*. I was as bad as they come, enthusiastically so, and *I* never took advantage of the sister of a friend."

It was either hit Lyndale or walk away. Nathaniel strode to the side of the room. Lyndale followed, as if the move had been a quest for a private chat.

"I did not know who she was, remember?" Nathaniel said, turning on Lyndale at the edge of a wall lamp's glow.

"And now you do. Since you have already broken the rule about a friend's female relatives—"

"There is no such rule. You made it for yourself but only so you could narrow the field to women who would cause the least trouble. You are the last man in Britain to criticize. Hell, it was *your* damned orgy."

Lyndale sighed with strained patience. "It was a good rule, as you have now learned. Have you spoken to her about it?"

"I offered to do the right thing, if that is what you mean."

"Very decent of you. I assume she refused."

Lyndale's confident tone raised the devil in him. "Why would you assume that?"

"Because the lady does not like you. A masked encounter is one thing, but a lifetime is another."

"She likes me better than you think." He heard himself sound like a petulant boy, and that made his anger rise more.

"Since she refused, what are you going to do about it?"

It was a good question, and not an easy one to answer. It was the question that distracted him. There had been much of the grand finale in that last night together. It was as if they had grabbed at everything because they assumed it was their last chance.

Lyndale rested his shoulder against the wall. He reached into his coat and withdrew two cigars. In companionable silence they clipped and lit.

"It would help if the two of you could tolerate each other. Although when one sees such blatant dislike, one always wonders if..." Lyndale shrugged. "Well, if the arguing is not a way of concealing a physical irritation, so to speak."

"If so, I will be bickering and arguing a long time."

"Ah." Lyndale looked down at his cigar. "Now you know why I never bought chambers at Albany. All those bachelors and servants. It is hard to be discreet."

Nathaniel realized that Lyndale had guessed all of it. That he and Charlotte had more than spoken of what had occurred, and that the bad play at the faro table was caused by a hunger to do more than talk again.

Lyndale pushed away from the wall. "I hear the lady has returned to London from a fortnight in the country. If you call on her, convey my highest regards." He walked away.

Nathaniel found a chair and finished his own smoke. Then he called for his horse.

He would return to Albany, where one could not

be discreet, and lie on the bed of nails that waited there. He would think all night about Charlotte and try to decide whether and how this affair could continue in town.

And he would conclude nothing, because the biggest obstacle was not Albany or her relationship to one of his friends. It was whether in her heart she would always be watching him as she had that night from the end of the table, worrying that he would have to know the truth.

It was time for him to resolve the desire and distraction, and find out if he did.

CHAPTER SIXTEEN

Charlotte waited for the girl to build the fire in the library. Usually she spent her mornings in her apartment, but today she had something to do.

Finally the servant left. Charlotte listened for silence outside the chamber, then rose and approached an old pedestal table tucked into a corner.

With its scrolled edges and Corinthian base, the table did not fit the decor. She had redecorated this room last fall in the Tudor style. Now turned legs and medieval floral carving marked the furnishings, and deep prints upholstered the chairs.

This classically inspired table should have been sold or moved. But it had always stood here, and it held Philip's private papers. It had seemed at the time that to remove it would be akin to removing the last of him and his ghost, so she had let it stay.

She grasped the two pulls of the large drawer beneath the tabletop. Her will hesitated. A fit of confusion and nostalgia made her heart pound.

She had not opened this drawer in six years. After Philip's death she had briefly assessed what lay in this drawer. Letters and papers and tokens of his childhood. Old school writings and missives from his father. It was the eclectric collection such as a person saves from habit or sentiment. She had been too grieved to read any of it then, and had never found the heart to do so since.

Now she wondered if there might be something in here that would explain Jenny's story about Mrs. Marden and Harry.

If there was, did she want to see it?

Her heart and better sense said no. The instinct born last night in James's presence would not quiet, however. It had to know. There could be something here that explained everything in ways that did not threaten anyone's peace or place in the world, after all.

She opened the drawer.

A scent rose from its contents. One of dust and staleness and something else. Him.

Her eyes blurred as her heart recognized the crisp scent, so weak now, so vague. It filled her head for a moment, calling forth images from the past. Then the atmosphere of the library absorbed it. The odors of polish and burnt fuel and her own perfume overwhelmed it.

She eyed the stacks of letters and papers. He had been her husband, but she felt like an intruder, sneaking into things she ought not see. He had never shared any of this with her in life, and it did not seem natural to read it now.

She lifted a stack of letters anyway. These were not documents that belonged to the estate, or Mardenford. They were Philip's intimate possessions, and now they belonged to her.

She shuffled through the letters, glancing at the signatures, wondering why he had saved these and not others. They all looked ordinary. Predictable. Letters from parents and friends, from his old tutor and nurse. She worked quickly, checking names and dates, fanning the sheets to find the oldest ones. Finally she saw a letter from a friend that must have been sent soon after Philip and James returned from their grand tour.

The tone was jovial and man-to-man. It referenced adventures and expressed envy. A few joking allusions implied this friend assumed all young men on tour experienced a carnal baptism. Nothing in the letter suggested that Philip had confided a great secret to this young man.

She returned to her search, looking for others from the time. She was concluding that she should give the drawer's contents some order, when the library door suddenly opened.

Feeling like a thief caught in the act, she slid the letters back into the drawer as a footman approached with a salver.

She raised her eyebrows and glanced pointedly at the clock, which showed it had just passed ten o'clock. The servant grimaced an apology for the rudeness of this early caller.

"He was most insistent, and said you expected him, and told us he would see we were all released if we did not inform you he was here."

She lifted the card but she already knew whose name it would bear.

There had been three letters, but no requests for a meeting. She had responded, but had not asked him to call, either. She doubted it was indifference on his part any more than it had been on hers. After a fortnight they both had affairs to attend to and things to think about.

She had mostly been thinking about him.

"I will see him," she said.

She snatched a book from a shelf and sat in a chair near the fire.

She could see the pedestal table out of the corner of her eye. It seemed to shine and call attention to itself. It really stuck out, now that she thought about it. Anyone entering this library would notice it and wonder what was in that drawer. Nathaniel would probably guess at once that she had been pouring over its contents and ask why she cared about letters written a decade ago—

Her attention snapped to the door as it opened. Nathaniel walked in, looking so handsome her heart jumped. He was dressed for riding, in a black coat and gray trousers and high boots. The day's breeze had mussed his golden hair and it looked too much as it did when a night of passion left it careless and free, with locks falling here and there to skim his brow.

He did not notice the table. His dark eyes locked on hers at once. He strode over and kissed her hand. They exchanged formal greetings for the footman's sake.

Nathaniel glanced at where the man waited for instructions. "Get rid of him," he muttered.

She dismissed the footman, who walked to the door. Very slowly. Each footfall took forever. All the while she suffered the full onslaught of Nathaniel's presence. Her body thrilled to the silent power barely leashed by propriety.

His dark eyes coolly watched the footman retreat. He waited until the door latch sounded. Then he turned his attention back to her.

His gaze slowly lowered from her face down her body, to her knees and along the diagonal line of her legs to where her feet tucked behind the chair foot. His expression grew severe.

"Did you deliberately take the same pose to taunt me?"

She flushed. She had not realized—

"How many letters were you thinking we should write to each other before I saw you again?"

He did not sound angry, just determined and crisp.

"I thought we understood that we both needed time to think about things."

He began his territorial pacing. Around her chair.

"Ah, yes. There are decisions to be made."

"Exactly."

"About *things*."

She glared at him. His aura might be thrilling, but it could also be vexing.

"Things that might divide us," he said. "So in order to think about things that might divide us, we must divide. Is that how *your* thinking goes?"

She did not care for his mocking tone. "It is not your place to scold me, least of all when I have behaved quite nobly and selflessly. Do not blame me for not knowing what to do now. I have no experience with liaisons at all, let alone with one that involves a man who might..."

He paused his steps in front of her and looked down. The *might* just hung there between them.

"So I am to retreat to my monk's cell and pray and contemplate my choices. You will wait on your decision until I have made mine, I assume."

The intensity of his attention had her swallowing hard. "I did not think it would be fair to seem to...I made it very clear that I will not have you blaming me for luring you to compromise. I will not be accused of trying to influence—"

"Any other woman would have extracted a promise from me in bed, damn it. But not you. Oh, no, you pretend it is separate instead of twisted together into a knot."

"You apparently intruded this morning to have a row. Well, so be it." She rose to her feet. "First, do not take that high-and-mighty tone with me. A woman who has Laclere as a brother grows immune to masculine demonstrations of pique."

"Pique? You have not driven me to pique, Lady M. You are driving me mad."

"I am trying to deal with you fairly. You should be grateful that I understand your need to make an honest decision and that I have given you the privacy to think clearly about what we learned and—"

"Think clearly? If you believe I have been thinking clearly for the last two days, or thinking about that great decision at all, you are much mistaken. The only thoughts I have had are of you naked and moaning and your mouth—"

"Mr. Knightridge." She glared at him, then to the door where who knew what servant listened.

"Damn the servants." He yanked her into his arms and created instant silence with a punishing kiss.

For an instant she was stunned. Then she was lost.

All thoughts of servants disappeared. His kisses were savage and his caresses bold. Fire burst in her. It did not matter where they were or who might intrude. His desire so dominated that she could barely reciprocate, but she could feel. Her fevered and reckless responses urged on his ruthless demands for her passion.

They went mad. Mad and hungry and impatient. His embrace lifted her off her feet. The world spun. Suddenly she was facedown, bent over the side of a desk, the smoothly polished surface beneath her hands and cheek. Fabric fluttered at her head and air breezed her legs and thighs. Firm hands pulled down her drawers and wicked fingers caressed down her naked bottom until he stroked where she pulsed and ached.

She bit her fist to keep from moaning and begging. His impatience matched hers. Their joining was as hard as the first kiss, long and thorough. Helpless, she abandoned herself to the pleasure and insanity and ultimately to the wild finish.

It took forever to return to her senses. First she heard his deep breath sounding out the time. His body hovered over hers. His hands flanked her on the desk where he braced his arms.

They were still joined. She sensed a warmth on her back, through her clothes. A kiss. Then he pushed away and left her. She heard the subtle movements as he fixed his garments.

She also thought she heard a knock on the door.

She jerked up her head and stared at that sound. She sensed Nathaniel freeze behind her.

"Yes," she called.

"The viscount is below," a muffled voice reported. "Lady Laclere is with him, and most insistent that they see you."

Nathaniel muttered a curse. He pulled up her drawers and lifted her to her feet. "Do you always receive them when they call?"

"Always. Oh, dear heavens." She fluffed out her petticoats and felt frantically at her hair. "Of course, bring them up," she called to the door.

With quick movements and hurried inspections, they assessed each other and smoothed hair and clothing.

"The servants suspect," she said, combing his hair into place with her fingers. "Otherwise the footman would have entered, and Bianca does not stand on ceremony. She would have been three steps behind."

"As I said, damn the servants. Although, almost being found like that by your brother—I think I am repaid for my father's intrusion. I had no idea families could be such a nuisance."

Despite his allusion to embarrassment, Nathaniel did not look the least bit chagrined. He wore an expression of utter confidence as he dealt with her skirts.

Actually, he looked like a man well contented. A man who had just settled something important.

He gave her a last inspection, then looked in her eyes. "I trust that we have an understanding about this thread in that knot, at least."

She was in no condition to disagree. Nor did she have time to do so. The door opened and Bianca sailed in with Vergil at her side.

"Forgive the hour, but when you hear why we came you will not mind," Bianca said. She strode toward them with a big smile. Her excited speed made the feather on her bonnet bob. Nathaniel's presence did not make her miss a step.

The same could not be said for Vergil. He specifically paused when he saw her company, then approached slowly.

"Knightridge."

"Laclere."

Bianca acknowledged Nathaniel, but her attention

was all for Charlotte. "Are you unwell? You appear a little flushed. No? I am glad. Now, here is the wonderful news that brings us so early. A week hence, on the coast, there will be a very special wedding."

"Pen?"

"Yes. It will be quiet, of course, but it is long past time."

Bianca's excitement could not be contained, and Charlotte tried to match it with her own. She truly was happy for Penelope, but watching Vergil's reactions to this visit distracted her a bit.

He kept looking at Nathaniel with a hooded speculation, and then at her with curiosity. She could see her brother calculating that this was an odd hour for Knightridge to be alone with her in this library.

She spotted the precise instant when the possible meaning of the closed door struck him. While Bianca chattered on about plans for the wedding, Vergil silently weighed the evidence.

He all but sniffed the air. Charlotte was heartily grateful he did not. It seemed to her that the scent of sex drenched the atmosphere.

"So we had to come at once and tell you," Bianca finished. "A note by post would never do."

"A note may have been more civilized and considerate, however," Vergil said. "We have interrupted a meeting, my dear."

Bianca brushed the admonishment aside. "Just as well, for Mr. Knightridge must attend if he can. He was important to the happiness that will be celebrated."

Nathaniel smiled noncomittedly. He was handling the awkwardness with aplomb, but Charlotte could tell that he was alert to Laclere's increasingly suspicious demeanor.

"All the same, we should excuse ourselves," Vergil said. "Although I am wondering if the meeting was already well concluded when we intruded." He gave Nathaniel a deep look on the last sentence that made Charlotte's caution prickle. She saw the big brother in him, thinking that a private chat with this man was in order.

Bianca still had not picked up the cue. "You are making plans regarding the petitions?"

"I trust that a petition came up at some point in the visit," Vergil said dryly. "Correct, Knightridge?"

Charlotte wanted to die. "Indeed one did," she said. "Mr. Knightridge is proving to be a great help in the cause."

Bianca beamed. "I always knew that the two of you would find common ground in something."

"Yes, we have discovered we think alike in one small area," Nathaniel agreed.

Charlotte wanted to hit him.

"Indeed," Vergil muttered. He turned his attention on her. She guessed he was looking for indications that she had not been importuned by this man whom she did not like.

Short of explaining everything, there was no way to reassure him. Nor did she feel an obligation to do so. She was a grown woman and her brother should not force his way into her house on a whim.

Fortunately, Nathaniel decided to make his exit. He took his leave of the others, and then of her. "We can continue our discussions another time, Lady M." His quick, deep gaze made it clear how hot those discussions would be.

As soon as he was gone, Vergil turned to Bianca. "I told you it could wait until calling hours. I also said that Pen might want to send the news herself." His palpable ill ease made his tone sharp.

The scold took Bianca aback. Suddenly confused, she looked at Charlotte. She glanced at her husband's stony countenance. She turned once more to Charlotte.

Charlotte watched the clouds part and a beam of illumination stream through. Bianca's eyes turned very shrewd. She examined Charlotte closely, her scrutiny pausing on every wrinkle in her skirt and every mussed tendril in her hair.

A little smile broke, one that only another woman would understand.

"Shall we take our leave now?" Vergil demanded. "I am sure that Pen will let you know all the particulars, Charl."

Vergil hauled Bianca away. Bianca looked back and cast Charlotte another womanly smile.

"Damned embarrassing," Charlotte heard Vergil mutter.

"I told you," Bianca muttered back. "I saw it at Laclere Park."

"It makes no sense. They have never liked each other."

Their whispers died away. The door closed behind them.

Charlotte returned to her chair and sat in a sated stupor for a long time. Eventually she remembered why she had entered the library this morning.

She rose and moved a chair to the pedestal table and opened the drawer again. She sorted the letters by date and began reading them.

At noon, she came to a flurry of correspondence between Philip and his tutor. The letters had been exchanged almost seven years ago, not long before she became engaged.

At five minutes past noon, some veiled allusions in the letters began making sense to her. A pattern emerged. Her instincts comprehended first and reacted with dread.

By ten minutes after noon she was staring sightlessly at those letters, now spread out on the table.

Shock immobilized her. Her soul screamed with denial. Her heart burned like it had received a raw cut.

She would never forgive Nathaniel Knightridge for starting his horrible investigation.

Never.

CHAPTER SEVENTEEN

⁓

"I remember it," Williamson said. "It was hard to get her out. The clothing was sodden, but she was not yet. Had we been quicker... Well, accidents happen. It is always a sad duty, but common enough. She was a striking young woman, however, and looked to be of good birth, so she was one I remembered."

"Her identity remained unknown?" Nathaniel asked.

"Nothing on her to send us looking for family. No one who saw her pulled out recognized her."

Nathaniel had left Charlotte's house the day before triumphant, sated, and of clear resolve. He intended to finish with the Finley matter as quickly as he could, but while he did he would no longer allow Charlotte to avoid him.

If their only common ground would be pleasure and passion, so be it. He would not relinquish that. He could not.

He had thrown himself into his investigation the last two days. With any luck he would lay the whole matter to rest in the most benign way. Even if the answers were bad ones, he had hopes they could not destroy the unmistakable hunger he and Charlotte felt for each other.

Whether anything more could survive, he did not know. An impasse had been reached on that score. Only settling the "much that divided them" would ever resolve it, however.

Focused now, ruthlessly so, yesterday he had set in motion some inquiries to learn the name of the tutor who had accompanied Mardenford on the grand tour. Today he had sought information on the death of Harry's mother.

The Metropolitan Police kept records like the good English institution it was. Although many members of that brotherhood did not like Nathaniel much, due to his defenses, a few of the inspectors had become his friends. By midafternoon he had the name of the constables who had helped drag a dead foreign woman from the Thames near the Salisbury Stairs four years ago.

He had found Williamson on duty at his post near Covent Garden. Williamson was an average-sized man, of placid appearance overall but with very intelligent eyes.

"It was kind of you to record it as an accident, so she could have a decent burial."

Williamson's mouth flattened into a hard line. "I

do not falsify my reports, sir. She fell in. The evidence indicated as much."

"Did people see that?"

"None we talked to. She wasn't the first dead body fished out of the river, though. We get to know the difference. Could be she was a suicide, but I doubt it."

"Why do you doubt it?"

"Wearing expensive clothes, wasn't she? Not normal. Ones who do themselves in don't want their best ruined. Usually they weight themselves too. Nor do they have gold pinned to their petticoats. This one did. Part of a chain, about as long as my finger. The links were found by the surgeon when she was delivered to him. It was used to pay for her burial, as I heard it."

"Perhaps that was why she wore it. To pay for her burial."

"Foreign woman, she was, from her face and clothes. What was the chance she knew it would matter? If you ask me, and you have, that woman fell in the river."

Nathaniel turned their exchange over in his mind while he returned to his chambers. Williamson's conviction that it had not been suicide made some sense. Would she bring the boy with her if she planned that? She had to know he would be left adrift in the city afterward.

She had put Harry at a spot nearby, and told him to wait, however. If she had not wanted him to see her jump, what was the purpose of bringing him at all?

The most obvious answer only heralded more trouble. Nor, he suspected, could it ever be proven.

Harry's mother had not gone to the river to kill herself. She had dressed in her best garments, and taken the boy, in order to meet someone. Someone to whom she had been writing for nearly a year, with no response. Someone whom she had journeyed to London to confront.

She had left the boy close by so that he could either be seen or fetched once that meeting began.

He saw it all play out. A woman in a dark, expensive dress meeting a man on the bank of the Thames. A quest for privacy, perhaps on the stairs near where her body had been found. Only she had received coldness, not welcome. Rejection, not acceptance.

Did she threaten him? Did she say she would let the world know?

Whatever had been said, she had not left the river's edge alive. Perhaps in a fit of despair at the results of that meeting she really had jumped to her death. Or perhaps she had fallen by accident.

There was another possibility, one that the Old Bailey lawyer in Nathaniel could not ignore.

She may have been pushed.

The letter did not arrive in his chambers by the post late that afternoon. Instead it was delivered by a footman whom Nathaniel recognized as one from Charlotte's house.

"I will be at Albany at ten. Please remove Jacobs," the note read.

Her message surprised him on several counts. Although he had been more than bold at her house, he did not expect her to return the favor and match his precipitous demands for passion with her own. Furthermore, her visiting him was potentially ruinous in ways his visit was not.

Finally, her abrupt note implied he had not established mastery of this affair quite the way his pride had thought upon leaving victorious yesterday morning.

He gave Jacobs leave to visit his sister in Middlesex for the night, then waited with distracting impatience for Charlotte. He left the door ajar so she would not need to stand outside even for one indiscreet moment.

The clock's chimes had not yet finished when she arrived. He had been waiting so hard, so completely, that he sensed her enter despite her silence. He shut his eyes, astonished by how thoroughly her presence entered him as well as the apartment.

He opened them to see her standing in the sitting room where he sat. Dressed in black, as if in mourning, she wore a veil that obscured her face. If anyone had seen her on the walk, that person would have observed no more than the shadows shifting in the night.

He rose to go to her. She held up a hand, stopping him. She set down her black parasol, then lifted her veil.

Her appearance stunned him. She might have truly arrived from a funeral, she looked so wan. Her eyes showed no light, but only dull distant thoughts. Her face had turned drawn and tired.

He went to her anyway and embraced her with concern. She did not soften against him. She seemed to stiffen a little, as if his hold hurt her.

"You are unwell," he said.

She extricated herself and stepped back. She regarded him with a cool expression, but her eyes glistened now.

"I am not unwell, but I am sick," she said. "You had to know, damn you. Well, now I am the one who knows, and I do not think I can survive the knowing."

"What are you saying, darling?"

Her expression folded into one of distraught grief.

"Nathaniel, it was not James who had that youthful liaison in Spain. It was Philip."

She had arranged this assignation in a fit of mindless fury. She had come here to berate him, to scream at him like a madwoman.

Instead, saying the words sapped her strength. She broke and tears poured out, even though she made no sound.

Strong arms surrounded her. That made it worse. She fought the desolation, and him. She pounded her fists against his chest even as she sobbed against his coat.

It felt good to be angry. To hit him. The hours

since reading those letters had been horrible. Frightening. She had felt dead all afternoon. Then, at night, the truth had begun slashing the picture of her life to shreds. The Charlotte she knew had been cut to pieces too.

She had not been able to accommodate it. Her mind refused. She had never known such confusion before. Thoughts jumbling, emotions careening, she thought she would die if she did not release the building shock and resentment.

There was only one person with whom she dared do that. Only one to whom she could confide and speak. The same one whom she wanted to thrash.

She thrashed now. She pounded him as she cried. He let her, holding her closer even when her flailing fists hit his face. She truly lost control of her senses and went mad for a moment.

Then it passed. Nothing remained in her. No tears and no thoughts. She rested her face on his coat, tired and numb.

She lifted her head. His expression was so concerned, so gentle, that her heart twisted. She hated him. *Hated* him. But her heart refused to understand that.

"Did you know? You said you did not believe it was him, but did you really, all this time—"

"No. I swear. The possibility entered my head, but I was sure it was James," he soothed.

"I wasn't." It was out before she realized the words had formed. She was too tired, too angry to lie to him. To herself. "Oh, I did not believe it, not really, but it was there, underneath all the other fear, like a dark, dangerous animal hiding in the cellar. My soul knew it was there. It knew just how dangerous you were to us. To *me*. I dared not contemplate all the reasons why."

He let the accusation stand. He did not attempt to mollify her with reassurances. Of course not. Nathaniel Knightridge was a man of honor, damn him. A man of truth and justice, by heavens.

"Can you speak of it?" he asked. "Will you tell me why you think this? You may be wrong."

"For once I wish I were." She moved to the settee and dropped into her familiar spot. The agitation that had left her walking for hours, unable to remain still, mercifully retreated. The exhaustion and limpness that claimed her was almost welcomed.

Nathaniel stood nearby, watching her closely.

He reached over and found the pins on her hat. He slid them out, then lifted the hat away. Its veil fluttered on its path to a table.

The gesture touched her. It did not imply seduction, although it could have. It said she would stay even if she hated him, and he would take care of her.

Perhaps that was really why she had come. To bask in his aura of command and confidence. To remind herself that there was more to her life than the past.

"Now, tell me," he said.

She explained the drawer and its letters. "They were private. I had never read them."

"Nor had you destroyed them."

"No."

Why not? She could not answer now, but she supposed she should someday. "I thought that perhaps, if something in Spain had transpired as Jenny's story implied, there might be information in those letters that explained it away."

His expression altered slightly. Mr. Knightridge, who could always spot her dissembling, knew he was hearing less than the truth.

He was good enough not to say so. "What was in the letters?"

"They were ordinary. Quite dull. Philip was not famed for his skill at the pen. There was nothing of interest from the years right after the grand tour. Nothing to raise concern or suspicion. Later, however—"

She faltered. She wanted to slide over the painful parts. The parts touching on *her*.

Except it all touched her.

"I found a series of letters from his old tutor, written very near the time Philip began courting me. At first they appeared dull too, as if Philip had written asking for news of a mutual friend. Then it became clear the tutor was making inquiries. Not in England. Finally a letter informed Philip that he had received confirmation that she was dead, lost in the war. That was what caught my eye. We had no war then, but Spain did."

"Did the letter say 'she'?"

"Yes. I might never have read those letters closely but for that one 'she.'" Seeing that word as she skimmed had made her head ring. "At the end, after writing of common things, his garden and a sermon he was preparing, the tutor closed with another reference. 'Be assured that the legality of the alliance is now an irrelevant question. There is no need to pursue that.' "

A question entered Nathaniel's eyes. She did not wait for him to ask it.

"I am quoting exactly. He used the word 'legality.' " Desolation flooded her again. "An alliance with a woman that had legal implications. Tell me there is another besides marriage, Nathaniel. I very much want to hear that is so."

He stepped closer and rested his palm on her cheek in comfort.

She grasped at composure. His touch helped. It should have repulsed her, not given solace. She had spent all day slicing him to ribbons with scathing accusations in her mind, but here she was drinking his sympathy instead of laying blame at his feet.

"Have you told anyone else?"

His concern remained palpable and his voice quiet, but she could tell his mind was working.

"I called on Bianca today, intending to confide, but found I could not speak of it. What would I say? I wanted desperately to share my shock with her or Pen, but if I voiced one word I would start raving. The implications are too shameful."

"It is not shameful. It was long ago. He thought her dead. If he returned to England without her, he must have thought he lost her to the war even before he left Spain."

"But she wasn't dead, so *my marriage was not legal*." Her voice broke as she spelled it out. She looked at her hands, knotted on her lap, and grit her teeth. "That is not the worst of it, however. I feel stupid and angry. I am unsure of every memory I ever had. It is as if I lived a lie every day of those three years."

He knelt on one knee so his head was level with hers. He covered her hands with his, forming a little mound of warmth. "With time, as the shock passes, you will find it less devastating. I also do not think this story would reflect badly on him if all of it were known. There is no reason for you to believe you lived a lie."

He was trying so hard to make it better that she had to smile. Her lips trembled, only half-willing to cooperate.

"My thoughts have been raining curses on you all day for starting down this road."

"I wish I had not. It grieves me to see you so hurt." His head dipped and he kissed her hands. "If you want to thrash me with your parasol, I promise not to resist."

She stretched her fingers into his hair as he kept his lips pressed to her hands. The sorrow in her still wanted to curse and hate him, but she had found a peace in this sitting room that she had not expected. *Comforting, but not comfortable.*

She had needed to share her distress with a friend, to confide a secret to someone who would help her regain some sense. And she had found that friend in this man.

Nor did he attempt to excuse his role in provoking her discovery. He had not said one word in his own defense. Instead he had sought to absolve another man, long dead, to whom he owed no loyalty.

He had done that for her. His only words had been ones that offered her a path to some relief.

Her heart filled with a glow so sweet, she could not bear it. She pressed a kiss to his bowed head.

He straightened and looked at her. An intense connection, raw and vital, instantly bound them. The intimacy deepened and invaded until she was helpless.

"I do not know what to do now, Nathaniel." She referred to her discovery, and also to the emotion leaving her defenseless.

"I do."

He rose, lifted her into his arms, and carried her from the room.

"His name is Yardley. The tutor, that is his name."

Her words broke the long silence. He nuzzled the head resting on his shoulder and caressed the shoulder under his hand. He had removed her dress and petticoats so they would not get ruined, but he had intended no grand passion tonight.

She had been the one to initiate a slow, careful joining, one that spoke of her soul's desire for distraction more than her body's quest for pleasure. Now they remained bound in this embrace full of human warmth and unspoken questions.

He already knew the tutor's name. His inquiries

had borne fruit fast, but then he and Mardenford lived in a very small world.

Her head angled back so she could see his face. "You do not seem interested. I thought you would be hesitant to ask, but that you would want to know."

"I do not care what his name is." Not now. Not anymore.

"You could find him and learn the truth."

"There will be no more finding and learning. The truth is that you married Mardenford and are his widow. Those letters were not explicit and you misunderstood them."

She pushed up on her arm and gazed down at him. "You do not really believe that."

"Here is the story I glean from those letters, Charlotte. He decided to marry you but had the decency to make sure his prior alliance permitted it. He asked his tutor to learn for certain if that woman had died, as he believed. He asked about the legalities of the alliance in any case, which means he had reason to think they were ambiguous. A foreign engagement could explain that. It did not even have to be a marriage."

Her fingers traced a long, meandering line across his chest while she thought about that.

"So it ends here? Now? Because of this?"

"It was time to retreat anyway." If he did not, it would only get worse.

"What about Harry? You said he was the real reason."

"I will take care of the boy. He will not want. He will not be alone."

She returned to his side and his embrace. "Your interpretation fits, I suppose. It is not such a bad story when seen that way."

"I am sure I am right."

"How are you so sure?"

"For the same reason I never thought it would be him. If you saw fit to love him, Charlotte, he could not have been a man without honor."

She snuggled closer, then went still. He wished he could believe he had convinced her, but he knew her thoughts still dwelled on hard questions.

"I think he loved her, very much," she whispered.

His chest knotted. There were some questions he could not talk into submission. He wished he could absorb her confusion and hurt into himself instead, to spare her. "You do not know that. There is no reason to think it."

"There is. Not in the letters, but in a memory. I see the light in his eyes as he describes a fire dance on the Spanish coast. She was there, I am sure. She was the reason for that light. The love he felt for me was honest, but different. She was the great passion of his life."

As you are mine. He did not say it. This night was not about him. Such an admission had no place now, while she struggled to make her peace with what she had learned.

He just held her, so she would not be alone in the dark as she negotiated with the ghosts of the past.

CHAPTER EIGHTEEN

~

Charlotte called at Mardenford's house two days later. She had promised to visit Ambrose, and her heavy heart lightened while she waited at the door. Ambrose was one small part of her past that she could still count on, and she needed badly to hold his innocence for a while.

The footman's face drained of color when he opened the door. Little beads of sweat popped up on his forehead. She waited for him to step aside. He didn't.

"My lord is not receiving," he finally said. His gaze sought a spot two inches beneath her eyes.

It was an odd thing to be told, and also irrelevant.

"I have come to see Ambrose. I do not require Mardenford's attendance."

When the footman still did not move, she tapped her parasol impatiently.

The man looked stricken. "My lady, we have been given instructions that you are not to enter."

"You misunderstood, I am sure."

"There is no misunderstanding. The command was very clear. You are not to enter, and you are not . . . you are not to see the child." His mouth firmed on the last words. So did his back, as if the cruelty left him no choice but a retreat into duty.

She stared at his suddenly crisp demeanor. Her battered heart took another blow, one that stunned her.

He was serious. James had really done this.

She glanced up the facade, to the nursery windows on the fourth level. Ambrose would wonder why she had not come today as she had promised. The poor child would never understand.

"Listen to me. I am entering unless you want a scandalous scene right here that the town will talk about for months. I am not leaving until I speak with my brother-in-law, so inform him of that at once. You will now stand aside and I will wait for Mardenford in the library."

He eyed her, to see if she meant the threat about a scene. She glared back in a display of vexation that masked the scathing pain this new loss created.

He moved aside. She sped past him and up the stairs to the library.

Whatever had caused James to issue such a strange order, she would make him change his mind. Still salving the wounds that those letters had created, she would not be able to absorb this grief as well.

James did not send a refusal to see her, but neither did he come to the library. She wondered if he planned to pretend she had not entered the house since he had decreed she should not.

She sat on a chair, determined to wait him out, impatient and agitated. James had ruined the fragile truce she had forged with her emotions while Nathaniel held her through the night two days ago.

She had emerged from that embrace still dazed but no longer so lost. A type of acceptance had begun forming. Voicing the worst of her fears had lessened the confusion.

Nathaniel had been very good to her. Very kind. He had sounded so confident that his explanation was correct. Very certain.

All night she had been certain too, and all the next day, while she sat in her chambers putting the memories back in some order. A new order, changed now. A new history and a new life, but not all that different from the old one in the important things.

Only when that was completed, only when she saw the road behind her cleared of debris, had her thoughts turned again to those letters and the alliance they revealed.

Nathaniel might be very sure he knew what had occurred, but she was not. She was still deciding if it mattered if she knew the particulars, or even the truth.

"I am expecting visitors this afternoon, Charlotte, so you will have to leave now."

James's voice spoke from the doorway. She turned to find him outside the library, addressing her as he passed by.

"It was good of you to take the time to throw me out yourself."

"I was informed you would not leave until I did."

"You were misinformed. I said I would not leave until we spoke about your command that I not visit or see Ambrose."

"Are you threatening another scene, such as you did at the door?"

"If necessary."

He strolled into the library but stopped a good distance from her. Head high, lids low, he gave her a critical inspection.

"The family did not want him to marry you. Bad blood, they said. A propensity for eccentricity and sin. Even your brother Laclere, who seemed fine at first. That marriage he made, and his factory in Manchester . . . They were all against it, but not me. I told him you were different. Pure and good and that you would bring no shame on the family."

"Nor did I."

"Not for a long time. But it seems bad blood wins out eventually." His pose got more rigid, if that were possible. "You are having an affair with Nathaniel Knightridge and I do not want my son under the influence of a woman who has lost her reputation and her morality."

His declaration startled her. She had no intention of lying, but she did not have to agree either.

"Why have you concluded I am having an affair, James? It is an odd accusation to make."

He crossed his arms. It did not make him look

strong, but only petulant. "He was with you on that journey. My aunt sent me word that his presence alongside you at some political meeting was noted in a county paper."

"He was helping with the petitions."

"He was also helping himself to your favors."

"It is disgraceful of you to make such rude accusations."

"He was been to your home at early hours. You have been to his at very late ones."

"How do you know this?"

"Your Mr. Knightridge is not the only one who knows how to investigate people, Charlotte."

Her heart skipped. She rose from her chair and advanced until she could see him very clearly. She noted the tightness in the long, sullen face, and the hot sparks in his eyes.

He knew. He had learned about Nathaniel's inquiries. He had possibly discovered the visits to the coastal villages.

"I am sure that you are superb when you investigate, James."

"Better than him."

"Whom did you quiz on my movements? My servants?"

"*My* servants, Charlotte. Not yours. Mine. Just as the house is mine, and the furniture, and the coach." He smiled slyly. "The coachman did not want to tell about your night visit to Albany, but then I reminded him who was lord of that manor."

"So you know of my friendship. I have been very

discreet, and that is no reason to close your door to me, to deny Ambrose—"

"It is not just any friendship, damn it." He shouted suddenly. His fury exploded so unexpectedly that it startled her. "It is one that is disloyal to me, and my dead brother, and even to my son. The bastard has been asking questions about the family. About me." He strode toward her, snarling as he spoke. "Why is he doing it? You know, I'm sure."

She backed up when he reached her. She had never seen James really angry before. He exuded a frightening energy.

She had not intended to lie, but she did now. "I do not know. Surely you misunderstand. He is probably only curious about my relatives."

"Curious enough to ask about my old tutor? That is a lot of curiosity regarding the relatives of a woman he is having his way with."

"If he has been asking questions, I am sure they will stop. Very sure." She tried to look beneath the mask of anger and find the man she knew. "It is cruel of you to separate Ambrose and me because of this. You know the child depends on me. He will never understand if I disappear from his life."

"He is too young to dwell on it. When he is older, I will explain how you traded our love for the cheap pleasure that you found with that scoundrel."

Our love. It was not the words that made her heart pound, but the bitter way he spoke them.

Suddenly another part of the past rearranged itself.

She had never guessed James had those kind of feelings for her. Never suspected that the little family they had formed was all the family he wanted.

If that drove his anger as well as his worry about Nathaniel's inquiries, she doubted she could sway him. She tried anyway.

"I am sorry you are angry, and disappointed in me. Truly, I am. Bar me from this house if you must, but let me see him. Allow his nurse to bring him to me at my house. I cannot bear the thought of losing him, James, and this will break his little heart. You are not so cruel as to require that."

"I am not being cruel. I am being careful with my son's upbringing and character." He turned on his heel and strode away.

At the doorway he stopped and faced her again. A nasty contentment marked his expression. He was glad he had hurt her.

"As for his visiting at your house, you have no house. You live in one that is mine. I have decided that I want to sell it. My solicitor will call and explain it all tomorrow, but you should pack your personal property at once."

He watched her shocked reaction at this last blow and smiled with satisfaction. Then he left her to her dismay.

"He is simply turning you out?" Bianca asked, incredulous.

"My abigail is packing even as we speak." Charlotte

said. She sat down beside Bianca on a patterned settee in Pen's dressing room.

The meeting with the solicitor two hours ago had been just shy of insulting. The man had not only informed her of Mardenford's decree but had quizzed her about the furniture and objects, taking inventory.

If he expected her to haggle, he had been disappointed. She would remove what was hers, clear and free. Later, she would send her own solicitor to embark on the unseemly task of settling the rest.

Rather than watch the packing, she had kept an appointment to meet Bianca at Pen's house to help choose her sister's wedding garments. Pen now stood with a yellow silk dress in her arms. A decision on the dress had been forgotten as soon as Charlotte entered the dressing room and impulsively blurted her news.

"You must come live with us," Bianca said. "At least until you make other arrangements."

"Thank you. I may have to accept but I do not want to. It is not that I question my welcome. I would feel like a girl again, returned to my childhood."

"Nonsense. Pen lived with us for a spell last year and she was not reduced to childlike dependency."

Charlotte caught Pen's eye. They exchanged a tacit acknowledgment of the disagreeable aspects of any dependency.

"Bianca, she is referring to Laclere, not financial matters," Pen said gently. "You know how he can be. I am his older sister and he still wanted to manage and protect. Charl is so much younger and he may not be as . . . accommodating with her."

Bianca turned thoughtful. She gazed down at the pattern on the upholstered seat of the settee and weighed that problem.

"Yes, I can see what you mean. Also, Laclere was very sure of Hampton, but wonders a bit about Mr. Knightridge."

Pen's brow furrowed. "What has Mr. Knightridge to do with this?"

"Oh, he is Charl's lover now."

Pen laughed. "That is a rare joke, Bianca." She began fussing with the yellow dress again. "Charl and Knightridge. Goodness, they can barely stand the sight of each other."

Bianca laughed too, carefully.

Pen laid the dress down. As she turned to the wardrobe for another choice, she shot Charlotte and Bianca a merry glance and grin. The outrageous suggestion of an affair with Nathaniel still amused her.

Charl tried to appear bland. Pen quickly assessed her studied passivity, and then Bianca's wide-eyed innocence.

She froze. Her face fell in shock. "Good heavens, is it true? You have a liaison with Knightridge?"

"I apologize for my indiscretion, Charl," Bianca said. "However, what fun is an affair if your best friends don't know?"

"You told Bianca and did not tell me?" Pen asked, looking hurt.

"I told no one. Bianca is guessing."

"Hardly guessing. It is mere luck that Laclere and I did not walk in and find you—"

"You are still guessing."

"My guess is you do not want to live with us because of what cannot happen there with the discretion you would like. Although midmorning in a library is hardly discreet, if you want my opin—"

"What I would like is to avoid having my big brother lecturing a certain friend on honorable intentions and whatnot. That is inappropriate and unfair."

Pen and Bianca exchanged quick looks.

Pen bit her lower lip, but Bianca had never been known to swallow frank questions. "Unfair? Charl, dear, are you saying there have been discussions regarding honorable intentions?"

"All I have said since entering this room is that I no longer have a house. Now, the problem I face is where I will live tomorrow, and how I will arrange to see Ambrose."

That turned them back to matters of substance.

"You will stay here, of course," Pen said. "In two days I leave for the coast, and when I return I will be living at Russell Square. This is not even a third as grand as your current home, but it has served me well over the years."

"Laclere will continue to maintain it, I am certain," Bianca added.

"I will not need his help. I am not destitute, just homeless at the moment. My settlement contained enough for me to live in style even without Mardenford's assistance."

She considered that assistance again, and how generous it had been. Unusually so. She should have wondered why. She prided herself on being astute, but her ignorance and blind faith in Mardenford's motivations had been unbearably naive.

"Most likely Mardenford plans to remarry," Bianca suggested. "Perhaps his intended wants to be queen, and demands the dowager be thoroughly un-crowned."

"Bianca is probably correct. His refusal to allow you to see the child is peculiar, however," Pen said. "Turning you out with only your personal property, severing you from the child you love—he never ap-peared to be such a harsh man. It is as if he were di-vorcing you."

Pen had no idea how accurate her description was, and how it touched on the reasons for this harshness. The implications left Charlotte a little sick whenever she considered them. Yet another set of memories had taken on new meaning in the last day.

She hoped there would be no more of that. An en-tire decade had been rewritten already.

"I must see Ambrose. I will not accept that part of Mardenford's plan." Not a plan. A punishment. For infidelity and disloyalty. His goal was to make her pay, no matter what the pain and distress to his own son. Already her heart mourned the loss of the child.

A warm hand reached and covered hers. She looked over to see Bianca's sympathy.

"We will find a way for you to see him, Charl. If we put our heads to it, we can devise some plan."

Charlotte hoped so. She had lost much recently, but most of it was in the past. Ambrose was part of her life now. Her heart might learn to accommodate the rest, but the grief forming over the child would never go away.

Nathaniel rode his horse slowly through Hyde Park. It had rained yesterday, so his rare participation in London's fashionable hour had been delayed by a day.

Carriages and horses filled the park. Society was returning to town in preparation of the season. Soon the park would be jammed on fair days, and even busy on those that threatened rain. Much had changed in the rituals in recent years, but not the desire to see and be seen while on parade here.

He greeted and chatted and flattered, as was expected. He avoided the lures of mothers looking to marry off daughters this year, and dodged the bait of ladies casting for amorous diversions. All the while he kept his eyes on the passing coaches, looking for Charlotte's.

A quick note two days ago had requested he meet her in the park yesterday if it did not rain, or today if it did. The weather's delay meant he had already learned the news she would impart. Word had reached his ears that Charlotte was leaving that big house after all these years.

He did not see her until she was almost upon him. She had not come in a coach, but was riding a pretty horse. Fine boned, compact, and spirited, the dark filly's lines matched Charlotte's own.

He moved his horse forward, and they "accidentally" met on the path.

"Lady M., this is an unexpected pleasure. I can see you agree that the day is too fair to be imprisoned in a coach."

"To be sure, Mr. Knightridge. It is also too brisk to be bound to this path. I have been looking for someone foolish enough to ride with me on the sodden fields, and your display of that quality on so many occasions suggests you might do."

"By all means. Lead the way."

"Aren't you afraid that lacking your leadership we will find ourselves in Canterbury? You strike me as someone who would not allow another male to lead, let alone a woman."

"I do not take the lead when I have four in hand, madam, but it is clear who is master on the road all the same."

The occupants of a passing carriage giggled at the sparring. Two nearby riders slowed their pace in order to enjoy the show.

Confident that they had shown society the bristling nature of their relationship, Charlotte turned her horse and cantered off the path and across the field.

She did not stop until they were a good distance from anyone, even if they were still in full view of the world.

"You are better?" he asked as he drew up alongside her and they slowed to a walk.

She had left him after their last night subdued and

thoughtful. He knew that his embrace had not resolved all her fears and questions, however.

"Much better. It will still be some time before I truly accept it all, but I no longer want to hit you. Or him."

"I am glad. However, it was not wise to confront Mardenford with your discovery, Charl."

"I did not confront him. He does not know that I learned about any of it."

"When I heard of your leaving that house, I just assumed—"

"He claimed he wants to sell the house, but that is a feint. He will no longer receive me. He knows about you and me, and that is partly why he has done this. He also knows that you have been asking questions, so our liaison is a special betrayal in his eyes."

He had been feeling guilty, and this added to the burden. "I am sorry, Charl. I was very discreet and am surprised he learned of my inquiries. Perhaps I trusted the wrong men."

"Or perhaps he went looking for evidence of inquiries. He implied as much. He mentioned the tutor. Maybe Mr. Yardley learned of your questions himself, and in turn informed Mardenford."

"Even so, turning you out is a harsh reaction."

"Pen says it is as if he is divorcing me." Her mouth tightened as she said it.

When he did not respond, she shot him a sharp glance. "You knew. You saw it, didn't you?"

"I saw enough to wonder. Nor do I think it is base lust."

"That only makes it worse, and more hopeless. It would help enormously if you had not seen it. Then I could pretend it was not so obvious that I should have seen too. I am feeling stupid again, and recently I have had enough of feeling stupid to last a lifetime."

"It was not obvious. No one whispers about it."

"Then how did you know?"

"It was in his eyes that first time I called on you."

She laughed, and her eyes glinted for the first time this day. "Oh, it feels so good to laugh." She gasped, catching her breath. "I must learn to trust what you see in all those eyes, Nathaniel."

"Despite your laughter, I see pain in yours, Charlotte. A new one."

The glint moistened. She stopped her horse. He paced around so he could face her as they sat side by side.

"In barring me from the house, he has also barred me from Ambrose. This divorce is quite thorough."

He barely bit back a curse. "Mardenford is a scoundrel to do this. You are like the boy's mother. He is sacrificing his child's happiness."

"Yes. It seems he loves his own pride more than his son. That shocks and worries me. I fear that Ambrose will have very little attention now that I am gone."

She contained her sadness, but it was there, brimming at her eyes. He wished they were alone, out of sight, and he could hold her again.

That would solve nothing, however. Once the embrace ended, she would still face the loss of the child she loved like her own. It was their embrace that had cost her that love too.

They sat in silence, surrounded by a brisk breeze carrying the scents of resurrection. The odors of spring mocked the hollow forming in his chest, where the echoes of nostalgia joined the slow, sad beat of a song's final notes.

He knew what he had to do, but a visceral rebellion resisted anyway. His gaze lingered on her face as time pulsed by.

"He will relent about the child, surely. If we end this affair, he will at least change his mind on that." The words felt thick in his mouth.

She did not respond at once. She gazed to the distant path and its parade of the fashionable world. Then she looked in his eyes.

"I considered it."

Of course she had. Any mother would.

"Short of moving to France, I am not sure that I can, however," she added.

Her gaze communicated her affirmation of their passion more clearly than her words. His pride soared at this acknowledgment that the hunger was mutual and impossible to deny, but he wondered if she would soon resent how much it cost her.

"I do not think he would relent, either," she said. "It is not only the insult to his pride, or his affections for me, that caused this rash move. He was very calm until he spoke of your inquiries. Then he became so angry it frightened me. He is worried, Nathaniel. He is so worried, it has made him a different man. What does he fear, that has transformed him so?"

"Perhaps he fears losing something valuable. You alone would qualify."

She shook her head. "He would have left the door ajar, then. He would have given me a way to return. Instead his repudiation is complete. He fears losing something else."

He had decided two nights ago not to contemplate what that something else might be. "Do not dwell on it. Who can know a man's mind in such things? It was probably just jealousy."

"I do not think you believe that."

"Lady M., you are trying to be vexing again, claiming to know what I believe."

She did not pick up the playful cue. "You are try- ing to protect me, Nathaniel, and it is very sweet. You said that the asking and the knowing were over, be- cause you want to spare me. However, I think one more inquiry is necessary."

He stifled a sigh. Whether in the lead or holding the reins, he actually had no control over this woman once her mind started working. "Which one would that be?"

"I want to speak with that tutor."

"No."

She raised her eyebrows at his blunt response. An- other glint, an old one that he knew very well, entered her eyes.

While it would help if she submitted to his dis- plays of mastery, he doubted he would want her so much if she did. He tried a more appeasing tone and refusal.

"I do not think that is wise."

"I do. Can you find him, Nathaniel? Can you learn where he is now?"

"Do not do this, Charlotte. It will change nothing."

"It will answer questions that I cannot live with forever. Even without Mardenford's repudiation, I would have sought that man out. My brother-in-law's fear only makes the mystery bigger, and has me thinking that my new view of the past is not the correct one at all."

He understood her need to know, but he wished she would retreat. He had rejected all the questions, to spare her. She had never requested that compromise, but he had embraced it without a second thought when the weight of the answers landed on her shoulders. Now here she was, forcing it forward against his better judgment.

She gazed at him so earnestly, so honestly. She appeared vulnerable and soft, but the formidable Lady M. still existed beneath the fragility. He saw her determination as well as her confusion.

With him or without him, she was going to speak with that tutor.

"I will find him," he said. "We will listen to his story together."

CHAPTER NINETEEN

~⌇~

It was not such a small wedding. The family alone made for a good group, and friends had traveled down from London as well. They all filled the small church in a town near the coastal property that Julian Hampton owned in Essex.

Charlotte watched the ceremony begin, thinking the simplicity of the setting was appropriate. Not because a grand London affair would have been wrong, and not because of the circumstances of this marriage. If ever God had meant a man and woman to be joined in life, it was Penelope and Julian.

Rather, the quiet nature of the wedding was like their love. The ancient stones of the church symbolized the longevity and faith of their affections.

Pen looked beautiful in the blush dress she had chosen, and Julian was equally handsome. If they had worn rags, however, Charlotte still would have felt the tears burning her throat. Their expressions garbed them in glory such as no clothing could. Pen glowed, and Julian's eyes reflected his triumph and awe that the woman he loved was finally his.

Charlotte was not alone in being moved. Pen and Julian exchanged vows in a church gone silent with emotion.

Charlotte glanced at the men who had stood by Pen's side over the years. Laclere's expression appeared tight, which meant he fought to contain what stirred his heart. Dante, who had left Fleur and the baby at Laclere Park in order to see his sister wed, smiled with contentment that Pen would now know the happiness she deserved.

Another man caught her eye. Not a relative, but much more than a friend. He sat at the side of the church, his dark eyes on the ceremony, his classical profile carving the air and his golden crown marking his spot. One might think him a casual acquaintance from his place in the gathering among the visitors.

He did not appear really engaged in the event. His expression seemed distracted. Was he contemplating his visit to her new home two nights ago? As soon as Pen left for the coast, they had arranged an assignation. There had been no conversation upon his arrival, but instead an immediate rush to bed and a tumultuous passion as they both quenched the mad craving that deepened with every separation.

Perhaps he dwelled on the little journey that would follow this celebration. He had located Mr.

Yardley, the tutor, and when he and she returned to town, it would be by way of Hertfordshire.

She returned her full attention to Pen and Julian. Suddenly Mardenford's words came back to her. *Bad blood wins out eventually.* No doubt he would see this marriage that way, as Pen displaying the Duclaircs' propensity for behavior less than acceptable.

She found herself smiling. Mardenford was right. Her family did have that tendency, and always had. But it had led her sister and her brothers to happiness that exceeded what most others knew. There was no doubt about the soul-stirring love shared by her sister and Hampton as they were bound by law. It affected the air and the light and gathered everyone inside its awesome power.

She looked at Pen and Julian with new eyes. How courageous they were. Not in refusing to conform, but in their complete love for each other. How brave to show another your naked heart and soul and embrace the danger as well as the joy. What occurred between naked bodies was a small thing in comparison.

She felt a stirring within the emotion-laden atmosphere. She looked to its source, and found Nathaniel watching her.

His gaze communicated more than memories of their recent assignation. There were depths and questions in his eyes that she could not read, but she knew they had to do with her. With the two of them, and what waited within their passion.

———

The wedding breakfast was simple but elegant. Nathaniel assumed that Bianca, Viscountess Laclere, had a hand in that.

The party gathered at tables set in the rustic, white-washed rooms of the coastal house that Hampton owned. The scent and sounds of the sea flowed in the open windows. The weather proved fair, as if heaven chose to favor the reason for the celebration.

Hothouse flowers joined native greenery in forcing the season's images by a month, and servants brought down from London cooked and served, making do with a kitchen never intended for such a fete. There was no attempt to transfer the formalities of a London wedding to this site. Instead it took the tone of an elegant country party being held in Tuscany or Provence.

Nathaniel discovered that his place was next to Charlotte's, at the main table that stretched through the sitting room overlooking the sea. They were seated across from the Duchess of Everdon and the financier Daniel St. John.

"I am honored," he said to Charlotte as he took his seat. She looked beautiful today. In that sapphire dress, she was a cool lake into which he longed to plunge.

Charlotte glanced toward her sister-in-law, Bianca. "She knows. I assume she approves, if she placed you here. Laclere must not mind too much if he did not object."

"That is a relief. I would not want him minding *too* much." He had received a speculative glance or two from Laclere since arriving at the wedding. "Lady Laclere has been indiscreet, I think. I suspect she has told your entire family and your closest friends." There had been additional quizzical looks from most of them. Right now the Duchess of Everdon was assessing him very critically from the other side of the table.

"We have such a contentious history that they find this friendship odd. Everyone is surprised." She laughed. "Even me."

He tilted his head so he could speak lowly. "I am not. That party was not the first time I desired you. You provoked me during that history in many ways, Charlotte. Perhaps the passionate provocations in turn provoked the history itself."

"Perhaps so, for both of us."

It was a strange moment to admit to each other that their little battles had been a way to hide other irritations. The ceremony, the fair day, even the joy filling the house made it easy, however.

She had a right to know his interest was not entirely recent, but he had never expected her to let him know the same thing.

She smiled impishly. "Now that the first provocation is satisfied, perhaps the others will eventually disappear."

"I hope not. How dull. I think you will always provoke me in all kinds of ways. After all, you know my game, just as I know yours. It is disconcerting to be so thoroughly comprehended by another. It is also very . . . compelling."

A sweet smile softened her countenance so much it bordered on indiscreet. "Most compelling, Nathaniel. Also a bit frighening. Like being on the brink of a cliff."

She looked in his eyes, and the party faded away for a moment. Her gaze shifted, first to Laclere and Bianca, then to Dante, and finally to Pen and Hampton.

"I realized something today, Nathaniel. There are no neat fits to these things. No smooth roads. A bridge does not appear suddenly to take you forward when you reach a chasm. One either retreats to safety, or one jumps and trusts the stride is long enough. I am thinking that I retreated too quickly, and too often, in the past."

The party intruded again, demanding their attention. He forced the necessary smiles, and joined in conversation with St. John. All the while most of his thoughts dwelled on the woman by his side, and her startling admission of the brink to which their affair had led her.

He pretended to hear something the duchess was saying, but he angled his head so he could whisper into Charlotte's ear.

"Jump with me."

Most of the wedding guests left by midafternoon. Finally, the family began taking their leave as well.

Charlotte strolled out to the terrace that overlooked the sea.

Jump with me. It was an astonishing invitation. A frightening one.

At the sound of a step, she looked behind her. It was not Nathaniel. Laclere had followed. He came to her side.

"This property is beautiful, isn't it?" she said, breathing the sea air deeply.

"Handsome and private and just a little wild, much like its owner," he said.

She laughed at the apt characterization of Pen's new husband. They enjoyed the view in silence while the vague sounds of final departures leaked from the house and the front drive.

"He asked me to marry him," she said. "Nathaniel did. It was out of obligation, of course. I refused."

"Obligation? What obligation?"

"That doesn't matter. I just wanted you to know that he did offer."

"That was very decent of him, I expect."

"Yes, it was."

"If you say so. I wouldn't know, since I have not heard the story behind this obligation."

Nor would he. Ever.

They watched a few more waves crash against the seawall beneath them.

"I will not be returning to London with you," she said. She had ridden down from town in Laclere's coach, with Bianca and Dante.

He did not respond. She turned her attention to his harshly chiseled profile. His piercing blue eyes did not show disapproval, just thoughts that made him look serious.

"I will be making a short journey before returning to town," she said.

"That explains the extra portmanteau. I trust you are not traveling alone. Did you tell me he had proposed so I would not object?"

"In part. You are not going to embarrass me by talking to him about it, are you?"

"Bianca asked the same thing. How did I acquire a reputation for doing such things?"

"Perhaps by being overbearing on occasion, especially when we all were younger. Also you look at him as though you disapprove."

"So Knightridge has been waiting for me to stick my nose into your affair, has he?" He chuckled. "I neither approve nor disapprove, Charl. I am merely surprised. It is not disapproval he sees when I look at him, but astonishment."

"Because we do not like each other?"

"Because you have favored no man all these years, even though half of London would have pursued you if given the slightest encouragement."

He spoke casually, as if they agreed on his observation. In truth, she thought it was a peculiar thing for him to say.

"I did not notice half of London waiting to pursue me. I did not even notice a tiny corner of London interested in doing so."

"Didn't you? Well, it appears that is over, and I am glad for it. You grieved longer than most, but you are at long last yourself again. If Knightridge finally drew you out of mourning, I have no quarrel with him."

He appeared relaxed and conversational. He had no idea he kept saying the most extraordinary things.

"I was not in mourning. I did not grieve long at all. I resumed my duties and my life faster than most."

Her firm tone surprised him. He studied her face with curious, concerned eyes. "Perhaps you would have done better to wail and get sick from it, Charl. If you have not been grieving these last years, what do you call it? What is the word given to the state that causes a young widow to not even notice for six years that other men want her?"

Had she been mourning? Was that the name for the even, dulled emotions of those years? If so, had she been mourning Philip, or the safety and comfort she had found with him?

The house had quieted behind them. She pictured Bianca watching them through the window, and Pen and Julian occupying Nathaniel.

She should let Vergil go, but it had been a long time since they had spoken like this, honestly and in confidence. Not since before her marriage, now that she thought about it. Not since the day when he had asked her if she truly wanted the man who asked for her hand.

The memory of that conversation came to her quite vividly. Vergil asked the same question in five different ways, as if he thought she did not understand it. He explained in detail how the family finances were much improved and there was no need to marry at all her first season, let alone grab the first proposal.

"Vergil, did you think it odd that I accepted Philip?"

He considered the question. Or else he considered whether to answer it at all. "A little. He was a good man, from a good family, but very sedate. You were brighter than he. Smarter, and far more spirited. I concluded his solidity appealed to you after all the disasters we had been through. Also, he could give you the unquestioned place in society that had been lost to us."

"Did you believe he loved me?"

His gaze pierced her. A subtle frown creased his brow.

"He did not speak of it to me, Charl. Not beyond expressing his high esteem of you, and his affections." He glanced to the house. Nathaniel's blond head was visible through the window. "Let me say, however, that such love manifests itself in many different ways. It is as varied as human nature. It is like music, I think. Some is loud and full of contrast and drama, but the simpler melodies still are meaningful."

It was sweet of him to try to help her reconcile how the current loud drama confused the memory of the quiet melody. He did not know that she suspected Philip had known deafening music himself, just with someone else.

She stretched up and kissed his cheek. "Bianca

must grow impatient. We should all depart, and give Pen her privacy."

They joined the others. With cheerful confusion the last of the party headed to the front of the house, where the carriages waited.

Dante strolled beside her and Nathaniel, asking about events in town. When Nathaniel bid farewell, however, she peeled away with him instead of following Dante to Laclere's coach.

She entered the carriage and peered out the window. Dante still stood on the drive, looking in her direction with surprise.

Vergil and Bianca emerged from the house and passed him. Still glancing toward Nathaniel's carriage in befuddlement, Dante fell into step.

His complaint carried to Charlotte on the breeze. "I am always the last in this family to learn anything."

"You were down at Laclere Park," Vergil said.

"You say that like I was in China. Someone could have written." The carriage door closed on him. "Charl and Knightridge?"

"I fear meeting him," she admitted that night. She and Nathaniel ate supper in a small, private room at a large coaching inn near Hertford. They had taken two chambers for the night, but Nathaniel had given false names. Married names.

Jump with me. If she did, what would it mean? A brief, intense love affair of the heart, or a more permanent alliance?

She had practiced with the idea of marriage on the ride here, imagining the day-to-day living with this man. It had been a startling experiment that provoked wonder and mystery. All she knew for certain was it would not be like the last time.

"You do not have to meet with Yardley. I advised against it," he said. "We will depart for London at once in the morning. Or I will speak with him alone."

He had turned her worry into retreat very quickly. "I cannot permit that. It would be cowardly of me. Also, I do not think you would tell me everything."

"You think I would lie?" He scowled deeply enough for the patrons in the last aisle of a theater to see.

"I think that you would tell me the truth, just not the whole truth."

He puffed up. "I am insulted."

She laughed at his theatrics. "No, you are not. It is your kindness that would make you choose which truth I hear, Nathaniel. I would wager that already there are some things you know or suspect but that I have not heard."

"No truths have been withheld."

"Mere speculations, only?"

The actor melted into the man. "I speculate a lot and am often wrong. Such speculations led us into this mystery, to my regret."

"Not wrong ones, unfortunately."

The air got heavy with the truths those speculations had revealed. A little squeeze in her heart reminded her that while she was no longer numb, and she no longer raved, it would be some time before her essence did not grimace when reminded of the shock.

His hand lay on the table mere inches from hers. A strong hand, masculine and handsome. Just seeing it conjured up sensations of the way he caressed her body, and how quickly she submitted to the exciting power his touch cast.

The lamp glow made his eyes very dark and his face very handsome. He gazed at her with the all-seeing warmth he so often displayed now, so different from the provoking amusement of the past. Or maybe not different at all. Perhaps the warmth had always been there, subtly, but she was too self-absorbed to notice. Or too cowardly to risk her dull peace for the turmoil that his gaze incited.

"After the truths of the past are discovered, we need to face the truths of the present," he said. "You risk much with this affair. I am no prize, but I would like to marry you. I would like to do so as our choice, and not in a rush when you find yourself with child."

It was a calm little speech, quietly and casually spoken. The servant standing near the fireplace would never guess it had included a proposal, and so much more.

She slid her hand over his. "I am flattered, Nathaniel. Truly so. However, since you are serious, I am bound to tell you that there is some question whether I will ever find myself with child."

He barely reacted, but a subtle surprise affected his expression. "He was ill for most of your marriage, Charl."

"I told myself later it was the illness beginning, or that whatever problem existed was not with me. I always knew there might be another explanation, however. Now there is a boy in Durham who proves it was not any lack in my husband."

"I believe you are wrong. If time proves you are not, that is how it will be. This is not about begetting an heir. And, since others will whisper, let me emphasize that it is also not about obtaining your fortune."

"We both know that if you wanted a fortune, an estate waits for you that requires much less disruption to your life than taking on a wife." Alluding to that caused a jolt in her heart. "Oh, my. If we discover that Harry's mother was indeed married to Philip, a marriage to me will close that path to you forever. A man of the Church could not have a wife stained by the scandal of bigamy, even if the fault were not mine in any way."

His response was a knowing smile. "I thank you for clarifying the cost, Lady M."

"You should have waited to make this proposal," she said, distressed by the implications that had not been foreseen. "You should have seen what transpired tomorrow first. You have said that you believe there was no lawful marriage, but—"

"Should you marry me, Charlotte, I will take great pleasure in laying down a few laws. The first will be that you do not tell me what I should do, or whom or what I should protect."

His scold left her chagrined. Of course he had

seen all the eventualities and costs, long before she had.

He spoke more gently. "I do not care what is learned tomorrow. I will not allow the truths of another man's past to create the truths of my future. I know it is harder for you, and I do not expect an answer now. I am only making my intentions plain so you do not doubt my loyalty or misunderstand the nature of my interest."

It was an astonishing declaration. An enormous commitment. He would stand by her no matter what was learned, and what scandal resulted. Her entire past might become the subject of gossip and public investigations, but she could anchor herself to his strength through it all.

His hand had turned, and he was holding hers. A sweet, wonderful ache filled her chest.

She could not answer until she knew what they faced. She had to do her own weighing once she saw all the costs. Until then, until tomorrow, she would not deny the profound emotions saturating her, however.

As always, he understood. He knew exactly what she was thinking, she did not doubt it.

"Shall we retire, madam?" He spoke almost formally, but his gaze said so much more. The whisper from the afternoon was in his eyes, seducing her to much more than pleasure.

Jump with me.

She both thrilled with and cringed from the

sensation of being poised on the brink of an unknown space, whose mist promised both wonder and danger.

They walked up the stairs in silence. She felt him behind her, benign in step and manner but not entirely in spirit. A caution, such as she had experienced the first night in Elmcrest, slid through her. The difference was that her vulnerability was not physical or sensual this time.

A loss waited in the mist as well as a gain. She had forever been separate, even in her prior, peaceful love. She had only relinquished a part of her essence to little Ambrose, not to any man.

It made her shy suddenly, that aura of decision behind her. For all their comprehension of each other, for all their knowledge of each other's games and each other's bodies, she became more virginal than she had ever been. Giving one's favors was one thing. Giving one's heart was another. Giving oneself was fearsome. She did not know if she had the courage for that ultimate selflessness.

She did not look at him when the door closed on the chamber. While he lit two lamps, she began unfastening her dress. He came up behind her and helped. His vitality encompassed her even though his hands barely touched as he tended to these practical matters.

She closed her eyes to both fight and absorb his energy, but it stirred all her senses and intuitions, provoking again the instinctive sense of danger that he had always called forth, and that had given rise to every other sort of provocation in turn.

"I am afraid of you," she said, admitting to herself what these reactions had always meant. "I am afraid of how I respond to you, and what it might mean."

He turned her around so he could see her face. "And I am a little afraid of you. But not enough, anymore."

He continued to undress her, his fingers calm and firm on the hooks and ribbons. His confidence unnerved her. *Jump with me.* He had made his decision, but she still experienced a visceral wariness.

Loud, dramatic music, Vergil had called great passion. He had also been describing Nathaniel the man. Such men drowned out the people around them with their mere presence. One had to struggle to avoid becoming a mere echo of their symphonies.

She barely knew who she was anymore. Revelations and new emotions kept remodeling her like so much pliable clay. If she allowed herself to love him, fully love him, she might lose any clear distinction. She might become a girl again, unformed and vague.

She stopped fumbling with her garments and allowed him to finish. He swept away her dress and petticoats, and released her stays. Sly fingers skimmed her drawers over her hips and they fell to her feet. She stepped out of them, wearing only her hose.

He embraced her from behind and the submersion became physical. That helped. His embrace had always defeated her hesitations. His physical strength comforted in ways his presence did not.

His embrace also aroused her more. She had been excited all day, all week—a long time, actually. Long before they ever found common ground, she knew now.

His hands moved wonderfully over her breasts and down her stomach. Warm, slow strokes caused her to sink against him. Into him.

"You are beautiful, Charl." His palms circled her breasts, sending luscious shivers down her stomach to her vulva. "You haunt me, day and night. I do not want to scheme at having you. I do not want the calculation and the deception."

Neither did she. Right now she did not want anything except his hands on her every day. That is what he did to her.

She turned and helped him, as he had helped her. Impatient now, the familiar craving beckoning, she plucked at his shirt buttons while he shed coats and cravat. She almost rent the linen to get to his warmth. When his chest was finally bare, she laid her cheek against it to feel him and smell him and hear his heartbeat.

He held her. Enclosed her, and his wrapping arms were a physical reminder of all the enclosures he might cause.

She assessed the incredible comfort she felt, and also the alarming excitement. A poignant sweetness drenched her. She pressed her hands and lips to his skin. Her heart smiled at her confusion and spoke its silent words.

She loved him. That was what this was, this lovely

ache in her chest. She looked up to find him gazing down, waiting. Soulful trust poured through her, as it had at that party and so often since. He might know her game, he might know she was helpless against all of his strengths, but he would never use them against her.

She could not help smiling, almost laughing. Her heart had already jumped. She only had to admit it, and allow her mind and will to follow.

She wondered what it was like to make love to the man with whom you shared both love and earth-shaking passion.

Her fingers sought the closure on his trousers so she could find out.

They made quick work of his garments, and their next embrace was all skin on skin. Her hands moved slowly over the hard lines and taut strength of his body. Pride of possession tinged her pleasure. Love gave her rights greater than any law's.

He carried her to the bed and laid her down. "Muslin and a lumpy mattress," he said as he joined her.

"It could be a rocky beach and I would not care tonight." She could not stop smiling. The sweet ache inside her had turned to joy. "I had no idea there were choices in these things, Nathaniel."

He covered her with his body, his skin warming her length and starting a hundred little happy shivers. He rested his weight on his forearms so he could look at her. "What choices have you made, Charlotte?"

She hesitated only a moment. Trust conquered her

shyness. "I suppose I chose to admit to myself that I love you, Nathaniel."

"As I love you, Charl." His gaze carried the old amusement along with a beautiful warmth. "We have done this backwards, haven't we? First a bond of the spirit, then one of pleasure and passion, then declarations of love. Perhaps, in the future, vows of marriage. It normally goes the other way."

"I think I have enjoyed our way better."

"For us, perhaps it was the right way, if it brings us here now." He kissed her so sweetly her heart sighed. "I would not have wanted to wait on your choices to have you. I might have waited forever then." His kisses sought her neck and shoulders. "However, I am glad for your choice, Charlotte. This is too right to deny what it is."

Very right, and so beautiful. He seemed to feel the new power within the passion, just as she did. His hands moved over her body very slowly and deliberately, wringing every emotional nuance out of the sweet pleasure. His mouth praised as much as aroused when his tongue teased at her nipples and his lips gently drew on her breasts. She held him to her then, her fingers stretched through the hair on his crown, while euphoria joined the desire that claimed her mind and body.

The passion could not be contained, but it never eclipsed the love. She lost herself in both, but the part of her that relinquished itself to love would never be reclaimed. She sensed that even as it happened. They both gave and took in that sharing, trading parts of their souls so they would be forever linked.

There were no erotic games this time. He took her like the virgin she had been on entering this chamber, his desire waiting for her at each step. She realized there had been love within the pleasure before, potent but unnamed. The power of this passion had always come from its seeds and growth.

The pleasure was sweet, but soon it would not do. It was not enough. She reached down and closed her hand on his phallus, near its base. She guided him to her, so he would fill her.

He looked down at her. Everything was in his gaze. She had never seen so much before. The essential things about this man, about the two of them, were visible.

He returned to her embrace. She held him during the long, beautiful union. His strength dominated her small size completely and his thrusts claimed new rights unmistakably, but she felt no threat and no loss. She absorbed him just as he entered her, and their comprehension of each other became complete.

They did not speak afterward. She felt no need to tell him how she had been moved. He knew, she was sure, just as she knew what was in his heart. His embrace was as encompassing as his spirit, holding her close as he fell asleep.

She looked into the night while snuggled in the security he gave. She understood much now, far more than he guessed. She suspected she knew why he had proposed today, why he wanted his intentions made clear. She understood why he did not want her meeting with Yardley in the morning, and why he had so quickly compromised when the inquiries touched on her life.

Love could be senseless in its desire to protect. Senseless and selfless. He did not count the cost to himself, and she would not count the cost to herself either.

She turned in his arms so she inhaled his breath and felt his skin on her cheek. Another choice was coming, about that proposal. Her love would make the decision easy, inevitable, even if it led to a new grieving that would never end.

CHAPTER
TWENTY

⌒

"If you are determined, then let us do it now."
Nathaniel rose and offered his hand. He had spent
the last hour gently trying to dissuade Charlotte from
calling on Yardley, to no avail.

It was not that he feared her learning the truth. He
merely did not want her *hearing* the truth. Yardley
could end up being like those witnesses in trials who
dithered and meandered in giving the facts, and
ended up revealing irrelevant, unwelcome, and damaging details amidst their verbal excess.

He would like to believe his love would make all
discoveries insignificant, but he had no secure confidence about that.

She took his hand. Her eyes and smile said that
she knew he wanted to protect her and she appreciated it. However, she would never let him shield her
the way he wanted. His soft little Charlotte could still
be the vexing Lady M.

The carriage waited outside the inn. Once it began moving, he explained the plan he had concocted in order to control events somewhat. "I will ask him the questions. If you do, he may try to dissemble."

"Are you saying I should be seen but not heard?" Her tone, while pleasant enough, carried a sardonic note that he chose to ignore.

"Exactly. Be there if you must. Listen to your heart's content, but I will direct the conversation."

Her mouth pursed with amusement. "You do not lose any time laying down those laws you spoke of yesterday. I am too besotted from last night to mention that it is premature to attempt such mastery of me. I will agree to your direction, but only because you are an expert at asking questions, and will no doubt do it better than I would."

He doubted any attempts at mastery would be well timed or very successful. He looked forward to having the right to try, however. It promised to be as much fun as their prior skirmishes had been, but with much more pleasurable truces.

They entered a large village five miles west of Hertford. As they drove down the main lane, Charlotte peered out the window at the thatched roofs and cross-timbers that they passed.

"What a charming and picturesque place. Is this our destination?"

"Yardley is the vicar of the church here."

"He has done well for himself. How did a tutor come to such a living?"

She *would* have to ask. "The living is controlled

by Mardenford. I assume once the young men were grown, it was arranged to give their tutor this income."

"I do not recall seeing anything in Philip's letters about this. Indeed, the few I did see from Mr. Yardley were not posted from this village. On the rare occasions that Philip mentioned him, it was not even by name. He was 'my tutor'—a servant from the past and not a fond old friend."

So much for controlling events today. He hoped he would have more compliance from Yardley. "He received the living later, from James."

She did not say that was odd, but a woman too clever by half would see that it was. There was the small chance she had been so well pleasured and loved last night that she was not thinking straight. That would be convenient.

"When did James give him the living? How long ago?"

Damn. "Four or five years, I believe. Soon after James inherited the title. No doubt he thought his brother should have provided for Yardley better, and rectified matters."

"Perhaps."

The carriage stopped. He handed her down and they approached the vicarage door.

The housekeeper took his card away, then returned to escort them to a little drawing room. It was too early to be making calls, but it appeared Yardley would receive them. Nathaniel assumed that meant Yardley knew who Nathaniel Knightridge was and what he might want. Which in turn suggested that Mardenford had been in communication with the tutor. If so, that would make this harder.

Charlotte waited calmly, perched on her wooden chair, exuding the formidable presence that far exceeded her size. She was not at all too besotted to think straight. He doubted she would miss the implications of every word spoken today.

Love and pride momentarily distracted *him*. He would forever thank heaven she had been so rash and so bold as to attend that sinful party.

Yardley entered the drawing room abruptly, as if he had paused in the wings to compose himself first. His long gray hair, receding at the brow, and his spectacles initially made him appear older than he was. A smooth oval face and spry step suggested he had barely passed his fortieth year.

He beamed exaggerated welcome and pleasant curiosity. Nathaniel recognized him at once as a fellow actor. This would be interesting.

"How can I be of service to you, Mr. Knightbridge?"

"Knightridge." The mistake with his name had been a nice, befuddled touch. "This is Charlotte, Lady Mardenford. You once served as tutor to her late husband, the sixth Baron Mardenford."

Yardley advanced on her with sympathy and deference. "I am undone to meet you. Your husband was a dear pupil of mine and, dare I presume to say, a dear friend."

"I am sure he would not have considered it a presumption. He spoke very highly of you."

Her warm acceptance of his greeting encouraged him. He sat nearby, as if he had found an ally.

Nathaniel did not sit at all. Donning his courtroom demeanor, he moved close enough so he would tower above Yardley. "We apologize for the intrusion, but Lady Mardenford has learned of events in the past that trouble her, and she desires some information."

Yardley cocked his head at her. "Events? Information? I am sorry, but I cannot imagine—"

"I think you can," she said.

An awkward moment pulsed. Nathaniel let Yardley contemplate just how awkward.

"There is no delicate way to broach this. The lady has cause to think that as a young man, while on his grand tour, her husband formed an alliance with a Spanish woman. She would like to learn what you know of this."

Yardley displayed true dismay this time. He may have been warned that a man named Knightridge had inquired about an old tutor, but he evidently had not been informed about the reason. That meant that Mardenford was not sure of the inquiry's purpose either.

He is afraid of something. Charlotte's observation repeated in Nathaniel's head. If not revelations about events in Spain, then what? The pit of his stomach soured as he tried to ignore the question.

Yardley bent toward Charlotte with great concern

and appeasement. "Madam, you say you have some cause to think. Surely you have misunderstood or—"

"*Good* cause, Mr. Yardley," she said firmly. "Not some cause. Good cause. You knew of this alliance. I have seen a letter from you that indicates you did."

His attempts to retreat into startled ignorance broke down. Mouth tight and brow furrowed, he suddenly looked much older. Old and worried.

"May I inquire what you think you know?" he tried.

Nathaniel commanded his attention. "We would prefer if you simply told us what *you* know."

Yardley stared sightlessly at the carpet, then glanced at Charlotte. His face flushed. He looked at Nathaniel helplessly. "Sir, the lady . . ."

"Mr. Yardley, I regret if my presence unsettles you, but I must hear all," Charlotte said. "Whatever you reveal can be no worse than my imagination's fears."

"I know very little, actually."

Nathaniel's patience began to ebb. "Mr. Yardley, we can hold these discussions among ourselves, informally, or official inquiries can be initiated. These concerns touch on a title, and if necessary the whole matter can be given over to the House of Lords."

The vicar's face drained of color. He peered over to see if Nathaniel was serious. Nathaniel glared back more resolve than he felt.

The man shrank, folding into his chair as if half the air had left his body. "It was not a typical grand tour. My fault there. I take full responsibility." The last was said to Charlotte. "Once we left England, I proposed that we alter the itinerary, and visit some adventurous spots along with the cultural centers. They were both so staid, you see. So...boring." He reddened and his eyes begged Charlotte's forgiveness. "Philip agreed, and James did not mind, so we circled the Mediterranean. It was wonderful, the colors and contrasts..."

He drifted off into a private reverie. Nathaniel called him back. "You ended in Spain?"

"Yes. Full circle then. Their civil war was localized. It came and went, so to speak, and we thought to make a quick visit, a few weeks, then sail home. Unfortunately, it flared up while we were there. Not only did it become difficult to find passage out, but there were other...developments." He grimaced at Charlotte again.

"Do not compromise the truth for my sake," she said.

"Who was she?" Nathaniel asked.

"Her name was Isabella Zafra, the daughter of a middling landowner. Unfortunately, her brother had revolutionary ideas that put her at risk. Philip formed an...infatuation for her. He did not want to leave her to an uncertain fate. He devised a plan to get her out."

"Marriage?"

"Not a real one," Yardley hastened to say. "She was Catholic, and only such unions are legal there. He was not. By being less than forthcoming regarding his station and religion, there could be a ceremony that would permit her to leave as his wife, when in fact she really was not." He smiled hopefully. "The small deception seemed minor in light of the goal. We truly feared for her life."

"Except such a marriage would be legal," Nathaniel said. "If legal in the locale in which it occurred, even here—"

"It would not have been legal there. One cannot marry under false pretenses in any Church. He said he was a Catholic, Mr. Knightridge. He did not reveal he was heir to the title. I am not even sure he used his correct family name. A sympathetic country priest did the deed. I do not even know if proper records were made."

Nathaniel kept most of his attention on Charlotte, looking for evidence she was convinced. Yardley could spin any tale so long as it did not distress her more.

"The passage was obtained. We were set to go. The night before our sailing she disappeared, leaving a note saying she was going inland to bring back her mother to accompany us and would return by noon. Philip had taken ill—the first time his later sickness manifested itself—so James went after her. We waited, poised to flee. James returned many hours later, right before the ship was to sail. Alone. There had been fighting at their property. The government was searching for the brother. She had been killed in the gunfire."

"James saw this?" Nathaniel asked.

He shook his head. "He heard the guns. A servant running away told him. We thought her dead. Later,

Philip sought confirmation. Like you, he wanted assurance that marriage might not have some legal validity. I assured him not, but..."

"But you are not a canon lawyer, nor qualified to say," Charlotte noted. "Did this woman think the marriage was valid, Mr. Yardley? Did she understand the plan?"

"We explained it clearly," he said.

"You were asked to make further inquiries some years later." Nathaniel repositioned himself as he spoke. He moved so that he faced Yardley squarely and could see his face, and his eyes, very clearly.

"Philip asked it of me when he contemplated marriage. For obvious reasons, he desired discretion. I corresponded with some friends visiting Spain, and asked them to look into her whereabouts. I learned she was indeed dead. That ended it." His gaze shifted here and there, but finally met Nathaniel's. His suddenly confident expression almost masked his thoughts. Almost. This actor wasn't quite good enough, however.

"She was not dead. She came to England five years ago. Did you know this?"

The vicar's face went blank. It was supposed to look like shock and disbelief. "Good heavens! That is impossible."

"She came. She is dead now, but she was not when you made your inquiries."

"I am truly undone. You astonish me. I am sure you must be wrong."

Nathaniel studied Charlotte. She appeared to

accept the story as told. She believed there had been a sham marriage to save the life of the young woman. She did not see the dissembling. Perhaps she did not want to.

"You are satisfied, madam?"

She rose to her feet. "I am, Mr. Knightridge. Thank you for your time, Mr. Yardley. I am glad to have met my husband's old friend, who showed him some adventure and helped him attempt to save a damsel in distress."

Yardley flustered under her attention and praise. Relaxed now, confidently so, he accompanied them outside and saw them off in their carriage.

Fifty yards down the lane, Charlotte called for the carriage to stop. She emerged from deep thought. "He was lying, wasn't he?"

Nathaniel exhaled a small sigh. Sometimes he wished she were just a little bit dimmer. "He was not lying."

"Then he was being careful in the truths he revealed."

"Charl—"

"There was a child. There was a woman who called herself Mrs. Marden, and who thought her child had claims. Mr. Yardley would not want to speak of such in front of me. He would not want to be indelicate when it no longer mattered. She thought she was married, however, even if she was not. I am quite sure of that."

"She spoke a different language. At worst, it was a misunderstanding."

"Jenny said she spoke English well enough."
Charlotte reached for a book that she kept in the carriage to read on long rides. "I will wait here while you return and ask him about it."

She settled in with her book. He experienced a wave of irritation, full of all the provocations she had ever caused.

"Charlotte, there are times like this when I want nothing more than to turn you over my knee."

She did not even look up. "Would that arouse you, Nathaniel?"

"*Jesus*, Charl."

She shot him a far too knowing look. "I see. You want it for more than excitement. You are vexed with me. Is it because I have told you what to do, or because I know that you intended to speak privately with him at some point anyway? Really, darling, there is no reason to make another journey. You may as well deal with it now."

Lord have mercy, the woman was going to drive him mad. He jumped out of the carriage and strode up the lane.

"He is in the garden, sir."

Nathaniel pushed past the housekeeper. "I will go to him. I forgot to give him a message entrusted in my care."

He was in no mood for formalities and niceties. He *had* intended to return at some point and have this conversation, damn it. Probably. Most likely. If he was going to have it now, he wanted to be done with it.

He found his way to the garden. Yardley sat on an iron bench in the midst of naturalistically arranged plantings of bushes and branches aching to bud. His eyes were closed and his face raised to the sky. He did not sleep, Nathaniel was certain. He appeared to be a man composing himself, searching for internal stillness.

Yardley did not hear the approach until Nathaniel was almost upon him. His eyes flashed open. Awareness. Caution. Fear. It was all there, plainly this time, before the actor could collect himself.

Nathaniel grabbed the shoulder of his coat and hauled him to his feet. "Come with me. This way." He pushed Yardley to the far end of the garden, to a wall obscured by a tall hedge.

He threw Yardley up against the wall. "Now you will tell me the rest."

Yardley tried to sink into the stone. He sputtered with indignation and objections. Nathaniel lost his patience.

"This living was late coming to you. It is a handsome one too. Very handsome for a tutor. You received it near the time that woman came from Spain. Not from Philip, but from his brother."

Yardley started crumbling. Shrinking. His fear smelled. He glanced around as if trapped, or worried someone might overhear. Nathaniel did nothing to reassure him. He stepped yet closer, so his size dwarfed the man.

"Isabella Zafra thought she was truly married. Tell me why."

"His honor," he croaked. The first words made it easier, like a blockage had dislodged. He inhaled deeply. "The night of that Catholic marriage, she went to him. A wedding night. He was an honorable man, but—well, he was young and infatuated and—the next morning, he demanded I perform another ceremony, an Anglican one. His sense of honor demanded it, since he had—they had—"

"You had taken orders already?"

He nodded. "I was ordained right after completing my studies. A position as a curate waited for me, but after several years it was given to another. So I took a position as a tutor."

"It was a legal ceremony then."

Yardley looked miserable. "I do not know! There were two witnesses, but local people and who knows if they even understood what they signed. James refused to witness or be present."

Of course he refused. He did not want to be the proof should this marriage ever be repudiated by his brother.

"I never registered the marriage." Yardley sounded desperate to make light of it all. "She was dead, the whole matter was full of ambiguities and—even the license was nothing more than a document drawn up by me as best I could, with their signatures."

"Where is that document?"

"I burned it."

Nathaniel looked over his shoulder, at the garden and handsome house. He reached over and fingered the edge of Yardley's silk cravat. "No, you did not. Or if you did, Mardenford does not think so. You have let him believe you still have it. You are blackmailing him."

"Blackmail! How dare—I have never demanded a penny—"

"Then you have a partnership. Or he has seduced your morals. He sees to your welfare and comfort with this living, to ensure your conscience does not lead you to something foolish. If your silence is this expensive, you must know about the boy."

"Boy? What boy? I know nothing about—"

"When I referred to an inquiry by the House of Lords, you knew what I meant. The title could only be in question if Philip had a son, unknown but legitimate."

Yardley's eyes widened in horror. He reddened. Nathaniel let him absorb his position for a ten count, then stepped back, physically untrapping him.

He did not want this man intimidated and cowering, but instead amenable to interrogation. He altered his stance to one less towering and lowered his voice to a friendlier tone.

"I will learn all of it. I am close already. You knew about the boy, which means James told you. He could only know because Isabella wrote to him when she arrived in England. It must have been a shock for both of you."

Yardley relaxed a little. He closed his eyes and

vaguely shook his head. "You cannot imagine the distress. He put her off, of course. Explained how it had been. I suggested he give her a little money, since the boy—it seemed only right. He refused to believe it was his brother's son. A by-blow of another man, he said. He refused to acknowledge what had happened or that he had any responsibility for her or the boy. He told her to go away."

"She did not go away, however. She continued writing for almost a year."

"It sounds as if you know more than enough and have nothing else to learn. Leave me in peace. I did nothing wrong. My role was small and long ago. I have told you all I know."

Nathaniel doubted that. He looked away, to a distant boxwood hedge along the eastern wall of the garden. Succulent green shoots rowed its bottom, as bulbs pushed up their leaves.

Did he want to know the rest? This had been enough to appease Charlotte. She could live with this story. Her husband had shown honor in a way, and that old alliance had been formed under extraordinary circumstances.

He could walk out of this garden now, and leave the final questions unanswered. Or he could ask the questions that might reveal truths that could not be ignored and that would bring Charlotte more pain and massive scandal.

His need to know had led to a horrible place. All he had to show for it was a history to give Harry, and a dreadful decision.

Yardley shifted his weight. Nathaniel glanced at the movement. Without choosing to, his gaze landed right on Yardley's eyes. On them, and in them.

The truth flickered out at him. It was visible beneath the relief now that Yardley's guard was down. Unmistakably there.

In that instant, the choice to walk away still ignorant, to never know, was lost.

"You met her," he said. "When he arranged to see her that day near the Thames, he brought you with him. He wanted a man of God to explain why she had no claims. You know what happened there. You saw it all."

Desperation replaced relief in Yardley eyes. Masks rose and fell in quick succession. Confusion, then indignation, then anger, then...nothing. No mask, and no strength. He looked at Nathaniel with a stricken, beseeching face. His eyes glistened and his mouth trembled.

He began sinking. His back slid down the stone until he sat on the ground like a big, limp doll. He looked up at Nathaniel with great sorrow, then gazed into the garden.

"I am ruined by my own weakness. May God forgive me."

Nathaniel climbed into the carriage and gave orders for it to move. Charlotte set aside her book. It had been a longer wait than she expected.

"Did he offer tea? Is that the reason for the delay?"

"Brandy, actually."

"It is early for brandy."

"I'll be damned, so it is. I clear forgot the time of day when I accepted."

His tone was not nearly as playful as normal when he pointed out her game. His expression on returning had been very thoughtful and displeased.

"Are you angry that I asked you to go back?"

"You did not ask. You demanded it. I am not angry that you did, but I am not happy that I complied."

"You would have sought him out again, Nathaniel. You would have gone back eventually."

"You do not know that, damn it. I do not know that."

She gave his annoyance some time to ebb. She waited several miles before speaking again. "Did you learn anything of significance?"

His jaw firmed. His gaze speared a warning at her.

"Are you going to tell me what it was?"

"It was not significant to you and your inquiries. I learned nothing more about your husband."

"I find it hard to believe a clear line can be drawn on significance. It is all a knot, you said. If you are not telling me to protect me, I remind you that I have chosen to hear it all, and can decide for myself—"

His sudden movement interrupted her. He reached, grasped, lifted. The world spun. Then she was sprawled on his lap, her shoulders supported by his strong arm. He cupped her face with long, firm fingers.

"I will protect you when I choose, how I choose. I will cut off my arm if I think it necessary. I will kill a man if I conclude I must. Do not dare to interfere with my decisions on that. Do we have a right understanding on that, madam?"

His lack of humor, his firm command, left her stunned. "Yes, Nathaniel."

"Good." His hold softened. His fingers slid down her jaw to her neck in a sinuous path. "Now, kiss me. We will spend this journey back to London on important things, not arguments about Mr. Yardley."

CHAPTER
TWENTY-ONE

Nathaniel finished dressing for dinner. He would be attending a private party tonight at Charlotte's house. A party for two.

Her move to her sister's home made their affair much easier. Too easy, perhaps. The inconveniences of a liaison no longer inhibited their meeting. He could call in the afternoon and simply never leave. Or arrive for a late dinner party at which there were no other guests.

He had done this twice now since their return to town four days ago. She had known better than to quiz him about Yardley, but he knew she wondered what else had been learned. He shut that away when he was with her, but otherwise had spent these last days in a long, internal moral debate. He had needed to make a hard decision, one that involved more than Charlotte and Harry. It weighed on him, and his choice still occupied him now while he fixed his cuffs.

He took his pocket watch from its case. Beneath it, the edge of a paper showed. He had debated how to handle Mardenford, and that paper would play a crucial role. He had settled on the best course, he believed—one that would protect Charlotte but still achieve some justice. His conscience had not yet accommodated the compromise, however. The final decision to act had not been made.

Jacobs left to tell the Albany grooms to ready his horse. Nathaniel finished with his neckwear, donned his coats, and walked to the front of the apartment.

Voices greeted him. A visitor had come. Jacobs stood in the reception hall, trying to block the advance of a tall man with steely hair and eyes.

"Father," Nathaniel said, interrupting the earl's intimidating orders. "You choose the oddest times to visit."

"I need to talk to you. It is difficult to find you these days. You are rarely here, or even in town."

It appeared that dinner would have to wait. Nathaniel led the way into the sitting room. "If you had written, I would have arranged to be available."

Norriston snorted. "At your convenience, no doubt."

"No, at yours." It would not have been the truth a month ago, but it was now. Nathaniel realized he did not mind this intrusion as much as he normally would.

"Brandy? Sherry?" he asked. "Have you come to offer another living?"

"I have come to talk about the affair you are having with Lady Mardenford."

His father had not taken him aback in many years, but this calm statement did. "As a gentleman, I cannot respond to that bald accusation."

His father sank into the chair that Nathaniel normally used. "As a gentleman, I cannot make it. I speak as a father to a son, however."

Nathaniel brought another chair nearby and sat. He could refuse this conversation. He could lie. He realized that he did not want to do either. "And here I thought we had been discreet."

"I am sure you were. I wouldn't know. I do not pay attention to the gossip on these matters. I am aware of this affair because Mardenford spoke to me. He is distraught that you compromise her reputation, and forced him to take steps."

"The steps he took were unnecessary, and cruel to his own child. He is very distraught, I am sure, but not for her reputation. He will be more so when you report that I have proposed to her."

Norriston's attention snapped alert. "Has she accepted?"

"Not yet."

"Is there a chance?"

"I am hopeful."

His father absorbed that. "It would be a good match. Not bad at all."

"I think so."

"Of course, her family—well, some odd doings there. I hear her sister recently married that solicitor.

I admit to less shock than some others profess. Never liked Penelope's first husband myself. I always thought there was something unhealthy about the man. But Laclere's wife, well ... and everyone knows that fortune is from trade, all of it, Laclere's now too—but Lady M. seems to have turned out fine and upright. Handsome woman too ..."

Nathaniel let his father meander through the details. He guessed where the twisting path was going.

"I should warn you that she will not aid you in turning me into a bishop."

Norriston raised his eyebrows, then sighed. "Too bad. Willful woman, from what I've seen. She would have been a useful ally." He shrugged. "If she will tolerate your ill-chosen employment, I can reconcile myself to it, I suppose."

The capitulation was so unexpected that Nathaniel grew suspicious. "If I had known a good match would sway you, I would have looked for a second prospect with more tenacity."

His father's face fell at the allusion to the first match that Nathaniel had planned. "She did not know what she was getting in you, that girl. Nor you in her. She did not know about your stubbornness, and your belief in truth and principle. Did you want her harping your whole life, once she learned what was yours for the taking?"

They had never spoken of his father's motivations in arranging that fateful visit where his intended learned what he could have with one word. The episode had created the final distance between them, and froze an already chilly relationship. Now the ice was melting rapidly in this sitting room with neither of them planning or expecting it.

Broaching that sorry episode, explaining the reasons, altered the air in the chamber. It stilled as if time waited for something to happen. For an argument to ensue. Or for a response that would move them closer to some common ground.

They were not so different, Nathaniel realized. Perhaps too much alike. Nor was his father a fool. He was an intelligent man whose judgment had clashed with his son's, that was all.

Nathaniel never expected to sympathize with his father's view, but he suddenly did. He understood the need to protect one's own now, and the desire to control the history they would live.

"I regret that my choices disappointed you," he found himself saying. "I do not regret the choices themselves, but..."

"They did not disappoint me. They annoyed the hell out of me. There is a difference."

Nathaniel laughed and his father did too. It had been years since they laughed together. No, not years. Forever.

"See here, Nat, I had visions for you. Canterbury eventually, I was sure. I do not like the notoriety of your defenses, that is true. It is unseemly for you to be in the Old Bailey. I understand that you do not do it for pride or fame, however. I know why you do it, and the sentiment does not disappoint me. You are a

man of honor and seeker of truth, and *that* is why I
thought you would make a good bishop."

Nathaniel rose and paced away. His father's words
moved him. He did not know what to do with the un-
familiar emotion. He gazed into the dark beyond the
window and waited for the intimacy to pass, for the
distance to return.

It didn't. In speaking man-to-man, they had become father and son again.

"I am learning that sometimes principle is a chain.
I am discovering that learning the truth can be destructive," he said.

Silence claimed the chamber after he spoke. He
sensed his father watching him.

"What is it, boy?"

"I cannot tell you. If you ever learn of it, it will be
along with the entire world."

Another stillness. Nathaniel turned to see his father pondering this cryptic statement, choosing the
words of advice that were the first allowed in both
their memories.

"There are some truths better kept from the world.
I know that sounds dodgy—"

"No, not dodgy."

"Is it better known or not? That is the question.
And if not, can right still be done? Not easy to decide."

No, not easy to decide.

"I have not helped you much." His father looked
more resigned than disappointed.

"You have helped me greatly. Mardenford would be surprised to know how much."

A dismissive wave of the hand greeted that. "He expected me to rave with shock about this affair, no doubt. He probably thought I would threaten your allowance. Little, purse-lipped squirrel."

Not a squirrel, but a close relative. A rat.

Norriston got to his feet. "You are dressed for dinner, and I am delaying you. My reaction to the squirrel's revelation was not what he thinks it was. I have long admired Lady Mardenford, and think she would suit you well. She has spirit and a sharp mind. I came to let you know that should you marry the lady, I will release the estate. I can't have you going to her almost penniless. That is too dramatic for me."

"You are being very generous. And if the lady refuses me?"

Norriston grinned. "I suggest you see that she does not."

"Bianca spoke with Ambrose's nurse in the park," Charlotte said as she undressed. "She plans to charm the young woman into letting me see him someday. The nurse said that James never visits with his son now. He spends no time with Ambrose at all."

"He never spent time with his son, darling. He spent time with you. Ambrose was just his excuse."

Nathaniel was probably right, and that made her sad. It was another reason to use subterfuge if necessary to see the child. She and Bianca had spent the afternoon concocting plans to do it. With James so indifferent to his son now, there had to be a way.

She cast her hose aside and approached the tub. Nathaniel already soaked there, reclining like a river god. He filled it, but there would still be room for her. Just enough to snuggle in his embrace.

He watched as she strolled toward him. His gaze scorched. A hundred tiny fires ignited in her body. Her love flamed too, the way it always did now when she saw the passion in his eyes.

"You have the most accommodating servants," he said as he reached up to help her step in. His hands guided her down so that she lay on top of him, her crown on his shoulder and her back along his length. He made room for her legs between his bent knees.

"My sister trained them well."

A toasty fire kept them warm in the tub. The house was not very large and had no grand dressing room. This little ritual had to occur in her own bedroom.

She had called for the bath when she saw Nathaniel's state upon arriving for dinner. He was very distracted tonight. Coiled tightly with that energy wanting to burst out. She could not decide if she preferred that to the thoughtfulness that he had carried to their previous meetings. The deep contemplation would fall away in her presence, but this pending vitality only seemed to grow as the dinner tonight progressed.

It encompassed her now, as surely as his arms crossed over her breasts. He reached for a sponge and began stroking her body with it, both cleansing and arousing.

"My father called on me tonight, before I came here."

"Is that the reason for your mood? Did you have an invigorating argument?"

"No argument. There was a rapprochement of sorts. A beginning."

She turned her head and gazed up at his face, so close to hers. "You did not give in to him, did you? I do not care about that estate, Nathaniel. It will make no difference to me—you must know that. If I have not accepted your proposal yet, it has not been because of your fortune."

The sponge rose and deliberately circled her breasts with wet, soft caresses. "Then what is the reason?"

She had not expected this conversation now. She had been weighing much since their return from Hertfordshire, including his proposal. She had been waiting to choose the time and place to discuss it all. It appeared he had concluded this night in the bath was the appropriate one.

"Did you agree to do as he wants, Nathaniel?

"No."

No compromise. Of course not.

His hand lifted one of her legs so her foot was propped on the side of the tub. With his long arm he could reach most of its length with the sponge. Little waterfalls trickled down as he stroked its length, all the way up. Her vulva flexed as the sensation neared.

The warm water, his embrace, the languorous caresses lulled her into a luxurious relaxation and purring sensuality.

He kissed her neck, then her ear. "Why have you not yet decided on my proposal, darling?"

She felt his erection against her bottom. She shifted so it rose between her thighs.

"Is it because of him, Charl? Do you still need time to explain our passion to the memories?"

"It is not that."

"Then what?"

She reached down and slid her fingertips up the length of his shaft. A tightening in his chest at her back, in his lap beneath her, spoke of her effect. "I have sensed a decision in you these last days. I thought to wait until you had made it."

He dropped the sponge and used his hands. Soaped and slick, they began moving over her with the deliberate, possessive caresses that she loved. The way he handled her said so much about him, and reflected the reasons she was helpless to this passion.

He nuzzled her ear and neck, his breath producing wonderful warm shivers. "You are right. I carried a decision in me. It is made, however."

That was the reason for this new mood, this contained energy. He said nothing more. He did not explain what the decision had been.

"You are very sure that you are done with your contemplations, Nathaniel?"

"Done and resolved."

"Then I accept your proposal. I will marry you."

His hands paused. They remained bound in stillness for a long moment. Then he turned her, gently but quickly. Water splashed over the edges as her body made little waves.

His arm held her to him as he looked in her eyes. "You do not care what decision I have made, or even on what question?"

"I care. It was not the choice that I waited to hear, however, merely that you had resolved it."

"Do you know what the decision concerned? It would be like you to guess."

"I know it does not involve me directly because you have said it does not. I suspect, however, that it touches on my life both past and present."

He moved her again so that she straddled his lap and faced him. He cupped her face with his hands. "You have stolen my heart, Charlotte. Knowing your answer to my proposal would not have affected me, and withholding it did not lessen my considerations of you. My love for you was influence enough."

His declaration both saddened her and made her heart swell with exquisite sweetness. "Was the influence a bad one?" she whispered.

"How could it be bad? Our love does not diminish me or my honor, Charl. It does not obscure the right path, but illuminates it."

He spoke so honestly that she did not doubt he was correct. In her small way she had been trying to protect him. She had not wanted obligations to her to interfere, to lure him to rationalize a wrong judgment. She had never considered that their love would help him to make a right one.

"What are you going to do, Nathaniel?"

His embrace lifted her so that his tongue could caress her nipples. They had become tight and sensitive from water and warmth and his seductive washing. The sensations made her tremble so much, she thought the water would make waves.

"Right now I am going to make love to my fiancée," he said. "Then, tomorrow, I am going to return Finley's ghost to its grave."

She wondered what that meant for a brief moment. Then the sensuality submerged all thoughts of tomorrow. His mouth teased her breasts until she rocked and cried. He held her firmly, his hands cupping her bottom, and she steadied herself by holding his shoulders.

It was too much. Too intense. Desire maddened her. Nathaniel's arm braced her back for support, and his free hand slid between her thighs. Slowly, confidently, he touched and caressed spots of unbearable sensitivity. Shudders of pleasure left her boneless, helpless.

Blind now, awareness blurred to everything but the desperate need consuming her, she saw nothing as he flipped her. Then she was kneeling in the bath, the water licking at her breasts. His body hovered over hers, and his arms flanked her own. The position both protected and dominated.

He filled her totally, touching her womb, titillating soft flesh with the best irritation. She met his thrusts with her own. The rhythm of give and take began deliciously slow but escalated as she sought to feel him more. Hardness entered the passion as they soared in mutual ecstasy.

She dipped her shoulders to accept him deeper, to take him into herself as thoroughly as possible. Water soothed her cheek and sloshed around their heat.

A gentle quake of pleasure trembled where they joined. She surrendered to its power as he made it intensify. The quakes continued on and on, rippling with a perfection she savored, until the ultimate pleasure broke with intense, beautiful waves.

Nathaniel normally left before dawn, for both discretion and practicality. He had business affairs to conduct, after all. He did not live only to attend on her.

He did not leave this time. He remained in her bed long after the sun rose. She watched him sleep, his dark lashes feathering his skin and his golden hair mussed on the pillow.

Perhaps he had stayed to celebrate their engagement. Then again, maybe he slept so soundly that he did not realize the hour. It had been a long night of love, after all.

She sat up on crossed legs and just watched him. He had asked if she still negotiated with the past. She would explain to him soon that she honored that past but she lived in the present now, thoroughly. For one thing, she was very sure that Philip would understand this passion. It helped to know that he had not been cheated, and that their quieter melody had been as much his choice as hers.

One of her little reveries claimed her, briefly but intensely, as his presence echoed in her heart. She expected that would keep happening on occasion. It was right that it should. He had been her husband, and they had shared a love.

He had been a good husband too. He had also been a good man who had once tried to protect another woman he loved. She was glad for that. Glad he had been heroic, as best he knew how. It pleased her that for a brief few weeks he had not been so staid.

She gazed at her lover, sprawled on her bed, his muscular limbs firm even in repose. The idea of a life with him thrilled her. The emotion was very similar to fear, just more joyful and optimistic and eager for the mysteries to be explored.

His eyes opened. They stayed unaware for a moment, then he glanced to the window and to the clock. He sat up and rubbed his eyes. "Past ten o'clock. I hope the servants will not be shocked."

"I believe they are used to it. There was a thick oilcloth beneath the towels surrounding the tub, so I think there is little they do not expect, and even anticipate."

He left the bed and walked to a window, indifferent to his nakedness. He parted the drapes and examined the day while she examined him.

"The weather is fair. Let us take breakfast out in the garden," he said.

They dressed and went down. They sat on two iron

garden chairs near a little table, and basked in the sunlight until a simple breakfast arrived. They did not speak much as they ate, but the silence was pleasant. He had never needed words to know everything about her.

Nor had she needed words to comprehend him. Right now she comprehended that he was waiting for something. The energy had never left him, not even in the exhaustion after passion. Here in the garden's silence it intensified as if the sunlight stimulated it.

A footman came into the garden, salver in hand. Nathaniel's lids lowered over glowing eyes.

She picked up the card and shot him a glance of surprise.

"Receive him," Nathaniel said.

She sent the footman away. "You knew he was coming?"

"I told him to come."

"Do you intend to confront him with what we know?"

"In a manner of speaking."

The approach of their visitor could be heard. Not only footsteps announced it, but also voices. A low rumbling one, punctuated by another high squeak.

She knew that squeak. She rose to her feet, not daring to hope.

The squeak got louder. It was a child's voice, asking questions.

Nathaniel sat calmly on the iron chair, drinking his coffee. She caught his eye, and her vision misted.

"Thank you, Nathaniel. However you did it, thank you so much."

The garden door swung. The footman escorted Mardenford outside. A little head peeked around the moving legs.

"Ancharl!"

He darted out of line and ran to her, his little legs working hard. She fell to her knees and opened her arms to him.

CHAPTER
TWENTY-TWO

Ambrose's joy filled the garden. Charlotte's happiness matched the child's. Their reunion moved Nathaniel and evoked images of her like this with other children, their children, and this love multiplied many times.

Mardenford remained rigid, his gaze on his squealing son but his thoughts clearly centered on himself.

The initial excitement calmed. Charlotte embraced Ambrose closely, pressing a kiss to his crown. She looked up at her brother-in-law. "This is a wonderful surprise. It was generous of you to bring him, James."

She released Ambrose and rose to her feet. The child darted down the garden path, daring her to chase him. She joined the game, letting him win as they ran around bushes and trees.

Nathaniel kept his gaze on their play. "I am glad

you chose to accept my invitation and brought the
child, Mardenford. It was good of you."

"Damn you." The mutter was not nearly as low as
it should have been.

"Sit down and have some coffee."

"I'll not—"

"Sit."

Mardenford lowered himself into the other iron
chair. Nathaniel did not need to look at him to recognize the mixture of anger and fear in the man. He
knew the smell well. It covered accused criminals
like a damp, sour mist.

Mardenford retreated into imperious hauteur.
"Your letter was damned impertinent, and close to
blackmail."

"I do not want money, but only a conversation."

"There is nothing to discuss with you."

"If you believed that, you would not have come,
let alone brought your son as I instructed."

*I know about Isabella and her son. Meet me at
Charlotte's house tomorrow at noon. Bring the child.*
That was the letter he had sent last night after his fa-
ther left Albany.

Charlotte was deep in the garden now, on the
ground with Ambrose, ruining her dress. Their laughter's melody rose and fell on the breeze.

Nathaniel tore his attention from them and fixed it
on Mardenford. "Have you received a letter from Mr.
Yardley?"

"Yardley? My old tutor? Why would I seek out the
man, or he seek out me?"

"For the same reason you gave him that living. I met with him five days ago, you see. I thought perhaps he had written to you about it. He said he would not, but one never knows. I suggested it would be in his health's better interest to visit Scotland for a fortnight or so, but old loyalties die hard."

Mardenford's face remained impassive, but his eyes revealed the first flames of desperation.

"It must have been a shock when you received that first letter from Isabella, addressed to Baron Mardenford and intended for your brother. What a complication to learn that she had not died. Or did you know that? It was your report of her death that got your brother on that ship to England."

Mardenford's jaw clenched at this evidence of how thoroughly Yardley had been indiscreet. He shot Nathaniel a dangerous glare. "She was a whore. A scheming whore. A false marriage, Philip said. A false wedding, just to protect her. I told him it was madness. The potential for trouble—" His mouth clamped shut suddenly.

"You do not have to parse your words with me. I know all of it. Much more than you would like."

A wary gaze slid to him. Nathaniel let the mind behind those hooded eyes work its way through just how much "all of it" might mean.

"What do you want, Knightridge?"

"I am sworn to want justice. It is my stock in trade, you might say."

"You have no proof."

"I have the boy. I have a signed document from

Yardley, in which he reveals all. I convinced him it might be wise to give that to me, in case your bad judgment got the better of you. A type of insurance, you might say."

He stiffened with indignation. "Blast, what are you accusing? Yardley has nothing to fear from me."

"I hope not. Forgive me, however, if my experiences in the Old Bailey made me cautious for his sake. He knows too much. It was generous of you not to remove him."

Mardenford reacted oddly to the peculiar compliment. A sneer twitched on his face. Not generous but cowardly, that sneer of self-disgust implied. "I don't know why you give a damn about any of this."

"There is a boy with your family's blood who spent four years living in a cellar with a half-mad thief. Your brother's son, as I now know. If you had dealt fairly with that woman, provided some support, I would have nothing to give a damn about now, because I never would have learned about the boy."

"He has no claims!"

His sudden fury sent his denial ringing through the garden. Charlotte stopped her play and looked in their direction, then Ambrose reclaimed her attention.

"His claim is ambiguous," Nathaniel said. "It is all ambiguous. That is my conundrum, and why I requested this meeting." He caught Mardenford's gaze in his own. "Even what occurred that day by the Thames is ambiguous."

Fear now. Naked fear. The attempts at covering it with feigned incomprehension did not work.

"Yardley described that meeting to me. Did you lure her down the steps for privacy, or with murder in mind? Did you grab her in a rage, or just to silence her loud denials? Did she lose her balance, or was she pushed? The lawyer in me can see a defense made of those ambiguities, you see. At least one good enough to save a baron's neck. Maybe."

"I did not kill her. How dare you—"

"I think you did. I think your anger, so rare but so explosive, burst forth when she would not accept your version of what had occurred in Spain. She thought her son was legitimate. When you told her Philip was dead, she thought her boy should have the title. Your title, your estate, and your fortune were at risk. Even raising the question would have been devastating to your name. The investigation would have humiliated you. Worse, it might turn out she was correct."

"She could not prove the boy was my brother's child."

"If the marriage was found legitimate, any child born within it would be your brother's child in the law. You know that."

Mardenford rose abruptly and walked away, as if seeking escape from a trap. Nathaniel followed him over to the wall and trapped him quite literally. "Did you see the boy? See the resemblance? He was there, positioned where you could see him before you went down those stairs."

"I saw no boy." Shaky now, he refused to look at Nathaniel. "You are going to do it, aren't you? Air it all, so the whole world pokes and talks and wonders." He turned his attention to Charlotte. Renewed confidence produced a smirk. "Then again, maybe not. If it is decided that either marriage ceremony with Isabella was legal, Charlotte was my brother's whore for three years. Her settlement is gone. Her reputation is gone. She will be humiliated and degraded by the investigation worse than me, no matter what its outcome. If she is more than a whore to *you,* you will not do it."

"You are a coward to hide behind her."

"I am protecting her."

"You are thinking of no one but yourself." He placed a companionable hand on Mardenford's shoulder, but gripped hard enough that the face above his hand blanched. "Listen to what I say, and believe it to be true. I do not seek to air this before the world. If you do not accept the resolution I offer, however, I will let it all come out. I will let the Church decide about that marriage, and the lords decide about your title, and a court decide about the day at the Thames. Charlotte's future will be secure in either case, because she will be my wife."

"You would not marry a woman so ruined."

"I would have her if she came to me in sackcloth."

"She will not have *you* if you do this. Look at her with my son. She will repudiate you if you harm him through me."

"Now you use your own son as your shield. You

disgust me." He released his hold and barely contained the urge to thrash the bastard. "Come into the house now. I will explain what you must do. Have no illusions that I will spare you if you refuse."

Ambrose finally tired of running and games. Charlotte sat on the ground and gathered him into her lap. He giggled while he pulled at ribbons and poked her face.

Nathaniel had taken James into the house some time ago. She guessed James was learning about the discoveries they had made. Maybe he was learning about the other things, too; the things that only Nathaniel knew.

She firmed her hold on Ambrose, giving a subtle hug. His visit was a perfect gift. He made her so lighthearted that she did not care overmuch what was being said in the house.

Ambrose began squirming. A sound caught his attention. Scrambling in his clumsy way, he tumbled out of her lap and ran toward the footman who had just entered the garden. A young man, little more than a boy himself, the footman laughed when Ambrose grabbed his leg. He paused and told the child to hold on, then proceeded toward her, carefully swinging the little body that wrapped and clutched his leg.

"My lady, the gentlemen request your presence in the library," he said, dutifully ignoring how Ambrose demanded a longer ride.

"Will you please take my nephew to the house-keeper? Tell her I will come for him shortly."

"I could bring him to the kitchen, if you prefer. Cook enjoys the little ones." His glance down at Ambrose suggested that the housekeeper would find this active, loud little one not much to her liking at all.

"I will defer to your judgment."

He turned to retrace his steps. Ambrose's squeals filled the air as the footman lugged his weight along.

Charlotte entered the house through the morning room's terrace doors and went up to the library. Nathaniel and James waited for her there. They stood silently, as if one chapter of time had finished and they anticipated the page's turn to the next one.

James looked her way briefly and blankly. She sensed he chose not to see her, or anything.

A peculiar pause ensued.

"I have been summoned, but no one has anything to say?" she asked.

"Mardenford has quite a bit to say, don't you, Mardenford? I think he hesitates because it requires a great favor from you."

"I would be happy to help you any way that I can, James."

Mardenford smiled weakly. He was not a happy man. No doubt it embarrassed him to request a favor of one he had so recently insulted.

He walked over to the desk. A stack of papers rested atop it. A lot of writing had been done during their meeting.

His face lengthened. His mouth pursed. He gazed

past her, at nothing. "I have decided to go abroad. I have agreed . . . I would be grateful if you would allow Ambrose to live with you until I return."

"Nothing would give me more pleasure, James. You know that."

He lifted a paper from the table. "I put it in writing, that he be allowed to stay with you while I am gone, so the family cannot object." He gestured to the other papers. "There is another one there, to my solicitor, and documents establishing a trust for the boy, so his expenses can be met."

She glanced at Nathaniel. He watched impassively but his gaze pinned James in place.

"A trust? How long do you intend to be away?"

"Some time, I expect. I really do not know." He cast a glare at Nathaniel but the flame of rebellion was extinguished by Nathaniel's cool stare. "It will be a great adventure. I am due one, I think," he muttered.

She asked for more particulars and received very few. This great adventure would commence immediately, however. James did not even plan to take Ambrose home with him.

"I will send his nurse, for now. You can then make what arrangements you wish."

"I do not know what to say, James. I am grateful for your trust."

He gazed at her, taking all of her in. His attention lingered on the stains her dress had received in the garden. "Yes. Well, do not spoil him."

"I will try not to."

Silence fell. James continued looking at her. Nathaniel quietly cleared his throat, breaking the awkwardness and jolting James out of whatever sad reverie had claimed him.

"Oh, yes, and the house. It is yours again, if you want it. I acted rashly, and since Ambrose will be living with you—"

"Thank you, but I do not think I will return there. It would be best if you sold it. I have concluded I stayed there overlong, you see. Wherever I go, I promise Ambrose will be comfortable and well loved."

James glanced at Nathaniel in question. Nathaniel shrugged.

"Well, that is settled." James barely voiced the words. They emerged on a deep exhale of breath. "I will take my leave now. I do not expect I will see you again before I sail." He moved abruptly, walking resolutely to the door.

She moved so he had to walk past her. "James."

He stopped.

"Ambrose is in the kitchen, if you want to say good-bye," she said.

He nodded dully. She stretched up and kissed his cheek. "Take care, dear brother."

He grasped her hand in both of his and kissed it. He strode from the room. She watched the door close on his back.

Nathaniel silently watched the end of the performance. She knew that he had managed this little drama, however.

"He will not return to Britain soon, will he?" she asked.

"No."

She strolled across the carpet to the window. James's crown emerged below her as he headed to his carriage. He had not even said good-bye to his son.

She turned to the desk. She leafed through the papers there. "You have been busy. Here is another trust, a handsome one, for Joseph, also known as Harry, who currently resides with Mr. Avlon in Durham."

"James saw the rightness of providing for the boy."

She could imagine how that happened. "Will Ambrose ever see his father again?"

He came over to her and removed the papers from her hands. "When he is older, he can visit Mardenford wherever he resides. It will be his father's choice whether to explain what happened."

"Are you going to tell *me* what happened?"

"I did not blackmail him, if that is what you think."

"It would be an odd blackmail, since you gained nothing in it but the presence in your new marriage of a small boy who is not your own."

He shrugged. "He is a nice enough small boy. He will stop squealing in a year or two."

She gazed at the documents. Trusts and letters ensuring the care of James's son and his estate. These were the legal remains of a man putting his life in order. "He is not going to do himself in, is he?"

"No. However, he will not be returning to England."

Not returning. Ever. She looked at Nathaniel. Not blackmail, but a bargain. A compromise. James had agreed to this to avoid a scandal about Isabella and Harry. To avoid the formal inquiries about that marriage in Spain.

Nathaniel had proposed this solution, she was sure of it. He had forged this plan to protect her and Ambrose from the same scandal and all it might reveal.

That did not explain why James had to accept exile, however. Either Nathaniel had forced James into a very bad bargain, or there was more at stake than she knew.

The answer stood in front of her, tall and confident, watching her.

"Do you think the marriage would be found to be legal?"

"Possibly. However, it would depend on whether the witnesses could be located, which is unlikely."

"Will Harry ever know about that possibility?"

"When he is of age, I will share what I know with him. He has a right to that. It will be his choice whether to pursue it. However, I think the trust will appease him enough."

"And if he does pursue it? Ambrose—"

"Ambrose will not grow up in an earl's household, but in ours. His trust draws on James's private wealth, not the title's estates. He will be wealthy and have your secure love. If he does not become an earl because it is discovered the title is not rightfully his, it will not be the end of the world for him."

"So all of these strategies may only delay the reckoning."

He drew her into his embrace. "I cannot lie to that boy up in Durham. This was the best I could do."

"I think you did very well. Eight years hence, I do not think I will care much whether my past is rearranged again." She took his face in her hands and gazed deeply into his eyes. "James must have done something very bad to agree to this, Nathaniel. I do not think he goes abroad only to suppress questions about his brother's Spanish alliance. Nor do I believe you would require it of him to buy our silence on that."

He did not reply, but she found the answer in his eyes. "He killed that poor woman, didn't he? That is what you learned from Mr. Yardley that day."

He nodded. "However, Yardley is not the best witness. His memories are confused and vague. Even I would have difficulty getting a conviction on his story alone."

She assumed he had considered trying, while he weighed his decisions these last days. He had tried it on and rehearsed that role. That meant he knew the truth even if Mr. Yardley was not enough. "Tell me, when you looked in James's eyes today, what did you learn?"

He gathered her hands in his. "I saw his guilt, and damned little repentance. I also saw very little love for his son."

"He is fortunate you chose this road for him, and not a more precipitous one."

"It was a road that spared the innocent. It was not a bad compromise."

His embracing arm guided her out of the library and away from those documents and the truth they buried. They went down to the garden again, and out amidst the plants under the sun.

The scents of spring drenched the breeze, creating the heady smell of a world embracing renewal. Nathaniel strolled beside her down the garden's length.

"James was right. You spoil the boy. We should marry soon so the child is not ruined before a man's influence saves him."

She laughed. "You are so selfless, Mr. Knightridge." She let the mirth die. "I am tempted to impose on that fine quality one more time."

"How so?"

"You must deny me if you even suspect it is an unwise request, one that might risk our happiness. It would be just like you to agree, just to be kind, when in your heart you wished you had not. If that happens it will be a sorry state we will find ourselves in, although you would never say so. Which means that I would know you were unhappy but you would deny it, and we would—"

"Heaven spare me, Lady M. In another two sentences you will have us doomed to misery because I am so damned good." A sardonic smile accompanied the scold. "I will weigh your request with due deliberation and answer honestly. I will never put our happiness at risk. Now continue."

She stopped and faced him. She moved close and toyed with the fabric of his cravat. "I have been thinking that I would like to make another journey. To the north. To hold assemblies for the petitions."

"Certainly. I assumed we would spend the summer on your cause. We can arrange it as soon as we are wed. Where would you like to go?"

She shrugged. "Durham would be convenient."

His hand lifted her chin. "A tour of Durham would never risk our happiness, so there is more to this plot, I think."

"Much more. I was thinking about Harry while I played here with Ambrose. I am sure that school is very good, and that he will be content there. However, I would like him to know he has a place in the world, and Mardenford's family will never accept him. Even the funds in that trust will not give him a real home." She bit her lower lip. "Do you think he could have a place with us, Nathaniel?"

He cocked his head in the due deliberation he had promised. "You astonish me, Charlotte."

"It will be a little odd; I know that," she hastened to add. "He is Philip's son, of course. Not yours and not even mine. But I want to do this, if you do not hate the notion." She also *needed* to do it, if she could. She faced the future now, but she still owed the memories some loyalty. "If it would be too awkward for you, I understand. It is only that—"

His fingers touched her mouth, silencing her with

a gentle caress. "You misunderstand my surprise. If your heart can open to the boy, I am glad. I am fond of him, and do not want him adrift either. We will visit him in Durham and propose he make his home with us."

His generosity moved her. She embraced him closely. Love's poignant ache swelled her heart. "We will have an unusual family. Larger than most marriages when they start."

"I am confident it will get larger. In fact, I wonder if it will not quite soon."

She looked up. "What do you mean?"

He smiled at her perplexity. "It has been a month since we began this affair, Charl, and you have never put me off for the usual reason."

"Usual reason . . . ?" Her mind snapped alert to his meaning. *"Oh."* She did some fast calculations, not daring to hope. "Oh, my. I have not . . . Well, it has been some time since I counted days or even paid attention and . . ." Startled elation made her head spin. "I think you are right, Nathaniel. I can't believe it, but I think you really are."

He laughed at her shock. "I found your explanation of your barren state very odd in Hertford, since the weeks were passing and—"

"You must think me very stupid."

"Never, my love. I only think you were too certain without fair proof."

She did not think she could contain the day's happiness. It threatened to burst her heart. Another child to love. Nathaniel's child.

She eased his head down so she could kiss him. She let her love and gratitude flow to him. "I cannot wait until this child is born and with us," she whispered. "A year from now our house will be so full of joy and love."

"And full of children. I trust that the formidable Lady M. can manage it all."

"As long as you love me, I am not afraid of any challenge, Nathaniel."

"I love you completely, darling. My heart and soul and body are yours alone, forever. You are my life's great passion."

His kiss contained the totality of his promise. She responded just as completely. Her spirit met his in the perfect emotion. Desire shuddered within their love, a storm approaching fast with gale winds.

He stopped before the tempest overwhelmed them. His arms wrapped her and held her close to his chest. She rested her head near his heart, awed yet again by how alive this man made her feel.

He kissed her crown and loosened his hold. He took her hand in his. "Let us go inside and find the boy."

ABOUT THE AUTHOR

MADELINE HUNTER's first novel was published in 2000. Since then she has seen twelve historical romances and one novella published, and her books have been translated into five languages. She is a four-time RITA finalist and won the long historical RITA in 2003. Nine of her books have been on the *USA Today* bestseller list, and she has also had titles on the *New York Times* extended list. Madeline has a Ph.D. in art history, which she teaches at an Eastern university. She currently lives in Pennsylvania with her husband and two sons.

Don't miss

Madeline Hunter's

upcoming tale of intrigue and passion

THE
RULES OF
SEDUCTION

Coming in Fall 2006

Read on for a sneak peek. . . .

THE RULES OF SEDUCTION

On sale Fall 2006

Mr. Rothwell waited in the reception hall, surrounded by walls that had already been stripped of paintings. As Alexia entered he was bent, examining a marquetry table in the corner, no doubt calculating its worth.

She did not wait for his attention or greeting. "Mr. Rothwell, my cousin Timothy is not on the premises. I believe he is selling the horses. My cousin Miss Longworth is indisposed and her sister is too young to assist you. Will I do for whatever your purpose in coming might be?

He straightened and swung his gaze to her. She grudgingly admitted that he appeared quite magnificent today, dressed for riding as he was in blue coat and gray patterned silk waistcoat. She suspected he dominated large ballrooms as thoroughly as he did this small chamber. His presence, bearing and garments announced to the world that he knew he was handsome and intelligent and rich as sin. It was rude to look like that in a house being deprived of its possessions and dignity.

"I expected a servant to—"

"There are no servants. The family cannot afford them now. Falkner only remains until he finds another position, but he no longer serves. I fear you are stuck with me."

She heard her own voice sound crisp and barely civil. His lids lowered just enough to indicate he did not miss the lack of respect.

"If I am stuck with you, and you with me, so be it, Miss Welbourne. My purpose in intruding is very simple. I have an aunt who has an interest in this house. She asked that I determine if it would be suitable for her and her daughter this season."

"You want a tour of the property so you can describe it to potential occupants?"

"If Miss Longworth would be so kind, yes."

"I doubt Miss Longworth would be so kind, although kindness is in her heart in most situations. She is also far too busy. Being ruined and made destitute is very time-consuming."

His jaw tightened enough to give her a small satisfaction. The victory was brief. He set down his hat on the marquetry table. "Then I will find my own way. When I said my aunt had an interest I did not mean a casual curiosity but rather that of ownership. This property is already my aunt's, Miss Welbourne. Timothy Longworth signed the papers yesterday. I presented my requirements as a request out of courtesy to his family, not out of any obligation.

The news stunned her. The house had already been sold. So fast! Alexia quickly calculated what that might mean to her plans, and to Roselyn and Irene.

She swallowed her pride. Its taste was growing increasingly bitter. "My apologies, Mr. Rothwell. The new ownership of the house had not been communicated to either Miss Longworth or myself. I will show you the house, if that will do."

He nodded agreement and she began the ordeal. She led him into the dining room where his sharp gaze did not miss a thing. She heard him mentally counting chairs and measuring space.

The rest of the first level went quickly. He did not open drawers and cabinets in the butler's pantry. Alexia guessed he knew they were already empty.

"The breakfast room is through that door," she said as they returned to the corridor. "My cousin Roselyn is there, and I must beg you to accept my description instead of entering yourself. I fear seeing you will greatly distress her."

"Why would my presence be so distressing?"

"Timothy told us everything. Roselyn knows that you brought the bank to the brink of failure and forced this ruin on the family."

He absorbed that. A hard smile played at the corners of his mouth. Really, the man's cruelty was not to be borne.

He noticed her glaring at him. He did not seem at all embarrassed that she had seen that cynical smile.

"Miss Welbourne, I do not need to see the breakfast room. I am sorry for your cousin's distress, but matters of high finance exist on a different plane from everyday experiences. Timothy Longworth's explanations were somewhat simplified, no doubt because he was giving them to ladies."

"They may have been simple, but they were clear, as were the consequences. A week ago my cousins lived in style in London and soon they will live in poverty in the country. Timothy is ruined, the partnership is sold, and he will have debts despite his fall. Is any of that incorrect, sir?"

He shook his head, nonplussed. "It is all correct."

She could not believe his indifference. He could at least appear a little chagrined, a bit embarrassed. Instead he acted as if this were normal. Perhaps he ruined families frequently.

"Shall we go above?" he asked.

She showed him up the stairs and into the library. He took his time browsing the volumes on the shelves while she waited, silently tapping her foot. She hoped he did not plan to open every book and memorize every title.

"Will you be going to Oxfordshire?" he asked.

"I would not allow myself to be a burden on this family now."

Most of his attention remained on the books. "What will you do?"

"I have my future well in hand. I have drawn up a plan and listed my expectations and opportunities."

He replaced a book on its shelf, quickly surveyed the rug and desk and sofas, then walked toward her.

"What opportunities do you see?" It sounded as if he knew the expectations were nonexistent.

She led him through the other rooms on the floor. "My first choice is to be a governess in town. My second is to be a governess anywhere else."

"Most sensible."

"Well, when facing starvation it behooves one to be so, don't you think?"

The third level was not as spaciously arranged as the public rooms. He cramped her in the corridor. She became too aware of the large, masculine presence by her side as she showed the bedrooms. It seemed very wrong for this stranger to be intruding up here.

"And if you do not find a position as a governess?" The casual query came some time after their last exchange. His curiosity raised her pique to a reckless pitch. It was unseemly for the man who caused this grief to want the details.

"My next choice is to become a milliner."

"A hat maker?"

"I am very talented at it. Years hence, if you

should see an impoverished woman wearing a magnificent hat artfully devised of nothing more than an old basket, sparrow feathers and withered apples, that will be me." She threw open the door of Irene's bedroom. "My fourth choice is to become a soiled dove. There are those who say a woman should starve to death first, but I have never held with that. One must be practical and I am very much so."

She received a long, sharp glance for that. One that managed to take her in thoroughly. Beneath his annoyance at how she mocked his lack of guilt, she also saw bold, masculine consideration, as if he calculated her value at the occupation fourth on her list.

Her face warmed. That stupid liveliness woke her skin and sank right through to churn in her core, affecting her in a shocking way, creating an insidious, uncontrollable awareness of her body's many details. The sensation appalled her mind even as she acknowledged its lush stimulation.

She had to step back, out of the chamber and out of his sight, to escape the way his proximity caused a rapid drumbeat in her pulse. In the few seconds before he joined her she called up her anger to defeat the shocking burst of sensuality.

She continued her goads so he would know she did not care what he thought. She wanted this man to appreciate how his whims had created misery.

"My fifth choice is to become a thief. I debated which should come first, soiled dove or thief, and decided that while the former was harder work, it was a form of honest trade while being a thief is just plain evil." She did not resist adding "No matter how it is done, or even how legal it may be."

He stopped walking and turned into her path, forcing her to stop walking too. "You speak very frankly."

He hovered over her in the narrow corridor. His gaze demanded her total attention. A power flowed, one masculine and dominating and challenging. An intuitive caution shouted retreat. The liveliness purred low and deep. She ignored both reactions and stood her ground.

"You are the one who asked the question about my future, sir, even though it does not matter at all to you what becomes of any of us." She peered up at him severely. "I hope that you are proud of yourself. These are decent, good people and you have destroyed their lives. You did not have to remove all your business from Timothy's bank. It is as if you deliberately ruined him and I do not know how you can bear to live with yourself."

He gazed down at her, his dark blue eyes almost black in the dim hall's lights and his jaw as set as it had been in the drawing room the other day. He was angry. Well, good. So was she.

"I live with myself very well, thank you. Until you have more experience in business and finance, Miss Welbourne, you can only view these developments from a position of ignorance. I am sincerely sorry for Miss Longworth and her sister, and for you, but I will not apologize for doing my duty as I saw fit."

His tone startled her. Quiet but firm, it commanded that no further argument be given. She retreated, but not because of that. She was wasting her breath. This man did not care about other people. If he did, they would not be taking this tour.

She guided him toward the stairs rising to the higher chambers, but he stopped outside a door near the landing. "What is this room?"

"It is a small bedroom, undistinguished. I believe it was once the dressing room to the chamber next door. Now, up above—"

He turned the latch and pushed the door open. She pursed her lips and waited for him to take his quick, mental inventory.

Instead he paced into the small space and noted every detail. The two books beside the bed, the small, sparsely populated wardrobe, the neat stack of letters on the writing table—all of it garnered his attention. He lifted a hat from a chair by the window.

"This is your room," he said.

It was, and his presence in it, his perusal of her private belongings, created an intimacy that made her uncomfortable. His touching her hat felt too much like his touching her. It created a physical connection that made the simmering liveliness more shocking and embarrassing.

"*For now* it is my room."

He ignored the barb. He examined the hat,

turning it this way and that. It was the one she had begun remaking in the garden two days ago. No one would recognize it now. "You do have a talent at it." He glanced to her sharply, then back to the hat, as if mentally putting the two together and picturing the hat on a head.

"Yes, well, but as I said, being a milliner is only choice number three. If a lady works in such a shop, she can no longer pretend she is a lady at all, can she?"

He set the hat down carefully. "No, she cannot. However, it is more respectable than being a soiled dove or thief, although far less lucrative. Your list is in the correct order if respectability is your goal."

That was an odd thing for him to say. It almost sounded as if he thought she should have different goals and a differently ordered list.

She still hated him by the time they were finished with the tour. She could not deny he was less a stranger, however. Entering the private rooms together, seeing the artifacts of the family's everyday lives, being so close, *too* close, on the upper levels, had created an unwelcome familiarity.

Her susceptibility to his overbearing presence had placed her at a disadvantage. She wanted to believe she was above such reactions, especially with this man who probably thought it his due from all women. She resented the entire, irritating hour with him.

They returned to the reception hall and he retrieved his hat.

She broached the reason she had agreed to receive him at all. "Mr. Rothwell, Timothy is distracted. He is not conveying the details to his sisters, if indeed he even knows them himself. If I may be so bold—"

"You have been plenty bold without asking permission, Miss Welbourne. There is no need to stand on ceremony now."

She grimaced. She *had* been bold and outspoken. She had allowed her vexation to get the better of her good sense. In truth, she had not been very practical in a situation where she badly needed that virtue.

"What is your question?"

"When have you told Timothy that the Longworths must vacate the house?"

"I have not said yet." He levelled a disconcertingly frank gaze at her. "When do you think is reasonable?"

"Never."

He smiled. "That is not reasonable."

"A week. Please give them a week more."

"A week it is. The Longworths may remain until then." He narrowed his eyes on her. "You, however . . ."

Oh, dear heavens. She had raised the devil with her free tongue. He was going to throw her out at once.

"My aunt has a passion for hats."

She blinked. "Hats? Your aunt?"

"She loves them. She buys far too many, at exorbitant prices. As her trustee I pay the bills, so I know."

It was an odd topic to start on the way out the door. In truth he sounded a little stupid.

"I see. Well, they often are very expensive."

"The ones she buys are also very ugly."

She smiled and nodded and wished he would leave. She wanted to tell Roselyn about the week's reprieve.

Once more she received one of his piercing examinations. "A governess, you said. Your first choice. Do you have the education to be a finishing governess?"

"I have been helping prepare my young cousin for her season. I have the requisite skills and abilities."

"Music? Do you play?"

"Yes. I am well suited to be a governess for any age, and especially young ladies. My own education was superior. I was not always as you see me now."

He looked right into her eyes. "That is clear. If you had always been as you are now, you would have never dared be as rude and outspoken with me as you have been today."

Her face warmed furiously. Not because she had been rude and he knew it, but because his invasive gaze was causing that annoying stimulation again.

"Miss Welbourne, my aunt will be taking possession of this house because she is launching her daughter in society this season. My cousin Caroline will require a governess and my aunt a companion. Aunt Henrietta is . . . well, a sobering influence in the household is advisable."

"One that would keep her from buying too many ugly hats."

"Exactly. Since the position matches your first choice in opportunities, and would ensure you need not contemplate choices four or five, would you be interested in taking it? If you are so honest with me in sharing your thoughts, I think that you would also tell my aunt when a hat is ridiculous."

A variety of reactions barraged her mind. At first she thought he was teasing her about her list of choices, but she realized that he was serious.

He was asking her to stay in this house where she had lived as a family member, only now she would continue as a servant.

He was asking her to serve the man who had ruined the Longworths and reduced her yet further, pushing her down the path of diminishment begun when her father died and his heir refused the support he had promised.

Of course Mr. Rothwell did not see any of that. She was merely a convenient solution to staffing his aunt's household. She provided a unique combination of skills that were perfect for the position. Even if he saw the insult, this man would not care.

She wanted to refuse outright. She itched to say something far more outspoken and rude than she had ventured thus far.

She bit her tongue and checked her anger. She could not afford insulted pride these days.

"I will consider your generous offer, Mr. Rothwell."